THE RAIDERS

Also by Alloway Publishing, Ltd.
The Grey Man by S.R. Crockett.

THE RAIDERS

BEING

Some Passages in the Life of John Faa, Lord and Earl of Little Egypt:

BY

S.R. Crockett

Alloway Publishing

First published 1894
by
T.Fisher Unwin
Paternoster Square,
London

This edition published

by Alloway Publishing, Ltd.
1992

Text printed by Bell and Bain Ltd, Glasgow
Cover printed by Walker & Connell Ltd

The Publisher acknowledges subsidy from the Scottish Arts
Council towards the publication of this volume.

FOREWORD

I, Patrick Heron of Isle Rathan in Galloway, begin the writing of my book with thanks to God, the Giver of all good, for the early and bountiful harvest which He has been pleased to give us here in little Scotland, in this year of His Grace, 17—. It is not the least of the Lord's mercies that throughout all this realm, both hill-land and valley-land, the crops of corn, Merse wheat, Lowden oats, and Galloway bear, should be in the stackyards under thack and rape by the second day of September.

So with a long back-end before me, the mind running easy about the corn, and prices rising, I am not likely to get a better season of quiet to write down the things that befell us in those strange years when the hill outlaws collogued with the wild freetraders of the Holland traffic, and fell upon us to the destruction of the life of man, the carrying away of much bestial, besides the putting of many of His Majesty's lieges in fear.

Now it will appear that there are many things in this long story which I shall have to tell concerning myself which are far from doing me credit, but let it not be forgotten that it was with me the time of wild oat sewing when the blood ran warm. Also these were the graceless, unhallowed days after the Great Killing, when the saints of God had disappeared from the hills of Galloway and Carrick, and when the fastness of the utmost hills were held by a set of wild cairds—cattle reivers and murderers, worse than the painted savages of whom navigators to the far seas bring us word.

It was with May Mischief that all the terrible blast of storm began (as indeed most storms among men ever do begin with a bonny lass, like that concerning Helen of Troy, which lasted ten year and of which men speak to this day). The tale began with May Mischief, as you shall hear. I keep the old name still, though the years have gone by, and though now in any talks of the old days and of all our ancient plays, there are the bairns to be considered. But it is necessary that ere the memory quite die out, some one of us who saw these things should write them down. Some, it is true, were deeper in than I, but none saw more or clearer, being so to speak at both the inception and the conclusion of the matter.

To

Alexander Whyte,

my friend,

I offer this story

of the hills of my Home land—

like himself, friends

ancient, unforgotten, well-beloved.

James, be the grace of God, King of Scottis: To our Schereffis of Edinburghe, principall . . . and to all otheris Schereffis, Stewartis, proveftis, auldermenne, and bailleis within our realme, greting.

FORSAMEKILL as it is huimlie menit and schewin to us be our lowvit **JOHNNE FAA, LORD AND EARLE OF LITTLE EGYPT:** I charge you to aſſiſt him in puneſſing all that rebellis againis him, and in the execution of juſtice upon his company and folkis, conforme to the lawes of Egypt.

Subfcrivit with our hand and under our Prive Seile, **AT FALKLAND** the fiveteine day of Februar, and of our reigne the xxviij year.

Subscript. per Regem

James R.

CONTENTS

CHAPTER 1

MOONLIGHT AND MAY MISCHIEF

It was upon Rathan Head that I first heard their bridle-reins jingling clear. It was ever my custom to walk in the full of the moon at all times of the year. Now the moons of the months are wondrously different: the moon of January, serene among the stars—that of February, wading among chill cloud-banks of snow—of March, dun with the mist of muirburn among the heather—of early April, clean washen by the rains. This was now May, and the moon of May is the loveliest in all the year, for with its brightness comes the scent of flower-buds, and of young green leaves breaking from the quick and breathing earth.

So it was in the height of the moon of May, as I said, that I heard their bridle-reins jingling clear and saw the harness glisten on their backs.

"Keep far ben in your ain hoose at hame when the Marshalls ride!" said my father nodding his head at every third word in a way he had.

I shall never forget that night. I rowed over towards the land in our little boat, which was commonly drawn up in the cove on Rathan Isle, and lay a great time out on the clear, still flow of a silver tide that ran inwards, drifting slowly up with it. I was happy and at peace, and the world was at peace with me. I shipped the oars and lay back thinking. A lad's mind runs naturally on the young lasses, but as yet I had none of these to occupy me. Indeed there was but one of my own standing in the neighbourhood—that Mary Maxwell who was called, not without cause, May Mischief,[1] a sister of the wild Maxwells of Craigdarroch—and her I could not abide. There was nothing in her to think about particularly, and certainly I never liked her; nevertheless, one's mind being contrary, my thoughts ran upon her as the tide swirled southward by Rathan—especially on a curious way she had of smiling when a wicked speech was brewing behind her eyes.

[1] May, the old Scots diminutive for Mary, was pronounced, not like the name of the month, but Mei—the German ie, a characteristic sound which occurs also in "gye", "stey", & c.

THE RAIDERS

My skiff lay just outside the loom of the land, the black shadow of the Orraland shore on my left hand; but both boat and I as clear in the moonlight as a fly on a sheet of white paper.

There was a brig at anchor in the bay, and it was along the heuchs (cliffs) towards her that I saw the horsemen ride. They were, I knew, going to run the cargo into shelter. I was thinking of how fine they looked, and wondering how long it would be till my father let me have a horse from the stable and a lingtow over my shoulder to out to the Free Trade among the Manxmen like a lad of spirit, when all at once I got a sudden, horrid surprise.

I could hear the riders laughing and wagering among themselves, but I was too far away to hear what the game might be. Suddenly one of the foremost whipped a musket to his shoulder. I was so near the shore that I saw the flash of moonlight run along the barrel as he brought it to his eye. I wondered what he could be aiming at—a sea bird belike.

"*Clip! Splash!*" went something past my head and through the bow of the boat. Then on the back of the crack of the gun came a great towrow of laughter from the cliff edge.

"A miss! a palpable miss!" cried some one behind. "Haud her nose doon, ye gowk!"

"Noo, Gil, ye are next. See you an' mak' a better o't."

I was somewhat dazed with the suddenness of the cowardly assault, but I seized my oars of instinct and rowed shorewards. I was in the black of the shadows in three strokes, and not a moment over soon, for another ball came singing after me. It knocked the blade of my left oar into flinders, just as the water dripped silver off it in the moonlight for the last time before I was submerged in the shadow. Again the laughter rang loud and clear, but heartless and hard.

"Guid e'en to ye, gowk fisherman", cried the man who had first spoken. "The luck's wi' ye the nicht; it's a fine nicht for flounders."

I could have broken his head, for I was black angry at the senseless and causeless cruelty of the shooting. My first thought was to make for home; my second to draw to shore, and find out who they might be that could speed the deadly bullet with so little provocation at a harmless lad in his boat on the bay. So without pausing to consider of wisdom and folly (which indeed I have but seldom done in this life with profit), I sculled softly to the mainland with the unbroken oar.

Barefoot and bareleg I got into the shallow water, taking the little cleek anchor ashore and pushing the boat out that she might ride freely, for, as I said, the tide was running upwards like a mill-race.

Then I struck through the underbrush till I came to the wall of the deserted and overgrown kirkyard of Kirk Oswald. There stands a great old tomb in the corner from which, it ran in my mind, I might observe the shore and the whole route of the riders, if they were on their way to unload the brig in the offing.

There was a broad splash of moonlight on the rough grass between me and the tomb of the MacLurgs. The old tombstones reeled across it drunkenly, yet all was still and pale. I had almost set my foot on the edge of this white patch of moonshine to strike across it, when, with a rustle like a brown owl alighting swiftly and softly, some one took me by the hand, wheeled me about, and ere I had time to consider, carried me back again into the thickest of the wood.

Yet I looked at my companion as I ran, you may be sure. I saw a girl in a light dress, high-kilted—May Mischief of Craigdarroch, what other? But she pointed to her lip to show that there was to be no speech; and so we ran together even as she willed it to an angle of the old wall, where, standing close in the shade, we could see without being seen.

Now this I could not understand at all, for May Mischief never had a civil word for me as far back as I remember, but so many jibes and jeers that I never could endure the girl. Yet here we were, jinking hand in hand under the trees in the moonlight, for all the world like lad and lass playing at hide-and-seek. Soon we heard voices, and again the bits and chains rattling as the horses, suddenly checked, tossed their heads. Then the spurs jingled as the riders dismounted, stamping their feet as they came to the ground.

Twenty yards below us a man set his head over the wall. He whistled low and shrill.

"All clear, Malcolm?" he cried. I remember to this day the odd lilt of his voice. He was a Campbell, and gave the word Malcolm a strange twist, as if he had turned it over with his tongue in his mouth. And, indeed that is to this day the mark of a Cantyre man.

A man stepped out of the doorway of the MacLurg tomb with a gun in his hand. May Maxwell looked up at me with something triumphant in her eyes, which I took to mean, "Where had you been now, if it had not been for me?" And indeed the two shots at the boat in the moonlight told me where I would have been, and that was on the sward with a gunshot through me.

A dozen or more men came swarming over the broken wall. They carried a long, black coffin among them—the coffin, as it seemed, of an extraordinarily large man. Straight across the moon-whitened grass they strode, stumbling on the flat tombs and cursing one another as they went. There was no solemnity as at a funeral, for the jest and laughter ran light and free.

"We are the lads," cried one. "We can lay the spirits and we can raise the dead!"

They went into the great tomb of the MacLurgs with the long, black coffin, and in a trice came out jovially, abusing one another still more loudly for useless dogs of peculiar pedigrees, and dealing great claps on each other's backs. It was a wonder to me to see these outlaws at once so cruel and so merry.

Some of them went down by the corner of the kirkyard opposite to us. May Maxwell, who had kept my hand, fearing, I think, that we might have to run for it again round the circle of shade, plucked me sharply over to see what they were doing.

They were opening a grave, singing catches as their picks grated on the stones. I shivered a little, and a great fear of what we were about to see came over me. I think if May Maxwell had not gripped me by the hand I had fairly run for it.

The man we had first seen came out of the tomb and took a look at the sky. Another stretched himself till I heard his joints crack, and said "Hech How!" as though he were sleepy. Whereat the others railed on him, calling him "lazy vagabond."

Then all of them turned their ears towards the moors as though they listened for something of importance.

"Do the Maxwells ride to-night?" asked one.

"Wheesh," said another. "Listen!"

This he said in so awe-stricken a tone that I also was struck with fear, and listened till my flesh crept.

From the waste came the baying of a hound—long, fitful, and very eerie.

There was a visible, uneasy stir among the men.

"Let us be gone," said another, making for the wall; "'tis the Loathly Dogs. The Black Deil hunts himsel' the nicht. I'm gaun hame."

"Stop!" cried one with authority (I think the man that was called Gil). "I'll put an ounce of lead through your vitals gin ye dinna stand in your tracks."

But the others stayed neither for threat nor lead.

"It'll be waur for ye gin the Ghaistly Hounds get a grip o' your shins, Gil, my man. They draw men quick to hell!"

So at the word there seized the company a great fear, and they took to their heels, every man hastening to the wall. Then from the other side there was a noise of mounting steeds, and a great clattering of stirrup-irons.

May Mischief came nearer to me, and I heard her breath come in little broken gasps, like a rabbit that is taken in a net and lies beating its life out in your hand. At which I felt a man for the sole time that night.

But not for long, for I declare that what we saw in the next moment brought us both to our knees, praying silently for mercy. Over the wall at the corner farthest from us there came a fearsome pair. First a great grey dog, that hunted with its head down and bayed as it went. Behind it lumbered a still more horrible beast, great as an ox, grim and shaggy also, but withal clearly monstrous and not of the earth, with broad, flat feet that made no noise, and a demon mark in scarlet upon its side, which told that the foul fiend himself that night followed the chase. May Mischief clung to my arm, and I thought she had swooned away. But the beasts passed some way beneath us, like spirits that flit by without noise, save for the ghostly baying which made one sweat with fear.

As the sounds broke farther from us that were in the graveyard the horsemen dispersed in a wild access of terror. We could hear them belabouring their horses and riding broadcast over the fields, crying tempestuously to each other as they went. And down the wind the bay of the ghostly hunters died away.

May Maxwell and I stood so a long while ere we could loose from one another. We only held hands and continued to look, and that strangely. I wanted to thank her in words but could not, for something came into my throat and dried my mouth. I dropped her hand suddenly. Yet as I searched for words, dividing the mind between gratitude and coltishness, not one could I find in my time of need.

May Maxwell stood a little while silent before me, her hands fallen at her side, looking down as though expecting something. I could not think what. And then she took the skirt of her dress in her hand, dusted and smoothed it a moment, and so began to move slowly away. But I stood fixed like a halbert.

Then I knew by the dancing light in her eyes that something was coming that would make me like her worse than ever, yet I could not help it. What with my lonely life on Isle Rathan I was as empty of words as a drum of tune.

"Guid e'en to ye," she said, dropping me a curtsy; "virtue is its ain reward, I ken. It's virtuous to do a sheep a good turn, but a kennin' uninteréstin'. Guid e'en to ye, Sheep!"

With that she turned and left me speechless, holding by the wall. Yet I have thought of many things since which I might have said—clever things too.

May Mischief walked very stately and dignified across the moonlight, and passed the open grave which the raiders had made as though she did not care a button for it. At the gap in the wall she turned (looking mighty pretty and sweet, I do allow), nodded her head three times, and said solemnly, "Baa!"

As I rowed home in the gloaming of the morning, when the full flood-tide of daylight was drowning the light of the moon, I decided within myself that I hated the girl worse than ever. Whatever she had done for me, I could never forgive her for making a mock of me.

"Sheep," quoth she, and again "Baa!" It was unbearable. Yet I remembered how she looked as she said it, and the manner in which she nodded her head, which, as I tell you, was vastly pretty.

CHAPTER II

JOHN HERON OF ISLE RATHAN

Just why my father called me Patrick I have never yet been able to make out. His own name was John, which, had he thought of it in time, was a good name enough for me. It may have been part of his humorsomeness, for indeed he used to say, "I have little to leave you, Patrick, but this auld ramshackle house on the Isle Rathan and your excellent name. You will be far on in life, my boy, before you begin to bless me for christening you Patrick Heron, but when you begin you will not cease till the day of your death."

I am now in the thirty-seventh year of my age, yet have I not so begun to bless my father—at least not for the reason indicated.

My father, John Heron of Isle Rathan, on the Solway shore, was never a strong man all the days of him. But he married a lass from the hills who brought him no tocher, but, what was better, a strong dower of sense and good health. She died, soon after I was born, of the plague which came to Dumfries in the Black year, and from that day my father was left alone with me in the old house on the Isle of Rathan. John Heron was the laird of a barren heritage, for Rathan is but a little isle—indeed only an isle when the tide is flowing. Except in the very slackest of the neaps there is always twice a day a long track of shells and shingle out from the tail of its bank. This track is, moreover, somewhat dangerous, for Solway tide flows swift and the sands are shifting and treacherous. So we went and came for the most part by boat, save when I or some of the lads were venturesome, as afterwards when I got well acquaint with Mary Maxwell, whom I have already called May Mischief, in the days of a lad's first mid-summer madness.

Here on the Isle of Rathan my father taught me English and Latin, Euclid's science of lines and how to reason with them for oneself. He ever loved the mathematic, because he said even God Almighty works by geometry. He taught me also surveying and land measuring. "It is a good trade, and will be more in request," he used to say, "when the lairds begin to parcel out the commonties and hill pastures, as they surely will. It'll be a better trade to your hand than keepin' the blackfaced yowes aff the heuchs (cliffs) o' Rathan."

And so it has proved; and many is the time I have talked over with my wife the strange far-seeing prophecy of my father about what the lairds would do in more settled times. Indeed, all through my tale, strange as it is (may I be aided to tell it plainly and truly), I have occasion to refer to my father's sayings. Many is the time I have been the better of minding his words; many the time, also, that I have fallen with an unco blaff (serious downfall) because I have neglected to heed his warnings. But of this anon, and perhaps more than enough.

It was a black day for me, Patrick Heron, when my father lay a-dying. I remember it was a bask day in early spring. The tide was coming up with a strong drive of east wind wrestling against it, and making a clattering jabble all about the rocks of Rathan.

"Lift me up, Paitrick," said my father, "till I see again the bonny tide as it lappers again' the auld toor. It will lapper there mony and mony a day an' me no here to listen. Ilka time ye hear it, laddie, ye'll mind on yer faither that loved to dream to the plashing o't, juist because it was Solway salt water and this his ain auld toor o' the Isle Rathan."

So I lifted him up according to his word, till through the narrow window set in the thickness of the ancient wall, he could look away to the Mull, which was clear and cold slaty blue that day—for, unless it brings the dirty white fog, the east wind clears all things.

As he looked a great fishing gull turned its head as it soared, making circles in the air, and fell—a straight white streak cutting the cold blue sky of that spring day.

"Even thus has my life been, Paitrick. I have been most of my time but a great gull diving for herring on an east-windy day. Whiles I hae gotten a bit flounder for my pains, and whiles a rive o' drooned whalp, but o' the rale herrin'—desperate few, man, desperate few."

"I hae tried it a' ways, Paitrick, my man, ye ken," he would say, for in the long winter forenights when all was snug inside and the winds were trying the doors, he and I did little but talk. He lay many months a-dying. But he was patient, and almost anxious that he should give me all his stores of warning and experience before he went from me and Rathan.

"No that, at the first go off, ye'll profit muckle, Paitrick, my man," he would say; "me telling ye that there are briers i' the buss (bush) will no advantage ye greatly when ye hae to gae skrauchlin' through. Ye'll hae to get berried and scartit, whammilt and riven, till ye learn as I hae learned. Ay, ay, ye wull that!"

My father was a dark man, not like me who am fair like my mother. He had a pointed beard that he trimmed with the shears, which in a time of shaven men made him kenspeckle (conspicuous). He was very particular about his person, and used to set to the washing of his linen every second week, working like an old campaigner himself, and me helping—a job I had small stomach for. But at least he learned me to be clean by nature and habit.

"We canna compass godliness," he would say often, "try as we may, Paitrick. But cleanliness is a kindly, common-like virtue, and it's so far on the road, at any rate." That was one of his sayings.

My father was not what you would call a deeply religious man; at least, if he were, he said little about it, though he read daily in the Scriptures, and also expected me to read a chosen part, questioning me sharply on the meaning. But he did not company with the lairds of the countryside, nor with the tenants either for the matter of that. He took no part in the services which were held by the Society Men who collected in the neighbourhood, and who met statedly for their diets of worship at Springholm and Crocketford. Yet his sympathies were plainly with those men and with Mr. Macmillan of Balmaghie who subscribed to them—not at all with the settled ministers of the parishes. On Sabbaths he always encouraged me to take the pony over in the great wide-bottomed boat to the shore, and ride on Donald to the Kirk of Dullarg or the Societies meeting.

"Ye see, Paitrick, for mysel' I hae tried a'ways o't. I hae been oot wi' the King's riders in the auld bad days. Silver Sand kens where. I hae been in the haggs o' the peat-mosses wi' the sants. I hae laid snug an' cosy in Peden's cave wi' the auld man himsel' at my back. So ye see I hae tried a' ways o't. My advice to you, Paitrick, is no to be identified wi' ony extremes, to read yer Bible strictly, an' gin ye get a guid minister to sit under, to listen eidently to the word preached. It's mair than your faither ever got for ony length o' time."

By bit and bit he grew weaker, as the days grew longer.

"Noo Paitrick," he said, over in the still time of one morning, at the hour of slack tide, when a watcher sitting up with the sick gets chill and cauldrife and when the night lies like a solid weight on the earth and sea, though heavier on the sea. At this time my father called to me.

"I'm gaun, Paitrick," he said, just as though he were going over to the Dullarg in the boat; "it's time I was awa'. I could wish for your sake that I had mair to leave ye. Had I been a better boy at your time o' life, ye wad hae had mair amang your hands; but then maybe it's you that wad hae been the ill boy. It's better that it was me. But there'll be a pickle siller in Matthew Erskine's hands for a' that. But gin I can leave ye the content to be doing wi' little, an' the saving salt o' honour to be kitchen to your piece, that's better than the lairdship o' a barony."

He was silent for a while, and then he said—

"Ye are no feared, Paitrick?"

"Feared, father," I said, "what for would I be feared of you?"

"Aweel, no," he answered, very calm, "I am no a man to mak' a to-do aboot deein'. I bid ye guid-nicht, my son Paitrick." And so passed, as one might fall on sleep.

He was a quiet man, a surprisingly humorsome man, and I believe a true Christian man, though all his deathbed testimony was no more than I have told.

CHAPTER III

DAWN ON RATHAN SANDS

If there be anything bonnier or sweeter in this world than a May morning on the Isle of Rathan by the Solway shore, I have yet to see it—except it be the blush that comes over a young maid's face when one that is not her lad, but who yet may be, comes chapping at the door.

Some months after my father's death I mind me of just such a morning. There had drawn to me in the old house of Rathan certain other lads of my age, of good burgher families, that did not find themselves entirely comfortable at home. The house and lands with all the sheep upon them and some six thousand pounds sterling of money in the public funds were left to me to deal with as I liked, though I was not yet of age. Matthew Erskine, the douce Dumfries lawyer, who was in my father's confidence, put no barriers on my doing as I pleased; and thus carried out my father's intentions, which were that I should neither be hampered in well-doing nor in ill-doing, but do even as it seemed good to me. For this was ever his way and custom.

"When I was a lad," he used to say, "I was sore hampered in coming and going, and most of the evils of my life have come upon me because I was not early left to choose right and wrong, nosing them for myself like a Scent-Dog after birds. So I will even leave you, Paitrick, as says the Carritches, to 'the freedom of your own will.'"

The lads who had come to bide with me on Isle Rathan, at least for the summer season, were Andrew Allison, that was a burgher's son at Carlinwark (where there are but few decent people abiding, which made his father the more remarkable) and his brother John. Also there was a cousin of the Allisons that came from the ancient town of Kilconquhar, high up on the Nith Water. There was also, to our joy, one Jerry MacWhirter, a roguish fellow that came to me to help me with my land-surveying, but was keener to draw with colours on paper the hues of the landskip and the sea. But he was dearest to us because of his continual merry heart, which did us good like a medicine.

So the five of us lads abode in that house, and of them I was much the biggest and oldest. Also the house was mine and it was my duty to rule, else had we been an unruly crew. But in truth it was also my pleasure to rule, and that with the iron hand. With us at times there was one Silver Sand, who deserves a chapter to himself, and in time shall receive it.

Now I must tell of the kind of house we had on the Isle Rathan. It stood in a snug angle of the bay that curved inward towards the land and looked across some mossy, boguish ground to a range of rugged, heathery mountains, on which there were very many grey boulders, about which the heath and bracken grew deep.

The ancient house of the Herons of Rathan was not large, but it was very high, with only two little doors to back and front—the front one set into the wall and bolted with great bars into the solid rock beneath and above, and into the thickness of the wall at either side. The back door opened not directly, but entered into a passage which led first to a covered well in a kind of cave, where a good spring of water for ever bubbled up with little sand grains dancing in it, and then by a branch passage to an opening among the heather of the isle, which you might search for a summer's day. But unless you knew it of others' knowledge, you would never find it of your own. The windows were very far up the sides, and there were very few of them, as being made for defence in perilous times. Upon the roof there was a flagstaff and so strong a covering of lead and stone flags that it seemed as though another tower might have been founded upon it. The Tower of Rathan stood alone, with its offices, stables, byres, or other appurtenances back under the cliff, the sea on one side of it, and on the other the heathery and rocky isle, with its sheep pastures on the height. Beneath the sea-holly and dry salt plants bloomed blue and pink down near the blatter of the sea.

Fresh air and sound appetites were more common with us lads on the isle than the wherewithal to appease our belly cravings. It was not our pleasure to be served by any woman. Indeed we could not abide the thought of it. It was not seemly that any young one should be with us, nor did we wish to put our wild doings under the observation of any much older than ourselves. So it came that we had to fend for ourselves, and as it drew near to term day, when I got my little pickle money from Matthew Erskine, the Dumfries lawyer (riding there on Donald, my sheltie), the living was very scanty on the isle. For when I had money, it was ever freely spent. But at the worst of times we had a stake salmon net which we fished every morning when the fish were clean, and there were flounders all the year round. Thus we lived, and, take it all in all, none so evilly, considering that the country was a poor one and we had no friends that bore any goodwill to help us—except May Mischief at Craigdarroch, who, for all her jeers, set a great tankard of milk aside for us every morning and night.

So on this morn in May I rose long before the dawn, and went out into the cool, camp air of the night. The tide was going back quickly, and it was this which had raised me at such untimeous hours. It has always struck me that when the creation was, and that justly, pronounced very good, sufficient attention was not paid to the matter of the tides. But in a great job like the making of the earth, small points are apt to be mislippened. For instance, it would have been a great advantage if the tides at Rathan had been regular in the morning, leaving the nets clear at something like seven o'clock in summer and nine in winter. But I was not consulted at the time, and so the matter rests as at present—a trifle inconveniently for all parties.

Now I am a man of my devotions, and render thanks to a kind Providence every morning for the preservation of the night. But I am well aware that the quality of my thankfulness is not what it should be at half-past two of a bleak and chill morning when the nets must be looked. So I say again that both parties suffer by the present arrangement.

But this morning of which I speak there was not a great deal to complain of, save that I left the others snoring in their hammocks and box-beds round the chambers of dark oak where they were lodged. The thought of this annoyed me as I went.

It was still dark when I went out with only my boots over my bare feet, and the chill wind whipping about my shanks. What of the sea one could observe was of the colour of the inside of an oyster-shell, pearl grey and changeful. The land loomed mistily dark, and there was a fitful light going about the farm-town of Craigdarroch, where the Maxwells dwelt, which made me wonder if it could be that hellicat lassie, who had called me a sheep, wandering abroad so early. For in spite of her smile she was a lass that none of us lads of the Rathan could abide. Still, I own that it was friendly-like to see at that dead hour of the morning some one else astir even across half a mile of salt water.

From Rathan Head I looked out seaward and saw one of the fast brigs of the Freetraders from the Isle of Man, or perhaps from Holland, manoeuvring out with the tide. Little thinking how much she was to cost us, against the swiftly brightening sky I watched her draw away from the land. None of us, barring the Preventive officers, had any ill-will at the traffic itself, though my father had taught me never to use any of the stuff, desiring that I should be hardy and thole wind and weather without it, as very well may be done. Still, when it was decently gone about, he did not see what right the Preventives had to keep other folk from doing in the matter as their fathers had done before them. King George, decent man, that was but lately come over the water from Germany, surely could not be much harmed by a poor man's bit still in the lee of the peat-stack.

But indeed there were good and bad, decent and indecent, at the traffic, as we were soon to learn.

It was cold and unkindly on the flats, and there was nothing except lythe and saithe in the nets—save some small red trout, which I cast over on the other side, that they might grow large and run up the rivers in August. So little was there that I must, with exceedingly cold feet and not in the best of tempers, proceed to the flats and tramp flounders for our breakfast. Right sorely did I grieve now that I had not awaked two of the others, for Andrew Allison's feet were manifestly intended by nature for tramping flounders, being broad and flat as the palm of my hand. Moreover, John his brother was quick and biddable at the job—though I think chiefly because he desired much to get back to his play about the caves and on the sand with his ancient crony, Bob Nicoll of Kilconquhar.

But I was all my lone on the flats, and it was sufficiently dreary work. Nevertheless, I soon had my baskets full of the flapping, slippery fish, though it was none too nice a job to feel them slide between your toes and wriggle their tails under your instep. That was what gave Andrew Allison so great an advantage at the business, for he had no instep—at least not to speak of.

When I got to the shore with my backload of breakfast I knew not whether I had any feet at all, except when I looked and saw my legs causing them to move and in some fashion to carry me. So I came to the house, which now stood up bright in the sunshine of the morning.

Going into the still curtained chamber out of the flooding morning sun was the strangest thing. It vexed me wonderfully to hear the others still snoring in their naked beds, and I so cold and weary with my morning's work. Moreover, the air had the closeness that comes with thick walls and many breathings.

Throwing down my fish and slipping off my dew-damp clothes

to be dried before the fire, I threw myself into the bed which Andrew Allison and I occupied together. He lay next the wall. Without a moment's delay I placed my ice-chill feet where it would do them most good. This caused my companion to awake with so great a shout that the others tumbled instantly out of bed, thinking that the Freetraders were upon us at the least. As for Andrew, he lay still and acted warming-pan being fortunately between me and the wall.

To the others I issued my orders as I grew warmer. "Lazy slug-a-beds"—it was my way thus to speak, ordering the youngsters about like a skipper—"get about your work! You, John Allison, get the boat and go over to Craigdarroch for the milk, and be back by breakfast-time; and gin ye so muckle as lift the lid of the can, I'll thrash ye till ye canna stan'—forbye, ye'll get no breakfast."

John got his cap, grumbling and shaking his head. But he went.

"You, Rab, clean the fish, and you, Jerry MacWhirter, get a fire started, and hae the breakfast on the table in an hour. Dry my clothes before the fire."

"It's Andra's day!" said Jerry.

"Maybe it is," said I, "but for the present Andrew has other business on hand. He was tired yestreen, and he's the better o' a rest this morning. Get the breakfast and be nimble. It'll be better for ye.'

"But, Rab says——" began Jerry, who was reluctantly putting on his clothes.

"Not another word out of the mouth o' ye!" I cried, imperatively.

It is wonderful what firmness does in a household. In this way I had a good sleep before breakfast.

When I awoke Andrew was on foot. He had stolen out of bed and taken a sea plunge from the southernmost rocks, drying himself on the sand by running naked in the brisk airs of the morning which drew off the sea.

There is no finer breakfast than flounders fried in oatmeal with a little salt butter as soon as ever they come out of the water—their tails jerking *Flip, flap*, in the frizzle of the pan.

"Gracious," said Jerry, "but it's guid. I'm gled I got up o' my ain free will."

Andrew and I being captain and lieutenant of the gang, had forks; the rest had none, by which lack for eating flounders they were the better off. It is most amazing the number of bones a flounder can carry, and that without trouble. Also it is a mercy that none of us choked on any of them, in so unseemly a haste did we eat.

CHAPTER IV

THE CAVE OF ADULLAM

Rathan Island lay in the roughest tumble of the seas. Its southern point took the full sweep of the Solway tides as they rushed and surged upwards to cover the great deadly sands of Barnhourie. From Sea Point, as we named it, the island stretched northward in many rocky steeps and cliffs riddled with caves. For just at this point the softer sandstone you meet with on the Cumberland shore set its nose out of the brine. So the island was more easily worn into sea caves and strange arches, towers and haystacks, all of stone, sitting by themselves out in the tideway for all the world like bairns' playthings.

In these caves, which had many doors and entries, I had played with the tide ever since I was a boy. I knew them all as well as I knew our own back-yard under the cliff. And the knowledge was before long to stand me in better stead than the Latin grammar I had learned from my father.

In fine weather it was a pleasant thing to go up to the highest point of the island, which, though little of a mountain, was called Ben Rathan, and see the country all about one. Thence was to be seen the reek of many farm-towns and villages, besides cot-houses without number, all blowing the same way when the wind was soft and equal. The morning was the best time to go there. Upon Rathan, close under the sky, the bees hummed about among the short, crisp heather, which was springy just like our little sheltie's mane after my father had done docking it. There was a great silence up there—only a soughing from the south, where the tides of the Solway, going either up or down, kept for ever chafing against the rocky end of our little Isle of Rathan.

Then nearest to us, on the eastern shore of Barnhourie Bay, there was fair to be seen the farmhouse of Craigdarroch, with the Boreland and the Ingleston above it, which is always the way in Galloway. Wherever there is a Boreland you may be sure that there is an Ingleston not far from it. The way of that is, as my father used to say, because the English came to settle in their "ton," and brought their "boors," or serfs, with them. So that near the English towns are always to be found the boor-lands. Which is as it may be, but the fact is at any rate sufficiently curious. And from Ben Rathan also, looking to the westward, just over the cliffs of our isle, you saw White Horse Bay, much frequented of late years for convenience of debarkation by the Freetraders of Captain Yawkins' band, with whom, as my father used to say quaintly, no honest smuggler hath company.

For there were, as every one knows, in this land of Galloway two kinds of the lads who bring over the dutiless gear from Holland and the Isle of Man. There be the decent lads who run for it for something honest to do in the winter and for the spice of danger, and without a thought of hurt to King George, worthy gentleman; and there are also the "Associated Illdoers," as my father would often call them in his queer, daffing way—the Holland rogues who got this isle its bye-name of Rogues' Island by running their cargoes into our little land-locked cove which looks towards White Horse Bay. These last were fellows who would stick at nothing, and quite as often as not they would trepan a lass from the Cumberland shore, or slit the throat of a Dumfries burgher to see the colour of his blood. But the Black Smugglers never could have come to such a pitch of daring and success unless they had made to themselves friends of the disaffected of these parts. The truth of the matter was that in the wilds of Galloway that look toward Ayrshire, up by the springs of Doon and Dee, there lies a wide country of surpassing wildness, whither resorted all the evil gypsies of the hill—red-handed loons, outlaw and alien to all this realm of well-affected men.

When a vessel came in these openly marched down to the shore with guns, swords, and other weapons—Marshalls, Macatericks, and Millers, often under the leadership of Hector Faa—and escorted to their fastnesses the smuggled stuff and the stolen goods, for there was as much by wicked hands reived and robbed, as of the stuff which was only honestly smuggled.

My father had fallen out with Yawkins when he began the robbing of man and the seizing of maids. I can remember him coming to the Rathan, a thick-set, dark man, with his head very low between his shoulders. He had a black beard on his breast, and there was a cast in his eye. He swore many strange oaths. Being a Hollander, the most of his conversation seemed to be "dam," but between whiles he was trying to persuade my father to something.

"It's clottered nonsense," said my father over and over to him; "and, more than that, it's rank black-guardism; and as for me, I shall have no trokings wi' the like o' ye aboot the maitter."

THE CAVE OF ADULLAM

From which and other things I gathered that in the days of his wildness my father had had his hands pretty deep in the traffic.

Away at the back yonder, across the fertile valley of the Dee, we could see from Rathan Head the blue shadowy hills, where, among the wild heather and the solitudes where the whaups cried all summer long, the hill gypsies had their fastnesses. On those blue hills, to us so sweet and solemn, no king's man had been of his own free will since the days of Clavers. Little did I think, as I used to sit and watch them, with Andrew and young Jock Allison, Rab Nicoll, and little Jerry, on the smooth brindled heather of Ben Rathan, that I should so often tread the way up to those fastnesses about the Dungeon of Buchan or all were done.

It was after the time of dishwashing, and the most part of us were out on the heuchs, looking to seaward with my father's old prospect-glass (which was ever one of our choicest possessions) when little Jerry, who had been drawing with pencils and colour the shape of the coast and hills—a vanity he was very fond of from his childhood—came up the hill in great spangs, crying that there was a boat coming round the point running against the tide, with two men rowing. I turned the glass on the boat as she came, and was soon able to pick her up.

"It's your mither, Andrew Allison," I said, "an' yours, Jerry, my lad. They'll be gettin' anxious to see ye!"

"Guid save us," said Andrew; "I'm awa' to hide!"

"Awa' wi' ye, then," I said; "but dinna inform me where, that I may not have more lies to tell than are just and needful."

I was well aware that there was some business for me to do during the next hour, for neither Mistress Allison that was a baillie's wife, nor yet Mistress MacWhirter, were canny women with their tongues when they got a subject to do them justice.

But my father set me on a capital plan, having regard to the tongue of a scolding woman. I know not how it would work if you had her always in the house with you. I misdoubt that in that case my father's receipt might need application and reinforcement from a hazel rod; but against the tongues of orra folk that you have only to stand for a while at a time it is altogether infallible. My father had a great respect for Scripture, and he had Scripture warrant for this.

"Mind ye, Paitrick," he used to say, "that the Good Book says, 'A soft answer turneth away wrath.' Now keep your temper, laddie. Never quarrel wi' an angry person, specially a woman. Mind ye, a soft answer's aye best. It's commanded—and forbye, it makes them far madder than onything else ye could say."

As we looked the boat sped nearer, and, peering through the prospect-glass again, I could see that it was rowed by a pair of folk—a lassie and a man. It was the Craigdarroch boat—white with a green stripe about it, very genteel. So that I did not need to be a prophet or other than my father's son to know that it was my daft Maxwell lass, whom they call May Mischief, that was oaring the wives across.

Now it made me vexed sore to think that she should hear all the on-ding of their ill tongues. Not that I cared for May Maxwell or any like her, only it was galling to let a lass like that, who was for ever gibing and jeering, get new provision of powder and shot for her scoffs and fleers. The last time I saw her, when I went over to Craigdarroch myself for the milk—one day that it blew hard and I could not send the younger ones—she had a new word for me. She would call me no word but "adullam." Well, any name was better than "Sheep," for when I saw her forming her mouth to say "Baa," I could have run and left her in fair anger. But this she did but seldom.

"Noo, Adullam," she cried, as soon as ever I could get near the onstead for *yowching* dogs, "this is a bonny business. I suppose ye think that ye are a great captain, like King David in the cave; and that a' that are discontented and a' that are in distress wull gather in till ye, an' ye'll be a captain ower them. A bonny like captain, Adullam. There's a braw big hoose up in Enbra', I hear, that's fu' o' sic captains. They pit strait-jackets on them there, an' tie them up wi' rapes."

This I did not answer, remembering my father's prescription.

"O, ye think ye're a braw lad," said the impudent besom. "Ye're a' braw lads, by your ain accounts, but some knotty twigs o' the bonny birk wad fit ye better than so mony 'captains.' I'll speak to my faither aboot that!" she said, making believe to go off.

Now when she spoke in this fashion I got a great deal of comfort just from saying over and over to myself, "Ye impudent besom! Ye impudent besom!" So before I was aware, out the words came; and then in a moment I was horrified at the sound of my own voice.

I had never so spoken to a young woman before; indeed seldom to the breed at all. For my father and I kept ourselves very close to ourselves in Rathan Isle as long as he lived.

But instead of being offended the daft lassie threw back her head and laughed. She had close curls like a boy, and her way of laughing was strange, and smote me as though some elf were tapping down at the bottom of my throat with his forefinger. There was something witching about her laughter.

"Weel dune, Adullam, ye'll be nane sic a *sumph* (stupid) some day, when ye get the calf conceit ta'en oot o' ye and your hair cut," said she.

"Let my hair alane—my hair's no meddlin' you" I said, so coltish and stupid that I fair hated the lass for humbling me that way—me that had so good an opinion of myself from living much alone.

So it was small wonder that the thought of her hearing what the pair of old randy wives had to say to me for leading their precious sons astray was like gall and wormwood.

CHAPTER V

AULD WIVES' CLAVERS

The boat was coming quickly in, and I could see that Mistress Allison, who had the steering, knew nothing at all of the matter, so that the boat in spite of the efforts of the rowers, was in danger of being carried past the landing-place on the northward side where the beautiful beaches of shell-sand are.

Now, although I wished the whole crew far enough, yet I did not want a drowning match on the Rathan heuchs, so I ran down alone, the better to pilot them in. The lads had fled; and, indeed, their room was better than their company. Only little Jerry MacWhirter sat calmly finishing his perspective drawing on the hilltop.

"Tell my mither I'll be doon the noo!" he cried after me as I ran. But I thought he was joking, and went on without reply.

At last the keel grated on the beach, and I pulled the boat ashore. Even as I did so the daft Maxwell lass that I was so angry with unshipped her oar, put her hand on my shoulder, and leaped on the shingle like a young goat. The two old wives were speechless with black anger.

"Good-day to you, Mistress Allison and Mistress MacWhirter, and to you, May Maxwell," I said, lifting my bonnet to each, and speaking as I ought, just to show that I was none so rough and landward.

"Guide-day to ye, Adullam!" says she; but the two old wives said neither "Fair-guid-e'en" nor "Fair-guid-day," but only sat and gloomed and better gloomed. I stood at the side of the boat to offer them a hand; but Mistress Allison waved me away, and asked the great stot of a farm lad that was at the oar to jump out and help them ashore.

"No, an' I'll no, eyther!" said that youth, pleasantly. "Wull Maxwell said that I was to bide by the boat—an' so I'll bide. Ye can loup!"

So help he would not. But he was willing to give his reasons.

"Wull is my maister, an' he's a man to be mindit, I'm tellin' ye!" he said, and that was all they could get out of him.

So the old wives, who could have eaten all they liked of me with pleasure and ease, had perforce to accept my helping hand to get them out of the boat, which had grounded high on the shell-sand and now coggled upon an uneven keel.

"Think on the honour o't, Mistress Allison", cried that randy lass May Maxwell, standing with her hands on her sides and her elbows crooked out in fashion of her own. (I cannot think what made me notice these things, for I fair hated the lass). "Think," says she, "on the honour of being handed oot by a laird on his ain grund, or raither a prince in his ain kingdom, for a' this isle will belong to his lordship. Ye're a big woman the day, Mistress MacWhirter!" And she pretended to look about grandly, as though taking in a prospect of wide dominions.

But never a word said I out loud, but in to myself I kept saying, "Ill-tongued hizzy!" And that I said over and over.

But she was not yet done, and went on, "Is't a captain or a general ye are, Adullam?—my memory's failin'. I think ye mentioned it the last time ye were ower by at Craigdarroch. Or is it nothing less than to be a king that'll serve ye? My faith," she added, looking round, "I'm thinkin' that your standing airmy's a' run awa'!"

She laughed elvishly here, though I, that am as full of appreciation of humour as any man, could see nothing whatever to laugh at.

"Here's the standing airmy, Mistress May Mischief!" cried Jerry MacWhirter, upstanding as bold as brass on the edge of the sea cliff which rose above the white sands of the bay.

"Guid mornin' to ye, mither," he said, lifting his blue bonnet politely; "and my service to you, Mistress Allison. your son Andrew sent his love till ye."

"Ye impudent vaigabond!'

At the word both of the women made a rush at him with so angry a countenance that, though a man grown, with (some) hair on my face, I gave back a pace myself. But as for little Jerry, he never turned a hair, but only sat down on the edge of the cliff, looking now at the group and now at his drawing. It was as pretty as a play.

"Dinna be in a hurry, mither," he said; "it's bad for the disjeestion; an' this bank's ower steep for twenty stone, Mistress Allison. Try roon to the left. There's a bonnier road there."

His mother's tongue got vent.

"Ye sorra' and vexation," she cried, "ye disgrace to a' oor hoose, that was aye decent grocers! Wait till I get ye hame. I'll wile ye hame wi' the strong hand, my lad, and lay on ye wi' a stout stick when I get ye there. Ye shall suffer for this if there's hazel oil in Dumfries, gibin' an jeerin' at your ain blood-kin."

Little Jerry had a piece of paper on his knee, and he made marks on it with a callevine (pencil) as if he were drawing a map. I admired greatly to see him.

"Na, mither," he said; "nae ill word did I ever speak to you, or aboot you. I did but advise ye for your health no to excite or overexert yersel', for, as ye ken, Doctor Douglas tells ye that it's ill for the bowel complaint. But my respects to my stepfaither the Doctor. I hope ye left him weel."

"I tell ye that as sure as my name's Sarrah MacWhirter, ye'll get sic a lickin' as ye'll no get ower for a month when ye come back to Dumfries. I'll get the burgh hangman to attend to ye, gin I haena the strength o' airm to gar ye lowp mysel'."

At this fearful threat I looked for Jerry to lower his colours, but he seemed more than usual calm, and turned his head sideways to look this way and that at his map, like a wild bird on a bough when it is not sure about you.

"Na, mither, lickin's dune noo! It's a' by wi'," says he; "so it's no for me to say whether or no yer name's properly Sarrah MacWhirter or Sarrah Douglas. I wasna at either o' your waddin's—at least, that I mind o'—but whether or no, strap, taws, birk, an' hazel, are a' by wi'; and I'll come nae mair hame till ye promise to let me alane."

"Ye ken, richt weel, ye vaigabone, that ye wad be let alane. Aye, an' made muckle o' gin ye wad consent to be a decent grocer in the Wynd, an' succeed yer faither in the shop."

"Na, mither, I'll never be grocer nor yet chandler. The provision line is a guid trade, but it's no for me. I was aye that hungrysome that I wad eat a' the profits. I wad cadge keel first, mither, like Silver Sand. Can ye no let me alane?"

His mother and Mistress Allison, quite aghast at the turn affairs were taking, had retreated, and were for making their way up the cliff by themselves. May Mischief had gone back again to the boat, and was lifting something heavy out of it. I went down to help her, for I never could abide to see a woman do man's work, even if I had reason to dislike her, as I had right good reason to do this lass from Craigdarroch; though, to tell truth, I had some better reasons also to think well of her, as I owned to myself, remembering the night by the tomb of the MacLurgs in the kirkyard of Kirk Oswald.

Then I heard little Jerry say from his post on the top of the cliff, "Might I trouble ye, Mistress Allison, juist to stan' still till I get your figure drawed? It disna look bonny withoot the head, especially as I hadna aneuch paper to mak' your feet."

I began to see that though Jerry might be an exceedingly useful ally with the tongue, his answers, though soft enough to satisfy Solomon himself, were not such as to turn away wrath. On the contrary, if the two ladies were angry when they came seeking their sons on my island, Jerry had made then ten times worse now.

All this time I was helping May Maxwell out of the boat with something heavy, wrapped in a white cloth. Whatever it was it gave out a rare good smell to me, who had breakfasted some hours before on plain flounders tramped on the flats at three in the morning.

Overhead the two good dames were labouring upward, Mistress Allison crying as she went—

"Andra! Jock!—wait till I catch ye!"

This mode of address struck me as, to say the least of it, unwise, and as one might say injudicious.

On the hillside Mistress MacWhirter made ineffective swoops at her erring son, who evaded her as easily as a swallow gets out of the way of a cow.

"And, my certes," cried the good dame, exceedingly irate, "you are michty wastefu', my laddie! What for are ye wearin' your best claes, I wad like to ken?"

"Because I hae nae better!" said her obedient son, for all the answer that was requisite.

The reasoning was excellent. Had he had better, he would have had them on. He had done his best.

I came up the path in the sunlight, carrying the Maxwell lass's packet under my arm, and mighty weighty it seemed to be. It was very hot underfoot with the sun reflected from the rocks. It was a clear, coppery sky overhead.

"What are ye gaun to say to them?" May Maxwell asked, looking across at me in a way that I thought kindlier.

"That I do not ken," said I; "I was thinkin' o' lettin' them get it a' their ain way for the sake o' peace."

"Man, Adullam, for a lad that sets up to be a general, ye hae little contrivance aboot ye. That's a' weel eneuch for a while, an' when there's but yin o' them. But there's twa auld wives' tongues here, an' it's a'thegither useless, for as sune as the breath o' yin gaes oot, the ither yin'll tak' up the tale, and the deevin' (deafening) will juist be eternal."

"But what will I do then, May Maxwell?" said I.

"Misca' their bairns to their face. Misca' them for a' the sornin' tinklers—the lazy, ill-contrivin' loons i' the country. Gin that disna gar their mithers change their tunes, my name's no May Maxwell."

"Your name's May Mischief, I see that weel!" I said, roguishly.

"What, ho, Adullam!" she cried, making a pretty, mocking mouth, "this will never do. Twa o' a trade will never agree. Dinna you set up to be waggish, like oor dog Toss that tried to play cat's tricks on the lip o' the boiler an' fell amang the pig's meat. Na, na, Adullam, stick to your generalin' and captainin'. Did ye ever hear o' the calf that tried to be humorsome."

"No," said I, "and fewer of your gibes." For indeed it was no time for tales.

"'Weel,' said the farmer body to the calf, 'I ettled ye for a keeping quey, but a coo wi' a sense o' humour is a thing that I canna hae aboot the hoose. The last yin ett a' the wife's half-year's washin'. I'll e'en hae to see what kind o' veal ye'll mak.' So the humorsome calf deed suddenly. It's a lesson to ye," said Mistress May, coming quickly to the end of her parable.

This, as all may see, was ever the way that she jeered at me, and I cannot think how it was that I was not more angered. Maybe it was because she was but a little supple bit thing, like the least of my fingers with a string tied round the middle of it.

When we two got up to the house we went directly into the kitchen. There we found the two dames standing in the middle of the floor, and, as one might say, each turning about on her own pivot, and sniffing loudly on the nose of contempt. I could hardly keep from laughing out loud. I looked to May Maxwell to see if she was at it already. I made sure that, as she saw humour in so many things, she would find this vastly amusing.

But I was never more mistaken. Her little nose was more in the air than usual. I always meant to tell her when she was going on to me that her nose turned up at the end. I never did, however, chiefly because I did not believe that she would have cared a pin if I *had* said it.

But her advice was worth the trying.

The kitchen, which had an oaken settle down one side of it, had also two box-beds let into the wall, and, in addition, two hammocks hanging for those of us who preferred the swinging beds. Now none of these beds were made, though the linen was clean enough, for Silver Sand took it over to a decent wife in the village of Orraland every three weeks to be washed. The bachelor ways of the house of Rathan did not admit of such a freit as bed-making. It was to us a vain thing. We rose up, and we heaved our coverings over the foot of the bed; or we left them lying on the floor beneath the hammock where they had slipped off. When we got in we drew them over us again. This was our bed-making. But in the two elder women, and even in May Mischief, this innocent and pleasing habit occasioned a new and more bitter indignation.

"And this is the place that ye hae wiled my Andra and my Johnnie to, puir lads!" cried Mistress Allison, her twenty stone of bulk shaking with indignation and the difficulties of the ascent.

"Will ye please to take seats, my ladies?" said I, standing as politely as I could with my hat in my hand, for I was in my own house.

The two dames looked at me, then at one another. Finally they seemed to make up their minds to seat themselves. This they did, each in her own manner. Mistress Allison took hold of a chair on which some books and drawings of little Jerry's were laid. As she tilted it forward these slid to the floor. The good lady let herself drop into it as a sack of flour drops on the ground when the rope slips.

The thin, spare, irascible Mistress MacWhirter took out of her swinging under-pocket a large India-red kerchief. Then she carefully dusted the chair, turning it bottom upward in a way which betrayed a rooted distrust of everything in the Rathan. May Mischief simply took a good look at the window-sill, set the palms of her hands flat upon it at her sides, and hopped up like a bird, but backwards.

Now the lads Andrew and Johnny Allison, with Rab Nicoll, their cousin, were hid at the end of the hallan, where the passage led from the back door out upon the moor. They were therefore perfectly within earshot.

As soon as Mrs. Allison got her breath she began, "Noo, Maister Paitrick Heron, could ye tell me by what richt ye keep my laddies here, that should be serving in their father's shop and rinnin' their mither's messages—you that caa's yersel' a laird? A bonny laird, quo' he, to wile awa' decent folk's bairns frae their ain door cheek to his ramshackle hoose, an' keep them there—a wheen puir bits o' boys to cut his firewood, and leeve in this fearsome-like hole."

"Aye," cried the shriller voice of Mistress MacWhirter, "and I'll e'en pit yin to that. It was him an' nae ither that pat my Jerry, that was aye a guid lad, past the grocering."

"Thank ye, mither; your obedient servant, Jerry MacWhirter," put in the little rascal from the outside somewhere.

"Ye are a regairdless hound, a black sheep in my bonny flock, a——"

"Puir lad that you an' my stepfaither lickit till he was black and blue, but that ye'll lick nae mair on this side o' the grave!" cried Jerry from the doorway, showing his witty, comical face round the corner.

I thought it was time now to try May Mischief's advice.

"Have ye said all that ye wad like to say?" I said, looking from one to the other.

Neither of them spoke, knitting their brows and glooming past one another out at the window. The lassie Maxwell, whom I gave a look at before I began, to see how she was taking the matter, had her fingers plaited together over her knee, holding it a little up and dangling her foot as she listened, innocent as pussy-bawdrons thinking on the cream-jug.

"Now, listen to me," said I, very slow and calm, and speaking as English as I could; "I have a question or two to put to you both. In the first place, did I ask or invite your sons to come to this my house on the Rathan Isle? As far as I ken they cam', every one of them, without ever so much as a 'By your leave!' They hae been here, a pack of idle vagabonds, eating me out of house and home for the better part of two months. What the better am I of that? They have finished a side of pig for me amang them. I'll be sending ye in a bonny account, Mistress Allison, for they're braw eaters, juist like yersel'."

At this Mistress Allison fidged in her seat as though something was rendering her uneasy. Things were not going just so well. It was one thing for her to abuse her jewels, but quite another to sit and hear an enemy give her sons the rough side of his tongue. Mistress May Maxwell looked on from her perch on the window-sill, but said never a word. Butter would not have melted in her mouth.

"And as for *your* son, Mistress MacWhirter, four times I have had to expel him out of my house for ill-bred conduct——"

"Five! Tell the truth when ye are at it, though ye be a laird!" corrected little Jerry from the door. "I stand upon my rights. Five, by Macmillan's cup!"[1]

"And I declare that I will no longer harbour such a nest of rogues and vagabonds on this Isle of Rathan," said I, "there has been no peace since any of the names of Allison and MacWhirter came hither. More nor that, I am fully persuaded that they are a' hand in glove with notorious Freetraders, such as Yawkins and Billy Marshall. And for aught that I ken they may be art and part in supplying undutied stuff to various law-breaking, king-contemning grocers and even baillies. I am resolved that I'll lodge informations with the officers of His Majesty's Preventive forces and get the reward."

When I had finished I took a glint of my eye at May Mischief to see how she was taking it. I was rather proud of that last bit about the smuggling myself, and I thought that she would see the humour of it too, but instead I saw that she was both pale and of a frowning countenance. Then I minded that the Maxwells of Craigdarroch, all the seven big sons of them, and even the dour Cameronian father, were said to be deeper in the Gentle Traffic, as it was called, than any others in the locality.

It was May who spoke first, and her words had a little tremor in them. "I wad hae ye ken, Laird Heron," she said, "that there are many decent men who do not allow that King George has any right to say 'Ye shallna brew yersel' a drap o' comfort or bring a barrel from the Isle withoot my leave, according to the ancient custom of your fathers,' and yet who have no trokings or comradeship with Yawkins, the Marshalls, and their like."

---

[1] A communion cup of ancient silver belonging to Macmillan of Balmaghie, the first Cameronia minister, to which a special sanctity was attached by the country folk.

She still sat on her perch upon the window-sill, but she did not swing her feet any more. Indeed she leant forward a little anxiously.

"Mistress May," says I, "I'm obligated to you for your word. Indeed it would ill become my father's son to think any such thing. Far be it from me to meddle with decent folk that have their living to get. But what I'm speakin' of is a very different maitter, here are three or four idle loons coming and sorning on me for months——"

"Three!" put in Jerry from the door; "*I* work hard! says he.

"Aye, so does the deil," answered I, dryly, for all his work was only slabbering with paint.

The two old ladies stood up together, as you have seen the sentries of a line of geese picking worms and gellecks (little beetles like earwigs) on the sand, stretch their necks at a sound of alarm.

"I wad hae ye learn, you that miscaa's my sons, Andra' and John, that they are decent lads, come of decent people, burgher folk, and your faither's son wull never be like them."

"God forbid!" said I.

"Nane o' your taunts," she said. "I'm sure nane o' my lads wull bide a day longer in this house when I tell them what language ye put upon them, puir ill-guided, innocent young things."

May Mischief seemed to incline her ear, tipping it a little to the side as if to listen. I knew well what was the matter. She was nearest to where these rascals, Andrew, John, and Rab were hid at the back of the hallan-end. I could distinctly hear that loon Rab laughing myself.

"There's rats in this hoose, I'll be bound! Ouch, I see yin!" she cried, following something with her eye along the dark of the passage as if terrified. "Mistress Allison, tak' care; I doot it's run in aboot your coaties!" she cried, pointing at the threatened territory with her finger.

That good dame rose once more with greater agility from her seat than one might have expected from twenty stone weight.

"Dinna tell me lees, lassie," she cried, switching her tails about with great fervour.

By mischance she whisked a ball of grey wool, which we had for darning our stockings, out from under her. It bounded away into the dark passage. The ladies caught a waft of it with the tails of their eyes.

"Save us!" cried both of them together, springing upon one chair and clutching one another. "There's a nest o' them."

May Mischief by this time was standing on the window-sill as terrified as the rest.

"Patrick Heron, tell me the truth," she cried, with her eyes like coals; "tell me the truth—are there rats in this house?"

"Plenty of them," quoth I; "they come on to the table at supper-time."

Now this is a great mystery, for in all else a braver lass never breathed. This I will say, and I should know. She gave me a look that might have bored a hole in an inch board, and drew her skirts very close about her ankles. It is my belief that she started the noise about the rats for mischief, as she does all things; but had gotten a glisk of the grey thing that louped from Mistress Allison's petticoat into the darkness of the door. Then the terrors that she had prepared for others came home to herself. At this moment through the dark passage at the back there came a noise of scufflings and squeakings such as rats make, and a terrible white beast, with long, scaly tail and red eyes, bounded across the floor past the two stout dames standing on the chair, and ran beneath the window-sill upon which the young woman was standing. A treble-tongued and desperate scream went up.

"Now I'll bid ye guid afternoon, ladies!" I said.

"No, no!" cried Mistress Allison. "I'll tak' back every word I said, laird—I wull indeed. I spoke hastily—I own it."

"Good-day to you, Mistress MacWhirter," I said, quietly, lifting my cap from the table.

There was more squeaking and scuffling, and, I fear, the sound of muffled laughter in the passage. I was only afraid now lest the rogues should overdo the matter, so I made haste to be going.

"Maister Heron, Maister Heron," cried Mistress MacWhirter, "my boy can bide here for ever gin he likes. I'se never say a word to hinder him."

"Thank ye, mither," cried that youth from the door; "ye micht send me half a dozen pairs o' socks when ye gang hame, just for a keepsake."

On the window-sill May Mischief was standing, the graven image of apprehension.

"Guid e'en to ye, Mistress Maxwell," said I.

The pet white rat, which the rascals in the passage had let loose from its box, gave a squeak of terror underneath. They had pinched its tail before they let it loose. This was more than enough for the young Amazon on the window-sill.

"Oh, Pat Heron," she cried, "dinna gang and leave me" Oh, I see the horrid beast! Dinna, Pat, an' I'll never caa ye 'Adullam' again. Mind the kirkyard o' Kirk Oswald."

I made as if to prove hard-hearted, and set one foot past the other in the direction of the door. Then, without a word or a look to forewarn me of her intention, she launched herself from the sill of the window and caught me about the neck.

"Keep that beast off me, Patrick!" she cried, clasping me tight.

How we found ourselves outside in the still, silent, rebuking sunshine after all this noisy riot, I never could tell. But before I knew where I was May Maxwell broke out on me in anger—she that had taken me soundly and honestly about the neck but a moment before. There is no end to the mystery of woman. Inside the wives were screaming both together; and then, for a change, turn about.

"Think shame o' yersel', ye great hulk; ye think it clever to fley a wheen silly weemenfolk. When I get time I'll tell ye what I think o' ye. Gang in and stop them."

Mistress Allison was crying "Murder!" and "Thieves!" time about without pausing a moment. May Maxwell looked so imperative and threatening that I went in again at once. I had meant to remind her that the matter was her own suggestion, and that she herself had begun about the rats. But her anger and her imagination were working so handsomely that I did not dare. Besides, it is no use casting up anything to a woman. She can always put ten to the back of anything you say. My father often said so.

So I went in.

No sooner was I within the dark kitchen than Mistress Allison, perhaps impelled by that terrible thing example, did as the Maxwell lass had done, and dropped upon my neck. I was under no illusions whatever this time as to the manner in which I found myself on the ground. Mistress Allison is no featherweight. But ultimately at the long and last I got them out, and on the green bank outside I gave them some refreshment. Then I went into the house and brought the evil callants out to make their peace and my own.

"I hae catched the rat," cried little Jerry, "but it was at the peril of my life. See here!" He showed red teeth-marks on his arm.

His mother screamed in mixed fear and admiration. "Oh, my laddie, hoo durst ye? A ratton's bite is poisonous!"

"D'ye think I'm carin' for that, mither, when I can do onything to help ye?"

He passed the limb round for inspection impartially, as though it belonged to some one else. There were certainly tooth-marks upon it, but they were broad and regular. I, who had seen many a rat bite, knew what the young scoundrel had done as well as if I had seen him do it. Round the corner he had set his own teeth in his arm. Then he had rubbed the place hard for a moment to drive away the blood from under the skin. So the tooth marks now stood out with alarming distinctness. It would not have imposed upon a man for a moment, but it did well enough with women.

Thus peace was arranged.

But not one of them would venture back into the terrible house of Rathan; which was a most strange and unaccountable thing, for in after days I saw with my own eyes one of these same fearful women-folk loading muskets for the fighters under a hot fire with the greatest coolness, yet at the mention of a white rat with red eyes any of them to the end of her days would have got out upon the housetop and screamed. The Almighty made all things very good without doubt, but He left some mighty queer kinks in woman. But then the whole affair of her creation was an afterthought.

When finally they rowed away with the morose keeper of the boat that evening all was kindliness and amity. May Mischief undid the great white parcel I had helped her to carry up from the boat. It was an immense pie with most toothsome, flaky crust. To look at it made our mouths water.

"That's no rat-pie!" she said, for all good-bye.

And the strange thing is, that from that day, though I was long in owning it to myself and abused her as much as ever to other people, I liked the lass none so ill in my heart.

CHAPTER VI

THE STILL HUNTER

But I promised Silver Sand a chapter to himself. Before all be done the justice of this will be acknowledged. Silver Sand was at that time and for long after, a problem like those they give to the collegers at Edinburgh, which the longer you look at, grow the more difficult. To begin with, there seemed nothing uncanny about Silver Sand more than about my clogs with their soles of birk. But after you knew him a while, one strange and unaccountable characteristic after another emerged and set you to thinking. We shall take the plain things first.

Silver Sand was a slenderish man, of middle height, stooped in the shoulders, and with exceedingly long arms, which he carried swinging at his sides as if they belonged to somebody else who had hung them there to drip. These arms were somehow malformed, but as none had seen Silver Sand without his coat, no one had found out exactly what was wrong. Also he was not chancy to ask a question of. If was curious, however, to see him grasp everything from a spoon to a plough-handle or a long scythe for meadow hay, with the palm ever downwards.

Silver Sand made no secret of his calling and livelihood. He had a cuddie and a dog, both wonderful beasts of their kind—the donkey, the largest and choicest of its breed—the dog, the greatest and fiercest of his—a wolf-hound of the race only kept by the hill gypsies, not many removes in blood from their hereditary enemy. This fierce brute padded softly by his master's side as he in his turn walked by the side of the donkey, not one of the three raising a head or apparently looking either to the right or to the left.

I had known Silver Sand ever since I was a lad. It so chanced that I had been over to the mainland by the shell-causeway that was dry at every ebb tide. I went to gather blackberries, which did not grow in any plenty on Rogues' Island. Now in the tangle of the copse it happened that I heard a great outcry of boys. I made straight for them as a young dog goes to a collieshangie of its kind—by instinct, as it were. Here I found half a dozen laddies of my own age, or a little older, who were torturing a donkey. There is no doubt that

44

the animal could have turned the tables on its tormentors but for the fact that it was shackled with a chain and block about its forelegs, so that every time it turned to spread its hoofs at its enemies, it collapsed on its side. When I got near to it the poor beast had given up trying to defend itself, and stood most pitifully still, sleeking back its ears and shutting the lids down on its meek eyes to ward off the rain of blows.

Now whatever be my own iniquities, I never could abide ill deeds done to dumb things. So I went into the fray like a young tiger. I had no skill or science of my hands, but with nails and teeth, with clog-shod feet and plenty of wild-cat goodwill, I made pretty fair handling of the first half-dozen, till a great lout came behind, and with the knob of a branch laid me on the grass. It had gone ill with the donkey and worse with me—for I was far from popular with the village lads—but for the advent of Silver Sand and his dog, Quharrie. Then there were sore dowps and torn breeks among the Orraland callants that night. Also their mothers attended to them, and that soundly, for coming home with their clothes in such a state. The donkey, Silver Sand, and I fell on one another's necks. Afterwards Silver Sand introduced me to Quharrie—that terrible dog—making him tender me a great paw in a manner absurdly solemn, which made me kin and blood-brother to him all the days of my life. And I have received many a gift which I have found less useful, as you shall hear.

In these troubled times to be a third with Silver Sand and Quharrie, was better than to be the Pope's nephew. So in this curious way began my friendship with Silver Sand.

From that day to this Silver Sand came to Rogues Island and Rathan Tower every month. He made journeys of three weeks' length to all the farm-towns and herds' cothouses in the lirks of the hills, with keel in winter and scythe-sand in summer—and it may be a kenning of something stronger, that had never King George's seal on it. But I asked him nothing of this last.

At any rate he had the freedom of the hill fastness of the gypsies up by the Cooran and Dungeon of Buchan, and he would make my blood run cold with tales of their cruelty and wrong-doing, and of the terror which they spread through all Carrick and the hill country of Galloway.

It was a heartsome sight to see the encampment of Silver Sand by the little burnside, that came down from the high spring on the top of Rathan Isle. It was aye like a breath of thyme to me. For one thing the place was really green all the year round, and seemed to keep hidden about it the genius of the spring.

Silver Sand and Quharrie, his great wolf-dog, appeared there with a kind of regular irregularity, so that we grew to expect them. Some morning, looking out of my deep-set wicket in the high old house of Rathan, there would be a whiff of blue wood smoke rising down upon the side of the Rathan Linn, which made me hurry on my clothes and omit my prayers, which indeed are not so pressing in the morning.

When I came in sight of the encampment I usually ran, for there I would see Silver Sand pottering about in front of his bit tent, with a frying-pan or a little black cannikin hung above his fire from three crooked poles in the fashion he had learned from the gypsies. Whenever I think of Paradise, to this day my mind runs on gypsy poles, and a clear stream birling down among trees of birk and ash that cower in the hollow of the glen from the south-west wind, and of Silver Sand frying Loch Grannoch trout upon a skirling pan. Ah, to me it was ever the prime of the morning and the spring of the year when Silver Sand camped on Rathan.

"Shure, the top av the mornin' to ye, Pathrick!" cried Silver Sand, as soon as he had sight of me. He had a queer, smileless humour of his own, and often used to pretend that I was an evergreen Paddy because my father, for my future sins, had dubbed me Patrick.

"Shure, an' the same to you, and manny av thim, Brian Boru!" it was my invariable custom to reply, which pleased him much. Then I would get a red speckled trout fresh out of the pan, which the night before had steered his easy way through the clear granite-filtered water of Loch Skerrow. It was hardly food for sinful mortals. And all the time Silver Sand told me strange tales and stirred the cold potatoes in the pan where the trouts had been frying till they were burned crisp and delicious. On such mornings there were no breakfasts for me at all in the house. Indeed as long as Silver Sand remained on Isle Rathan, I only looked in occasionally at the tower to see that all went well, but if the weather were good I did not trouble the inside of it.

As for Silver Sand he never was comfortable inside a room for more than half an hour together. The wide lift was his house, and sun or shine, rain or fair, made little difference to him.

The tales he told about the wild country by the springs of Dee set me all agog to go there, and I often asked him to take me with him.

"Ah, Pathrick, my lad, it's no for me to be leading you there, and you with neither father nor mother. It's a wild country and the decent folk in it are few. Wi' man, I dinna even take Neddy into the thick of it. 'No farder than the Hoose o' the Hill for Neddy,' says he, 'and thank you kindly.' But Quharrie and me's another matter. Where Quharrie and his master canna gang, the Ill Thief himsel' daurna ride. For Silver Sand can fill his bags o' the fine, white granite piles on Loch Enoch shore, watched by a dozen of the bloody Macatericks and the wilder Marshalls, an' no yin o' them a hair the wiser."

And this was no idle boast, as you shall hear ere the story ends.

Here I drew a long breath. These tales made my quiet life here on the island seem no better than that of the green mould which grew on the "thruch" stones in the kirkyard.

I longed for the jingle-jangle of the Freetraders' harness or the scent of the outlaws' camp-fires among the great granite boulders.

"No yin o' them a hair the wiser," said Silver Sand, striking a light with his flint and steel, and transferring the flame when it lowed up to the bowl of his tiny elf's pipe, so small that it just let in the top of his little finger as he settled the tobacco in it as it began to burn.

So the days went on and the lads at the house buzzed about and went and came to their meals—the Allisons and Rab Nicoll. Only little Jerry came down to us by the waterside, for Silver Sand could be "doin' wi' him"—boys in general, and even those under my protection, he held in utter abhorrence. Once Jerry brought tidings.

"There's a sharp-nosed brig with high sails setting in for Briggus Bay or Maxwell's landing. She's been beating off and on a' day with her tops'ls reefed," said Jerry, in a careless way which intimated that he was of opinion that his news was important, but which yet left him a porthole if it did not turn out so to be.

In a moment Silver Sand sprang up the side of the bank to a favourite lookout station of his own.

He came down shaking his head. The news appeared important enough to Silver Sand to please even Jerry, who loved excitement of every sort.

"There's deviltry afoot!" he said. "That's Yawkins and his crew, an' Silver Sand kens what they're after brawly, the ill-contriving wirricows—but we'll diddle them yet."

Then looking down at the great dog, he cried, with a kind of daft glee—

> "Up an' waur them a', Quharrie,
> Up an' waur them a', man;
> There's no a Dutchman i' the pack
> That's ony guid ava, man—*Hooch*!"

And Silver Sand, usually so dignified, executed a fandango on the beach, his long arms hanging wide from his sides and his light and limber legs twinkling. Quharrie also lifted up his forepaws, moving them solemnly, as though he wished to join his master in his reel.

So it wore to evening and the stars came out. Silver Sand seemed far from easy. He ran repeatedly up to the lookout place, which he called Glim Point, but ever came back unsatisfied.

"It's no dark aneuch yet to see weel!" he said, for his eyes seemed to be of greatest service at night when the light was shut from the eyes of others.

"We'll hae veesitors the nicht, doon by the Rogues' Hole, I'm thinkin'," said Silver Sand.

It was about half an hour past nine o'clock when Silver Sand's nervousness became very apparent and unsettling to myself. He ran about his camp and up to the hilltop—in and out all the while, like a dog at a fair. Quharrie also bristled up his hair and shot his short, sharp ears forward, and under his black lips there was a gleam of white teeth, like the foam line on the shore on a dark, blowy night.

Quite suddenly a light flickered out of the gloom across the water in the direction of the farmhouse of Craigdarroch, and then Silver Sand's agitation became pitiful to see. He ordered me about like a dog—nay, like a very cur, for never a word uncivil did he say to Quharrie that was a dog indeed. The beast seemed to understand him without a word, watching his look with fierce eyes that shone like untwinkling stars.

"Gae to the House of Rathan, and bid the lads bar every door and no sleep a wink the nicht. Tell them to loaden a' your faither's guns, but no to shoot unless the ill-doers try to break in the door. It's little likely that they'll meddle wi' the big hoose o' Rathan, that has no store of nowt or horse beasts. But wha kens?—wha kens?—the gleds are gatherin' frae the north an' frae the sooth. Ootland Dutchmen an' French Monzies—broken men frae a' the ports o' Scotland, and the riff-raff o' the Dungeon o' Buchan.

I ran to the house and startled the lads with my news. And here again was a strange thing. The boys that had hidden from their mothers so lately brisked up, and if any of them were downhearted about their position, they did not let the others see it. It had been recognised among us that we might have some trouble with the bad crew of smugglers, whom my father's reputation as a marksman and past-master in the Freetrade craft, had hitherto kept at a distance. But even I had no small conceit of myself, and I thought that I could soon make myself as respected among any Yawkins and his crew as ever my father had been. In which, as it happened, I was grievously mistaken, for without Silver Sand, I had been no better than a herring hung by the gills in the hand of these unscrupulous men. I named Andrew Allison captain of the stronghold of Rathan till my return, for we did everything in military fashion; and gave him the key of the glazed press of guns, which we often spent our wet days in oiling with immense care and forethought. It gave me pleasure only to look upon the row of them, shining like silver on the rack.

For myself I took a pair of pistols, and was for bringing the same out to Silver Sand, when I remembered that without doubt he had his own by him.

CHAPTER VII

THE RED COCK CROWS AT CRAIGDARROCH

When I got back again to the shore Silver Sand was already in the boat, Quharrie crouching in the bow.

I offered one of my pistols.

"Leave thae nesty things at hame," he said, with unusual shortness of temper. "They'll be gaun blaffin' aff when there's mair need to be as quiet as an ash-leaf twirlin' to the grund in a windless frost. Tak' a durk, man, instead!"

He handed me a long, deadly-looking weapon in a leather case, the look of which I did not like at all; yet, for the sake of peace, I stuck it in my black belt with the brass buckle, alongside of the pistols in their cases.

Silver Sand took the oars. He did not stick his weapon—a dirk like mine—into his belt, but held it gripped between his knees as he rowed. His oars made no noise, neither on the rullocks nor yet when he drew them into the boat to ship them when I had got the little rag of a sail far forward to fill and draw. Then Silver Sand steered with an oar. He made direct for the Maxwells' landing-place. The star before us at Craigdarroch grew larger and larger. Flames shot up far into the sky, so that the sea was lighted up for miles. Only under the shadow of the woods of Orraland, where the trees almost dipped their branches in the salt water at high tide, was there the safety of darkness.

So we kept far to the right, and skirted the shore almost under the trees. As we came close in, we lost the light wind which, a hundred yards from the cliff, seemed to slant upwards and leave the shore line breathlessly still, while from the burning onstead of Craigdarroch the flames and smoke were tossed westward in the strong breeze.

Situated as I was in the bow, I could not ask questions, and Silver Sand had not volunteered me any information; but I remembered that there was bad blood between the lads of Craigdarroch and the evil crew who went under the name of Captain Yawkins' gang. It might well be that they were now taking their revenge on the house; and little as I cared, in the way of love, for May Maxwell, it made my blood run cold to think of her at the mercy of these sea scoundrels and hill gypsies, who thought no more of carrying away a lass from the Lowlands than of killing one of their neighbours' sheep.

When at last we got into the shadow of the trees, and ran the boat safely ashore in the slushy sand of the little cove under the beeches by Orraland Gate, Silver Sand whispered in my ear that we must "keep wide," which is a herd's term for keeping some distance from the flock in order not to alarm them.

"It's likely," said he, "that ye may hae some wark wi' your shootin' airns. Keep them handy, an' when ye hear me cryin' like a hoolet, ye can rin in to me, but dinna fire gin ye can help it. The seven Maxwell lads are a' awa' ower at the Isle o' Man, an' thae vaigabones are dootless makkin' the best o't. It's the lassie that I'm vexed for; the rest might snore up in reek for me!"—a thing which I wondered to hear him say.

Quharrie and Silver Sand sprang clear of the boat, and I followed, knapping my toe on a stone as I did so. I uttered a sharp exclamation.

"My man, it's as weel to tell ye sune as syne. In ten minutes as muckle noise as that will get ye sax inches o' smugglers' jockteleg in the wame o' ye. They're no canny, thae boys, when onybody comes across them. There's Dago thieves amang them, ootlandish jabberers wi' the tongue, but gleg wi' the knife as a souter wi' his elshin."

When we got up on the hillside clear of the woods, we could look down on the farmsteading of Craigdarroch. The ricks of corn which had been left unthrashed from last year's harvest were in a blaze. Black figures of men ran hither and thither about the house and round the fires. We could see them disappearing into the office-houses with blazing peats and torches. The thatch of the barn was just beginning to show red. Narrow tongues of fire and great sweeps of smoke drove to leeward against the clear west. It was strange that there seemed no help coming from the other neighbouring farm-towns. We heard afterwards that the Black Smugglers had sent a man with a loaded gun to stand at the gate of each farm close, and keep all within doors at the peril of life.

"It's the auld man's brass kist they're after, I'se warrant," said Silver Sand; "and maybes the bit lass as weel."

I had not the least conception what he meant by the "brass kist,"

but it grieved me to see the bonny corn that had grown so golden on
the braes anent the isle screeving up in fire to the heavens; and when
he mentioned the lass my heart sank within me, only to kindle again
like fire the moment after.

"Yawkins threatened that he wad gar the Red Cock craw on
Auld Man Maxwell's rooftree afore the year was oot, an' faith, he's
dune it. But the seven bauld brithers, sirce me, but they'll be wild
men when they come hame."

We were now on a heathery eminence, dry above and wet
beneath.

"Here's a hidie hole for ye, young Rathan," said Silver Sand,
giving me even at that moment my laird's title, which he did not do
often. "Clap close and bide till Quharrie an' me comes for ye!"

With that he pointed with his finger to his great wolfhound, and
away in opposite directions the two set at top speed, the man
bending nearly as low as the dog. The east wind whipped the bent,
and the crackling of the burning rafters and blazing stacks came most
unpleasantly to my ears. I wondered at the time why there was no
noise of men crying. That was, I knew afterwards, due to Captain
Yawkins of Sluys, a very notable sailor, who forbade it. When he
was hanged, some time afterwards, for piracy at Leith, there were
seventeen warrants out against him for all manner of crimes, from
trepanning a lass on the Isle of Gometra (somewhere in the
Highlands), to bloody piracy on the high seas. When I was in
Edinburgh last I saw him swing in chains on Leith sands, very well
tarred, and the flesh dried flat to the bones with the bensilling[3] wind
off the Baltic lands. And he is more comfortable there than he had
been in old Richard Maxwell's hands that night.

This, at least, was his doing, and even then the cup of his
iniquities was brimming perilously near the lip. Captain Yawkins
would not much oftener seek the port of Sluys.

It behoved me, however, to lie low among the heather, and
watch warily the tarry scullions that were making such a hash of the
bien and comfortable homestead. Only about two hundred yards from
where I lay in the sheuch of the moss-hagg, I could see, plain as
black on white, a sailor man with a musket which he took over his
shoulder as if he had been one of His Majesty's red soldiers—as
indeed he was, but deserted and waiting for the tow-rope or the
ounce of lead which, in good sooth, and in the fitting time of an
all-wise Providence, he received in due course.

[3] A "bensil" is a cold, bask, dry east wind.

The place where I lay was on the edge of the wild country which stretches along the shore, very close in all round Galloway, save only about the estuaries of the rivers. From it the moors run back, in broken moss-hagg and scattered boulder-stone, to the Screel o' Criffel, which is the highest hill in that locality, and as they say, stands up from Solway, watching the tides and spinning the weather.

I was to do nothing except lie thus prone on my forefront, with my nose cocking out of the heather, and keep a watch till Silver Sand came back. It grieved me to be so actionless. It would have suited me better to be up and doing, if it were only to escape that lass's tongue. But my heart grew sore for the thought of her among all these regardless men.

Now there were a number of low, dwarfish *currie* thorns, bent away from the sea by the wind, on this waste place—the moor being generally very flat and bare. I remembered that I had come over to harry gleds' nests here in the years when yet my father was alive, and I could think on such things.

It came to my mind also at the same time that that was both a higher and a safer place for my watch quite near, by reason that it stood on a little mound that had been made by the hand of man, some say for the purposes of baron's justice in the old time of pit and gallows. There was also a stone dyke round a well, which always flowed cool and clear from under a great rock in the midst of the bit scrunts of birks and flat-lying, ground-creeping thorns.

I did not think that Silver Sand would be disappointed or angry, because the place where I designed to go was but a few hundred yards further west, and at the head of a glen which led up from the shore. This would also, as I well knew, be our best road to the boat we had left on the shingel. So, as silently as I could, I retreated through the long trough of the cold, black-looking moss-haggs. I had not gone far, progressing, as the partan-crab is said to do, backwards, when a rush of escaping cattle tore over the face of the moor, and one great stot coming my way trod upon me and *"gorroched"* me deeper into the black peat broth. For a long while I lay still as death, but as there seemed to be no pursuer, more stealthily than ever I resumed my way.

Soon I was climbing, a fearsome spectacle of dirt, up the side of the knowe of the "scroggie thorns." Suddenly, as I crawled, I was seized from behind in a grasp that threatened to dislocate my neck-bone, and a voice in my ear said, very low and deadly—

"Yae word, ye crawlin' blastie, an' I'll let the life oot o' ye!"

Now this was not at all a useful observation. It was a perfect impossibility for me to utter a word had my life depended on it, for the thumbs which were choking me had been at the work before, and the pressure on my windpipe threatened to shut out the breath of life from me in a few moments. There were flashes of fire in my eyes, and stars that fell and burst; a sound as of a great spate of waters roared in my ears; then darkness.

To all intents and purposes I died then, for to lose consciousness by violence is to die. What more is there left to experience—in this life, at least?

CHAPTER VIII

NIGHT ON THE MOOR

When I came to myself it was through the buzzing of a hundred million bees, each as large as my hand. It was a cold country I travelled through back to this earth, so cold that I wondered how such great bees came there and what flowers they were that they fed on, and who hived them, and what would happen if one of them stung me. Also many other things I saw which it would be tiresome to write down, even if there were a winter's forenight to do it in. But after the bees there followed a thought of pie, and what a pity it was that I had not got that lass Maxwell's pie eaten before I died. It was a good pie. It was warm, too, when she brought it, and I was so cold. Then at the last I wondered where I might be. I said to myself, "I know not where this place is, but it is not heaven, at any rate, so I must e'en content myself." Yet I remember I was not very much alarmed, nor yet very much disappointed. It was, in fact, as I had expected, or so like it that there was no need to make complaints. I had a comfortable sense of being somehow provided for.

When I came alive again there was a light on my face from somewhere, and somebody's arm was round my head, and there was a stronger suggestion of pie in my mind than ever.

"Is he come to?" said some one in a man's gruff voice, but yet softly.

"No yet, faither. I think he's comin'; but he's gotten an unco chirt "puir laddie."

"It was a muckle bullock, May," said I, as hoarse as a crow, the words whistling in my throat like the night wind in the keyhole of the outer door. Being awake now I was aware how it was that my thoughts had run on pie, which, when you come to think of it, is a sufficiently curious thing to think upon when you are dead.

"Aye, it was my faither," she said, quietly, and quite in earnest, transferring my head from her shoulder to some kind of pillow made of young bracken and a shawl—no kind of exchange at all, to my thinking. "He thocht ye war yin o' the robbers."

"An' weel it is for you, youth Rathan, that my dochter kenned

55

ye; for had ye been yin o' that accursed crew o' Yawkins', ye wad hae suppit in hell the nicht," said the old man of Craigdarroch, solemnly and without heat, simply stating a fact which might be relied upon. I wondered to hear him, for though he had been a wild man most of his days, in his later years he had become a great professor and a regular attendant on the Cameronian meeting at the Nine Mile Bar.

There was a cut on Richard Maxwell's forehead, done, as his daughter presently told me, with a seaman's cutlass when he broke away from them. They had been awakened by the herd-boy crying that the outlaws were come down from the hills to drive the cattle. Maxwell wakened easily, being a light sleeper, and his daughter was soon beside him, and that in much better order of apparel, as my own observation told me, than might have been deemed possible in such hasty and sudden deray.

Her father cried to her to come and help him to carry away a chest of papers and valuables which the robbers were coming to search for in his house at Craigdarroch; for this Captain Yawkins had often threatened to do, swearing that he would harry Maxwell the Psalm-singer (for so they nominated him) with fire and sword, with the driving of cattle, and the hamstringing of horse. So ere the mounted smugglers arrived, May and her father got clear of the steading, and came out here to the moss-haggs where for the present they were safe. But it happened that her father, not content with what he had possession of, ran back that he might get his Bible. Then some of the outrunners of the robber band coming or he was aware, thrust in on him before he could win clear; but he broke through them, leaving one on his back at the steading gate, which is called the White Liggate; it is on the way to the watering-place where the plough-horses drink. And so he came hither with his coat most torn off his back, a great ragged cut on his brow, yet holding his Bible in one hand and a naked sword in the other.

This was the substance of what I learned lying there on the moor on May Maxwell's shawl, while old Richard Maxwell in a low voice cursed the destroyers of his home and plenishing with great curses out of the Book of Psalms. It made me admire greatly to hear him so ready with his Bible words.

To us lying there in a little came Silver Sand and Quharrie, breathed and "peching" with the race. Silver Sand looked a sharp reproach when I told him how it was that I cam hither, out of the place and duty in which he left me; but he said no word, neither then, nor yet afterwards. May Maxwell and her father did not take his appearing as at all a strange thing; of which I now think the reason to be that all Silver Sand's movements were so still and secret that no one would have been much astonished at any hour of the day or night had he appeared at their door or suddenly vanished from their sight. Yet to me he was always good and kind; and, indeed, so remains to this day—though now he is, as he says, so stricken in years that the tether-rope is round his foot, with rheumatism in the joints for clog and shackle to keep him nearer home, which means near the old house of Rathan.

We maun quit from here and that right speedy," said Silver Sand, "for they are firing the heather and bent, and it will run like February muirburn in this dry, easterly wind."

"What is it they want?" said I to Silver Sand, for I could now sit up, and was feeling infinitely better. In truth it was more the surprise of it that hurt me than the old man's thumbs, or even the cloots of that great rampaging stot which trampled me into the moss-hole when the drove went over me.

"What is't they want?" said Silver Sand, testily. "The outlaws, what they can find—but Yawkins, he wants that bit kist" (pointing to the brass-bound box on which old Craigdarroch was sitting), "an' anither lad that I ken o', he's mair anxious to fa' on wi' the lass, I'm thinkin'."

At this May Maxwell, kneeling by her father, seemed to draw nearer to me in the darkness; but whether it was from curiosity to hear, or only for company and the sense of safety, I could not at that time rightly understand.

The old man was keeping straight on, interposing prayers among his curses in a manner which, had the matter been a trifle less serious, might have produced laughter. But none of us had even a trifling sense of humour among us that night.

"Curse them," he said, hissing his words—"curse them root and branch! But I maun try to be patient. It's doubtless the Lord's will that my seven braw sons should be awa' at the Isle o' Man when this comes upon me in my auld age. I maun e'en try to bear this. *It's after a' the Lord's will*—but wait till they get hame, thae seven braw lads, an' come to the blackened waa's o' Craigdarroch, and see the grey ash on the rick-bottoms that their ain hands laid, an' a' the bonny sheaves gane luntin' up into the sky—there'll be a vengeance that day so that they shall tell it to the babe yet unborn—yea, for many days. But, after a', it's a mercy it's nae waur, an' we maun try to be patient. It is the Lord's will!"

CHAPTER IX

IN RAMSAY BAY

How all this came about I did not learn for long after, nor what was the pick that the Black Smugglers had taken at the Maxwells, though I was about to put my hands so deep in their quarrels. Nor, in truth, did I greatly care; but it is a good tale, and necessary to the proper understanding of the whole matter from the beginning. It was told to me severally by Ebenezer Hook, who on that day steered the *Van Hoorn* in action (which, at that time, was the name of Captain Yawkins' brig), and also by Kennedy Maxwell, the youngest of the seven brothers who had gone for their spring cargo to the Isle of Man.

I shall try to straighten out these two tangled stories as best I may. The motive of the Maxwells was plain. Will, the eldest, had news of a tidy cargo of French brandy, German perfumes, and Vallenceens lace snug on the northern shore of Ramsay Bay. So his brothers and he set sail in the *Spindrift*, the little lugger of fourteen tons, which had run many cargoes and brought much joy and sorrow to the adventurous house of the Maxwells of Craigdarroch.

Now it so happened that in Ramsay Bay at that time Captain Yawkins (the head of the "Black" side of the traffic, as the Maxwells chieftained the "White") lay becalmed, with his boats out for towing and his sentinels on Maungold Head lest a ship of war should come and surprise him within the harbour.

It was the great Yawkins' custom to ask for what he wanted, and if he did not get it—why then, with no more words to take it with violence superadded to revenge the ignominy of the refusal. Word was brought to him that the Galloway Maxwells were just about to lift a "square" cargo of the finest ever run from the island. Some enemy no doubt took to Yawkins this news—as might well be, for the Maxwells were a little over-fond of the strong hand themselves.

Forthwith came Captain Yawkins in the grey of the morning, and from their snug hiding-place in lee of the Red Fisherman's cottage, took the linen-wrapped webs of the fine Vallenceens, the ankers of French brandy, and the cases of the sweet-smelling water of Cologne. The Red Fisherman ran to the shore as the men from Yawkins' longboat were landing, and with his fingers to his mouth gave the "gled's whistle"—the piercing signal agreed upon between himself and his employers, the Maxwells.

Up tumbled these seven dark-haired men from the tiny forepeak and from under the spread sail. In the stillness of the morning they could hear the rattle of their own beloved casks as they were swung into the boat of their adversary. Now the Maxwells were no long-suffering persons, and it had not been like them to let their goods go without an effort.

With his sheath-knife ready at his hip, Will Maxwell cut the rope of their small anchor as it ran over the stern.

"Away with the foresail!" he cried.

In a trice the great brown sail, barkened with tanpit juice as was Galloway wont, mounted steadily aloft and took the wind. Will Maxwell ordered his crew to haul the sheet aft, and in a moment the dainty little lugger was dancing over the ripples, running straight for the robber longboat, which was now reaching out for Captain Yawkins' ship that lay in the offing at the mouth of the bay, just under Maungold Head.

Will Maxwell handled his little craft well. She came away with the breeze in her great square of sail faster than anything else would have done in that light wind, the ripples talking briskly under her forefoot, lapping and making a pleasant noise. So Kennedy Maxwell says, and he wonders how he had time to think on these things. He also admired much to see a black corbie of the great sea breed chase a pirate gull, and force it to drop a fish it had just taken from one of the white-breasted sea-birds which were wheeling and plunging about. Kennedy Maxwell says that he felt himself upon a similar quest.

But the bay was so narrow and the rowing boat came on so fast that the man in the stern sheets had only time to cry, "Hold off, you lubbers, or you'll run us down!" before the prow of the *Spindrift* crashed right along the larboard side of the ship's longboat, carrying away the oar-blades before there was time to ship them. Six of the Maxwells tumbled into the longboat in a moment and were hard at it with fist and whinger, while Will stayed aboard and made fast to the stern with his boathook.

The brothers had a great advantage in leaping from a height, and it may be that the Black Smugglers did not fight at all up to their reputation. Indeed, except that peppery Welshman, Ap Evans, in the stern sheets, no one of them had much heart in the business. Moreover, a jollyboat did not give them fair scope for the display of their powers. They required the sweep of a ship's deck, and there, as we shall see, they were no cowards.

Ap Evans gave David Maxwell a long, slashing cut down the outer arm, which bothered him for many a day. But he was soon held by Kennedy, who had never before seen the blood flow, and was therefore the most heedless, while black-bearded Will from the lugger kept the others quiet with a pistol. It took no long time for the active brothers to get their cargo on board their own boat again and sail away, feeling themselves very big men indeed—a sentiment which, however, did not make them any the safer.

As they cast loose Will Maxwell cried, "My compliments to Captain Yawkins, and thank him kindly for his assistance in getting our stuff aboard. It was freendly done. Say that I'll no forget it."

"The devil fly away with you, for an ugly Galloway stot!" cried Ap Evans, the Welshman, his twinkling grey eyes contracted as to their pupils till the black within them shrunk to the merest pin-points. Kennedy says that he noticed this particularly, for it reminded him of their grim-cat Toby when he was watching the cage-bird.

So the seven bold brothers bore away with no greater damage than a cutlass slash, which did not yet bother David much, the wound not having had time to stiffen.

All this time Captain Yawkins was not idle. He had been awakened from his morning sleep by the news that his attempt on the Maxwells' cargo was likely to fall awry. So being, like all his kind, both swift and energetic, he at once ordered his boats out, made haste to get his anchor up, cast loose his Long Toms, and prepared to intercept the daring lads of Galloway as soon as they came between him and the shore.

This he might possibly have done, but it so happened that just when Will Maxwell was bandying compliments with old Ap Evans, the smugglers' watch set on Maungold Head signalled that there was danger approaching. Thrice the signal came, in a way that could not be misunderstood. Indeed it had been made before, but so intent were the men aboard of the *Van Hoorn* on watching the affray of the boats that not an eye had seen the first signals.

Round the Head, beating up from the south in the light wind, came a vessel with tall spars sweeping the sky.

"A myriad devils," cried Skipper Yawkins, "we have watched these landlubbers overlong. We shall lose our ship. Here she comes. By the weathercock of Krabbendyk, 'tis the *Seahorse,* boys—sloop of war of eighteen guns. See the jack at her mizzen. Mark their sky scrapers. She means to have us boys, but then *I* mean that she shall not. Captain Yawkins is not the man to be fooled twice in a morning."

The men bustled about the decks—Dago rats and broad-beamed Dutchmen, hill country gypsies taken to smuggling—and the whole crew of outlaw men gave a rousing cheer, for they were angry and wanted to have it out with some one. Before the guns were cast loose and their muzzle sheetings removed Ap Evans came on board, and his strident voice was to be heard setting the men to their quarters, for Captain Yawkins fought his brig like a king's ship. Indeed many a king's ship was less well found. Two Long Tom stern chasers looked over the taffrail, six twelve-pounder carronades grinned through the ports; and besides these there was Yawkins' pet, a fine new twenty-four pounder on the forecastle, just shipped and never yet fired.

Out between the heads of Ramsay Bay the Galloway lugger went spinning. In ordinary times she would have got a shot across her bows to heave her to, but Lieutenant Mountenay of the *Seahorse* had mettle more attractive than a possible score of brandy ankers under the sheepskins and bullock-hides of the lugger *Spindrift.* So the Maxwells tossed their bonnets in an ecstasy of salutation, and bore away north for White Horse Bay. It happened, however, that at the Point of Ayre they saw the spars of yet another king's man, waiting in the seaway with her topsails backed, keeping in the clear morning a bright lookout upon the four coasts. It was not in their mind to run any more risks when they had once come so well off. So Will Maxwell turned the head of the *Spindrift* southward in the direction of Derby Haven, where for safety they landed the goods again; and by the time that the second king's ship, which proved to be the preventive schooner *Ariel,* sent a boat aboard, the Maxwells were once more peaceful, coast-wise traders, with a cargo of salt, alum, barytes for the men of Mona, and hides and sheepskins to take back in exchange to the tanneries of Dumfries.

So the young offer who came on board was obliged to report all right upon his return. But MacCallum, the boatswain of the *Ariel,* said to Kennedy Maxwell—

"My lad, this may do yince, an' twice, an' gin ye hae luck three times; but at the hinder end ye'll cool yer heels in Kirkcudbright jail.

An' that's no a bonny place, I can assure ye."

"Hoot, Rab," said Kennedy, "it's no sae lang since ye war rinnin' the bonny faulds o' lace wi' the best o' us. Ye canna hae muckle to say."

"Aye, Kennedy, to my shame that's ower true, but I hae seen the error o' my ways in time!"

"Likely that," returned Kennedy, dryly, "an' the guid o' a pound a week and a pension at the hinder end."

"Aweel, Kennedy, say as ye like, my word was kindly meant, lad," said the boatswain.

"An' kindly ta'en," said Kennedy, nursing his arm with his other hand; "but gin I war you I wad come nae mair to yon toon. My faither's a passionate man, in spite o' havin seen the error o' his ways."

"What for should I keep awa' frae your hoose or ony ither hoose?" cried Rab MacCallum. "Ye ken Deputy Dallas, the gauger, is there every ither nicht."

"I ken that," said Kennedy. "Ye see the way o't is this, MacCallum—my faither can be doin' wi' preventive men, an' at a pinch he can put up wi' maybe a smuggler or twa. But the man he canna do wi' is the man that has been yae thing an' noo is anither, an' wha tries to keep a fit in ilka camp!"

"Naebody ever said that I gied information," said MacCallum.

"Na," said Kennedy, "but ye come frae Rerrick and the sted o' the gallows that hanged Henry Greg is atween yer een."[1]

The boatswain flew into a passion.

"I'll catch ye yet, you Maxwells; you an' your prood sister. Ye a' hae the gibin' tongue an' the pridefu' e'e that scorns honest fowk. But I'll hae ye laid low some day yet."

"That shows," cried Kennedy, "that ye hae tried to do it afore. A fig for your threatenings. Ye're like daft Tammy Norie's bladder that he carries daudin' on a stick—fu' o' wind, and maybe a pea or two rattling i' the wame o' ye! Nocht else!"

---

[1] A dark hint at a supposed local propensity for underhand work.

CHAPTER X

SMUGGLER AND KING'S MEN

Meanwhile there was a braver job going forward between the Heads of Ramsay. For the account of this I am obliged to Ebie Hook, who all that day was at the tiller of the *Van Hoorn,* stretched whiles across it, with a strong Dutchman to help him to twirl it round, and whiles steering her with his finger and thumb to sail her within a cat's jump of the orders of Captain Yawkins.

Now there have been many things said against that wondrous Dutchman, and no doubt he had many a sin on his soul, forbye murder in all its different degrees; but there are two things that no one could ever lay to his charge—that Yawkins was either coward or bad sailor.

Many a time in the ward-room when retelling the story of how the Dutchman ran athwart his hawse off Ramsay Heads, Lieutenant Mountenay would admit—

"Tarred, wizened, sun-dried, and smoke-dried, if you were to take down old Yawkins from the shore end of Leith pier, you would have a better sailor than I or any man on King George's navy roster."

Nor did any say him nay, for it was about his sixth glass that he was in the habit of saying this, and he was a stark carle in his cups.

So on the quarter-deck of the *Van Hoorn,* which was kept like that of a man-of-war for whiteness, Ebie Hook stood picking his orders from the captain himself, and crying, "Aye, aye, sir," like clockwork.

He said that it was a pleasure to see the ship fall into her marks like a racing cutter, and stretch away on another tack as steady as one's married wife.

"She was the sweetest boat that ever sailed, was the *Van Hoorn,* and Yawkins was the very son-of-a-gun of a fine seaman—not an ounce of tallow about him anywhere."

"Man, Rathan," Ebie would say, "the way he sailed that ship in the freshening breeze that blew between the Heads was a miracle.

Every time we wore ship I saw the wuddy plain afore me, for it wasna only smuggling, it was black piracy they had against us had we been ta'en, wi' the plunder of a sunken Greenock barkanteen in oor hold. Man, I tell ye I was feared. I misdooted I wad never mair get merry at Stanykirk Sacrament, or foo at Keltonhill Fair. 'It's a' up wi' ye noo, Ebie,' says I; 'I hae telled ye mony a time it wad come to this. The teuch tow-rape an' the weary wuddy hae gotten ye at the hinder end.'

"But oh, man, it wasna to be at that time, whatever; an' it was by clean-run seamanship that we wan clear."

Now, being a landsman, I have not the skill of sea-terms to tell the story as Ebie told it, but the gist of it was as follows:—

"The way out of the brulzie was this," Ebie Hook would begin (I see him yet, though he went to his account years ago. He sat ever by the chimney corner and lunted away on his cutty pipe, using tobacco of prodigious blackness and strength, such as he had learned to smoke in foreign countries when he was a traveller—so vile that it was evil enough to the stomach to stand the reek of his pipe after it had passed out of his mouth). "The bo'sun of our ship was Abraham Anderson, from the Crae Brig. As the king's man came nearer he piped to quarters; and it was a pretty sight to see, though being at the wheel I had little enough time to be seeing it. 'Twixt watching the binnacle and jumping to auld Yawkins' word I had enough to do. It wasna playing at x's and o's to be steerin' for that crossbones of a Dutchman, whether in a chase or a battle. He would have stuck a knife in you as quick as get married on shore—and they say he was married as many as sixty-seven times, the old Mahommetan!

"And it was bonny to see the boarding nets triced up and the pikes ready, the pistols all primed and the matches burning, ilka yin stuck in a linstock on the deck.

"The gunners were dumping round shot on the boards, and the grape and cannister were coming up from below. Outside the harbour, near the entrance of the bay, lay the king's ship, waiting to catch us as we cam' oot, with all their guns trimmed to rake us as we gaed by them.

"It was doubtless mighty fine, but the king's officer was a fresh youth to think of old Captain Yawkins stepping canny to his ain destruction like that.

"So in the lee of the land under the great rise of Maungold Head we lay with our topsails aback, waiting for the enemy to come in and lay us alongside.

"Now, though the Captain was cursing the Maxwells and their impudence, and blaming them for sending the revenue men on us, it so happened that it was really through them that we were preserved frae the gallows for that time at least.

"Now there is no doubt whatever that had the *Seahorse* but kenned that the preventive boat *Ariel* was within as short a distance o' Ramsay as the ither side of the Point of Ayre, she wad simply hae lain still where she was and waited for her consort, which wad hae compelled us to come oot and gie her battle on her ain terms. But luckily for us the *Ariel* was at that moment spanking away to the south'ard on a wild goose chase after the lang-shanked Maxwell lads. So we were left to fecht it oot on something like equal terms.

"It was awesome to hear the captain. He never stopped blasphemin'. And the curious thing about the matter was that it wasna the king's men that he was wild at, but the Maxwells, and more especially auld Dick Maxwell that had been his partner and sailed the seas with him in the days before he got the brig *Van Hoorn* for himsel'.

"He cursed him for a thief, and there was something aboot a brass box and a treasure, and something, too, aboot a lass; but the ower-word o' his sang was juist this, 'Be the day dark or clear, the nicht star-shine or pit-mirk, an' the Red Cock craw not on the rooftree of Richard Maxwell by the heuchs of Craigdarroch, may I turn for ever and ever frae side to side between the red coal and the brimstane flaming blue ayont the bars o' muckle hell.' A dreadfu' oath to speak, but he spak' it often.

"It was indeed maist fearsome to hear him. He was swearin' like that a' the time, even when we could see the king's ship coming through the narrows at the head o' the day and settin' in for us wi' every steek o' canvas set.

"Man, she was bonny as she cam', the foam reamin' white under her forefoot. The white toorock o' her snow-white claiths blawin' licht an' airy frae masthead to bowsprit and jib-boom-end. Then as soon as she cam' roon the point she began to fire the single guns, and the shot to whustle through oor riggin'. Aboot this time the job o' the man at the wheel is no to be recommended as a means o' livelihood, for the sharp-shooters they fire at him, and gin the ship gets raked fore and aft, he's the lad that kens aboot it first, for they hae e'en to soop a' that's left o' him owerboard wi' a besom.

"But there was no fear of any disobeying in Yawkins' ship. Ye *micht* be killed by the enemy if you obeyed; but ye *wad* be killed of a certainty gin ye didna, so ye micht lay your accoont wi' that.

"'Put her about,' he cried, suddenly, and wi' that ran right across the bows of the *Seahorse* as she came swiftly, swaying with the undercarry of the sea into the harbour mouth. She brought the wind with her, for as she closed on us we seemed to get it as weel; and the sudden shift in our helm, instead of landing us becalmed, steadied us to send a broadside doon her decks and yet draw clear before she could alter her course.

"We were running now as if to beach the *Van Hoorn* on the slushy sand of the southernmost bay; but in a moment, just when it seemed that we had caught ourselves, 'All hands wear ship,' cried our captain, and the mates gave the orders while the Dutchman and I burst ourselves to bring the helm sharp a-weather. Down dropped the peak, round went the spars, the yards were braced, and away we swung through the rising lift of the harbour bar till the wind caught us as she passed the Heads, and, like a sea pellock, buried her nose in the heaving smother where the wind and the tide met.

"As we left the king's ship astern, old Father Yawkins sprang on our taffrail, and waved his hand—'Out-sailed, out-fought, out-witted—such a set of kiss-my-loofs, you king's men. That's what I think of ye! Hae!'

"And with that he leaped down, and snatching off his wig and broad, flapping hat, he crammed them into the right-hand Long Tom, and with his own hand shot them aboard the king's man.

"Now this insult put more anger into the heart of Lieutenant Mountenay, commander of the *Seahorse* than all the men that he lost. It was in part this that caused the great eagerness which there was among all the king's navy men to capture Captain Yawkins—an adventure which afterwards succeeded to admiration in spite of many failures.

"Sae it was even in this way that the *Van Hoorn* ran direct north to land her cargo at the Brigghous', and to burn the bonny stackyaird o' Craigdarroch."

Ebie here took breath and blew upon his reeking pipe.

"But what hindered the *Seahorse* from chasing you?" I asked him. "She could not have been such a distance ahint you as to lose ye in a run of less than thirty miles, and its little mair to the Brigghouse?"

"Weel, an' that's a funny thing too," said Ebie; "it is just like a play. They tell me that the verra last shot that was fired—the yin that Captain Yawkins fired himsel"—carried awa' the halewar o' their steerin' gear, and left them withoot poo'er to do more than put down an anchor. So they tell me. I kenna. But gin that be the reason, it wad seem that some o' the auld man's brains had stucken to the auld man's wig.

"Eh, sirce, but there's mony wonderfu' things in the warld.

"An' my bacca's dune. Hae ye a fill aboot ye, think ye?"

CHAPTER XI

THE GREAT CAVE OF ISLE RATHAN

Certes, but it was good hearing when we got under the brow of the land and underneath the shaggy shadows of the trees, to hearken the sough of the water below the keel of the boat. We had Richard Maxwell and his chest, and May with her bundle of sarks tied in a spotted napkin. That boat was the wholesomest place that I had found since I saw the red star of a godless night rise over Craigdarroch.

Silver Sand rowed us back silently as we had come. As we went I saw that he was not taking us to the house, but down towards the sea point of Rathan Island where the rocks were at their wildest and the surge for ever fretted and boiled about the perpendicular cliffs.

"What for are we no going to the House Bay?" I asked Silver Sand.

"Because I dinna want my throat cutted," he said. "D'ye think Yawkins and his sea-thieves will no find out the first thing in the grey o' the mornin' that something heavy has been carried to the shore between twa men, and that three men, a lassie, and a dog hae gotten intil a boat under the trees by the White Horse Bay? It's so plain to be seen that even a gamewatcher could make oot as muckle!"

"But what then?" I asked, the project not yet being clear to me.

"What else?" said he. "Sorrow am I to have ocht to do wi' sic a pack of brainless loons withoot contrivance or gumption. Whaur wad they look for a boat to come frae but the Rathan? Whaur wad they be safe in seekin' but on the Rathan? Hae ye a regiment o' horse and foot on the Rathan? Do the officers o' King George's peace pay ye a veesit ilka day? It was on the Rathan whaur in auld days yer faither set ashore mony a braw cargo, and it's on the Rathan that they'll seek for us."

"Then what for are we going there; could we no make for Killantringan, or even Dumfries?" I asked, being still unsatisfied.

"Hoot awa', Laird Heron," said Silver Sand, "ye haena the heid o' yer faither ava', or ye wadna need to hae so many questions answered. Gin we gaed to Killantringan, we wadna be a bit safer than we are here. The hill outlawry could a' catch us or ever we wan twa mile if we had to carry this bit boxie. And as for Dumfries, it wad be as feasible to try the moon. There's but twa roads than I ken to Dumfries—yin alang the shore, and we hae nae horses bena my cuddy and wee Donald, and the ither road by the channel o' the Nith Water, and it's a braw wark we wad mak' racin' wi' the *Van Hoorn*, or even wi' her pinnace, that won the race at Rotterdam frae the crews o' a' the Dutch men-o'-war."

"Then there's nothing for it but the cave," I said.

Silver Sand pretended a great admiration of my talent and perspicuity.

"Preserve us a', Paitrick, but ye mauna pit sic a strain on yer uptak. It's no human to understand a' that! Aye, as ye say, it's the cave, and nocht else but the cave."

"But what's to come of the house of Rathan?" I asked, for though I was willing enough to take part in the quarrel of the Maxwells, now that I was in for it, I did not want all my earthly possessions burned within half a mile of me without doing my best to save them.

"Ye'll e'en hae to trust the hoose to me and Quharrie," said Silver Sand, still drolling. "Ye'll find that *we* are none so stupid watchers."

The night was already turning to bright yellow low on the west, and the red glow of the dying fire at Craigdarroch lay in a low "skarrow" of lurid light on the water, as we began to draw near to the sea caves at the foot of Rathan Island. There were many tales about these caves. They were miles long, according to the ignorant. They were inhabited by the most terrible of sea beasts, by mermen and sea-lions of fearsome presence and exceeding ferocity.

But of a truth they were rather pleasant places as caves go. Of one of them especially I was fond, for not only had it a sea entrance wide and high, which made it safe to enter by boat, but after one had penetrated a long way through passages and halls, mounting ever upward, he came to a space of clear yellow sand, from which there was an opening to the sea, for all the world like the window in a house high up above the doorway.

The cave entrance beneath was, as it were, the door of the house, and within it the tides for ever surged and swirled, while the window at the top looked out to sea midway down the cliff, where not even the samphire gatherer could come nor yet the sea eagle build her nest.

This was the Great Rathan Cave, and it was into this cave that Silver Sand conveyed his boatload.

The wild outcry of the gulls and gannets on the rocks struck us very strangely coming from the night quiet of the moors. May Maxwell had been very silent, as one might well be who has lost her all and sees herself in the midst of blood and threatenings. But the pleasant break of morn and the cheerful nature of our surroundings seemed to awake a kind of interest in her.

The lower end of Rathan Isle toward the sea is almost separate from the rest, and is called the South Stack.

South of this again was an isle, or rather a high single rock, whereon the sea-birds built. We left this isle of rock to our right hand as we passed into the entrance of the Great Cave of Rathan. And as we went by, the cloud of gulls rose with astonishing clamour, their many wings making a melodious thunder of flappings like the beating of innumerable sails when a ship stands shivering in the eye of the breeze.

There was a clear, brisk air, but the night dew had left a sticky "glet" on the face and hands. A black diver ran hither and thither and tried to make away with his life by staying under water long enough to drown himself; which it is indeed a wonder that I took notice of, save that I have ever minded my father's precept—"Mind a' that ye see, but forget a' that folk say aboot ye!" There are not many wiser observations than that to be got for nothing.

High up among the rocks a couple of ravens looked sneeringly and overbearingly down from the edge of their nest, and barked hoarsely at us as we went by. They had been watching all night with joy the burning of the decent folks' house, for that is the nature of the corbie.

"*Glock! Glock! Glock!*" they cried at us, as they do in the saga tales of the Northmen when the heroes are lying on the field of blood.

Now these caves of the Solway are in a different rock to that which goes along the greater part of the seaboard. There comes in here and there a softer rock, of the nature of a freestone, which the water makes great play to excavate.

I would that I could take you to see these wonderful spurs and arches that have been cut out of the rock by the genius of the water.

THE GREAT CAVE OF ISLE RATHAN

There are many sorts of caves there, and in them I used to play many a day by the length on the Isle Rathan. There was the Great Cave, that might have housed a thousand men in its depths, yet which ten could have defended against any number who knew not its ways and outlets. In it there was the outlook to the sea, and the hall which I called the Hall of Ossian.

The most part of these caves are sea caverns as on the coast of Antrim in Ireland, which is the only other place where I have seen these resounding halls of native rock, with the green water booming solemnly into them, and the sough of their roaring carried far along the coast. Some of these are deep, dark dens, accursed and gloomy, in which the tide sways blindly at all times, horrible to look upon from the sea, showing cruel teeth like an old wolf-dog that has drawn up its lip so that one may see the broken fangs and the cavernous dark behind. The dank, clammy air is compressed by the tide. A horrible ooze clings to every part of the rock, as though ugsome things, slimy worms from the sea-bottom, had overcrawled it all. There were on Rathan many caves and those of all sorts. But most I loved the tiny cavelets in the White Sand coves, where the waves of a sheltered sea beat all day, lisping and lapping with a pleasant sound. There, on warm days, it was my habit to lie even mother naked, half in and half out of the water, the whole isle being so lonely.

We now drew quickly from under the frowning face of the South Stack.

As Silver Sand brought the boat near to the Great Cave, the entrance rose so high above us, and the swaying of the waves in the mouth of it was so grand, that I felt proud of the Isle Rathan, and as glad that I possessed it as if I had made it myself.

Silver Sand, indeed, never glanced either aloft or alow. But then he had no need, having a circle of eyes all about his head. Richard Maxwell seemed to be muttering curses on his foes; and, by the jerking of his eyebrows and the twitching movement of his lips, I judged that he had fixed them severally in a locality where they would certainly have found pleasure in the cold salt water that sobbed and heaved into the cavern.

But May Maxwell, out of whom the mischief had died, glanced more than once up to the frowning portals, which opened for us like that water gate I have read of into the White Tower in London town, by which go in the traitors who come no more out. But she said no word.

Now the upper arch of the cave is not less than forty feet above the floor of uneasy water, and the sea entrance beneath is but three times the breadth of a boat. The cliffs rise so high above that seen from beneath, they hold up the sky as on pillars. As we steered our way carefully into the mouth of the cave, we passed through floating balls of sea-spume so large that the prow of the boat was whitened with them. I have often taken them in my hands, chasing them, as puppies do, along the shore when the wind comes in off the sea.

The rock is infinitely worn all about into a myriad holes and crevices, in which are sea-pinks with dry, flaky heads. I saw tansy also far above, yellow like fire, and on the sheltered crannies, where a little earth collects and the birds leave castings, there was some parched sea-grass, and I think that I caught the pale-blue glint of the sea-holly—a favourite plant of mine. I remember that I thought it early for it to bloom, and my mind ran on climbing to get a piece for May Mischief. This, too, in the midst of infinitely graver things to think about.

Quharrie sat beside May Maxwell in the boat with his paws on the seat, heaving his head aloft and sniffing in an uncertain fashion, as if his experience, though a wide one, did not include sea caves.

May Maxwell settled her shawl closer about her as we drew away from the wholesome light of day, and the greenish glimmer grew about us. It made my heart waver to and fro within me like a sunbeam in a basin of water, tingling and quivering, when she laid a little hand on my arm. It was but that she trembled as a maid will, for it was a cold hand, and it shook. But it made the last remnant of my dislike flee away. Nor do I think now, looking back, that I ever disliked her greatly. In my heart of hearts I aye liked her—not that ill even when she pursed her mouth and cried "BAA!"

It was sweetest, perhaps, when out of the depths of the great cave burst a clamorous cloud of rock pigeons. As we entered we could hear their voices *peep-peeping* and chunnering to their young, some of the old cockbirds meanwhile *roo-hooing* on the higher ledges with a sound wonderfully varied and pleasant. There were also at the entrance a few solitary maids and bachelors sitting in the clefts sunning themselves with drooping wings, like barndoor hens in the dust. Some were preening their feathers, the sheen on their necks being the redder because at that moment the sun was rising.

When the boat got well within the cave, where the narrows of the passage open into the wide Hall of Ossian (so we called it), the boat ground harshly on the sand and shingle. At this the doves took instant alarm, and with a startling whirr and clang they swooped down on us in a perfect cloud, their shining breasts extraordinarily near us, so that the wind came in our faces as the living stream poured out of the narrow and fetid darkness of the cave into the splendid sunshine of the young morning.

Then it was that May Maxwell cried aloud, as a lass well might. Indeed the clamour startled even me that was well accustomed to it, let alone a young lass that had seen her home burnt over her head that night. There was no shame or wonder in it. Nor is there any need that I should write about it, except that I could not just hear what name it was that she cried out. But I had hopes that I knew.

CHAPTER XII

MORNING IN THE CAVE

The entrance was indeed the grandest part of our cave. It was not very wonderful inside—a way that caves have. There was this dark hall of sand and pebbles, in which the water broke either at the end of the long sea passage or half-way up the incline of the floor, according to the state of the tide. But except for purposes of landing or defence we never stayed long in this dank and cold place, but climbed directly up to the little chamber, which might have been the cave of an anchorite, so comfortable was it in all weathers, save only when a heavy wind blew in straight from the south, when the large window faced the gale. But mercifully during the time we spent there the airs were fairly still, and we only heard the swell sobbing and swishing along the edges of the rocks far beneath us.

So at last we mounted through the dank and dripping passages, which indeed did not seem long, I carrying May Maxwell's parcels and guiding her. But it was pleasant to emerge opposite the window into the sunlight of the early morning upon the sea, coming across from Satterness and turning the cold, white crests of the chilly indigo waves to a rosy colour. I took pleasure in leading her to the window, which was of a shape nearly oblong, with sea-rockets and stonecrop growing about it. I shall always consider it as a special providence that, upon my looking past the end of the ledge, I saw growing in the cleft a little sod of heather, and in the midst of it, early for the season and the Solway shore, a few waxen lobes of bell-heath, perfectly white. So holding her still by the hand, lest the sudden coming into the light might cause a giddiness, I laid down her bundle, and, pulling the white, waxen bells, I presented them to her with all the courtesy of which I was the master. This she took not amiss, for she looked at me with eyes that were full of tears, and said, speaking not at all in her former way—

"Thank you, Patrick; what makes you so mindful of me? I dinna deserve it."

I meant here to have said something exceedingly fine and appropriate but all that I could get out was just, "Aye, but ye do!"

And even that I stammered. However, I am not sure that I could much have bettered it after a week's consideration.

So in the early morning we sat and looked away over the sea. The air was still caller, but the sun had already taken the chill off. The sea was like a painted cloth hung up before us, so high were we above the water—a cloth on which the ships and boats were drawn prettily one above the other.

The natural window at which we sat was oblong, as I have said—that is, not so high as it was broad—and there was a stone shelf before it, whether made by man's hands, I know not.

"It is very quiet and peaceful here," May said; but Richard, her father, said nothing. I think he hardly saw where he was being taken. He had lived at Craigdarroch all his life save when he was on the seas, having indeed been born there. It went hard with him to lose it all in a single night.

Thinking of what May said now, it strikes me that to look through a high, narrow window at a landskip framed in it gives one an impression of surprise, as though the outlook were upon an unknown country; while, on the other hand, to look upon the same scene from a broad window, as we did now, makes one think of still Sabbath mornings and the bees humming among the clover.

"As peaceful," May continued, "as though there were no wicked men in the world."

This time now seems to me so strange and peaceful—the thunder-slumber before the storm breaks and the lightning flares.

She shuddered slightly, for I knew afterwards that at Craigdarroch Hector Faa himself would have laid a hand upon her, but that she had broken from him, fleeing hot-foot into the wood. Hector Faa it was who, outcast with all his tribe from sweet Yethom, had sent a message to Richard Maxwell that he was coming to the low country for a wife, according to the custom of his tribe. For he and his mother made it their boast that never had a Faa bride been led home save with her hands tied behind her back. This was Faa custom, and that, among these wild gypsy clans, made it sacred. The Faa blood was so high that it could absorb and cause to return to itself all poorer fluids. So Black Hector, who was the brother of John Faa himself, was but doing the bidding of his mother, as well as following his own inclination, when he sent this message to Craigdarroch. His mother had proved the way of the clan and become more Faa than the Faas themselves, as they say all these abducted gypsy wives do become.

The curse that Richard Maxwell sent back is remembered yet in the hill country, and his descendants mention it with a kind of pride. It was considered as fine a thing as the old man ever did since he dropped profane swearing and took to anathemas from the Psalms—which served just as well.

The answer that came back was short and sweet.

"Tell the auld carle at Craigdarroch," Black Hector sent his message, "that I'll hae the lass in spite of him and the seven braw brithers."

And so it is likely that he would, had it not been for one that was no brother of May Maxwell's.

Once we were safe within the cave, Silver Sand went away with Quharrie, taking the boat with him, and leaving us shut in without a chance of escape, if so be the Black Smugglers followed us swiftly to the Stacks of the Isle Rathan. But I had my pistols, and now looked well to the priming, and with some ostentation also to the condition of the locks, for indeed I took no small pride in my marksmanship. As a boy I had set a stone on the dyke and knocked it over with another at thirty yards' distance, four times out of five. In later days, since my friends came to reside on the isle with me, I constantly used a pebble as an argument. Indeed there were few places about the Isle Rathan from which I could not reach an erring youth with pebble cunningly "henched." Then with pistols Andrew Allison and I had practised a great deal since he came, and it was with some pride I considered that a smuggler, great or small, would have little chance with me at twenty yards. I had also skill of the claymore and small sword, for my father had taught me these in the wet days of winter, keeping me at it till my limbs ached and my back was like to break.

It was not long before Silver Sand fetched back his boatload of provender from the house. He brought with him Jerry MacWhirter alone of all our reinforcements, with the news that in the morning the father of the Allison lads had appeared with two stout apprentices and a very large whip, and had driven the three boys—Andrew, John, and Rab Nicoll—before him to his boat. Jerry had stood meanwhile on the cliff above, and, according to his own account, had exhorted their father to lay on them soundly. Which I have small doubt that he did.

It was a loss, but one I was not sorry for. There was the less responsibility were the smugglers to come, for Jerry was of age to decide for himself as to his movements, and, besides, he had never been under control in his life. He would give us no anxiety, and also make us often merry. I think we were all more cheerful and hopeful as soon as he came among us.

But Silver Sand brought also another passenger, a bare-footed, barearmed lass, blowsed and freckled, with arms and legs like those of a man.

"This is a lass," he said, as soon as he came in, "that I fand chappin' at Rathan front door, which is not a very fitting thing. So I fetched her wi' me. She can speak for hersel'. She disna' appear to be troubled wi' blateness."

As soon as May Maxwell saw her she got up off the stone shelf by the window and ran to her—glad-like, as you have seen a bairn among grown folk do when another child comes in.

"Faither," she cried, "d'ye no see this is Bell MacTurk?"

"Aye," said the old man, "I see that!"

But apparently the sight did not do him much good, for he sank again into a morose silence.

"Bell," said Mary, "shake hands wi' Maister Patrick Heron this minute, for ye're on his Isle of Rathan—or, rather, in it—an' gye far ben too!"

Bell came forward and shook hands.

"Laird or no laird," said she, "ye micht hae as muckle sense as to gie a bonny lass a salutation.

Mary Maxwell laughed.

"Oh, Bell, Bell," she said, "is this a day for your daffin?"

"Hoot, awa' wi' ye' Mistress May. It's no ilka day Bell MacTurk gets the chance o' a bit cheep frae a laird! An' what for should ye greet? There's some gear an' plenishin' brunt, and the thack's aff the byre, and the stackyaird's empty; but there's them comin' hame that will big it a' up again, and pit a bigger harvest than ever under thack an' rape. For there wad no end to the wickedness o' that crew o' Black Smugglers and robbers. But noo the hale country will rise again them, and there will be an end to them."

While she was speaking thus Richard Maxwell looked at her from under his hoary eyebrows. There was a grey pallor about his countenance that did not look bonny in the full light of the morning as it came into the cave, for the sun had now worn round so that it shone upon the face of the cliff.

"Aye, lass," he exclaimed, rising to his feet, "These are words wise beyond your years. They shall be rooted out, for the destruction o' the bonny onstead that has been hame to me and that reared my bairns. This I swear and declare before the Almighty."

"Noo, sit doon, faither," said May, anxiously, "dinna walk aboot, ye are no minding your feet, and ye micht faa' doon oot ower the heuch. Forbye ye are pittin' them that's helpin' you so kindly into danger with the loud sound of your voice."

The old man sat down without another word, and wrapt himself again in his gloomy reflections. But all the rest of us were visibly cheered by the advent of Jerry and Bell, as well as by the food which they had brought from the house. The only sore thing that lay on my heart was the thought of my own Rathan house, which was my all, lying vacant and open to the crew that had burned Richard Maxwell's onstead and all his gear.

But Silver Sand relieved some part of my anxiety by declaring that he meant to remain outside, and be at once scout and watchman.

"The house if perfectly safe in my hands. I'll set Quharrie to watch it," he said, "and the smuggler doesna wear tarry breeks that will come near it when Quharrie is lookin' after it."

So it was arranged that if the waterway should be shut Silver Sand was to lower any message or package for us over the cliff in such a manner that it would swing opposite the window—a plan which was afterwards carried out with complete success.

For all that I thought it strange that Silver Sand should take no part in the real warfare against the outlaws, while giving us other help of every kind.

CHAPTER XIII

THE DEFENCE OF THE CAVE

But our content and mirth were of short duration, for we were to hear from the enemy in a very sudden and surprising manner. How Yawkins got track of us to this day remains a mystery. Not even Ebie Hook, to whom I owe the solution of so many things, can unravel this, for he was not present at the attack, being one of the watch who remained on the *Van Hoorn* by order of Captain Yawkins.

It is likely that one of the lookout upon the mainland saw us go into the cave, or noted Silver Sand's return from the house with his load.

At least, certain it is that it had not passed nine o'clock of the morning, before the *Van Hoorn,* having embarked those of her crew who had joined with the gypsies in destroying the homestead of Craigdarroch, bore up to the south of Isle Rathan under easy sail. When she came abreast of the entrance of the cave a puff of white smoke rose from her side, and a great round shot came plumping into the mouth of the cavern, breaking away a fragment from the cliff, which plunged like thunder into the deep water of the entrance. Myriads of chips flew every way, but not so much as a feather-weight of dust reached the great centre hold called Ossian's Hall, where only the echoes reverberated, and the swells raised by the round shot and the fall of the great fragment came rolling up to our feet in an arching wall of green water crested with white.

From our secret watch-tower window on the face of the cliff we could see the brig hanging in the wind to give her stern chasers another chance. I therefore judged it wise to send May Maxwell and Bell into the little passage at the back, where even in the event of a ball striking through the window of our retreat, they might be tolerably safe.

As soon as the noise raised by the second round shot died away—it struck the cliff without doing any harm—we saw two boatloads of men from the brig putting off with the evident intention of attacking us. The *Van Hoorn,* so far as appeared from her deck, had been firing uselessly at a vast hole in the sea cliff. Even so the men at quarters on board of her regarded it; and some of them muttered to one another that it had been better to have 'bouted ship and borne away with what plunder they had before the king's ships came up with them. But the captain, it is said, had private information of the chest which Richard Maxwell had carried away, and cared for no other part of the spoil. At any rate he resolved to try the entrance of the cave, having little doubt that so large a force would be able immediately to subdue our weak defence, which must have appeared still more feeble to him who knew not the strength of our position.

Now there was nothing very wonderful about the cavern in which we were concealed. It consisted simply of a sea entrance practicable for boats, and a cliff entrance practicable only for gulls and pigeons. The passage between the two chambers was narrow, but with many turns and twistings, having small chambers and one or two side ways which returned back upon the main one. At the bottom of this natural winding stair there was the large hall which we called Ossian's Hall, where was the end of the sea passage and where the swell broke upon a beach of shingle and sand.

Now there was no foothold for any along the cliffs that lined the sea edge, so steep, black, and slippery were they. You may find the cave of which I speak, the second on the right hand in sailing along Rathan, between the South Stack of Rathan, and the east point that looks to Killantringan and Satterness. Indeed, the entrance is so wide that you cannot miss it.

The arched cliff that is called the Needle's E'e is within fifty feet of it, and the reverse suction of the sea pouring out of the Great Cave of Rathan sets through the Needle's E'e in a jumping jabble at every turn of the tide. It is thus easily found. The only caution is that is must not be mistaken for the Caloman Cave, or Pit of Pigeons (as the word means in the Pictish speech of ancient Galloway), which has its entrance high among the rocks and allows no opportunity for the breaching of the sea waves. So that by going to the place it is easy to prove the exact truth of this history. This I say at length lest any should think that the cave is some wonderful thing. For the glosing of the common people has raised a great number of legends in the countryside—as that when we were besieged in this cave by the Black Smugglers we escaped inland by the space of three or four miles and came out by an underground passage at the Old Pict's Tower or Orchardton, with other stories that have no truth in them. Indeed the whole cavern, as it was known to us, did not extend more than two hundred yards in all its turns and windings, entrances and passages. So much, then, for our situation. A word concerning our dispositions for defence.

We had plenty of arms and ammunition, and, speaking for myself, a kind of gladness in the fray that I am sure I should not have had in the open country where a hundred might fire at you from all sides. I thought it better that Richard Maxwell, Jerry, and myself should go down to the great hall called Ossian's, and by getting as far out into the passage as possible, kneeling upon ledges and jutting rocks, be ready to beat back our assailants as they entered.

There was, indeed, about thirty feet from the Hall of Ossian a kind of platform on which two of us could stand. This commanded the entrance, and from it we could see the wide span of the outer arch and the rock-doves flitting to and fro in the sunshine. May Maxwell came with us to help in loading the guns—in which she was exceedingly expert, having been trained to the way of it by her brothers when they went shooting at birds or at the mark, which latter they often practised on wet days or in the dull winter season.

Bell remained in the chamber over the gate, both to give us intelligence of the approach of the enemy and also to receive any message from Silver Sand on the cliff above, which he might swing downwards in the way indicated. We had hardly gone to our quarters before one such message did reach us. It was wrapped about a stone and tied with withes. This ball swung clear of the cliff, so that Bell had to take the *cleps* (or crooked links which were used for hanging the porridge pot upon the wooden crossbar of our cave fireplace), in order to draw it in—an action which, had the smugglers been on the lookout might have proved dangerous to herself and hurtful to our interests.

But in a trice she had detached the stone and brought me down Silver Sand's message, which said in correct enough English but in a curious ancient hand and without punctuations—

"IT IS THE CHEST THEY WANT AND THE LASS THE HOUSE IS SAFE ENOUGH FIRE AT THE HILL FOLK THEY ARE THE DEYVILS THE TARRY BREEKS HAVE NO HEART IN THE MATTER. YOUR OBLIGED SERVT. SILVER SAND."

With this we had to be content. Of one thing I was well convinced, that Silver Sand would be of greater service free and aboveground than down with us in the sea cave. So that we were all in good heart, and that more especially when Bell came down with the letter and served us with a little heartening of the Dutch sort out of a square, wide-mouthed case bottle, scandalously overserving

Jerry because he was a favourite of her own—which she thought that I did not notice; as indeed I did, and that carefully; and besides, these things are not good for boys.

So we went to our posts to be ready, for the boats were approaching. From the vantage ground of the window in the cliff we could note their numbers and bearing. There were about twenty of them in two boats. The most part were no sailors, but wild fellows from the hills, bonnetless and unkempt. Yawkins himself was in one boat and Hector Faa in the stern sheets of the other, monstrously fine in a buff coat and a shirt with lace upon it, both of which he had taken from the house of Richard Maxwell at the burning of Craigdarroch.

When I told this to May Maxwell she ran her ways up to take a peep at the window, and came down main angered, saying, "That is the sark that I got ready for my faither to gang to Staneykirk Sacrament in, and to think that that regairdless loon should wear it upon his back!"

"Deil scoup wi' him," cried Bell, "an' I turned it and bleached it on the green an' sprinkled spring water frae the well upon it."

"Load the muskets, May," said I. "It's sma' use cavillin' aboot the man rinnin' awa' wi' yer faither's sark, when he wants to rin awa' wi' you yersel'."

But she did not somehow seem to think that this last was nearly so heinous a crime as wearing her father's shirt on his dirty caird's back.

"It took me two hours to do the ruffles," she said. It is a strange thing, but this kind of foolish care for a trifle made me almost angry.

"Maybes ye wadna hae been so very vext gin he had run aff wi' ye!" I said, with as ill-natured an expression as I could compass, for such superfine care for her father's ruffles was beyond me at such a time.

"I wadna wonder," says she; "it's weel that some folk in the world think something o' me."

"Even a broken land-loupin' Cheat-the-wuddy like Hector Faa!"

"Aye," says she, "him better than naebody!"

At this moment came the roar of the third shot from the brig. She was firing again into the cave, and the shot, being aimed low, came skipping in, rebounding from side to side of the cavern and filling the long sea passage with dust and the clamour of echoes. But it did no harm, for the first time it touched the roof it rebounded and plumped to the bottom where, without doubt, it lies to this day to prove my story.

Upon this Jerry cried, "I am going up to see what they are doing. I have a biscuit up there I would like to toss them for their breakfast."

"Come back to your post, ye wull cat," I shouted after him. "Gin ye run ony o' your rigs at sic a time I'll break the back o' ye!"

Now I knew how he must have angered his mother and relations, and for the first time I had some sympathy with them and their overfree use of the birch rod.

"I'll be back the noo!" he cried, far up the passage. I could only girn my teeth at him and go over in my own mind what I would give him when I got him quietly by himself for all this. Then the first musket-shot went off outside.

There was a crash and a loud yell.

"That will be Jerry's biscuit!" said May Maxwell, who knew something of his intentions, having heard Bell and him talk together. Now there was evidently wild work at the outer gate of the cave; though being in the dark far back and standing to our posts with our muskets ready, we could see nothing. Yet we could hear shoutings, cursings, blasphemings, and multitudinous squatterings in the water as of a thousand wounded wild ducks.

"They've sunk the boat, blood them!" cried some one, hoarsely.

"Let us on board, Yawkins!" cried another.

"We've ower mony here already; shift for yourselves!" was the answer. Then came a burst of swearing and more of the squattering.

"Back her! Back her!" cried the strong voice of Yawkins. "Keep the rascals off wi' your boathooks; here comes another stone."

There was another resounding splash, and a loud, universal "AH!"

Then a cry of "Into the cave mouth, lads, and ye'll be oot o' the reach of the stanes!"

I could have bitten my thumbs that I had not thought of this plan before. I was indeed, as Mistress MacWhirter had said, "a bonny general."

I was also angry with Jerry for being quicker in the wits than I. It turned out, however, that the plan was May Mischief's, communicated first to Bell and afterwards assisted in and carried to success by Jerry and Bell together.

All this was indeed mighty fortunate for us, for the first great stone descending fifty feet sheer, drove a hole in the leading boat—that of Hector Faa—and in a moment he and all his ragged regiment were struggling in the water. They scrambled upon the rocks, however, swimming with one hand and holding their matchlocks above their heads with the other, for that is the manner they use in swimming across the narrows of Loch Enoch and Loch Neldricken in their home country.

But the swell and jabble of the sea water was puzzling to them, and many of them got their tinder wet as well as their powder; so that their pieces were no use to them, which was presently a most fortunate thing for us in the cave.

In a trice we could see them against the light climbing and crawling like wild cats of the hills, as indeed they were, on the knobs and ragged edges of the sea entrance.

We could also hear the grating of the oars of the boat against the sides of the cave as they scraped along, and the voice of Yawkins ordering his men to take their oars out of the rullocks and push the boat along by hand. Then came a splatter of musketry up the passage, and May Maxwell cried out in a way that went to my heart.

In an instant both her father and I set our Queen Anne muskets to our shoulders and fired. This stopped the boat, for one of the smugglers dropped forward, and falling among the feet of the others grievously impeded them with his moaning and catching at them as they trod upon him.

Some of them cried "Back!" and some "Have at them!" So there was a great confusion among them. I did not fire again, hoping that there might not be need for any more bloodshed. But Richard Maxwell was not at all of my mind, for right nimbly he climbed down with the discharged pieces and ran up again with the loaded ones which his daughter had prepared for him. He took not the slightest notice when she cried out, for as soon as he had fired his first shot he broke out into a great rapture of singing. This was his song:-

> "There arrows of the bow He brake,
> The shield, the sword, the war;
> More glorious Thou than hills of prey,
> More excellent art far.

THE DEFENCE OF THE CAVE

"Those that were stout of heart are spoil'd,
They slept their sleep outright,
And none of those their hands did find,
That were the men of might."

It was wonderful with what vigour the old man sang this psalm, never for a moment stopping his musketry practice, and at the end of every verse dropping a deadly shot among his enemies.

The boat's crew soon had their bellyfull of fighting in the dark, and were now only anxious to get off with whole skins. Some of them lay down in the bottom of the boat, while others stood up and fired into the darkness of the cave; but except that a pigeon or two fell flapping and struggling into the water no one was a penny-piece the worse, for May Maxwell's cry was only a sudden exclamation at the crack of the musket, though it had sounded to me so exceedingly lamentable.

The boat backed out, narrowly escaping another or Jerry's dangerous biscuits, and in a little while we heard the noise of shooting above us, which made me fear that the gypsies had found means to scramble down the cliff. It was no more, however, than Jerry trying his hand at the gun, for in a little Bell came flying down in a high state of excitement for more ammunition, crying, "We dowsed them a'. Hector Faa gat his bonny French coat drookit." And this seemed to her somehow the cream of the jest.

Our cave, which was shaped much like a tadpole, with a very wide head and a very long body, was full of the white smoor of gunpowder smoke, so that we could not see those we were firing at. But Richard Maxwell continued to discharge his gun as often as he could get it loaded, bitterly winging each shot with double powder and a text of Scripture.

Presently another great gun went off from the *Van Hoorn,* but there was no lead or iron in it this time. It was the signal of recall, and in a few minutes the single boat's crew which remained was taken on board, and the brig stood away to the south; and that not a moment too soon; for the outsailed *Seahorse* and the deceived *Ariel* had forgathered off the Isle of Man and were speeding north to hem the Black Smuggler into the blind alley of the estuary of the Solway.

Now, though Yawkins was no doubt eager for revenge, and still more eager for the brass-bound box which Richard Maxwell carried with him so carefully, he had too great a respect for his neck to risk hanging on the bare change of either. He ran, therefore, towards the entrance of Wigton Bay to turn the point before the slower king's ships could trap him, whence he held south to escape for this time. His day was not come. But the shadow ship was following hard after, and the Fate that grips by land and sea, but most surely and completely by sea, waited to lay the final arrestment upon him, and on Leith Sands she hove him to. Where to this day he stays.

CHAPTER XIV

THE HILL GYPSIES

Then for some hours we had peace.

As Silver Sand had foretold, there was little heart for the onset among the "Tarry breeks!" They fought best on sea. But the gypsies of the hills, accustomed to the crags and caves, the screes and precipices of the Dungeon, were quite other adversaries.

Since that day the countryside has settled down so fast that it is hard to realise that but a few years takes us back to the time when the Marshalls and Macatericks levied mail and drave cattle from half the land of Galloway. Many of them were gypsies *pur sang,* as Faa himself, and Marshall—the Faas indeed, though expelled from the Border country, accounting themselves above the Stuarts or Douglases, or any other name in ancient dignity. In which I do think honestly that they have the right of it; but whether the blood be improved in quality by this long descent through cattle-thieves and wizards is a moot point. But Hector Faa was a little above the chicken-coop thief, and confined himself to maids of the Lowland and droves of cattle from anywhere; and as for the lost John Faa himself, did he not still hold King James' patent of nobility, and belt himself with justice and full heraldic right "Lord and Earl of Little Egypt"?

The greater part of these tribes that herded together in the upper hill country—the No Man's Sheriffdom, on the borders of the three counties of Kirkcudbright, Wigtoun, and Ayr, were broken men from the Border clans and septs—wild Eliots, bystart Beatties from the debatable land, and outlaw Scotts fleeing from the wrath of their own chief, the Warden of the Marches. With them there were the Macatericks, a sept of cairds, sturdy rascals from the wilder parts of North Carrick and the Upper Ward.

All these outlaw folk used to plunder the men of the middle hills till the Leshmahago Whigs rose into power in the high days of Presbytery before the return of Charles Stewart, the second of the name, weary fa' him. Then these, being decent, God-fearing men, of a dour and lofty spirit, and all joined very close by the tie of a common religion and by the Covenants (National and Solemn

League), rose and made an end of the Macatericks, driving them forth of their country with fire and sword.

Those that escaped betook themselves to the wilds of the moorlands, where no writ ran, no law was obeyed, and no warrant was good unless countersigned with a musket. In the dark days of the Killing, this country (which seems fitted to be the great sanctuary of the persecuted), was more unsafe for them than any part in the wilds; for the reason that there were always informers there who for hire would bring the troopers on the poor, hunted wretches, cowering with their ragged clothes and tender consciences in the moss-haggs and among the great rocks of granite.

Then in the times which followed, as some yet alive are old enough to remember, all the land was swiftly pacified save only in the "cairds"' country—the cairds being the association of the outlaw clans that had gathered there. It appears strange that, so long as their depredations were within bounds, no man interfered with their marauding, so that they took much cattle and as many sheep as they had need of. As to their country itself, no man had the lairdship of it, though my Lords Stewart of Garlies have long claimed some rights over it. For centuries the whole of it was of the country of the Kennedies, and all the world knows that they were no better than they should be. As for lifting a drove of cattle from the Lowlands, it had been done by every Macaterick for generations, though generally from Carrick or the Machars, where the people are less warlike than in Galloway itself.

It was therefore not of the nature of a mere bravado that Hector Faa should send word to the Maxwells, the strongest of all the patriarchal smuggling families of the Solway seaboard, that their only sister was intended for the bride of a gypsy chief.

Hector Faa had seen May Maxwell at the great fair of Keltonhill, whither she had gone every year since she was a girl under the guardianship of her bodyguard of brothers. Only a year ago Kennedy had smitten Hector on the mouth to the effusion of his blood, and Hector had drawn his knife on the Maxwells, who, however, at Keltonhill, were in their own country and in overwhelming force.

"Till another day!" cried Hector Faa, as they dragged him away.

The other day had come.

I have no doubt that the gypsies knew well enough that the Maxwell brothers were at a distance or they had been far less bold and infinitely more wary.

All this takes a long time to tell, yet the sailing away of the smugglers, and the second attack of the gypsies followed within a few minutes of each other.

We were yet standing in the Hall of Ossian waving our hands before our faces to clear the cave of the sulphurous smoke of the powder.

"Run," said Richard Maxwell to his daughter; "bring me my canister. I left it at the cave-head."

I myself had started to obey him, when he called sharply to me, "Dinna leave your stance. I hear them coming again—ah, if I could but see them!"

A moment afterwards there came out of the smoke, floating as it were upon the water, half a dozen heads, black and fierce, with long hair dabbling in the tide as their owners swam towards us.

Richard Maxwell, Jerry, and I fired, but what with the darkness of the place, the thickness of the smoke, and the horror of shooting at men's heads so close, I think that no one of us except old Richard hit his man.

In another moment they were on us with the dirk, all except one of them who swam last and seemed to be grievously hurt.

It was a dismal enough fight in that crowded little cave, and I was nonewise expert at the dirk. Indeed as it was I stood in the corner in front of the niche where May had been loading the muskets, and swung my sword in that St. Andrew's cross which hardly even a skilled swordsman can beat down. I felt it strike flesh once and again, and the cave was full of confused darkness and flashings. The oaths of the gypsies, the shouts of old Richard whose pistols cracked again and again, the crying of the womenfolk, all dinned in my ears, and in the midst of all the sulphur of the powder set me a-sneezing.

'Tis not what one would choose twice to undergo, though indeed I had not chosen it even once. It had come to me without seeking, ever since I saw the twinkling star over Craigdarroch grow into a lowe of the cruelest and most cowardly fire-raising. In a little the light grew clearer in the cave, and I could see dimly. Richard Maxwell was in death grips with a tall gypsy, and little Jerry was engaging another. One lay on his face at the edge of the water, and one at my feet. The fifth was nowhere to be seen. I rushed to Richard Maxwell's assistance, but the man at my feet gripped me in the act to run and I came down over him.

Outside there was a noise of guns—an irregular dropping fire, and the sound of a boat coming up the passage.

"This is the end," said I, within myself, for it would be as much as we could do to be quit of those who had already gained access to the cave. We could not hope to beat back another boatload. The man who had brought me to the ground could only grip and hold. He had apparently no weapon. Nor was I conscious of a wound, but the horror of his face so near my own, put me in a fever lest I should faint. He drew me nearer and nearer to him as though he would bite. I had heard terrible rumours of the ferocity and cannibalism of the folk of the hills. A loathing came over me that was near to fascination, like the tale of the serpent and the bird. I could not resist with my full strength, and I verily believe that by strength of arm the fierce wounded gypsy had drawn me quick into his embrace and met his teeth in my face, had not the boat we had heard coming along the cave at that moment discharged her cargo of men, who, springing out, soon put an end to the combat.

I must have swooned away before I knew my fate—but more from unusual excitement than from any hurt, and also because I was green and had not yet come to my strength.

When I awoke Kennedy Maxwell was bending over me. He shook me roughly.

"Where is my sister?" he said.

What I said in answer I know not, for my head ran round, and the darkness of the cave, together with the turmoil of the struggle and the lashing of the sea on the pebbles, set me in a swither.

Kennedy, seeing that I had no certain word to speak, instantly ran from me, leaving me lying. I tried to rise; and in a little, holding by the rock and leaning my shoulder against it, I stood upon my feet. Two of the Maxwells, Will the eldest and his brother Patie, next in years, were bending over their father where he had fallen at the other side of the wide room where we had fought. Silver Sand knelt on the opposite side, and the old man appeared to speak to him earnestly but with great difficulty. The other five of the Maxwells—Kennedy, and young Richard, David, Archibald, and Steenie—were nowhere to be seen.

"Is he sore hurt?" I asked, seeing them so stand about with grave faces.

Silver Sand looked up quickly and motioned me to be silent,

moving the fingers of his right hand quickly up and down. The old man was hurt nigh to death, if not indeed in the act to pass.

Richard Maxwell looked around, as if seeking what in the dusk of the cave he could not see.

"Where are the rest?" he said, speaking with difficulty.

"They are lookin' for May!" said Peter, incautiously.

His brother Will turned on him with a frown of fierce threat.

"They may look but they'll no find her," cried the old man. "Alas, I am like Job, stricken in my house and my children at once! Bring in the lads."

Silver Sand went and called them in. They were scattered through all the passages, but no trace of May Maxwell could they find. Jerry also had vanished, and there was no way by which they might have left the cave. Bell came reluctantly out of the nook where in the thick of the fight she had hidden, but could tell nothing.

The seven Maxwells stood about their father, who sat half supported in the arms of Silver Sand. Only Kennedy hid his face, and he was the youngest. The rest stood stern and calm, accepting the fact without repining.

"Me have they bereft in one day of my home, of my daughter, and of my life. The Lord knows that never have I done harm to those that sought my blood. Listen, my sons; forgiveness belongs to the Lord, and I forgive these sons of Zeruiah. I, that am about to pass, and shall never carry spear or pistol more, forgive them. But see that ye meddle not with such matters, at least till ye be as near the presence of the Judge as I. Follow after them with a great vengeance. Vindicate the right. Smite with the sword of the Lord and of Gideon. Let the Lord smite an He will, or hold His sword an He will; but see ye that ye be Gideons and spare not your swords to strike. Let not your eye pity till that evil tribe be rooted out—robbers of house and murderers of men."

He paused, his hand on his side.

"I see," continued the old man, "a time coming, horses and men upon the green. I see the waving of their banners. The companies are marching to the tuck of drum. They are clattering up the Wolf's Slock. I see them go."

"It is the second sight," whispered Silver Sand. "List to him. No horses can go up the Wolf's Slock."

"I see them go," he cried, turning sightless eyes upon the roof of the cavern, in so vivid a manner that we all turned our eyes also that way; but we saw nothing there save the tremulous gathering and scattering of the light which came out of the deep water at the cave's mouth.

"I hear the horses' cackers ringing on the granite. They slide and scrape the corklit[1] from the stones. O Lord, let me see the brunt o' the battle and wha is the victor afore I gang, and then I'll e'en go quiet, like a lamb. Dinna smite unless it be justice, Lord, but gin it be, sheath not Thy sword. Ah, I see them, I see them. Help, Lord, for Thy servant faileth. The bloody and deceitful man shall not live half his days. Their winding-sheet is drawn, and is sleekit white and fair. The Lord has let down His corpse clout upon them."

There was a long silence, very still, in which I could hear the breathing of the strong men within, and without the pulsing of the sea. Then the high-pitched old man's voice, that was like the crying of an elricht wind about the housetops, again took up the vision.

"They hae gotten the dead stroke. Thou has done it! Death and destruction are written on our Lord's banners. The brunt of the battle is ower. The shower is slacked. The on-ding will come nae mair! Loch-in-loch! I see thee, little loch. Thou art clear this morning. Thou art red at even, and there is a pile of haggled heads by thee. Praise to the God of battles. I see the end. It is a Pisgah glimpse. For me I am in His hands. I see the victors come riding home. There is a maid first on a white horse."

He sat up of his own strength, Silver Sand keeping close behind him to catch him in case that he should fall.

Waving his hand, he cried, "It is my ain lassie. Praise the Lord, Himself has cast the lap o' His cloak aboot the bairn. pure within and without, I see her come hame, for the intent of the wicked is holden. The Lord that is a strong Lord deals tenderly with the young plants and waters them oft."

He fell back, but his voice went on, though the tide was plainly on the ebb.

"But there is much to do—little time to do it in. Up and awa' back by the east door, the dry door, that we hadna the gumption to see. Follow them that gate. Leave me! leave me!

---

[1] "Staneraw," or lichen, used for dyeing, found on the hills of the Outlaw country.

Can ye no let an auld man dee his lane? It's atween him and his Maker at ony gate. Let the dead bury their dead, follow ye the living! Gang ye! Gang ye! Lord, into Thy hands I commit my spirit."

For a moment only he rallied, opening his eyes on the dusky cave, and seeing the light at the far end of it which came in from the wide sunlit sea.

"Ebb tide and a dark, misty morning!" he said very quietly and wended on his way towards the light.

CHAPTER XV

THE DRY CAVE

The dead father lay in the cave. The living sister had gone from it. The Maxwells stood all about their father as Silver Sand, in whose arms he died, laid him down softly and closed his eyes.

"And now concerning May," said Will Maxwell, like one who passes calmly to the next subject. "Who saw her last?"

"She was in the corner where the guns were loaded when the rush of men came," I said; "she passed me a gun just after we saw the black heads on the water."

"And she was not in the cave when we entered, neither did she pass out by the way we came," said Will.

"There is a hope for her," I said; "Jerry is also missing. He may be with her." For I knew the tricks of the youth.

"You heard my father's words," continued Will Maxwell. "It is for us to follow after. We are all fit and able. The track is plain. Why stand we here?"

"Whom shall we follow?" said David Maxwell. "Sea or land—Yawkins or Marshall?"

"She's never with Yawkins. He was doon the wind afore ever she was oot o' the cave. It's wi' the outlaws we maun seek," said Kennedy.

The Maxwells made no parade of their intentions, but forthwith settled among themselves how they were to follow. Four were to ride the Raiders' track, while three were to gather wide and raise the country. And they were all to meet at the Bridge of the Black Water of Dee.

"And you?" said Will Maxwell, looking to Silver Sand and myself. Silver Sand answered for both of us.

"We are with you immediately. As soon as we have searched the cave for Jerry, we will follow after you."

"Why will you not be of our company?" said Will.

"Because," said Silver Sand, "if the outlaws have taken May

with them, they would split, and some would leave the cattle-trail to seek the fastest road to the Dungeon of Buchan. We will seek the track of the riders. Follow you the cattle as you say."

Will Maxwell still appeared not to understand. He had little thought of any refinement of pursuit. He desired only to come swiftly to blows with the outcasts and have the matter over. He doubted not that he should then find his sister, if indeed she had been carried off.

Silver Sand, being versed in the ways of the hill men, read deeper, and was determined to follow his own counsel.

But concerning the steadfast purpose of our search we all made a vow, standing about the dead body of Richard Maxwell, to seek until we found and to strike until we made an end—all excepting Silver Sand, who had gone aloft to search the higher chamber, whence Jerry, earlier in the combat, had thrown his biscuits.

On the sandy knowe behind the cave at the farthest end of Rathan we laid Richard Maxwell to rest. As we came out the seagulls clanged about, and a rock dove flew down and perched on the brow of the boat above the dead body, which was strange, and mightily admired, for never did any of us see such like before. But the Maxwells took it as a sign not of this world, so they all of them took off their bonnets and put them in the bottom of the boat; for which I thought none the worse of them, though I kept mine on (for, indeed, it was but a pigeon and a young bird that was tired flying, which presently was gone), and so we drew to the shore. We buried him with haste and without ordered preparation, but with all reverence, and Silver Sand put up a prayer that moved me strangely, for I knew not even that he was a man who held religion in honour. Then I bethought me on many things I had said to him that were no credit to me to say, and I wished I had not said them. Yet I remembered that he had never rebuked me as a strict professor would have done.

Thus ere we departed we made a grave for Richard Maxwell, and I went for spades and shools, which I brought from the House of Rathan. When I was in the house I took a hasty look round to see that all was right. Nothing had been touched. There was not so much as the track of a dirty foot. But in the kitchen I found Jerry lying in a wet pool on the floor. I thought him dead, but as I pulled him to the window he recovered somewhat, and said, lifting up his hand to the light and letting the moisture drip from it, "It is only sea water. It was a fine morning, so I took a dook for my health."

This made me glad, but I could not wait to ask him further, having come for the spades.

"Ye saw nocht o' May Maxwell?" I said.

"I left her in the cave," he said, glancing quickly up; "she'll be there yet."

Knowing this not to be so, I left him hastily, commending him to a square bottle of Hollands to recover him from his dwam.

So we laid old Craigdarroch in a fine sandy grave. We had no grave clothes, saving a sheet which I brought from the house, but his face and wounds were washen clean, and he had the look of one that dies well pleased. So we left him without coffin, to the kindly chemie of the mools. For me, I would not have silver plate or polished oak retard by one day the solemn "dust to dust" which is the requiem of us all.

But we could not start on our search till we had gone back to the cave and resolved the words of the vision concerning the unknown entrance which the old man spoke of.

So Silver Sand and I took the boat back where I, for one, had no desire to go because of the blood, the bodies, and the keen, fetid stench of gunpowder, which was not yet cleared away. We made a complete search, beginning at the uppermost chamber. We went into every cranny that would admit either of ourselves creeping on our knees or of Quharrie, going forward with his head down, and growling as though to track out a wild beast.

But not so much as an outlet for a rat did we find on either hand till we came down to the great cave where the strife had been so deadly.

"The dry door—the east door!' quoth he," muttered Silver Sand, musing. Suddenly he clapped his hand on his knee like a man that solves a riddle.

"What gomerils!" he cried, and with that he got him into the boat as though to leave the cave. But he put no oar into the water—only felt with it along the dark rock above his head on the right hand, pulling the boat along by his left hand laid on the projections of the rock. The oar scraped and slid along the ledges, bringing down the straws and dirt of the doves' nests into the boat. He went two or three yards in this fashion, pulling the boat with him. Then he came to a sudden dark bend of the rock which looked no more than as it were an aumry or corner cupboard to the cave. All at once his oar, which had been scraping and rasping along the dead wall, fell forward till the leather that lay in the rullock rested on a ledge of rock.

"I though as much," cried Silver Sand; "this is the way we lost our maid. The old man saw clearly, as the dying ever see."

He put his hands as it had been on a breastwork and leapt up, pushing the boat back as he did so till she sent her stern against the opposite wall.

"Cast me a rope," he cried from above, "and come hither and see!"

I did so. He caught the rope deftly, and in a few moments I was up beside him. What I saw surprised me that I had not seen it before. For I had passed a thousand times that way, and even taken my skiff round, sitting in it and feeling with my hand if there were any way or any chance of adventure; for in those days I expected to find a wondrous mermaid in every sea hole. Now I discovered that the rock barrier, which seemed continuous to the roof to one sitting in a boat, was little more than breast high, when one was standing erect. I called myself a fool for not having seen it before.

"Ye're nocht to me," said Silver Sand, "that has been here before, and that no in good company. More than that, I have seen the very make of this in Antrim, which is in Ireland, at a place they call Port Coon, where much good stuff used to be run."

This, then, was the "dry door—the east door" that the dying visionary had spoken of. Silver Sand went back to the cave again for a candle, and indeed I was glad to remain by the boat, for I had no stomach any more for the Hall of Ossian. I would not have gone even for all the contents of the brass chest which lay hidden in the sand there.

When Silver Sand came back, he lighted the candle. Standing still in the boat and shielding it with his hand, he looked narrowly at the rock, with his eyes within an inch or two of the wall.

"I thocht as muckle," he said. "Hector, my man, this is the gate ye gaed." And he pointed out to me a series of irregular steps, not greatly larger than notches, that went up from the water to the edge of the rock breastwork. They were not one above another, like steps in a ladder, but more like the steps over a stone dyke. Some of them might be natural, but the best part were made. No wonder Hector Faa knew of these, for was it not the Isle of Rogues?

"Up, my man!" cried Silver Sand to me. "Gin ye want yer lass, ye hae nae time to waste. The Faas bides na on priest nor presbyter when they marry or gie in marriage!"

"*My* lass," he said. May Maxwell was no lass of mine, and at another time I should have said so. But she and I had been friendly during these last days, and I had done her a good turn according to my ability, which always breeds kindly feeling. But *"My* lass,*"* quoth he. "My faith, that was an over-quick word," I said to myself.

Yet it was no time to argie-bargie about words and sayings if we were to save this young maid that was so bright and cheery, though a kenning mischievous, from the grip of the wild and ungodly gypsies of the hills. With the candle alight we looked narrowly at this new cave, which was bone dry on the other side of the barrier. The bottom was a smooth bed of freestone rock, as if the water had worn it, but there were no pebbles upon it.

"Hector Faa was rinnin' barefit, and carrying the lass," said Silver Sand.

"How do ye ken that?" I said, for I could not conceive how he knew.

"Because there's neither nail nor shod marks, but yet the limpet fish have been started here and there, so somebody has come by this way middlin' fast, and that at no long time's distance."

We tracked the dry cave some way till we could hear the wash of the waves again. Then we came to a narrow opening very low down, through which the tide was rippling brightly and softly. The roof of the cave came to within three feet of the water, like the blue hood of a packman's waggon. Silver Sand stepped down and out. I followed him, and we found ourselves standing in the broad sunlight in a little bay that looks to the south-east, among the high craigs of Rathan Island. Silver Sand was gazing all about him, looking so extraordinarily foolish with the lighted candle in his hand in the broad sun, that I laughed aloud.

He looked at me cross-like. "What may it please ye to be so merry about?" he asked.

I said no word, but pointed to the candle in his hand. He blew it out, and looked at me with his eyes drawn to pin-points, like a cat's in the sun.

"Gin she were my lass, it's no laughing I would be."

This he said nettled-like, in a way that I had never dreamed of, for it was strange to me that such a man as Silver Sand, who could be so mysterious and uncanny, should mind being laughed at like an ungrown girl.

Meanwhile his eyes, roving everywhere quick as thought, landed on something that seemed to take him greatly. He pointed with his finger to the bottom of the water in which we stood up to our knees. Looking, I saw a little shoe sitting on its sole on the sand, as though it had been set afloat to sail for sport and had softly filled and sunk. I lifted it and held it in my hand, and from that moment all that day I had no thought of merry-making. Silver Sand had indeed struck the laugh out of my face. It was May Mischief's shoe, and it looked so pretty and simple with its little wet silver buckle glinting in the sun that I could not forbear weeping. It seemed mortally affecting to me because it was the shoe which she wore the day I called her "Impudent Besom." I could see her as she sat on the window seat, dangling her feet in the air, sitting on the fingers of both hands turned with the palms down on the sill, her hair like a boy's, and she with a very pretty mouth piping away like a blackbird at "The Bush abune Traquair." All this came so sore upon me that it was a comfort to greet and make myself small before Silver Sand, who stood looking at me, not waeful, but as one might at a child who has broken his toy and thinks he will never be happy any more.

But for all that I was glad now that he had said "Your lass!"

So we waded our way to the shore, and before we came out Silver Sand threw the old tin candle stock into the tide, which I went and carefully picked out again. There was no service in being wasterful that day or any other day, for it was the candle which used to sit on the stone shelf of the milkhouse at Rathan in my father's time. And it stands there to this day.

When we got to the house we found Jerry MacWhirter much recovered, but not able yet to move far.

"I'll take care o' the house for ye till ye come back," he said. "It'll be as muckle as I'm good for. I'll be obliged to you for the loan of the cellar key, and if ye'll reach me down that side of bacon ham, the frying-pan, and some butter, I'll manage brawly," said that cheerful youth.

"Have any of the Maxwells been here?" I asked of him as I gave him what he asked for.

"Aye," said Jerry, "an' they hae ta'en muskets an' ammunition, an' aff to follow the chase. O that I could gang after them, but faain' bellyflaught on the water like a paddock is no chancy for one's inwards."

This was all that Jerry had to tell, and not a word more could we get out of him. He did not seem at all concerned that May Maxwell should have been carried off. He treated it as an excellent jest to laugh at.

"Weel, it's dootless a queer taste to rin aff wi' a gypsy, but I've heard o' sic like," he said.

"I'll thraw your neck for that, Jerry MacWhirter, when I come back!" I cried as I went out of the door.

"Tak' care that ye ever come back on your legs," he cried. "Gin ye're gaun to hie after hizzies that rins to Gretna wi' gypsies, ye are more like to come back wi' your feet foremost, or I'm mistaen."

The last I heard of Jerry was some words that he cried after me as I went along the stone passage: "Ye micht leave me a scrive o' yer pen, Laird, that wad serve me heir to Rathan—in case like——"

And I heard no more. I had, however, heard enough to make me swear to twist his neck on my back-coming—which, indeed, I may say in this place, I lived creditably to perform and like one that is a man of his word.

CHAPTER XVI

THE CAMP OF SILVER SAND

But fast as I might go, with my pistols new primed and an extra powder flask at my hip, Silver Sand went the faster. We were to take the boat over to the Orraland Cove, where were the white shell sands.

Quharrie was in the boat before us, and a fearsome-looking beast he was, for he had somehow been in the fray and had gotten a lick with a whinger on the chops, which his master had made shift to stitch in a neat and surgeon-like manner, doing it like one bred to the business, as indeed he did everything to which he set his hand.

As we went, I at the tiller, Silver Sand at the oars, as was usual (for Silver Sand liked exercise, while I was in no wise partial to it), I said to him, "We are to follow the Maxwells, I suppose?"

"Suppose here, suppose there," said Silver Sand, who seemed a little discomposed in his temper for some reason that I could not divine; "gin ye want to play follow-dick to the Maxwell lads, ye can do it. That's the way to find the beasts, gin it's the nowt ye're wantin'. But if ye want the bit lass, afore Hector Faa's minnie ties him an' her up ower the tangs, ye'll hae to try anither way o't." Being wise I said nothing, but waited for explanations, knowing better than to interfere with Silver Sand when he was in such a good mood.

Suddenly a thought made me strike my pockets. We had no money, and though steel blades and steel pistol barrels were imperative, some of the coin of the realm might be useful. I mentioned my distress to Silver Sand and he smiled.

"Tak' ye never a thocht for the siller," said he, "there's a guid steeve purse inside this sleeved waistcoat that is at your service every doit and boddle!"

I must have looked very queerly at him, I daresay, for he made answer—

"Ye needna turn up your een at me like tea-dishes. I am neyther thief nor robber—though I bena a laird wi' an island that I can nearly cover wi' my breeks when I sit doon on it. Think ye I hae no siller because I am but a packman an' a seller o' scythe sand and keel?" said he. "Forget na the keel!"

"Whiles I am thinking, Silver Sand," said I, quietly, without any show of temper, "that you are very different from what you appear to be."

A very futile and foolish remark, as I now perceive. "Dod, d'ye ken," said he, pleased-like, "but I'm whiles o' that opeenion mysel'."

He quite recovered his good-humour in a moment. I think it was that the matter of the candle still stuck in his throat, so terribly was he set against being laughed at.

"But hae ye really siller enough for us baith?" I asked, just to make sure.

Silver Sand put his hand into his pocket and poured out of a purse a full gowpenful of golden guineas, such as I had never seen before.

"Keel's remarkable profitable," he said.

"'Deed aye," I replied wistfully; "I'd swap Rathan for your cuddy at that rate. An' by the ribs of the Curate o' Carsephairn, there's that same cuddy!" But I knew well he was but daffing about the profit on keel.

As we landed and pulled up the boat Silver Sand's donkey, a beautiful beast of a dun mouse colour, and far larger than common donkeys, came frisking down to meet us.

"It's weel," said I, "that the gypsies didna get their fingers ower the bit cuddy or ye wad hae had to buy anither."

"Aye," he said drily, "but I'm thinkin' that the dourest catheran that steps atween here an' John o' Groats will think twice afore he meddles wi' Silver Sand his cuddy."

Then we took our ways up to the tent in the wood which Silver Sand had pitched the morning before opposite to the Isle Rathan. It was standing intact, without confusion inside or out. There were, however, many footmarks about it, as of clooted feet of cattle, broad pads of unshod horses, sharp steds of horseshoes, and the slipping prints of bare human feet over all.

The mystery was more mysterious than ever to me now. The wild gypsies had indeed been in this quiet nook of Orraland Glen. It was here that they had gathered their drove to make for the hills. How came it then that all the property, left here so openly with only a cuddy and no other warden, was as secure as though locked in Kirkcudbright jail? The solution was beyond me. I saw, however, that the answer was bound up with the manner in which Silver Sand undertook to keep Rathan House safe against hill gypsy and black smuggler. The two things hung together. But as I was the one to profit, I had nothing to say in the matter. As we came near to the tent (which was bell shaped, with a pole of untrimmed birch stuck through the roof), I saw a plain saugh wand, peeled white, leaning against the door flap. It was stuck deep into the ground, and was easy to be seen by all that came near. Then on the flap itself there were curious signs, like those they say are to be seen in the land of Egypt, the country out of which the children of Israel escaped. In the centre of these was the sign which is known among Eastern peoples as the Shield of David. This was painted in black, but there were two bars of red across it, a thick and a thin, the thick being topmost. Strange letter-signs as of lions and gryphons, and many eagle-faced things were also painted on the canvas in outline.

"What might these be," I asked of Silver Sand, somewhat incautiously. I might have been well aware that if there were any secret in the matter worth knowing, it was not likely that he would be telling me his mysteries then.

"Well," said he, "they micht be drawed to amuse the cuddy, or they micht be made by the birds o' the air drappin' fairings on them, or aiblins they micht be mysel' tryin' the quality o' my tar and keel; but ye see, they're nane o' a' thae, an' thank ye for speerin'."

Such an answer I might have expected, but the truth is I asked the question without thinking.

He paused a moment as though to ask himself if it were worth while to give me any information.

"They're just my lock and key," he said, drily, and that was all I got out of him.

He went into his tent, putting aside the peeled rod, but he did not ask me to enter; yet, when he came out, he brought a bottle of foreign wine with him and some sweet cakes, of which he bade me partake.

I objected that I did not care for wine, and indeed never used it.

"Ye'll be the better o't or ye get to your journey's end," he said; "them that gaes linking thorough the moss-haggs and the muirs wi' Silver Sand and Quharrie has need o' some steeve belly-timber, whatever."

So I took a little, and what with me being unaccustomed to it, and the rarity of the vintage, it ran through my veins like soft liquid fire, exceedingly heartsome and vivid.

"That's surely by-ordinar'," said I.

"Aye," he said, "there's no the like o' that in braid Scotland. That comes frae whaur the swallows gang in the winter time."

"And where's that," I asked, more anxious than ever to hear him speak of it, for indeed it was a thing that I had often wondered at but could get no satisfaction about.

But he did nothing but laugh and say, "Maybes at the bottom o' Carlinwark Loch!"

And though that was the currently reported opinion, I knew well that he was joking, though he liked my quip about the candle ill enough. It is a strange thing that the folk that are aye taking their nap off other folks are the thinnest in the pelt themselves. But it is a thing I have noticed particularly, and that many times.

CHAPTER XVII

COUNCIL OF WAR

So we set out, travelling forward with all speed, but, as our custom was, talking as we went. We spoke of the daring of the outlaws. No raid for fifty years had reached so far south as the shores of the Solway, though the smugglers and the gypsies had a regular route by which they conveyed their smuggled stuff to Edinburgh on the east, and Glasgow or Paisley on the west. So complete was their system, and so great their daring, that it is safe to say that there was not a farmer's grey-beard between the Lothians and the Solway filled with spirit that had done obeisance to King George, and not a burgher's wife that had duty-paid lace on her Sabbath mutch. The gaugers were few and harmless, contenting themselves for the most part with lingering round public-houses in towns, and bearing a measure cup and gauging-stick about the markets—occupations for which they were entirely suited.

The remark that I next made to Silver Sand was that such actions as kidnapping and fire-raising ought to be punished with hanging.

"That observe has been made before, Laird Rathan," he said in an ironical manner; "but as for me, though I'm trying to get ye back your lass, it's for the love I bear to you and the bit lass hersel'—no that I hae ony fault to fin' wi' Hector Faa or ony o' his clan."

"But it's cruel abduction and murder," said I, "and it breaks my heart to hear you upholding sic ongoings."

"Ye're young, ye're young, Rathan," said he, "an' in time ye'll learn sense. Man, whaur did a' the gipsy wives come frae that hae keepit the Faas in being for so mony generations. They were a' liftit, yin an' a'. There's Meggat Faa, that is the mither o' Hector and John Faa himsel'. Do ye think Meggat is a Faa by birth? I tell ye, not her—she's come o' decent Border folk as ever was—Kers o' Blackshiels ower by Yetholm. But she's mair Faa this day than ony o' her sons. Noo, what is't that brings aboot the like o' that? I can tell ye that; an' in this age o' ill-doing and ill-thinking (wi' the tales that we hear aboot the wee, wee German lairdie an' his Dutch women—an' maybe ithers no sae far frae hame), let me tell ye that there's no a Faa that wadna mak' a guid man, leal and true-hearted, kind too at the feck o' times. Faith, let me tell ye there's mony a lass that micht be prood to be in the place o' Mistress May Maxwell the nicht."

"Then if that be your key, I'm lang aneuch wi' you," cried I, hotly flaming up at the way he spoke about the man who had abducted by force the daughter of Richard Maxwell, who lay coffinless in his shroud under the sands of Rathan. But as I grew hot Silver Sand grew cool.

"Na, na, laddie, I'm wi' ye to the neck, dirk and dagger, I hae thrown awa' the scabbard; but I'll never say that the Faas are ill to their wives, or, 'deed, that they are sic ill folk ava'."

"Wha does the murders, then, that they are blamed for?" said I.

"Deed, there's bluid shed a plenty, and the Faas nae doot hae their hand in't, and they shall be hangit and headed for it, an' it's no me that shall peety them; but O man, I like ill to hear folk that bien and cosy, hiveing thegither like a bee's byke, cryin' oot on them that's lying amang the hills. Man, I've been there mysel', an' I ken what it means never to get justice nor the chance o' justice—to be tried by sherras and judges that hae ye judged and condemned afore ever ye win into the coort."

"But ye wadna condone murder and robbery, man, surely, wad ye? for if ye say 'Aye,' muckle as I loe ye, you an' me maun twine," said I.

"My lad," said Silver Sand, "you an' me will agree. I'm as great on the side o' the law as it's siccar to be in thae uncertain times, when wha kens when they gang to their naked beds whether they'll wakken under King or Pretender, or indeed wha's richt King an' wha's wrang Pretender."

"As for me," said I, with a self-righteousness that I wonder Silver Sand did not kick me for—"as for me, I am at *all* times on the side of the law."

"My gracious, think o' that!" said Silver Sand; "they'll mak' ye a gauger! Ye hae a rare job afore ye wi' thae brithers-in-law o' yours, the Maxwell callants. They're nane sae fond o' the law, that I ken."

I declare that I could have pistolled him there and then for saying such a thing about the kin of a poor young lass that had lost her father, and was at that moment in the hands of a ruffian.

COUNCIL OF WAR

I said as much to him, whereupon he laughed, having regained more than his former goodwill, and treated me with a fine and glancing affection, which, from one so strange in appearance and mysterious in antecedents as he, made me wonder that I liked it so well.

"Come noo, Paitrick," he said, "you and me has kenned yin anither a gye while. Ye ken that I am wi' ye to the last gasp—aye, an' ayont it, if they'll let the like o' me through Peter's White Yetts. I'll fecht wi' ye again' Faas and Macatericks and Marshalls, and especially again' Marshalls; but I'm thinkin' that you and me had best stick thegither. Ye are a braw lad an' a bonny bit fechter, but ye want the judgement. Man, the great art is to keep clear o' fechtin' till ye canna help it. An' then—why, then—dinna mak' twa jobs o't."

He clapped me on the shoulder. "Sit ye doon. There is a council o' war called," he said.

Having said all this so rapidly that he left me breathless, he plumped down on an anthill, and motioned me to do the like. But I sat on a stone and said nothing. I watched for the ants to come out, but the hill was empty and none came, which vexed me.

The night was drawing down apace, and we were in a very desert place under the fine rocky hill that is called Screel, which rises from the Solway side, and is visible like a great blue potato-pit against the sky all over the southland of Galloway. We had made our way among rocks that crumbled under our feet, and rang with a kind of iron clang as we trod across them. I was most exceedingly hungry, yet in this place no victual grew, and there was no farm town within our sight. It seemed, however, but a little way to the clouds.

"Let us reckon the chances," said Silver Sand. "The first thing is to make up our minds what the enemy is likely to do, and then we can plan our own course. First, then, there's the smugglers wi' their casks and ankers of brandy and wine. We may let them gang. They are far on the road to Edinburgh wi' the Preventive men keepin' weel oot o' their road. Then, in the second place (this is like preachin'), there's the cattle reivers. They had a lang start—mair nor fifteen hours, mind ye, for they never cam' near the Cave o' Rathan. They wad start when the onstead o' Craigdarroch was in a bleeze. Then there's oor freen that ye are mair particularly interested in, Hector Faa an' his bridal company—that has, ye may depend, the best horses and the best of advice and assistance on the road. They'll be the hardest to mak' up on!"

"Silver Sand, I ask ye no to speak o' the young lass like that."

"Aweel, aweel, Rathan, then I'll no; but dinna fret, I'm kind o' sib to the gypsies mysel', an' I can tell ye that till the marriage is by at the end o' the three days o' feastin', May Maxwell will be attended and 'kuitled' like a leddy—an' after that mair nor ever, for she'll be a Faa hersel'."

"God forbid!" said I, fervently.

"Amen to that!" said Silver Sand. "We'll e'en make her a Heron, though the Herons are but lang-nebbit paddock-dabbers to the Faas."

All the same I was extraordinarily relieved to know that the young maid was safe from insult, and also that we had at least three days after Hector and his prisoner reached the outlaws' hold on Loch Enochside. It was not much to be thankful for, but it was so much better than my fear, that I almost counted it an actual deliverance.

As Silver Sand sat on the ground, he laid his long arms, from the elbow to the wrist on the heather before him, as though they were actual weapons; and sitting there, I saw that the joints seemed to be set the other way, either naturally or through some extraordinary torture. Seeing which a great pity took hold on my heart, and the tears came into my eyes. I remembered all his kindness, and so without more ado I set my arm round his neck and said to him earnestly, "Forgie me for every ill thing I hae said to ye, for O man, I like ye—I like ye!"

For a moment Silver Sand glared at me as if he had been angry, then suddenly laid his face between his hands and sobbed as if he would tear his throat. It was terrible. I knew not what to do in that lonely place, but I laid my head on his shoulder to see if that would comfort him.

"O man Paitrick!" he cried at last, "ye hae given me back my manhood. I have been treated like a beast. I have been a beast. I have lived wi' the beasts, but you are the first that has drawn close to me for thirty years. Paitrick, ye may want a friend for you and yours, but it shallna be as lang as Silver Sand can trail his auld twisted banes after ye. Man, I wad gang for ye into the Ill Bit itsel', that's fu' o' brimstane reek, the reed lowe jookin' through the bars, and the puir, puir craiters yammerin' ahint."

He turned away for a moment, and when he looked up again all trace of his emotion had gone.

"But this is no what we are here for," he said, with one of his quick changes; "we didna come here for oor healths, as Jerry

Macwhirter jumpit oot o' the cave-hole." He went on calmly. "The question is, what road gang we? I'll tell ye what I think, an' then I'll hear your mind on't. The cattle are easily trackit. Ye canna drive cattle withoot leaving plenty o' marks. There's but yae road for them, and that's the straughtest. Gin they pass the fords o' the Black Water, an' get by Cairn Edward and the Black Craig, the Maxwells may say, 'Fare ye weel, Kilaivie,' to every hilt an' hair o' them. Noo, second, ye may depend that Hector, the lass, an' yin or twa mair are doin' no cattle drovin', but killing horse beasts on the road for the Dungeon o' Buchan and the Kames o' Loch Enoch. What road they wad gang, I kenna, but I hae my ain opeenion. It'll no be the direct road; ony way ye tak' it, for weel wad Hector ken that the country wad be raised ahint him, an' that the Glenkens wadna be safe for horses. Noo, a horse is just a necessity to him. The lass wadna walk, and they couldna carry her fast for twenty mile. I'll guarantee that they're by the Gate House o' the Fleet by noo, and streekin' it for the Ferrytoon o' Cree as fast as the horses can birl. Then they'll bide for an hour or twa up at the Herd's Hoose, or Cassencary belike, that's a graund hauf o' smugglers and gypsies. Mistress Ogilvy will look after the lass, an' clap her on the back when she greets, an' tell her tales o' the braw wives the Faas has gotten, an' hoo mony grand lasses wad be keen, keen o' Hector."

"The fause randy," quoth I, exceedingly angry; "I'll hae her indicate as a witch."

"Na, na," said Silver Sand; "ye'll no do that, for Mistress Ogilvy's a freend o' mine and a decent woman forbye."

But I was of a very different opinion.

Silver Sand paused a while, considering and pondering till I was weary. At last he appeared to reach a decision, for he took a piece of oaten cake out of his pocket, halving it fairly as he did so.

"I doubt that you and me maun twine afore we hae gane mony mae miles. I am wae to think on it, Paitrick, but it is the best that I can think on. I maun get there by the heather and my legs as quick as a horse wi' six hours' start can gallop by the Cree road. Noo that is juist possible for Quharrie an' me, but no possible ava' for you. What ye maun do is to get afore the cattle, that's making for the auld Brig o' Dee four mile on the far side o' Clachanpluck, atween that an New Galloway."

"How do you manage to make out that, man?" I asked. "Is it not more like that they wad tak' straight to the hills."

Silver Sand turned on me a look of scorn.

"It's weel seen that ye are shore-bred, and no Bloom-o'-the-Heather, or ye wadna speak o' drivin' cattle fast through the moors. Man, to gang fast they're mortally bound to follow a drove road. Noo they maun keep the west side o' Ken, and the east side o' Grenoch Loch by Clachanpluck. They darena keep the Parton Road, for that's ower public, and beside, Ken Brig is easy stoppit and sure to be guarded. They canna tak' the Lochenbreck hills, as I mean to do, straight from here, for the cattle wadna drive ower the braid muir."

"Noo, ye maun get to the Dungeon o' Buchan afore the cattle; they'll no be expectin' rescuers afore that, and I maun get with speed to Eschonquhan by the Loch of Trool. Whatever yin o' us finds the lass maun hing aff an' on till the ither comes, unless a chance opens by-ordinar' sure."

"But how shall we find one another?" I said, for in that wild, unknown country it seemed a madness, especially for me who had never been there in my life before. I saw myself already a poor lost for-wandered lad, out on the hungry hill, and May Maxwell the bride of the Faa.

Indeed, the thought of parting with Silver Sand, and even from the companionship of Quharrie, dauntoned me so sore that I could have wept; but I remembered the grey hair of Richard Maxwell, dabbled with his blood, his roof-tree blazing the while with the red flame, and I resolved that whoever should have mercy on the wild gypsies, I at least should strike and spare not.

The bushel-stoup of their iniquity was nearly full measure, heaped and running over, and it would soon be straked with the Lord's own level and plumb line.

CHAPTER XVIII

TO INTRODUCE MISTRESS CRUMMIE

So, as night fell on this most eventful day in my life, Silver Sand and I, Patrick Heron, set forward over the dreary stretch of Ingleston Moor that lies on the hip of Screel. Though it was the May time of the year and the green leaves were shooting out from the branches, yet the air was shrewd as it breathed from the north; and I wished for my great sea-cloak, that had been my father's before me, having with me only a plaid, and that a small checked one, which was made for my father to look the sheep in when he left the sea and came to Rathan. But Silver Sand had no cloak or plain whatsomever; yet he did not appear in the least disconvenienced. Now I am reminded by one that looks over my shoulder, without ever speering the leave of me, that those who use to read in tales, love to have a description of the dresses of the heroes. But I am no hero, God wot; and as for Silver Sand, he was not dressed fitting to be described in print.

Yet because the old fashion is passed away with the old lawless time, it may advantage to mention the ancient style of dress. Silver Sand was clad in a rough cap of badger skin with the fur out, and the ears cocked up on either side above his own, which gave him an appearance extraordinarily alert. For the rest he had on knee-breeches of hodden grey, and a round coat of the same without tails. His arms stood through his tight body-coat a great way, and when he travelled he was wont to take off his loose surtout and travel in his sleeved waistcoat, carrying his coat over his arm, as is the summer fashion in Galloway even to this day.

It so happened that on the day before I had put on my best suit, having regard to seeing May Maxwell—not that I had any desire to find favour in her eyes in the way of love, but because she had scouted and despised me when she came to my own house with Mistress Allison and Mistress MacWhirter, and I was resolved that she should do so no more.

I wore my own hair without powder, which indeed also my father never used nor any of our house, so far as I know; but I had it clubbed behind in a ribbon band. My body-coat was of the fine blue cloth, rather light blue than dark blue, long in the waist, with large silver buttons of pierced work, and creamy lace at the sleeves, monstrous fine. Underneath I wore a waistcoat that fitted me very well, as I thought. It was cut with long flaps on the thighs, in which were pockets, with broad mother-of-pearl buttons. Then as for my legs, they were covered with breeks of strong hodden grey, but of finer make than usual, which they weave somewhere near the Border. I wore pearl buckles at the knees. Long knitted "rig-and-fur" stockings had I also, sharp-pointed shoes that I bent upwards with care and labour—silver buckles also on these. Thus was I dressed in an attire more befitting the kirk of Dullarg on a Sabbath than nights and days on the wild hills of the Dungeon of Buchan.

In the fray of the cave, and during my adventures of the night before, the lace had been so torn off that I judged it better to take it all away, and so safely stowed it in my pocket, designing to have it stitched and put on again in due time.

Upon first setting out upon this quest I was careful of my attire, but ere all was done I gave no thought to it, more than if it had been a corn sack with leg and arm-holes pierced at the four corners, which some landward men in the remoter parts of Galloway still use. So under the cloud of night, and with some comfort from the little provision Silver Sand had brought, we set out over the heather-bushes of Airieland Moor. We went down a little glen side which opened from the hill where there were trees, birks, and oaks, I think—as near as I could tell from the sound that their leaves made in the dry, cold, north wind of night.

We passed a row of cot-houses by a mill-dam, and came down to the farm-town of Airieland, where is a great steading. We heard the cows tossing their heads and jingling their chains in the byre with a homely and friendly sound. So I took an extraordinary grooing in my inside for a drink of warm milk, such as I was accustomed to get from May Maxwell along with many disdainful words when I rowed across to Craigdarroch in the morning.

So I said to Silver Sand, "Can we not waken the people here and ask for a drink of the good new milk?"

"Ye may," says he, "but, mind you, Hector Faa waits na for new milk—his new milk is ayont the hill, an' he's runnin' for it!"

"But," said I, "unless I get something I fear that I am done, and that I can go no further.

"If that be so, we'll sune fettle that!" says he, and with no more words he turned aside into the byre, drew a milking stool down from between the thatch and the wall, and looked about for a vessel to milk in. In the dim light that was in the byre he could see none; but after looking at his own hat he said, "Gie me haud o' your bonnet!" which, when I had given him, he carefully knocked in the crown, then out of the high peaked cock that stood upwards with a gay air he made a tolerable drinking vessel. This he set on his knees, and went briskly to milking a cow into it, which I marvelled to see, having had little experience of cows myself. But Silver Sand was at no loss, and in a few moments he handed me the full of my hat of most excellent warm milk, which, when I had taken, and another like it, refreshed me extraordinarily.

Then I urged upon Silver Sand to take the like himself, and to use my hat, which had twice been used before.

"Na," he said, slily, "it's better to keep the stock separate. It saves marking them wi' keel, and keel, ye ken, is extraordinary expensive."

Then, having refused my hat, he showed me a trick that I had never seen, though how he managed it is more than I can say in the darkness of the byre. I heard the *sough, sough* of the milk streaming into some receptacle.

"Have you found a vessel to hold the milk?" I asked, thinking that he might just as lief have found it before he spoiled my hat.

"Ay," said he, "I have found a vessel, but the mischief is that there's a hole in the bottom of it, and it a' rins out as fast as I can milk it in."

"Then," I asked, in my simplicity, "why do you do it?"

He laughed, but made me no answer. Then, as my eyes became accustomed to the dusk of the byre, and the long rows of cow's hurdies, I saw that the madcap was making an extraordinarily wide mouth, and milking sideways into it, which made me much admire why the cow did not kick him. For the only time that I had tried the milking was at Craigdarroch, being persuaded thereto by May Maxwell with many smooth words; but the cow, that was a noted kicker, spilled me and the milking-pail heels-over-body, which caused a great laughter—at which I laughed also, but privately thought it a poor joke to spoil my suit of clothes in the gutter of a shippen. But this trick of Silver Sand was new to me, and I stood and gaped till, seeing with his cat's eyes that my mouth was open he suddenly directed a stream of milk therein, to my great inconvenience, for I was not expecting it. This seemed to me also an unfitting jest, considering the gravity of our situation. Besides, I feared that some drops had fallen on my coat. So I said to him, with some sharpness—

"Now, when you have quite done playing the fool, perhaps you will tell me how you mean to pay the goodman of his house for his hospitality."

"Hoots," he said, "wha pays for a drink o' milk?"

"I do," said I, "and I shall wake up the good man of the house and give him a penny."

"Do," said Silver Sand, "and I'll tell ye what ye'll get, and that's twa ounce o' lead drops in aneath your coat-tails for disturbin' the hoose at this time o' nicht. That's what auld Airie gies to young birkies like you that come in graund coats to play 'Jook my jo' wi' his lasses. See, that's his window," he went on, "but just be so kind as to let me ahint the midden first, for I'm no fond o' lead draps mysel'."

He skipped off behind the shelter of a mountainous fastness of some dark material that was piled in the yard.

"Noo gae on wi' your penny," he cried, "I'll see fair play. Naething like honesty."

His high spirits made me exceedingly angry.

"Come away," I cried, "let us have no more tomfoolery. I believe ye juist want to taigle me here till your fine friend, Hector Faa, the murderer, gets the lass."

"Taigle ye," he said; "far frae that, Laird Rathan; it's yer fine sense o' gentrice that taigles ye—that ye canna tak' a drink o' guid sweet milk till ye hae wakened the goodman o' the hoose frae his bed to introduce ye to the coo! Hoot awa', I can e'en do that mysel'."

And with that the madcap (who had the fit upon him) went to the door of the byre, and, lifting his hat with the air of His Majesty's Lion-King-at-Arms, he said—

"Mistress Crummie Cooshairn, let me mak' ye acquainted wi' the Laird o' Rathan, that did ye the honour to drink a drappie o' yer ain brewing to your good health, and mony o' them, Crummie!

I turned on my heel and walked away, for I had no words to express my indignation.

He called after me, "Paitrick, dinna sulk, man. It's no bonny. Tak' a lesson frae this sonsy wife Crummie. *She* bears nae malice. Hae, Crummie, my lass, there's a handfu' o' girse to brew mair milk, an' there, guidman o' Airieland, is a bawbee to pay for the girse. An' so a's correck, an' we're honest, honest—and gentrice to the back o' that, whilk is a great matter!"

Somewhere about the steading I heard a window go up, and a bellowing of ill talk, the purport of which was to ask what night-hawks of not doubtful parentage we were that came crawling and troking about his premises, and that he would have the blunderbuss on us in a moment.

"Guid e'en to ye, Airie," said Silver Sand, crying back from the little narrow stile that led over into a field among trees—"Guid e'en to you, and a' your bonnie lassies. My service to them, and tell them I canna bide the nicht, but I'll caa again sune."

The roaring of oaths from the window became a very thunderstorm.

As we went down the banks of a bonny bit burn that flows through a smooth meadow beneath the house, we heard behind us still the wrathful gollying of the great voice yet unappeased. Silver Sand chuckled to himself as if he had done something very clever.

"What for didna ye stop an' explain?" he said. "Ye micht possibly hae juiked the blunderbush and gotten time to pit in a word to satisfy your kittle honour afore he got time to load again."

But I scorned to say a word to him on the subject. So we went on our journey.

Now, though these episodes on the way take a long time to tell, and mayhap occupy overly much space, yet they took hardly any time in the doing, so quick was Silver Sand. I do not believe that we were a quarter of an hour about the onstead of Airieland in all.

Now, when I think on the matter at this distance, I cannot sufficiently admire the wonderful foresight and patient kindliness of Silver Sand. These halts I should never have taken willingly, and so in a short time, what with weariness and the want of sleep, I should have worn myself out long before we reached the hill country.

So we pursued our way, going over a levelish, boggy country, where there was some cultivation, and some cattle in the field. Coming past the farm of Auchlane I jumped a high dyke to show my agility, for the double draught of Crummie's milk had quickened me very greatly. Also the night was not yet quite set it, though the folk had gone to bed, for it is the custom in Galloway to bed very early. So, as I say, I leapt a stone dyke, but found one side much higher than on the other. I alighted on my feet, but fell forward against something that routed and rose instantly beneath me, throwing me off and running across the field. This gave me a great startle.

"Did ye think the bit stot was the Foul Thief himsel' that ye gied that skelloch?" cried Silver Sand, who had climbed the dyke quietly with Quharrie.

I answered that it was not I but the stot that made the noise.

"It was extraordinarily like you, Laird!" he said.

These were the sort of things that used to keep me wondering whether Silver Sand was the best of good company or the most insolent and forward of tinklers. Yet five minutes after he had said such things I would laugh at them in my heart, though I still continued to hold down my head like the sulky dog I was.

At the poor little hamlet of Brig o' Dee we crossed the river, which looked cold and grey, the night wind ruffling it beneath us, Beyond this we got into a most bleak, unkindly country, and so continued for more than an hour. It was all of wet, marshy peat, with black haggs; and, what were worse, green, deceitful "quakkin-qua's," covered with a scum that looked like tender young grass, but in which, at the first step, one might sink to the neck. Here and there we came upon some sheep grazing as best they could on the wet, sour grass. Nevertheless it was pleasant and cheery to hear them cropping the herbage with short, quick bites, then moving on to another clump. One of them gave a cough, mightily human, as we passed by, just as a man does in church behind his hand so that he may not disturb the worshippers.

In a little we were among the lochs of Bargatton and Glentoo, dreary stretches of reedy water in the midst of marshy ground, so that in the night it made one shiver to look at them. But ever our feet went onward to the lilt of Silver Sand's song or the rise and fall of Silver Sand's voice, as he told stories of the old Killing days, and the pallid men who had lain in these wildernesses to which we were going before they were utterly given up to the reivers and outlaws.

In front stalked Quharrie, never coursing about after rabbits and hares like other dogs, even when they popped out just under his nose, but following his master's eye and hand. With his head very high, his sharp ears set forward with a cock like the feather in a Highlandman's bonnet, his legs wide apart as though to guard against sudden surprise, he would run ahead and then stand a moment till we came up. In this manner he scouted in front of his master, so that there was nothing, not even a grouse cock, that was not indicated before we came to it. As we reached the little steading of Drumbreck, where the moss ends in a great flow of black peat, in which are deep and dangerous holes half full of water from former fuel cuttings, Quharrie stopped and growled.

Motioning me to stand where I was, Silver Sand passed the dog and went carefully to the dyke to look over. Then he waved to me to come on. It was but a tinkler and his family encamped under three great beeches that grow in the courtyard of the little farm, for Drumbreck has ever been a well-kenned place for the keeping of "gaun bodies."

"It's just Tyke Lowrie an' his brood," said Silver Sand; "no harm in them, though a deal *on* them. The mistress o' Drumbreck is well guided not to let them in amang the sacks in the barn."

The little village of Clachanpluck, inviting enough to weary limbs, with its whitewashed houses, and trees growing about the little fringes of garden, lay before us, and the curs barked as I went down the long street. At the end, where the roads separated, it was time for Silver Sand and me to part.

The "Lord keep us both!" said I, and parted without shaking hands, yet not so fast but that I heard Silver Sand say "Amen!"

I am sure he was a Christian man, but there are many queer Christians in this land of Galloway. Indeed I fear that I am one myself.

CHAPTER XIX

ON THE TRACK OF THE RAIDERS

It had darkened slowly, and now the night was at its prime when I passed down the street of the little clachan. The north wind met me in the face like a wall as I made my way alone on my quest perilous through this hamlet of sleeping folk, stilled under the peace of their cottage eaves of thatch—too poor to be worth the robbing, and numerous enough to render a good account of themselves in case of an attack.

Now while the wilder spirits of the smugglers and the gypsies attacked the cave for the purposes of which we know, there was a much larger number of both who devoted themselves to the easier work of driving off the cattle of the Maxwells and others of the country, and packing the cargo of the brig upon horses, with the view of clearing the country before the alarm rose.

They were the safer in this respect that in those days news did not spread with the extraordinary rapidity with which it does now. The dwellings of men were scattered sparser on the waste. A man might ride a long day among the hills of heather and see not one reeking house or any place where kindly folk dwelt. There was a district of thirty miles square in Carrick, in Galloway, and the moors of the Shire, over whose border never exciseman put his nose, except with a force of red soldiers at his tail, which did not happen once in twenty years. Moreover, the farmers and small proprietors of the day were better content to pay a kind of mail to the hill raiders than be in constant fear of them.

So long, therefore, as their own cattle were let alone, the bonnet lairds and farmers of Balmaghie and the Glen Kens were little likely to come to blows with the gypsies or the smugglers in defence of other people's flocks and herds. But murder and house-burning were quite different counts, as the outlaws were presently to hear. The chief desire of those who were driving the cattle was that they might get to the Craigencallie and Loch Dee drove-road before the country rose behind them. And this is how they set out from the Craigdarroch beach.

From the coves by the shore a great number of men came

running with the cargo—kegs of spirit, Hollands boxes wrapped about with wheat-straw—strange cases from the Indies, where the Hollanders have many plantations—iron-lined boxes of lace, most precious of all. As many of these as the horses were able to carry were loaded for the northward journey. The rest were taken to pits dug out under the scarps of precipices, or on the sides of the glens, and covered again with green turf.

So the long train set off, a bevy of wild loons keeping the pack-horses moving with slender pointed goads, cut from the nearest coppice. The horsemen of the smuggling party clattered ahead with great barrels slung at each side of their horses, secured under the belly with broad leather straps, and clinched by strength of arm and the leverage of foot against the side of the poor beast—the worst of whose sufferings were past, however, as soon as they were upon the way, for the jolting of the load soon eased the straps and fastenings.

The smugglers were the jollier of the two parties, for the gypsies had their hands deeper in crime than the Freetraders, having been art and part in the house-burning and the cattle-stealing, and so rode with their necks in danger. But the land smugglers, many of whom had no interest in the affair save to get the goods comfortably stowed, were more than merry, for it was their custom that a cask should be kept free and open for use by the way. And as they went they sang—

> "Where'er we see a bonny lass, we'll caa' as we gae by;
> Where'er we meet wi' liquor guid, we'll drink an we be dry.
> There's brandy at the Abbeyburn, there's rum at Heston Bay,
> And we will go a-smuggling afore the break o' day."

Now we have no further concern with them. They ride out of the story as soon as they cleared the cattle and the raiders who were at the driving of them. As they went the jingling of their horse-harness told the country folk that the Black Riders were abroad, and in the night many a goodwife reached over her hand to feel if her goodman were in his place; for though none of them objected to the anker of spirit which they would find at the back of the high road dyke the next morning, nor yet failed to place the money for it in a cup in the same retired position, it was not a business that the douce housewives wanted their own goodmen mixed up with.

But with the cattle drovers the case was different. They could only pick the best and speediest of the stock, and drive it with the horses going on before, and a regiment of half-naked loons from the hills keeping the poor beasts on the trot. If a Galloway cow lagged and threatened to keep back the troop, she received a sharp lash across the nose and was driven into the darkness. Sometimes, however, after a drink at the wayside burn, the terrors of loneliness so pressed upon her that she would come racing after the company, bellowing as loud as she could, and so rejoin the herd.

As soon, then, as I had passed the little forge at the lower end of Clachanpluck, where there are a great number of trees planted, and beneath which a pleasant burnie was making a singing noise, I became aware that I must be close upon the track of the stolen cattle. The road was deep trampled, and in the softer places there were many signs of a large herd having passed only an hour or two before.

It was now that I felt my lack of Silver Sand, my companion, for he could have told the number, condition, and intentions of the herd and their drivers, and even how fast they were going from the marks on the road. I had no such skill. But on the other hand I have always had a considerable idea of my own luck and resource in emergency. So that on the whole it was with a beating heart, but with a certain sense of elation, that I went forward along the road.

The track ran between two rows of trees—beech for the most part, as I knew by the dry clash and rattle of their leaves when the winds brushed them against each other. I could see over the low hedges into the meadows, and a bloom of the fair blonde flower that is called Queen of the Meadow looked over and nodded at me, which I thought to be very early for the season, being but the end of May.

As I went on a curious thought came over me, that I had come this way before with May Maxwell, though very well I knew that it was not so. Yet the phantasy so took hold on me, that as I footed it I looked from side to side, saying within myself, "Here she and I plucked the honeysuckle and the bindweed in the hedge. Here we sat and wove them into crowns on this low bridge of turf. Up this bramble-interlaced brae we wandered, our arms entwined." Yet all the time I knew full well that never had my eyes seen these places before. Though there was no reason why the thought should so pleasure me, yet I do not deny that it did comfort me in an especial degree; so that I continued to walk with satisfaction along the highway—such as it was—till I came to the side of the long narrow loch that is called Grenoch, which is yet not the same as the larger Loch Grannoch that lies among the granite hills at the head end of Girthon parish.

But soon I was meeting the backward-straying cattle too often to make it very safe for me to pursue my way further along the road. I mounted, therefore, to the moorland above the loch, where, from the ridge, I had a lookout in all directions, keeping the crown of the heather under my feet all the way.

So now I can see myself speeding along, like a beast that has had both drink and victual, pretty brisk with the thought of coming back this way again with May Maxwell at my side. Which, indeed, I never did—at least, not till long years afterwards, when all things were changed. But the feeling did me good at the time.

I looked to the priming of my pistols more than once, as well as the dim light would let me. There was a beast routing at the foot of the Duchrae Craigs, where the road kept away to the right straight for the old Brig of the Black Water. The cattle were upon the road immediately before me now. I could hear them quite plainly. A low and continuous moaning came backward upon the north wind, mixed with sharper noises of the shouting of men and the barking of dogs. It was but seldom that I heard these, and they were not, I think, the gypsies' dogs, which are trained to hunt silently, but dogs that had been gathered up of their own accord from the farm towns on the way. These did not bark long, however, either falling behind or getting a knife in their ribs from a gypsy driver that silenced their yelping for ever. As at this point the drove-road took over the Folds Hill, I desired to get upon the river side of the herd, to escape being driven upon the moors and away from the bridge, so that it was necessary for me to cross the road. This I did at the little hut which I now know to be the farm of the Clownie—a ruin of walls only when last I went that way. I made no haste, thinking myself safe, being so far behind, but stood at my ease on the dusky white road with dark patches upon it, looking both ways.

CHAPTER XX

THE GREAT FIGHT AT THE BRIDGE-HEAD

But I had not stood long there when a voice from the dyke foot, by the well of excellent water that lies by the path over to the Duchrae, cried to me to stand or take the consequences. Though these were not condescended upon, I elected to take them, and so ran whatever I could towards the loch, which I could see of a dull red colour beneath me.

Apparently the consequences spoken of were up a gun-barrel at the time, and consisted of two ounces of lead, for "Crack!" went a musket, and something whistled like a bum-clock[1] past me. Putting my hand down, my finger encountered a hole in the flap of my blue coat. It was warm at the edges, and appeared to be clean cut. In a moment I was in the heart of a saugh-bush, where I sat giving thanks to God for my escape. Now I should have been better pleased with a preserving Providence if the bullet had gone through my breeks, for I had more pairs of them, and besides, they were only of hodden grey when all was said and done. But I had only this one coat, and that of fine blue cloth.

The saugh-bush by the waterside was safe, but ignominious. From its depths I could see nothing, and I knew that every moment the dumb, hard-driven herd of beasts was drawing away in the direction of the bridge, and I not there to cross before them. But for that unlucky business of standing on the road I might have done it easily, for I was deceived by the great turn which the way makes at Parkhill towards the Folds of Tomorrach Wood. It is always thus with running after short cuts and taking off of corners to make new ways. When will I learn to walk in the old and be content? Possibly in the next world, when I shall not be able—for there, as we are told upon authority, all things shall be new.

As I went the light wind bore a strange, low, continuous moaning to my ears. From the saugh-bush I went slowly along the waterside till I lost the track of the cattle. Then, when the loch had narrowed into a lane of running water, I struck up through the tangled brush of the thick wood which is called the Duchrae Bank,

1 Dor-beetle

where many hazels grow, to the top of the hill that looks toward Bennan and the valley of the Ken. Day was just beginning to show, which it does in early May about two hours before the sun rises. The cold grey of the sky became the colour of a Water of Dee pearl—silken grey shot with quivering rays of white.

The moaning grew as I ascended into a hoarse, tumultuous routing. There they are at last! It is so dark that I can only guess at their position, but I can see that the head of the column is making for the bridge. The riders ride before, their heads low between their shoulders, glancing forward. The whippers-in run tirelessly on the flanks, dressing the uneven files. The moaning of the herd comes to me on the wind like the crying of a single mighty beast in pain. It is pitiful and heart-touching.

The Black Water looms dark—the bridge a grey purple arch spanning blackness.

But a row of sparks flashes out at the bridge-head. *"Crack! crack! crack!"* go the guns. There is a sudden turmoil in the densely packed herd. The horsemen at the head of the column form up, and from them too the red sparks, with the clang a little behind them, spit angrily out.

"Hurrah!" I cry aloud, not knowing what I did, for my friends are there, and at that bridge-head. They are fighting it to turn the robbers. Perhaps Hector and May are among them. Fool that I was that I did not hasten and get before them!

Ah, there they are at it! Hark to the rattle of the guns, the splutter of the pistols—how they go! I find myself running forward at full speed, keeping close to the water, and alongside the Holland Isle. I wonder as I run, if I shall ever come there when the nuts are ripe, for I have ever heard that it is a famous place for them. In a little I am abreast of the packed and frightened cattle. The outlaws are playing a bold game. Their mounted fighting men are pushing along the front. The silent, eager dogs and the limber gypsy laddies are dressing the sides of the column, which, indeed, is naturally held by the very formation of the ground—the rocky glen of the Black Water being in front, and the deep, dark lane of Grenoch on the other side. The unmounted men who are without guns keep circulating along the rear. Between them and the bridge there is a lowing, roaring, horn-tossing sea of wild cattle, the best and the strongest in Galloway.

I get down by the water's edge, for I am pushing on all the time. I hear my feet crash on the shingles. I fall on my face among the hard stones before I am aware. That is my safety, for with the instinct of a sea-bred boy I feel for the water. It is within ten feet of me, roaring deep. With my belt-thong of leather I fasten my napkin, filled with my powder-flask and pistols, upon the top of my head. The strap is caught in my teeth, and without a moment's delay I push off. Though I can wade nearly all the way, at last I am swept off my feet. Ten strokes, however, take me over, and I stand shivering on the north side of the Black Water.

But my powder and my pistols are dry, though I myself am streaming wet. Crying my name, to let the Maxwells know not to shoot, in a moment I am at the bridge-end and among them. As I had imagined, the defenders are my friends, with other ten men whom they had gathered as they came along, mostly kinsmen of their own, Maxwells and Sproats, from the coastlands. Kennedy Maxwell, who was the one I came nearest, had only time to say—

"Dinna throw a shot away, Patrick. We're turning them. This is the third time they have come at us."

Even as he spoke the mounted men did come on again, but a storm of balls tore through their ranks, and set the horses plunging and the cattle wild with terror. So again they were driven back. The men hung over the parapet of the bridge and kneeled with their muskets upon it, yelling with challenge in their voices.

"We have them," cried Will Maxwell; "we'll not let one o' the cowardly crew escape!"

The word was ill-chosen, the rejoicing premature. Again the mounted outlaws drew off to the rear, and for a space only the dogs kept the column within its lines.

Gradually their front widened, as though to flank the bridge and make for the water. We spread out to meet them. The others were soon blazing away, but the gypsies were far behind, and I saw small service in maddening the poor dumb beasts with pistol balls.

Yet it was an amazing sight—Dee Bridge that night, with its high-arched span—men standing two deep in the centre of it; men stride-leg on the parapet of it; gunshots cracking, pistols spitting. Then in front of us the white, pitiful eyes of a myriad (so they seemed) of wild cattle—maimed and tortured they knew not why, sending up a great routing of dumb prayer to the God of all ill-used, over-driven beasts that never did a sin. Beyond these the dark forms of the mounted outlaws contriving new plots in the rear.

I wanted the Maxwells to charge and break the column of cattle,

but Will Maxwell overruled, saying, "No; we will hold the bridge."
So the bridge was held.

Then suddenly a great fierce light arose in the rear. The outlaws
had kindled a fire, and the red light burned up, filtering through the
ranks of the cattle, and projecting great horned shadows against the
clouds. For a few minutes this picture stood like a painted show,
with the Dee Water running dark and cool beneath—a kind of
Circe's Inferno where the beasts are tortured for ever.

Two half-naked fiends ran alongside the column of cattle,
carrying what was apparently a pot of blazing fire, which they threw
in great ladlefuls on the backs of the packed beasts that stood
frantically heaving their heads up to the sky. Then in a moment from
all sides arose deafening yells. Fire lighted and ran along the hides of
the rough red Highland and black Galloway cattle. Desperate men
sprang on their backs, yelling. Dogs drove them forward. With one
wild, irresistible, universal rush the maddened column of beasts
drave at the bridge, and swept us aside like chaff.

Never have I seen anything so passing strange and uncanny as
this tide of wild things, frantic with pain and terror, whose billows
surged irresistibly to the bridge-head. It was a dance of demons.
Between me and the burning backs of the cattle there rose a gigantic
Highlander with fiery eyes and matted front. On his back was a black
devilkin that waved a torch with his hands, scattering contagious fire
over the furious herd. The rush of the maddened beasts swept us off
the bridge as chaff is driven before the wind. There was no question
of standing. I shot off my pistols into the mass. I might as well have
shot them into the Black Water. I declare some of the yelling devils
were laughing as they rode, like fiends yammering and girning when
Hell wins a soul. It is hard to make any who did not see it, believe in
what we saw that night. Indeed, in this warm and heartsome winter
room, with the storm without, and the wife in bed crying at me to
put by the writing and let her get to sleep, it is well-nigh impossible
to believe that any of these things came to pass within the space of a
few years. Yet so it was. I who write it down was there. These eyes
saw the tossing, fiery waves of maddened creatures than ran forward
seeking death to escape from torture, while the reek of their burning
went up to heaven.

I looked again. Beneath at the ford I saw (as it were) a thousand
wild cattle with their thick hair blazing with fire, their tails in the air,
tossing wide-arched horns. I saw the steam of their nostrils going up
like smoke as they surged through the water, a hundred mad Faas
and Marshalls on their backs yelling like fiends of the pit. In a score

of pulse beats there was not a beast that had not forced the bridge or crossed the ford. We who defended were broken and scattered; some of us swept down by the water, powder damp, guns trampled shapeless—dispirited, annihilated, we that had been so sure of victory.[1]

---

[1] But before I tell of other things let me add how the outlaws scattered Greek fire over their cattle, using unwittingly a stratagem of the ancient world. In a field by the waterside, within a hundred yards of where the column halted, were the Duchrae Ewebuchts, and there were kept in store pitch and oil for sheep dipping and cattle marking, of which, in some devilish fashion of their own, the outlaws, skilled in such horrid chemistry, made their cruel fiery brew.

CHAPTER XXI

SAMMLE TAMSON FETCHES A RAKE OF WATER

When I came to myself (for indeed I was mad as the beasts themselves while the turmoil lasted), I found myself tossed out on the heather from a bull's back that had landed me there. My hands were burned and black where I had slapped the poor beast's fell to put out the flames. But for all that, it had not known me from one of its persecutors. I think the mad impulse of the herd did not arise so much from pain as from the sudden unreasoning fury, which at any moment may seize a large crowd of half-wild cattle in presence of the unknown. Once there was a herd of cows in Parton, up Peathill way, that ate a man—chased him and ate him bodily. Their reason was, because the man belonged to a different denomination. But that is not my story. For that tale you must ask one of the red Wardhaughs. It comes not into my book, though I believe the man was a cousin of the Marshalls.

How I came on the beast's back, unless it were to save myself from being trampled under foot, I know not; but hither upon this shaggy charger I had come so far in safety, and now found myself between Mossdale and the Stroan Loch pitched out upon the heather, falling almost upon a grouse cock that had heard only the blatter of a bullock's heels, and no doubt wondered where the blundering beast was coming to. His cockship got something of a surprise, I am thinking, when the enemy of his kind was shot out upon the top of him with pistols shining in his belt. At any rate, he rose with a strong protest of *"Geck-kek-kek-a-kek!"* that such a deceit should be played upon him—as quiet a self respecting bird as ever was.

In a few minutes I was chapping at the door of Mossdale house, that sits all its lone on a pleasant braeface looking to the sun rising; and as the sun was so engaged at the time, I thought the long, low, whitewashed cottage a picture exceedingly quaint. There was a man just coming to the door with a wooden platter of hens' meat in his hands. His eyes were red with sleep, and as he came his jaws opened like a rat-trap, for he was gaunting as if he had not had nearly enough of his bed.

"Good morning, guidman," said I.

"And ye hae brocht the tap o' the mornin' wi' you, freen'," he said, but not at all suspiciously, passing by me with the hens' meat. I stood at the door, not venturing in. The man, who was built long and thin with a stoop in the shoulders, opened a little door in a wooden erection of boards. A hen or two with many chickens came tumultuously out, making that *scraiching* noise which tells of an empty inside among all the hen-tribe, as much as to say, "I'm as toom as a whistle! Are ye going to be long with that meat?"

The man put down the little trencher and stood over them with a long wand, putting back the greedy and making room for the poor, puny, backward ones, that could not elbow forward with their short, callow chicken wings. The scene was one of most exceeding peace, and affected me strangely, having yet in my ears that wild riot at the bridge-head, and the sound of that mighty bellowing, like the roaring of all the bulls in Bashan.

"It's been a fine nicht!" said he. "Whaur travelled ye frae this mornin', freen', so early. Lay ye a' nicht at the Duchrae?"

"'Deed," said I, frankly—at least with more frankness than I had intended when I chappit at the door, "I slept but little, for there were a feck o' wild men on the road yestreen, and peacefu' folk were better to keep a calm sough."

"I'm wi' ye there," he said, scraping up some of the *daich*, or hen meat, that had fallen on the ground, and giving it to a peeping, peevish little chicken that came complaining and pecking about his feet. "Neither troke nor traffic wi' the like o' them. For me I keep oot o' their gate."

"Heard ye nocht yestreen ava'?" I asked, eyeing him pretty carefully, for my own back was to the sun.

"I was thinkin'," he said, "that Dee Water had come doon in the nicht, and that I heard the falls roarin'. I thocht I wad try the fishin' in the mornin'. I micht get a fine fish."

"Ye micht catch a four-leggit sawmon, wi' horns," said I.

"Say ye sae?" said the man. "Then Sammle Tamson will be for bidin' close by his ain door check."

For the first time there came a shade of suspicion over his face as he glanced at me from head to foot.

"Ye're brawly airmed, freen, to be so early astir."

He looked at my pistols and silver-mounted whinger.

"I'm an honest man," said I, reassuringly.

"Likely," said he that had called himself Samuel Tamson, "there's a feck o' honest men gaun the road. I never met wi' yin that gied himsel' the contrar' name."

But nevertheless he viewed me again with a somewhat reassured look.

"Ye'll no be a Faa?" he asked, in a sly, pawky manner.

"Na," says I, "I'm nae Faa, thank Heaven!"

"So I was jaloosin'," answered he. Then he added reflectively, "The Faas are a weel-favoured race when's a's said an' dune."

He looked at me still longer.

"Ye kind o' favour the Macatericks—lang an' flail-jointed, but your mouth's ower big to be a Macaterick, an' nane o' the Marshalls hae turned-up noses!"

Which (I may remark) neither had I. Sammle Tamson seemed reassured. But he still had native caution.

"Ye'll hae a name o' your ain," said he; "let us hear it."

"My name is Patrick Heron!" said I, a little nettled at the man's patent suspicion, though indeed I would never have so much as looked at any one coming in such a case to my own door.

"Ye'll no be ony freen' to John Heron o' Rathan Isle?"

"I am his son," I replied, briefly.

"D'ye tell me so, O man——" said Sammle, yet seemed disinclined to take any action beyond the exclamation. He still stood with the empty trough of hens' meat in his hand. A voice from the house cried behind us, sharply—

"What's a' that cleckin' aboot? Am I to wait a' day for you to licht my fire, Sammle Tamson? Was it for this that I marriet you, an' me had so many better offers? I wish to peace I had never left Parton!"

The voice was sharp, but by no means unkindly. On the contrary, it liked me well.

"There's a young man here, guidwife," said Sammle Tamson at the door, leaning from the outside to put his head within, as one might set the bending top of a fishing-rod into an upper window.

"Fetch him ben, and let us see what like he is," said the voice.

Sammle silently motioned to me to put down my pistols and whinger on the window-sill without, which indeed I would not have done on his account; but the voice from within was extraordinarily reassuring. Then he stepped ben before me, and I followed. hardly had I got inside when I would have been out again, for I caught sight, for the first time in my life, of a goodwife in some disarray sitting on the edge of the settle engaged in completing her attire. I had fled on the instant, but the voice said, encouragingly—

"Hoot awa'; sit ye doon, young man——"

"But, wife——" began Sammle Tamson, in an ex-postulating tone.

"Haud your tongue, guidman. I'm nane so unsonsy yet, though I be auld eneuch to be the laddie's mither.

Ye wad think I was a quean in a cuttie sark to hear ye. Be na so nice wi' Eppie Tamson."

"He says he's a son o' the auld laird o' Rathan's." This came sulkily and somewhat grudgingly from Sammle.

"Come by here an' let me look at ye, laddie!" commanded the dame, from the bedside.

I had been standing modestly with my face to the window, looking over the wide moss, now bright with the red of the sun rising. I turned at the word with some diffidence. But the dame was already in her drugget short-gown, which she was busy buckling at the waist. She was a plump matron of forty-five, with a pleasant apple-red in her cheeks, and very bright blue eyes. Even while I turned she took her feet, one at a time, into her hand, and shod them with a shoe neater than I had ever seen on the foot of a Galloway wife—one of whose wonted household gods is the "bauchle," or shapeless slipper, often with a "hoshen," or loose double stocking, within. Altogether Eppie Tamson was a dame both douce and sonsy—a desirable friend, as I knew from her voice.

Sammle Tamson was blowing up the fire—on his knees, with his back extraordinarily high in the air, and his head so close to the bars that it seemed as though he were endeavouring to crawl between them. And he did not seem much over stout to succeed.

So I went biddably enough up to Mistress Tamson, who, rising from the oak settle on which she had been sitting, took me by the shoulders, led me across the room to the window, and looked at me a moment in a way which made me blush. I blushed still more when she took me fairly round the neck and gave me a sound kiss, saying—

"Aye, laddie, what wad I no hae gi'en for a boy like you! Get up, there, aff your knees, lang Sammle Tamson; ye canna even licht that fire. Ye are but a feckless lown. Lat me at it!"

Sammle rose in a discouraged way, as one that was not appreciated in life, and proceeded to put some water in the porridge pot.

"Gang to the well for fresh," his wife flung at him over her shoulder as she puffed and blew.

"But I brocht in fresh yestreen late," he said, complainingly.

His wife rose off her knees rapidly. Like a flash Sammle ran to the back of the door, and seized a couple of wooden water-cans. He was making out of the door with them when his wife came at him with the besom shank. Sammle guarded himself instinctively with the cans, and the stick rattled harmlessly on the staves. Yet he did not smile as he hurried down the path, nor did his wife fling a single word after him. It seemed entirely a piece of routine.

"Saw ye ever sic a man? queried the dame, as she returned to the fire. "He canna do ocht but he maun stand and talk and 'argie-bargie' as lang. And that thochtless and unmindful that he can hardly be lippened to do onything but feed the hens"—here she paused; then, as if something had been called to her mind, she added—"*if that!*"

"Just step to the door," she continued, after another pause, "and see gin he has gane to the well. He generally gangs to the midden for worms for his fishin' when he's sent for water," she explained.

I looked and saw Sammle Tamson standing by the well, emptying the water out of the cans. I came in and reported accordingly.

"Aye," said his wife, "sic a man—Lord, sic a man! It's juist mortal like him. He wad never think o' emptying yestreen's water at the door here. He bood carry it to the well and empty it there. It's a mercy he did even that. The mornin' afore last, ken ye what he did? He took the water-cans to the well wi' the water that had been standin' a' nicht, and he brocht them back as they gaed awa', with the selfsame water in them!"

The goodwife paused.

"But he catched it for that!" she said, righteously.

"But he canna mak' ony mistake this time," I said.

"I dinna ken—I dinna ken!" she said, shaking her head. "It's barely possible; but gin it be possible ava' to mak' a mistak', Sammle Tamson's the man to mak' it."

The fire was blazing up the chimney now, and the house of Mossdale, on its sunny braeface, was very cheerful. I saw a prospect of porridge.

My heart was opened. I began to tell, of my own accord, all my story to the good dame. She heard me with constant expressions of sympathy and pity, standing with the porridge spurtle in her hand in the middle of the floor, while the water in the pot steamed away unregarded.

I told more of my story.

"Say ye sae! Dear sirce—to think on that! An' the wull cats burned the hoose——"

I told still more.

"An' ye focht them in the cave for the sake o' the lass. My word, but she'll be a good lass. Lovenenty me! but she'll hae gi'en ye anither kind o' a kiss than an auld wife like me."

I said "Not so," but went on with my tale.

"The Almichty preserve's a'," cried Eppie. "An' the misleared heather-cat ran aff wi' the bit lass, an' noo ye're seekin' her. Heard ye ever the like o' that! My man shall gang an' help you. Oh, that he war ony guid! Gin I had a pair o' breeks, I declare but I wad gang wi' ye mysel'! An' ye hae nae mither, ye tell me. Puir laddie! puir laddie!"

The white apron went up to the eyes that were not merry any more, and she took me in her arms and kissed me again.

Then she ran to the door, and cried out loud, "Sammle Tamson, ye muckle sloyt, come hame wi' the water this meenit, or ye shall get 'Nickie Ben' frae your Jo Janet!"

Through the window I could see Samuel Tamson standing gazing moonstruck at the well.

"Ye great moidered nowt ye, d'ye think that this is miracle mornin', an' that the guid well-water is gaun to turn into wine?"

Samuel recovered his cans in haste and started for home.

His wife saw his legs beginning to move like compasses, and

then, thinking all was at last well, she came back in to the fire. She said no word of good or bad as Samuel came within the door and set down his cans behind it, with a look of self-righteousness which did one good to see.

Eppie took the great tankard from the shelf and went to get it filled with the fresh, cool water from the well. She thrust her dish into the nearest can. It struck the bottom with a hollow sound. In great surprise she looked within.

The can was empty and dry.

It was too much. Iniquity such as this was far beyond besom shanks. She gave her husband but one look that would have speaned a foal. Then with great politeness, she turned to me and asked if I would be so kind as to fetch a rake of water from the well.

When I was gone on my errand, my heart was wae for the poor man within. I expected that I should have to collect the fragments on my return.

But what really happened I know not, for when I came back Sammle was sitting on the wooden bench in the corner of the fireplace with an extraordinarily subdued face, and his wife was standing, silent also, by the inglenook.

It was Sammle who looked up first.

"It's fine caller water," he said, "and a nice heartsome walk i' the mornin' to gie ye an appetite for yer porritch—it's pleasant to fess in the water."

But his wife said no word; she only stirred in the meal.

In a few minutes there was a great reeking dish of porridge on the table—the delightsomest of scenery to a famished man.

Then as soon as I had finished Eppie came to me and said, "Noo, aff wi' yer claes, into my warm bed, an' get ye a sleep for four hours, at the least."

"But," I urged, "I dare not lose a moment. I maun tak' the hills for Loch Enoch this very instant."

"Ye'll do no siccan thing. I ken the look o' a laddie sickening for trouble. Ye'll do as Eppie Tamson bids ye in her ain hoose of Mossdale. Better to lose four hours than lose the lass. Ye hae had nae sleep for twa nichts, and ye'll never see Loch Enoch or your May if ye carry on as ye are doing."

All the while she was unbuttoning my coat and waistcoat as if she had been my own mother, which I thought a strange thing—but a moment after it seemed perfectly natural to me.

"Ye see I hae nae bairns o' my ain!" she said for all explanation, which somehow, perhaps because I was fair dead with sleep, seemed perfectly competent reasoning.

I think I was asleep before I was out of her hands. At least I have no memory of my head ever touching the pillow. I was rising up, up—on warm, white, fleecy clouds—up, up, till I put out my hands to keep from being squeezed flat against the arch of the blue sky. I saw angels. I remember what they are like. There are two kinds of them. One pattern has merry eyes and white teeth, with sunny curls cropped short like a boy's. The others are about forty-five, very buxom, and are all named Eppie. I did not hear the name of the first sort.

CHAPTER XXII

I GET THE RIGHT SIDE OF EPPIE TAMSON

It is a strange thing that when you are very tired folk will never let you sleep five minutes. You have noticed that. So have I. As soon as you drop asleep, in a quarter of an hour or less they are at you, saying that it is some frankly impossible time, and that you must get up.

As I lay asleep I heard some one say, about a million miles away (or maybe more), that it was eleven o'clock of the day. I turned over, for this was no concern of mine.

Somebody said, a little nearer this time—not over a thousand miles away, "Poor laddie! anither half-hour will no hurt him."

So I turned over again and went to sleep for a year.

But the contrariness of things is such that in less than three moments (and short ones) some one had taken me in a pair of strong arms—comfortable things too—and was raising me gently up. Angels again; but the warm, fleecy clouds were better even than these strong arms.

"My laddie, sorrow am I to wakken ye, but it's chappin' twal, an' the denner's ready, an' the guidman is ready likewise to tak' ye to the Wolf's Slock, that is your best road to Loch Enoch. He kens that gin he disna tak' ye safe, he need never more show his face at Mossdale or caa Eppie Tamson his ain guidwife!"

I sat up. The house was running round about in a breathless kind of whirling silence, as if the very plates on the dresser were waiting for me to speak, and I had nothing to say.

Wakening from a deep sleep in a strange house is the eeriest of things. I do not think that Lazarus had any different feeling when he awoke after his four days in the tomb with that big *thruch* stone covering him in.

Eppie helped me on with my things as she had helped me off, with the same air of having been my mother in a former existence. It was so wonderful to me, who had been a man's bairn all the days of my life, to have some one to lift my socks and undo the tags of my boots.

While she was bent over me in this way, once actually tying my shoe, I saw Samuel Tamson lift his head and give a look at her, both wistful and pitying, though I could not for the life of me understand why—his being the need of pity, to my thinking.

So being dressed, there on the table was dinner; and ere I sat down I noticed that my coat was neatly pieced and mended where the bullet had cut through the night before, at the Clownie dykeside, when I ran headlong into the saugh bush by the waterside. This pleased me as much as anything. Also that my clothes were clean brushed and exceedingly neat and snod.

I was about to thank her, but she cut me short.

"Get your denner, laddie, and see and no file your claes. I hae had siccan a wark wi' them."

"I am sorry to pit you to so muckle inconvenience," said I, politely.

"Havers! 'inconvenience,' quo' he, the boy wants wit. Glad and proud am I to do what little I can for your mither's son."

"Did you ken my mither?" I asked, for my father had spoken but little of her, and I would gladly have heard more.

"Na, it's a way of speaking just," said Eppie Tamson; "but I ken her son, and if ever there was a laddie needin' somebody to look after him, it's that same callant. Oh, but ye need that lass sair aboot the auld Isle o' Rathan. Guid keep ye and help ye to get her gin she be worthy o' ye. Gin ye win her oot o' the gleds' claws, she's no gang hame withoot a ring on her finger, or my name's no Eppie.

After dinner she had a great number of directions to give to her husband, who said not a word, but only looked at her and me time about in the same extraordinary wistful and mournful way. Then she gave me my pistols. They were cleaned and oiled, loaded and primed.

I was about to thank her again for having put them to rights, when she said, "Na, no me—I wadna touch the nasty things. It was him that did them, and I howp to your satisfaction?"

I hastened to assure her.

"It's as weel," said Mistress Tamson.

Then she pressed on me a fine engraved silver flask, which she said she had gotten from the Laird of Parton when she married, for that she had been a servant in the big house there.

"It's fu' o' the best. *You* carry it!" she said, pointedly.

Also she had scones and oatcake done up with fine bacon ham between the slices in a toothsome manner I had never seen before, but which she had no doubt learned in the kitchens of the great.

As I went out she asked if I had any money. I showed her Silver Sand's handful, and she was in a manner satisfied.

"Aweel!" she said, with a kind of disappointment, that told me as plainly as large print that she had meant to supply me also with that, had I been in need of it, which made me grateful all the same.

Then when she bade me good-bye, after giving me a fine hazel staff with an iron shod on it, she burst out crying like a bairn and went indoors without speaking, shutting the door.

But we had not got our feet off the little green loaning that goes towards the great hill of Cairn Edward, before Eppie came after us again with something bright in her hand.

"I brocht this," she said; "it micht be useful to ye."

It was a brass prospect glass, very short, but as thick as my wrist. It was of many draws, all shutting up into one, and closed with brass caps at both ends.

I did not want to take so many things from her, and began to say so. But I saw her husband motioning me to be silent from behind her back.

Following the direction of my eyes (for I have not the art of looking without seeming to look that some folk have), she caught him in the act.

"Gar him tak' it," she said.

"Ye had better——" said Sammle, feebly.

So I put the glass in my tail-pocket, where, to tell the truth, it was an extraordinary weight, and as I feared at the time of but little use.

Then, standing there before me on the heather (that was not yet full in bloom, but only brown and purple black with little dots and dashes of living green among it), this woman, whom I had never seen before that morning, made me promise, if I were alive, to come this way as soon as I got clear.

"Mind you," she said, "gin ye're no here by Wednesday, I'll

come amang the gypsies to look for ye mysel'—breeks or no breeks!" Saying which, she went into the little cottage at Mossdale that you may see above the Flow to this day. Only you need not call, for Eppie Tamson is not there now.

So in the brisk noon of a fine birling day in May, Sammle Tamson and I took the hill. At the first I misdoubted him, and thought myself a better mountaineer than he. But I was soon to learn different. Samuel Tamson walked with a strange forward stoop which approached a right angle. He leaned heavily on his shepherd's staff as he went—his thin, pallid face with its lack-lustre eyes going before him. He had the air of a man who carries his own head for a hand lantern. It was a tall stick which he carried, and oftentimes the hand that grasped it was higher than his head. Yet he could beat me on the hill without turning a hair. His legs moved over the heather and stones as though they could not help it, and would never stop. He carried his left hand pressed into the "small" of his back.

And as we went the man that had been so silent and distraught began to talk without ceasing, walking all the time and speaking as though talking on the slope of a Galloway hill, up to the knees in heather and shin-twisting holes, were as easy as breathing. The matter of his discourse, its temper and drift, also astonished me. It was all about Eppie.

"She's a maist extraordinar' woman, the wife. There's no the like o' her in the sax pairishes. Through-gaun, tight and clean, clever wi' hand and tongue, and wi' a heart as kind as—weel, ye hae seen yoursel'. It's an eternal wonder to me how she ever took the like o' me, or how she puts up wi' me when she has me."

"She was exceedingly kind to me," I said.

"Hoot na," said Sammle, speeding up Cairn Edward side at a pace that made me *pech* like a wind-galled nag, "man, I saw that ye had the richt side o' her from the start."

Then he stopped for a moment, so that I thought he was weary with the short, hot burst uphill. But this was not the case. He only wanted to assure himself of my attention.

"Ye mauna think she's sair on me," he said, earnestly. "I'm aye pleased when she tak's eneuch notice to look after me in the way o' keepin' me to my wark. I ken I wad try a sant. I hae nae memory ava, and the mind that I hae is no worth a buckie. Whiles I think I maun hae hidden my talent in my sleep, and forgotten whaur I put it, for I canna see hilt nor hair o't. And a' folks are born wi' yin, the

138

minister says. He has speaking aboot that verra subject in Kells Kirk, Sabbath was eight days. What think ye o' that question yersel' na, Laird Heron?"

This with the earnestness and desire of a Scot for a theological discussion. But I had small store of theology, and smaller desire at that moment to engage in any debate. So I tried to keep him to his story.

"'Deed, aye, I'm a sair trial and vexation to her, I ken, that was used to better things. Ye see the way o't is this: I had been a widow[1] three years when I began to gang aboot Parton Hoose to see her in the forenichts. I had yae bit lassie, that was five year auld. Weel I asked Eppie, and I better asked her, but she aye said me nay. In fact, she made fun o' me to my face; till I plucked up heart to say that I wad come nae mair to be lichtlied afore folk. Na, nor I didna look near for a fortnicht. Then I met her on the Boat O'Rhone road, at the edge of the Big Wood of Turnorrach.

"'Guid e'en to ye," says she, 'hae ye lost the road to Parton?'

"I said, 'No, I haena, but I was well aware that I wasna wantit at Parton.'

"She made answer that she was none so sure of that.

"Now, I'm not a bright man nor a forritsome man, but I'm no exactly a fool, so I took her round the neck, and that you'll find a better argument wi' a lass than ony talkin'—that is, gin she likes you ava'. That's my advice to you, Laird Rathan."

We were now on the brow of the high, rocky hill that is called Cairn Edward, or Cairn Ethart, which rises bleak and grey above the rushing of the Black Water of Dee.

"We'll keep high," said Sammle. "It'll be the better for seein' and less kittle for being seen."

So as we went, he took up again the burden of his tale.

"Sae, or course, after Tornorrach Wood, there was nae mair ado but to get married. And married we were as soon as the cries were through, and a braw wedding there was at the big hoose. The leddy was awfu' ta'en on aboot her, and amang ither things that she got awa' wi' her was the flask ye hae in your pooch, and the object glass. Aiblins ye wadna be the waur o' a drap the noo? No—weel, weel!

---

[1] "Widower" is a vain word in Galloway to this day

"But there was the lassie, Marion, that was mine an' my first wife's—a bonny wee bit lass; noo the silly, ill-contriving folk had been tellin' her aboot a step-mither, and when we rade up to the door, or as near it as the laird's powny could tak' us, here's wee Marion sitting on the doorstep (and ye could see that her heart was like to break, though she had the greetin' by wi' and only a begrutten face turned up to us as peetiful like). Waes me—to mind on't!

"Then when we lichtit doon, here wee Marion comes to meet us, wi' her bit underlip quivering and the clear water standing in her blue e'en—O man, man, to think on't! And, says she, as clever as if she had been sayin' it ower an' ower to hersel' to learn it by heart afore we cam—'

"'This hoose is yours noo, I ken,' she says to Eppie (she was but five year past in September). 'But, maybe, ye'll let wee Marion bide in the hen-hoose aside the calf. I'se no asturb him ava',' she says. 'Marion will be rale quiet, and see, I hae ta'en Black Andra' there already!'

"Black Andra' was her bit bairn's dolly that I had made oot o' a bit stick and pentit for her red and black.

"'See,' she said, 'Black Andra's there the noo, waitin' amang the hay, an' him an' me will never say cheep—wull ye let us bide in the hen-hoose?'

"O man, O man," burst out Sammle Tamson, sobbing to himself in a passion as he leant on his staff, "it was like death to me to hear the bit bairn.

"And the wife, Eppie, oh, but she took it sair to heart. She sat doon there on the doorstep and sabbit till she took to the laughing. And then she couldna stop. Never in my life had I seen onybody ta'en like that. It was a maist peetifu' hamecomin'.

"Then, when she came to a wee, she took the bit lass in her airms and kissed her; but Marion had been talked to by silly folk, and had gotten her mind fu' o' the going to the hen-hoose, so she would not come willingly to Eppie.

"But I sent Marion to bed in the spence, and saw her snugly happit up wi' Black Andra', that was a gruesome-like tyke pented wi' tar and cart-red, and shrouded in an auld clout—yet she took him in her airms and grat quately on the pillow, for she loved him.

"So I left them.

"But in the mornin' it happened that I had to rise early—and it ser'ed us richt for marryin' in the lambin' time; so it was in the very earliest blink o' day that I took the door ahint me, an' gaed my ways unwilling to the hill.

"Eppie was lying wide awake in the dark o' the morning, thinkin', nae doot, and no the pleasantest o' thochts, aboot what she wad do wi' Marion.

"When, as she has telled me fifty times, and fifty to the back o' that, the spence door gied a bit cheep as gin the cat were coming ben. Then a wee white facie lookit round the corner o' the door, and wee bare feet paidled across the floor till they stoppit by Eppie's bed.

"It was Marion. She looked a while afore she spoke, but Eppie said no a word.

"'They say that ye are my mither noo,' said wee Marion, haudin' up yae bare foot aff the cauld stane.

"'An' what if I war your mither?' said Eppie that is my wife, as kind as she could say.

"'WI' THAN,' says Marion, emphatically, 'gin ye be my mither, I thocht that I wad like to creep in aside ye a wee into your warm bed, for it's cauld, cauld in the spence.'

"Eppie was oot o' bed in a moment, and had the bairn in her airms, greeting ower her and rejoicing a' at yince.

"'Can I come in, then?' said Marion.

"'Aye, blessin's on ye, ye can that!' said Eppie, heartily.

"'And bide?' continued the wee lass in white.

"'Aye, come awa',' quo' Eppie.

"'And pit my cauld feet on ye?'

"'Hoot aye, bairn, onygate ye like.'

"'Then I'se come and bring Black Andra'!'

"When I cam' back frae the hill there was sma' room for me, for Eppie and Marion and Black Andra' were a' lyin' sleepin' wi' their arms aboot ither!

"And that was the beginning o't!" said Sammle Tamson of Mossdale.

"And where is the lassie noo? I wad like to see her. Is she up and married, or oot to service?" I said, without due caution.

Sammle shook his head. He did not sob again, but there was a look of wae on his face that was very touching to the heart.

"She's gane!" he said.

"Gane!" said I, startled. "Did she die?"

"Na, no that; she was lost on the hills—it's a lang story, and we're getting ower by the Black Craig o' Dee noo. We'll hae to be cautious."

But he went on.

"So, sir, for a year that bit lass was the very apple o' Eppie's e'e. We never had ony bairns o' oor ain, an' Eppie was juist wrapped up in that lass Marion. I often spoke to her aboot it, but as ye may understand, I micht as weel hae saved my breath."

I understood, and signified it with a nod.

Sammle Tamson went on, feet and tongue plying together, till we drew towards the verge of the Black Craig of Dee, and saw beneath us the whole of the land backwards, with its lochs and lochans, clints and mosses, away to the little white house of Mossdale itself, where I doubt not there was one looking up for us as we journeyed.

CHAPTER XXIII

THE FORWANDERED BAIRN

And this was the further matter of his tale.

"When the wife had been nineteen months at the Bennan, it was her custom to let Marion come oot ower the hills wi' my dinner-piece in a napkin. It was but seldom that I gaed so far away that she could not see me from the doorstep; for the most feck of my herdin' is done within sight of the house, by reason of the country all sloping to the Water o' Dee, where sits the wee hoose o' Mossdale, as ye are weel aware.

"But it happened on a day that I had a job up at the Englishman's Dub, that is at the back o' the Bennan hill, up by the springs o' the Lowran Burn.

"I mind the day as weel as if it was yesterday. I had an e'e on the sheep, of course; but I was cutting a bit birk, that was crooked, to carry it hame to mak' a 'creepie' stool for wee Marion.

"An', faith, here comes the bairnie hersel', liltin' blithe wi' my broth in a milk pail that she was carryin' by the bool, careful no to spill—my bit piece in a wee bag that she caa'ed her schule bag, though there was no schule near hand for her to gang to. I can see her, happin' and juikin' ower the muir—for a' the stanes and the deep heather that whiles cam' ower her heid—linkin' alang and singin' like a laverock. Oh, but she was a blithesome wee lass."

I will admit that I found all this extremely interesting, more perhaps than my readers may when it is told; but maybe to hear it from the strange, humorsome man on the great hills of heather made all the difference.

Sammle Tamson went on. "While I was at my denner, she sat an' talked bits of bairn's talk, and ate scraplets that I gied to her, or that she pu'd off for hersel', for she ever took great pleasure in sittin' by the bakeboard and eating the crumbs.

"I mind weel she asked aboot the wee crooked birks—gin God made them crooked. Or if it was their ain badness that made them crooked, or whatna way was it? Na, an' she wadna be pitten aff wi' nae answer ava', but pressed me so that she had me clean oot o' my depth, and I had to say—

"'Weel, Marion, ye'll hae to speer at the minister when he comes to catechise ye. Ye'll hae to speer him *his* quastions as weel!'

"'Deed, wull I that!' says she.

"So when I had ta'en my fill, I buckled on the bag and gied her the can, and the wee leddy took the road hame as canty as a lark."

As Sammle Tamson got so far in his tale we were in the great Corry that lies to the west of the Black Craig of Dee, between the Hill o' the Hope and the Rig o' Craig Gilbert. We could see the reeking chimneys of the steading of Laggan o' Dee, that was said to have decent folk in it, for all so near as it lies to the outlaw country.

Sammle stopped deliberately, and faced me in order to say impressively, "So I saw wee Marion gang frae me, her white bit legs twinklin' amang the heather aneath her short skirts. She gaed ower the knowe, standin' on the tap juist lang eneuch to wave her can, and cry a word that she had learned from Eppie—

"'Noo, Sammle, see an' be hame in time o' nicht.'"

"'Ye wee besom!' cries I, an' she juiked doon."

Sammle looked me in the face. I had not thought he could look so solemn.

"From that moment to this," he said, "have I never set e'en on my bairn."

We were silent a space, Sammle Tamson looking fixedly at me as though he had forgotten to look away, while I was trying to keep back the water from my face, for I cannot bear folk that are aye greet-greeting.

"But did you not seek for her?" I asked very foolishly, and without thinking.

"Seek for her—aye, far and near we seekit. There was parties oot on the hills for ten days. I wasna in my bed mysel' for near three weeks. It was then that I got the income in my back. The wife gaed oot o' her mind a'thegither. She was fair wild, and sair set again me, though I could little help it. The bairn had come hame farther nor that fifty times.

"But I gang ower fast," said Sammle; "I'll tell ye the tale.

"The day after Marion was lost on the moors, Eppie is lost as weel. She had risen and ta'en the hills afore the break o' day. My sister frae Clachanpluck, a married woman, was wi' her; but Tibby

144

was aye a sound sleeper. So when she wakkened Eppie was up an' awa.

"Then there was another hunt.

"Up a' the Dee Water side I tracked Eppie, here by a fit-mark, there by a screed o' her druggit goowon tangled on a blackthorn, till the next day at noon I fand her awa' up on the links o' the Cooran Lane far ayont Loch Dee, clean gane oot o' her mind a'thegither. As far as I could mak' oot the ootlaw folk had been at her, but she had fleyed them. A' thae kind o' folk are awfu' feared of them that's oot o' their mind, and disna think it canny to meddle wi' them—or itherwise, I dinna like to think what micht hae happened.

"When I fand Eppie she was lyin' on a bank, wi' her heid bare and the sun on her. As soon as she saw me drawin' near, she gied a skelloch an' ran whatever she was fit.

"Noo, it's a queer-like thing when a wife o' nineteen months rins like a tod frae her married husband. That took me at the hert, but I saw there was nocht for it but that I maun juist rin her doon. But it was a lang chase.

"She had the strength o' six. I dinna believe I wad hae grupped her awa', but for her lettin' something faa' she carried in her hand as she ran.

"So in a howe o' the heather I got Eppie in my airms, and caa'ed her 'my dawtie,' and spoke to her as I used to do in the hay-neuk at Parton on the nichts when I first gaed doon to see her.

"Bit by bit she cam to a wee, till she saw the thing that she had fand. It was the same can that Marion had ta'en wi' my denner broth that day her mither sent her. Every time that her e'en fell on that can, she wad gang aff again in a swarf, and speak wild, wild words when she cam oot o't.

"But at lang and last I gat her hame. That was nae joke. It was the hardest job that ever I had. The can was half fu' o' blackberries that the bairn had been gathering (as we jaloosed), because Eppie had said that she was fondest o' bramble-berry jelly o' a' the sugar conserves that are made. So the bairn nae doot had thocht to please Eppie and so gane to her death.

"And the strange thing is that even when Eppie cam to hersel', she threepit and better threepit, that she had seen the lassie rinnin' afore her ower the *quakkin quas* and the green morasses o' the Silver Flow o' Buchan. Oh, I ken it's a moral impossibility, but this is what Eppie declares to this day: She was on a hill that they caa'

Craigeazle, and doon below her she saw oor bit lass rinnin', and she cried to her, and her heart was glad. She ran doon the hillside amang the rocks and clatterin' slate-stanes, but aye the wee lass ran on. It was terrible-like grund, lairin' at every step, but the wean ran on licht-fit; when suddenly something like an airm shot up oot o' the quag an' poo'ed the bairn doon, and Eppie saw nae mair but the oily bubbles rising oot o' the black glossy glaur o' the wall-e'e.

"O man, Laird Heron, I ken brawly it's no a faceable story ava'. It's only a distrakit woman's dream; but gin she mentions it to you, ye mauna contradict her, for she believes it like her Bible. Na, na, sir, it was a pleesure to me to see her tak' sic' an interest in ye this day. It tak's her mind aff what does nae guid to think upon. Mony is the time that I'm gled when my stupidity angers her, an' it's a mortal pleesure to me when she comes at me wi' the besom shank. Whiles, maybe, I mak' mysel' a kennin' stupider than I need be, just to humour her."

Sammle Tamson finished here. What a dolt and ass I had been to look on this man as no more than a mockery and a laughing-stock! Underneath that strange outward appearance and behind his comical relations with his wife lay, unsuspected, a whole world of tragedy. The Lord keep me in the future from hasty judgments. We see our neighbour's face, but what is underneath is his own. Truly a stranger intermeddleth not with another's heart bitterness.

We had been out from the house at Mossdale more than two hours, when we came suddenly to the crest of the ridge and looked over the other side ere we were aware. As soon as Sammle got his first look he dropped like a shot.

"Clap," he said under his breath; "for the love o' God, clap!"

I was beside him in an instant. Together we peered cautiously over the worn and water-pitted edge of the blue whinstone rock, our bodies buried up to the chin in the heather.

Sammle pointed with his long whaup's nose.

"There," he whispered, as though we were not a thousand feet in the air above the drove-road, "d'ye see yon?"

This is what I saw. I saw the Links o' the Black Water o' Dee shining amid the dull yellows and greys of the grim mosses through which it slowly made its way. I saw the untenanted onstead of Clattering Shaws and the drove-road to the Cree Bridge wimpling across the heather. But what I mainly saw was a straggling line of black dots (as it were both upright and long) crawling irregularly over the moor by the waterside.

"There's the drove, and there's your Macatericks and Marshalls, an' I doot na a Faa or twa amang them," said the goodman of Mossdale.

I had out the prospect glass in a flash, and Sammle, being acquaint with its ways, set it for me. But he let me look first, for he was a thoughtful man.

I soon caught them up, and though they were but blurs when I first got them upon the eye-piece, by dint of a little screwing of the slides and learning how to shut one eye, I was soon able to see quite clearly. There were ten or twelve mounted men in the party, riding loosely behind; but on two of the horses wounded men were carried, who seemed unable to sit on themselves, and were held up by a man at each side. Then there were a great many cattle, some limping wearily on, and others trying to snatch a bite of fodder by the way. It astonished me to find that I could see all quite plainly at this distance. Never on Solway side had I seen so notable a glass. Then fore and aft of the herd there were raggety boys holding the beasts in check and playing pranks among themselves. But what I most longed for, yet feared to see, was not to be seen, for Hector Faa and May Maxwell were not of the party.

Silver Sand had been correct in his premises; it would yet be seen if he were also as faithful in his conclusions.

"The Lord grant it," said I aloud.

It is at the Clattering Shaws that the Edinburgh road takes a bend, and there too is a wide plain where the country folks say that Good King Robert fought a battle. But it was a difficult place for us to cross to the other side of the glen; yet cross we must, and that speedily, for it was evident that the outlaws now considered themselves perfectly safe and would not hurry the cattle, being in their own country.

I told Sammle as much of Silver Sand's plans as I thought prudent—which, to be honest, was nearly as much as I knew myself. He approved of them generally, and was able to shed a great deal of light upon the intentions of the gypsies, the lie of the country, and on what my own movements ought to be.

The cattle reivers would certainly, he said, take the easiest road, and slowly find a track by the Loch Dee and Loch Trool, past Bongill, and up the narrow defile of the Gairland Burn, into that tangle of lochs and mountains under the brow of Merrick, which formed their robbers' fastness. There would be better grazing by the loch shores than anywhere else, though indeed the Faas never wanted for fodder so long as there were hay crops on the Cree water or corn in the Glenkens. It was easy work taking down a bevy of horses and bringing up a supply—easier than cutting and winning the meadow hay upon their own sparse watersides.

It was therefore necessary for me to cross and take to the hills on the eastern side of the Dungeon, then make for the Wolf's Slock as fast as I could, and trust to Providence after that. At least, so said Sammle Tamson, evidently thinking that Providence would be no great improvement upon himself as a guide among the hills of the Dungeon.

CHAPTER XXIV

A MEETING WITH BILLY MARSHALL

As we went I began to see my guide hanging back and halting on one foot, instead of bravely striding forward as had been his wont.

"What is the matter, Sammle?" said I.

"We'll hae to cross the open," said Sammle Tamson, "and I like na the job."

Yet there was no one in sight to the east or south. We stood alone in a wide vacant world, or often rather crawled in the heather, only our noses peeping out.

"Ye see that muckle V the road maks here," said he; "noo that's a king's highway, though there's few o' the king's men ever sets fit on it noo. D'ye no jaloose what for it disna gang straight forrit, like an ordinar' road. It's because that bog doon there is no safe. They say that King Robert, that was a Carrick man in the auld days, laired and bogged a hale army o' the English there. Noo, my man, gin ye are to try the Wolf's Slock, there's but twa chances for ye that I can see. To gang forrit and cross, that's mair danger, but also a great deal mair speed. To gang back and cross, on the ither hand, ye maun gang to the Black Craig o' Dee afore ye hae a chance o' crossin' that weary road that rins like an ether beneath us."

Sammle looked at me to choose.

"On!" I said briefly.

"It's as I wad hae expected, but I'll no deny that in half an hour the baith o' us may be pechin' on the heather like a couple o' shotten pairtricks."

Sammle began to crawl cautiously among the boulders, keeping to leeward of every stone. The dots of cattle and men were now so far away that caution seemed needless; but I did not ask the reason of his extraordinary care, for I had great trust in the moorman. It might be that the outlaws had watchers on all the tops, who could discern every movement of both beast and body on that great empty waste.

In ten minute we were crossing the little Dee water, which here flows sluggish and brown from the peat mosses. It was deeper than I thought, and I had to hold my powder and pistols high up in order that they might get no hurt. While we were in act to cross, we saw two decent-like men come out of the little steading of Craignell (so Sammle called it) and wave to us with friendly gestures. They were so near that we could see them distinctly, to the very colour of their hair and the pearl buttons on their coats, and I was for turning back to see what they wanted. Sammle Tamson, however, became a different man as soon as he saw them.

"Rin for't," he cried, and instantly turned his nose to the hill and went upward like a fox, turning and twisting so quick that I could hardly follow him. Over my shoulder I could see the men running through the heather, and waving on us to stop. It seemed a mighty silly thing to be running from men who by their appearance should be decent moor folk, though at least one of them wore matted unkempt hair like the outlaws.

But since Sammle ran, I ran too; and it was as well, for in a little, *Whang! Crack!* came a bullet and the sound of guns hard on the back of each other. Sammle was going at top speed, digging his staff into the earth as he went up the side of the hill, as if he were running with an extra leg.

Presently we got upon what was one of the roughest parts of the country for heather and stones that I have ever seen. It is called, I hear, the Rig of Drumquhat, and I do not know who is laird of it; but one thing I know, that he has a barren heritage and routh of heather. If it had not been for this latter, indeed, I fear we had been as good as dead men. As soon as we had darned ourselves into the thickest of it, Sammle dropped on his knees and put his hands on the ground and panted with his head down and his tongue out.

"Keek oot," he said between his gasps, "and see gin ye can see the ill-contriving blasties."

I made answer that I did, but they were far away, and going very slowly, as men that were not keen about their job.

"Na!" he said, "Young Billy Marshall is ower fond o' the brandy bottle and the hizzies to be a good hill rinner, whatever."

"Billy Marshall!" said I, looking, I am sure, very queer at the name of the great catheran; "Billy Marshall's in Holland, and dare nae mair show his face on Scots grund than Johnny Faa himsel'."

"Weel, Laird, believe me, yon chap wi' the Roman nose that

was the better put on, verra decent like, was nae ither than Billy, or else I'm Billy mysel'. Just keep track o' them, will ye?"

And he lay down flat on the bent, with his arms wide and his hands flaccid and open.

Out of my heather bush I watched the glen. They had turned back to go into the house of Craignell again.

"There's mettle mair attractive inside there, ye may depend," said Sammle. "Ye'll no be bothered wi' Billy amang the rascals ye hae to fecht up by the Dungeon."

Then we set off again over two very desolate hills that have for names, as Sammle told me, Craignell and Darnaw. We were high up on them and keeping the crown of the causeway, the brown moors and grey rocks running from horizon to horizon beneath us.

So we felt ourselves safe for the present. The sun was now beginning to sink, and a great bank of cloud was gathering over in the west, from which pieces were ever and anon blown off, though only the gurgling sough of the wind came to us, even on these mountain-tops.

"Ye'll hae a dark nicht o't in the Wolf's Slock. It'll be as dark up there as the inside o' that beast himsel'. But a' the better for you. Keep a guid heart and your breast to the brae."

I had a question to ask.

"I heard ye say, guidman, that Billy Marshall could easily come across the Channel frae Holland. Noo, are ye of opinion that Faa himsel', wha's heid is forfeit, micht come as weel?"

"There's nae kennin'," said Sammle. "Faa micht never hae been oot o' the country since he broke wi' his clan. Ye ken thae Faas are gentrice ower by on the Border side. And they say that Johnny Faa keeps wide o' his mither and brither since they took to cattle-liftin' and murder, but yet gets aye his share o' a' that's gaun, that comes honestly. He tak's no shares in the cattle; but there's no a penny that rattles in a beggar's wooden cup, no a boddle that is gi'en to him at a changehouse, but Johnny Faa himsel' gets his tenth o't. He's a kind o' pope amang them, though the ragged clan wadna be keeped to gentrice, nor fecht for the Pretender instead o' liftin' nowt, as Johnny wad hae likit. Faith, they say that Billy Marshall is feared o' the Faa himsel'. Johnny Faa is no canny. He comes an' gangs like a wraith, or like the wind—no man knoweth whither he goes or whence he comes."

151

Soon we were on the height above Cairndarroch Ford. Sammle did not cower now, but strode boldly down, staff in hand, and kicking up the dust of the heather with his feet, so that I wondered to see him. Then I asked him the reason of his change of bearing; he said—

"I carena noo. Their tail's guarded by Billy Marshall at Craignell, where he is safe in hold by this time, birling at the wine—a doxy set by ilka oxter. Gin ony was to see us, they wad gang on a' the faster, thinkin' Billy was keepin' braw watch, screevin' ower the country to keep a' safe."

And it was as he said. When we got to the ford of the Dee Water, Sammle went plashing through, his feet casting up the water about him in a kind of glee, like a horse trampling into the Solway tide for a bath. Far up on the hillside somebody waved something white.

"Hae ye a napkin?" said Sammle. "I hae lost mine, and I'm loath to pu' aff my ither sark tail. Eppie made sic a wark aboot the last yin. I'll tell ye the story some ither day, when we hae less enterteenin' things aboot us."

I handed him my handkerchief that was none so white, but served his purpose, which was indeed no more than to wave back to the rascal who saluted us from the hilltop as we went through the ford. Sammle waved the napkin twice to his right hand once to his left, touching the heather on each occasion.

"That means 'All well,'" he said; "three times roon yer heid is 'Danger—Rin!' an' haudin' the napkin oot at airm's length frae yer left haun' is 'Bide till I come'; but that last will be no muckle use to ye."

We were now among the burnt heather, whistling as we went, and kicking up the ashy dust of the March muirburn with our feet. This dust or "stoor" got in Sammle's throat and kept him coughing.

"It behoves me to be turning, Rathan," he said. "I may hae been a help to ye so far, but ony farder I'll be but a burden and a danger. I can do mony a thing, but neyther in kirk or market can I keep back the barkin' when I get that dry yeukin' in my thrapple. I doot I'm to be hanged, for it's aye in my Adam's aipple that I hae a pricklin' like eatin' pepper-pods."

We were now high above the misty basin of Loch Dee, which we saw shining blue away in the hazy south, with the burn running out of it into the Cooran Lane, We could see with the prospect glass the drovers letting the cattle stray wide, watched only by boys on the green meadows of the two Laggans by the loch side. A very great number of the poor beasts were standing in the water of the loch cooling their travel-weary feet and drinking deep draughts.

We were now on the smooth side of the furthest spur of Millyea, the last of the Kells Range, which pushed its wide shoulders on into the north, heave behind heave, like a school of pellocks in the Firth. I was astonished at their height and greenness, never having in my life seen a green hill before, and supposing that all mountains were as rugged and purple with heather or else as grey with boulder as our own Screel and Ben Gairn by the Balcary shore. But these I found were specially granted by a kind Providence to afford *yirds* and secret caves for our Solway smugglers.

It was always counted a Divine judgment on the people of the Glenkens that their hills are so smooth that the comings and goings of men and horses upon them can be seen afar, and the smoke of a still tracked for a summer day's journey. But then, again, if the Glenkens folk had been able to supply themselves with whisky, the Solway farmers, like my friends the Maxwells, would have had to go farther afield in order to seek a market for their wares.

But things are wisely ordered, and amongst other things it was ordained that I should now be on the side of Millyea looking towards the great breastwork of the Dungeon of Buchan, behind which lay the outlaw country shrouded in dark and threatening mist.

CHAPTER XXV

THE DUNGEON O' BUCHAN

Now, because nothing can be more uncertain and uncanny than the changes of the weather in the Dungeon of Buchan, it behoved that Samuel Tamson, that very honest man, and I should part. The thought of the poor lass, May Maxwell, was heavy on my heart, and I began to desire with a great desire to see her, even if I could not come at the winning of her—which in the disturbed state of the country, and the mountain men having won so great a victory at the Black Water of Dee, did not seem likely.

It was time to part, so we looked at one another and found nothing to say. Sammle Tamson turned on his heel. When he had gone maybe ten steps, he looked back and said to me, still standing in the same place—

"The God of Jacob be your rereward."

But even then I found not anything to say, and so parted very heavy at heart. The great clouds were topping the black and terrible ramparts opposite to me. Along the long cliff line, scared and broken with the thunderbolt, the clouds lay piled, making the Merrick, the Star, the Dungeon, and the other hills of that centre boss of the hill country look twice their proper height. The darkness drew swiftly down like a curtain. The valley was filled with a steely blue smother. From the white clouds along the top of the Dungeon of Buchan fleecy streamers were blown upwards, and swift gusts spirted down. Behind, the thunder growled like a continuous roll of drums, and little lambent flames played like devils' smiles about the grim features of Breesha and the Snibe. Yonder were the frowning rocks of the Dungeon itself farthest to the north, and that great hollow-throated pass through which still a peep of sunshine mistily shot down, bore the grim name of the Wolf's Slock. Thither I must climb. Yet though there was no light in it, it was through it that I could best see the hell-brew of elements which was going on up there. Here on the side of the opposite brae did I lie face down on the grass and heather and look upward. The wind came in curious extremes—now in lown-warm puffs and gusts, and then again in sharp, cold *bensils* that froze the blood in one's veins.

Then it was that for the first and last time, a kind of shuddering horror came over me, which now I shame to think upon. What right had I to be there?—I that might have sat safe and smiling on my Isle Rathan? Had any meddled with me there, that I must go and take up a stranger's quarrel? What a fool to bring myself so to the dagger's point—and that for a girl who had no thought or tenderness for me, but only scoffs and jeers! I did not even know that she had not been playing with me. For aught I knew she might have gone willingly enough on the pillion behind handsome Hector Faa, that was own brother to John Faa; a gentleman born upon the Borders; and who might even, when the turmoil died down, succeed to the dignities, such as they were. What had I, who might have been sailing in the tall ships to see strange lands (for so my revenues permitted)—eating of the breadfruit and drinking of the coco brew that is as wine and milk at once—to do here on this Hill Perilous on such desperate quest among desperate men?

But, truth to tell, I believed not in my own unshakable logic, and in this I was even like a woman. I believed not in my own caution, and in my heart I only longed to meet Silver Sand and to come to grapples with a dozen Faas on their own ground—at least if I could get first sight of the self-same smile that was on May Mischief's face when I called her "Impudent besom!" aloud that day, when my tongue slipped and I let the words from me unawares.

Thus I let Satan tempt me, for the sake of setting my elbow in his face; but he was not so easily deceived, for he flew away out of my heart, crying, "Fool, thou hast the desire to go only that a light girl may lead thee to the death—one that cares naught for thee." But I said to him, "Thou liest, Foul Thief, and if thou didst speak truth I do not care. Go I will!" Whereat I fell mighty manly, and so rose and went.

But to resolve is ever easier than to do. Between me and the frowning ridges—now the colour of darkest indigo, with the mists clammily creeping up and down and making the rocks unwholesomely white, as if great slimy slugs had crawled over them—were the links of the Cooran winding slow, leaden, and dangerous. And there beyond them was the Silver Flowe of Buchan, where the little Marion had been drawn to her death either by the clinging sand or the dread arm of the water kelpie.

As I went the ground became wetter and boggier. My foot sank often to the ankle, and I had to shift my weight suddenly with an effort, drawing my imprisoned foot out of the oozy, clinging sand with a great "cloop," as if I had begun to decant some mighty bottle.

Green, unwholesome scum on the edges of black pools frothed about my brogues, which were soon wet through. Then came a link of silver flat where the sand was firm to the eye. My heart beat at the pleasant sight, but when I set foot on it a shivering flash like lightning flamed suddenly over it, and it gripped my feet like a vice. Had I not been shore bred, and that on Solway side, I had passed out of life even then. But I knew the trick of it, and threw myself flat towards the nearest bank of grass, kicking my feet free horizontally, and so crawled an inch at a time back to the honest peat again. Then I found a great shepherd's stick lying on a link of the Cooran—a wide, black, unkindly-like water, seen under that gloomy sky, whatever it may appear in other circumstances. It had been placed there by some shepherd who had business on the other side, or mayhap had been cast up by that dangerous water after it had drowned the man who used it.

But at any rate it was a fortunate case for me, for this "kent," or great staff, was more than two yards long and prodigiously stout, with a pike at the farther end, and a "clickie" handle, made closer at the lower part for catching sheep by the leg. I took it with gratitude, and I hope the man who left it there has never missed it. It was assuredly of great service to me, and, moreover, the chances were a hundred to one that the fellow was a Marshall, a Miller, or a Macaterick, for on the handle was a great M very rudely cut. Yet it was a good "kent," and served me well, so why all this bother about who made it? So it is also with the making of this world. Thus in time, by the grace of God, and by taking great pains, I crossed both the Silver Flowe of Buchan and the Links of the Cooran. It is ever the nature of Galloway to share the credit of any victory with Providence, but to charge it wholly with any disaster. "Wasna that cleverly dune?" we say when we succeed. "We maun juist submit," we say when we fail—a comfortable theology, which is ever the one for the most feck of Galloway men, whom chiefly dourness and not fanaticism took to the hills when Lag came riding with his mandates and letters judicatory.

CHAPTER XXVI

THE WOLF'S SLOCK

But I had no such reflections as I went up the side of the Dungeon towards the Throat of the Wolf. It was indeed dourness and not courage which took me there. I had done no harm that I should be afraid of any Faa that lived. But all the same there was a small cold contracted feeling about the pit of my stomach, where ordinarily my courage lies. Other folks may tell that they feel bold as lions—at the heart—or have a mortal fear—at the heart. These are differently made from me, for it is low down, even in my stomach, that my courage lies, though it is oftenest rather the empty want of any that pinches.

The truth is I was most mortally afraid. To begin with, I was wet through—not that I minded that much in itself, for so I was usually all day at the shore; but there the salt in the air, and the kindliness of the sea breeze, make it a comfortable wetness. Here, on the other hand, the wind off the hills had a cold nip about it, and seemed to freeze the very clothes on one's back. I felt also a sting of sleet on my face.

I clambered upwards through the great boulders and loose stones.

It was not jesting now. I could see only a hundred yards or so above me, but overhead the thunder was moaning and rattling, coming ever closer. There was a faint blue light, more unpleasant than darkness, high in the lift. Then little tongues of crawling cloud were reaching down as it seemed, to snatch at me, curling upward like the winkers of an old man's eye as they came near me. I hated them.

As often as they approached there was a soft hissing, and the rocks grew dim and misty blue. My hands pricked at the thin fine skin between the fingers that we call the webs. I had a strange prickling tightness about my brow, and my bonnet lifted. So for all my new stubborn stoutness, I liked it not, and know not how I went through with it. Were it to do again, I trow that I should instantly turn tail and make for Rathan's Isle, and Patrick Heron, his most defenced turret. But indeed I cannot tell how I went on. Certainly it was not out of courage.

What I liked least were the little spouts of stones that discharged themselves downward with a crash and a rattle. I know not why, for the waterspouts in the clouds had not broken. They came with a dry noise, like bones rattling into a vault, as once I heard them when they were clearing the Dullarg kirkyard to make room for new parishioners—a most unholy sound. I have wished many a time since that I had bided at home and not gone to hear it—as indeed my father had bidden me. So I was properly served.

Most of these spouts of stones fell on great tails that spread down the mountain steep, like rubble from a quarry toom (or dump, as they call it in the sea-coal district). Some of these I had to cross, and a most uncomfortable passage I made of it. Little sharp slate stones came down with a whizz, spinning like wheels, and passed quite close to the ear with a vicious *clip*; as the teeth of a dog snap when he bites and misses, yet means to do your business the next time (and you know he will)—a most vile feeling. One went past like a bullet of lead and clipped a piece of skin from my ear, which came near to make me swear—a habit in which there is no profit, and which therefore I never use. But I ought rather to have said a prayer and given thanks, but that I did not either.

Then I came to one very wide spout, and my feet plunged into it quickly and eagerly, because I was wishful to get across with all speed, for, indeed, I liked not the place. But just when I was in the midst, the whole began to move slowly beneath my feet, with a feeling that sent my heart into my mouth, and made me faint and sick at once, for nothing is so discouraging as to lose faith in the solid earth underfoot. I stood a moment till I felt the whole side of the hill, as it were, moving downward. Then I minded me of the sand, and when I felt the push of the stones growing quicker, slithering all along of a piece, and heard the ominous rattling at the edges, I can take my oath that I said my prayers at the run. More, I flung myself out as flat on my belly as I could and dug fingers and toes, aye and face too, into the moving stone slide.

We went slowly and slowly, and for some years (so it seemed, and I took careful note of the time), I could not tell whether we were going faster to fall or slower to stop. But I prayed heartily as I had not done for months. I resolved that if I could only get out of this I should be quite a different man. I promised as many as sixteen promises that I would give up various sins (which indeed I had been meaning to do for a long time, and cared nothing about). Then when I was sure that the slide was going quicker, I added other sixteen sins that I really cared about. After that I called on Providence to do so to me and more also, if I did not give all these sins up (having no intention of ever coming that way again, if only this once I could win clear). Then suddenly in the midst of my promises and petitions I minded me of the great precipice which was below me, and how I had admired as I lay on the brae opposite, to see the spouts of white stones shoot over it and clatter against the rocks down, far down at the bottom. There were ravens, too, flitting heavily about the face of that cliff, and eagles balancing themselves above, and I cursed my imagination that saw these things all too clearly.

Would we never stop?

We must be near the top of the sheer fall by now—we were still moving, slowly and bit by bit it was true, but still moving. Would the thing never come to an end?

I began to long for the fall and wonder if it would hurt much. One thing came into my mind and stuck there strangely. I was glad I had called May Maxwell "Impudent Besom," but I regretted that I had not then and there kissed her where she stood. It ran in my head that she might have liked it. And I should, certainly. But now it was too late.

We had stopped! No, we were moving on again. Stopped again! It was dark now for several years more, and I lay as one dead with my hands dug into the sharp-edged flaky gravel, my arms stiff-set in it to the armpits, my toes also covered, and all my soul and body on the strain, as one that is ready to be broken on the wheel and sets his teeth to bear the first wrench, praying only that it may be soon over.

How long I lay thus I know not, daring no breath or movement. Then with infinite softness and caution I began to move off, drawing out my arms inch by inch, and quivering with fear if a single slate stone the size of a crown piece clicked away downwards, or the gravel moved an inch to fill up my empty arm holes. I did not so much mind about dying, but the picture of that great corbie calling lustily to his mate, and plumping on the ground within two yards of me, sat chill in my marrow. Again I cursed my imagination—which, indeed, has been no friend to me, making me to endure not one but many deaths by anticipation.

For as I lay there I could see the black fiend alighting with an interrogative croak, cocking his rough head to the side. I could note him keeping his wings a little off his sides ready for flight, the purple gloss on his black satin cloak, his beak sharp as a chisel. He waddled a foot nearer, gave a 'Craw' to alarm me, if I would be

159

alarmed, then hopped to my head, took a look round, and——— .
There was, I declare, a horrid pain in my eye as I lay on the loose
slate heaps. Of a truth I thought for the moment that the corbie had
struck it out. And that is but a specimen of the way my vile
imagination served me.

I seemed altogether empty of all my interior and necessary
parts, as I crawled and wriggled myself off that wide spout of rock.
Now I would crawl a yard; then lie all so cold and empty within, that
the stones felt warm and soft though they were cutting my hands,
and the ice was glassing them where they had been wet.

Then in a moment more I was clear and sat on a solid knuckle
of rock that shot up from the ribs of the mountain, which was more
comfortable to me at that moment than the great armchair at Rathan
that once was my father's and which now is mine, in which indeed I
now sit and write.

I was trembling like a leaf. One moment I chittered with heat,
and the next shivered with cold. I was drenched with perspiration,
and then when I had time to look I saw that my hump of rock was
quite on the edge of a deep gulf. The blue-white reek was surging up
from beneath on some reverse current and boiling over the lip of the
cauldron. The reason I had not heard the stones falling over the edge
of the slide, was that they fell so far that they returned no noise up
here. There, too, was the raven, black against the darkness, sitting
like the very devil I had dreamed of, cocking his eye at me from a
neighbouring rock.

Whereupon such is the nature of man, or at least of me who
count myself one (and, says my wife, like all Galloway men, no
ordinary one), that my spirits rose swiftly. I taunted the raven with
names. I threw stones at him. I pulled out my silver flask and
pledged him, calling him "old Mahoun"—at which he seemed much
put out, for he rose abruptly, which he had not done for all the
stone-throwing, and sailed away, crying as he went something that
sounded like, "Till another day!"

Whereupon I was again full of courage, and pressed upward into
the belt of cloud. I was fairly within the Wolf's Slock now, and
found it as dark as many a lamb has done that was more innocent
than I. The iron pike of my staff shone with lambent light as it
touched the rocks, and I had again the prickling feeling all over my
body. But the tingling air somehow dried me, and thus probably kept
me from taking my death of cold.

And so upward ever I went. I rested none, because I had a kind of strength and a desire to see the thing through, which supported me mightily so long as it lasted.

I was in comparative quiet where I was, but the wind shrieked and "reesled" among the teeth of the shattered rocks above. It yelled overhead as I got nearer to the top. Yet hardly a breath reached me, save and except those hissing down-drives of chill wind that were over again in a minute. I thought that I should do well even in the darkness if I got the bield of a rock, or the space between two that might act as a shelter from the rain. But suddenly I had news of that.

I came to the summit as quickly as one gets to the edge of a wall when a comrade gives a hoist up. The wind met me like a knife, and cut me as it were in two—the lower part of me being warm behind the wall of rock and the top half nearly devoid of feeling; also the rain drops drove level like bullets. I had on a coat that buttoned, a waistcoat with flaps, and other things beneath; but the rain drops played "plap" on my naked skin, as though I had no more on me than a dame's cambric kerchief for holding scent to her nose in church. As for my face, I had to bend my neck and put the crown of my hat to the blast.

Yet I could not so stick all night like a fly to a wall, and though the discomfort was infinite, the fear I was in of another stone spout was far greater. So without stopping to think, I set my elbows and then my hands upon the brink and pulled myself up. Arrived there, I could do nought for some minutes but lie prone among the rocks, gasping for breath like a trout on the bank.

However, there was no advantage in that, but very much the reverse, for it was as chill up there as it is an hour before a March snowstorm. I got me on my feet and went stumbling forward, feeling all the time with my pike for the stones and hollows. Sometimes I fell over a lump of heather. Sometimes my foot skated on a slippery granite slab and down I came my length; yet strange to say I felt no harm thereby, either then nor afterwards, perhaps owing to the quivering excitement I was in.

Thus I went forward a great way, blindly and doggedly—so beaten deaf and dumb, dazed and stupid by the tempest, that I knew not whether I were living or dead—nor cared.

CHAPTER XXVII

IN WHICH BY THE BLESSING OF PROVIDENCE I LIE BRAVELY

All at once my pike struck something that was neither stone nor peat bog. It seemed strange to me, striking through the prolonged strain of unaccustomed things, with the surprise of something familiar. I struck again and yet again. It was like an outhouse or a door of wood. What good fortune, I thought! Some shepherd's shelter about a sheep ree, left from the nights of the recent lambing time, hardly yet over upon the hills.

But I heard a noise and a pother within that was not of the storm. I struck again and louder. Like a flash a door opened, as it were in the side of the hill, and a great light blazed in my eyes, so that I could not see. A number of men sprang on me all at once, and dragged me in. The door was shut to, and there was a knife at my throat.

Then I prayed for the stone spout of the Wolf's Slock. I was out of the throat truly, but I was among the wolf's teeth here. I had scouted the corbie, but I was in the erne's claws—which neat expressions I did not think of at the time.

But all the more that I did not observe anything clearly then, all being a dazzle—the whole of what I saw as they dragged me within is printed on my memory ineffaceably vivid, white and clear as the angry sea with a struggling ship upon it nearing the breakers, which I once saw off Rathan Head by a flash of lightning. So, though blurred at the time, the outlines of all that passed have now come out clear to my mind.

As the dark men dragged me forward I saw other two of the same breed, curly-haired, olive-skinned men, hastily crushing something heavy into a chest in a little back room, on the floor of which there stood a candle. A smooth-faced old woman with white hair was sprinkling sand all over the floor of the kitchen, and a great butcher's knife lay plain to see on a deal table. A fire blazed in a wide ingle, and the roof was hung with hams—a cheerful place on such a night, yet somehow it liked me not.

But while I saw all this the knife was at my throat. The point drove inward and pricked.

The old woman seemed to finish her task, and looked up.

"Let be, Gil," she said, standing with a handful of white sand in one hand and a foul red cloth in the other. "Let be; ask him first his name."

The word "first" stuck in my throat, further in than the knife.

"Your name?" said one of the men kneeling on my breast.

Right gladly I would have answered, but instead I only rooped like a rough-legged fowl.

"Your name?" cried he of the long locks again, setting his knee in my ribs till I thought he had sent the immortal soul flying out of my mouth as a chewed tow bullet is shot from a boy's popgun.

"Speak!" he yelled, more fiercely than ever.

It was a most unreasonable request in the circumstances, yet as my eyes goggled I tried to speak, but instead I only crowed like a cock. The others pulled the man off and propped me up against the ingle cheek.

"No hurry," said they, giving him a look that went to my marrow more than the knife. I began to like Gil's ways best. I was ever for getting medicine over quickly, and there are worse ways of dying than the knife—which indeed is nothing after the sharpness of it, as a pin does not hurt when you put it into the thick of your leg up to the head, after the first prick of the skin. A ploy which you can try or take my word for, just as you please.

"Hand him a drench," said the old woman, bending down a face as smooth as an eggshell and as false as a deal door painted mahogany.

They gave me something that tasted like liquid fire and burned as it ran down. I began to pick up my power of words.

"Now, honey, your name?" said the old woman softly, putting back her white locks. Her hair was yellow white of a strange dry texture, but there was a dirty rusty mark across it as if she had wiped something upon it—her hand or a knife, belike. They were altogether too ready with both in this house for me.

"Patrick Burgess," said I, telling as little of a lie as I could. Burgess was my mother's name, and as I was her sole heir and successor, surely that name was mine too—if it was anybody's, which I fear it was not.

"Aye, Paitrick Burgess," said she. "It is a bonny name, and whaur micht ye come frae, Paitrick?"

The dialect reassured me amazingly. No one could speak good Galloway Scots and be a complete blackguard. But concerning this also I had early news.

"I come from the New Aibbey," I said.

"Ye are far frae hame, bonny laddie," said Mother Eggface, speaking softly, but with a dangerous glinting glance in her eyes that I liked not. "What brocht ye sae far on sic a nicht?"

She might well ask that.

So I prayed the Almighty that I might be enabled to lie well. For my own part I intended to do my best, and I think I got grace.

"I am a peddler by trade," said I. "I am on my way to Dalmellington, and I have lost my way."

This last statement comforted me mightily, for by accident it was true. I had indeed lost my way and had most foully sped.

"Good Master Peddler, Patrick Burgess, bound from the New Abbey, and where might your pack be? Hast lost that also?"

She had fallen back into the English, which I like not, save in the Bible. There was also a dry and deadly mockery in her tone, which made me dislike this old woman worst of them all.

"Settle him first, and seek his story after," said one of the men genially. "He'll carry it about him somewhere."

Eggface looked at him with a glance like the light on a new knife when the blue sky is reflected on the untarnished blade, and he sat down and took a drink, saying no more for a while.

But I lied on and on for my very existence, never ceasing the praying, and I think, getting aid to lie, though whether from above or below I cannot for the life of me say. Yet sometimes the devil plays pranks upon his own, and if he helped me with my fictions that time, I do declare that I shall never speak a bad word of him as long as I live—which indeed is little use at the best of times, and shows neither forecast nor service.

"I am on my way to Dalmellington to take delivery of a new pack of goods brought by the carrier from Glasgow," I ventured.

"What is the name of that carrier?" put in a man from the back.

"Richard Brown, and a decent man," said I, like a flash.

Now either Providence or Ye-ken-wha was at my elbow, and I answered like the carritches (Shorter Catechism). Never was such lying since the Garden of Eden. I did not know I could master it so well.

The man at the back grunted and began whittling a stick.

Knives again—routh of knives.

I give thanks, not so much that Silver Sand had told me, in one of his many stories of this Dalmellington carrier's name, as that my memory had served me—for it plays me awkward tricks sometimes, specially with strange folks' names, and that more especially of late years.

"What said ye yer name was?" said the old dame again, looking at me with her gimlet eyes. What business has a woman to have eyes with three-cornered pupils that look at you like baggonets?

"Patrick Burgess," said I.

And I had nearly said "Heron" before I remembered, and would too but for the thought of the knife. Iron sharpeneth iron, also my wits.

She turned round. "Ivie," she said abruptly.

A great hulk lying in the corner grunted.

"Kick him awake somebody," she ordered, without looking at the lout, still keeping the gimlets fixed on me.

The long-haired tyke called Gil took my piked kent and thrust it into his ribs, which made the giant to grunt, exactly like a great swine that lies all abroad in the filth of the ree when you put your stick into it.

"Rise and speak to granny," said he of the locks.

"A sweet granny," thought I, but all the same I tried to appear happy, thawing myself serenely before the fire, and thinking of more lies. Now lies like mine will not be thought upon. They must come spontaneously or not at all. I was in danger of spilling my cup of sack by running on to show how well I could carry it.

The hog arose.

The hog rubbed his midrib and grunted an interrogative. He wanted to know why he had been awaked.

Granny turned her eye on him and said, "Dost know any of the name of Burgess at the New Abbey?"

The hog scratched among his bristles, grumbling.

"Give him the kent!" she said; "he'll be asleep again."

Gil took up the kent and dug it in once more, strong and good.

Whereat Hog turned like a heathercat, snarling with a flashing of white teeth, and red murder leaping up in his eyes like flame at the touch-hole of a musket.

"Let a man be, canna ye; I'll knife the next brute," he said, recognising his comrade's rank in creation.

Then he rubbed his head, and said slowly, "Man o the name o' Burgess at the New Aibbey? Aye, there's Isaac Burgess, the pig dealer—a fine man, an' a freend o' my ain."

For my sins—my uncle, brother of my mother; as rank a rogue as ever smelled Hollands gin.

"Here is a neffy o' his, or says he is. Sit up an' see if ye ken him."

It was a trying moment.

"Aye," said the hog, slowly, "ye favour him—ye'll be the son o' John that gaed awa' and took to the pack!"

"A good hog i' faith!" I thought, but yet if so be that I favour mine uncle, it is little wonder that my success has been small among the womenkind. For, indeed, he was as ugly as the man of sin.

But so far I was saved. I was a pedlar, and I had told the truth. At this there was a general relaxing of strained attention. The men began to polish up their guns and pistols.

As if the occupation of the others struck him, and the subject reminded him that I was inconvenienced, Gil—that long-haired thief—walked over to me and said, "Your pistols are in your road. I'll take care o' them for you."

The other men turned to see how I would take this. I gave the weapons to him, pulling them out of my belt, as well as my jockteleg with the horn handle, which I also gave him in hand.

Then I lay back and stretched all my bones as though I were glad to be rid of them. But I now kept feeling my throat grow sorer than ever where Gil's knife had been. I was reeking all the time like a lime-kiln before the fire. The old woman came to stir the pot now and again. She kept eyeing me as I toasted first one foot and then the other, taking off my wet brogues to do it, and commenting on the cleanliness of the house at my leisure. I told them what a night it was outside, and how glad of heart I was to have a roof over my head.

"'Deed," said Granny Eggface, "it's no' a nicht to set a dog oot o' doors—let alane a lad like you. But you are far oot o' the road to Dalmellington, laddie. What took ye up the Wolf's Slock? Da'mellington disna lie on the top o' a hill that ever I heard!"

"I was striking a short cut for Loch Doon," said I, for lying now came as easy as breathing. I toasted my feet at the fire, setting them on the hot hearth-stone to dry. The pot boiled and fuffed out little puffs of steam, and gave forth a warm and comfortable smell, full of promise. I began to feel more at home.

Eggface went to the foot of a ladder that reached up to a room above—a mere garret it seemed to me, under the roof. "Come doon, bairn," she said in a more human tone than I had yet heard her use.

"Come now, we'll do yet. When a child comes in the devil flies out at the window!" said I within myself, as I heard a light foot on the stairs. But I forgot that he came in again.

A little girl came downstairs, looking terribly thin and pinched; yet a well-grown girl withal, and one that would soon fill out with due nourishment.

The old woman set her to washing the tables and laying wooden basins round the board. I counted them. There was none set for me. This was not so good, for my inside cried aloud for lining and cargo.

But I kept watching the child. She was, as I said, pinched and haggard. Her eye was full and clear. Yet she shrunk at the least sound, and only answered "Yes" and "No" when she was directly spoken to. One of the men kicked her as she passed, because that in looking at her plates she had stumbled over his foot. The kick was but a slight one, and did not hurt, even if it reached her. But the girl winced and moaned, with a look of fear that went to my heart.

Granny Eggface turned sharply with inquiry in her look, holding a heavy potato beetle in her hand. Her eye flushed into sudden anger as she noted the cause. With a strength that I could not have believed to reside in that skinny form, she delivered the fellow the heavy end of the beetle on the side of his thick head with a dull sound, and stretched him senseless along the wall.

"I'll learn you to meddle the bairn," she said. "The next time we'll see what ye hae inside ye, ye sumph!"

The other men laughed a little at this, saying, "Served him richt, Granny, the muckle hullion!"

And the Good Hog laughed aloud, till the stricken man, arousing, looked evilly at him. Gil, who, under granny of the Eggface, seemed to be somewhat of a leader, set a fiery brand to his tail and bade him rise. This he did right sulkily, and with no pleasant expression in his face.

When the supper was served it was a fragrant stew of all sorts of meat, boiled with vegetable to a kind of pottage, very nutritious.

The men spoke among themselves in a language of which I could make nothing, the old woman joining them with a stray word.

The little girl and I sat apart. She dipped a tin skillet in the pot and gave it to me with a whole partridge in it, and much of the fragrant stew. I thought it was a good opportunity to thank Eggface for her hospitality, and to say that it was a blessing that there was such a house in so wild a place.

"Aye," she said, dryly, "it's fortunate in mair ways than yin. We often hae a veesitor for a nicht, but they seldom stay muckle langer. The air's tryin' to the health up by Loch Enoch and the Dungeon, ye see!"

"What kind of travellers come mostly?" I asked, as carelessly as I could.

"Oh, nearly every sort," said Eggface. "We had a stranger last nicht, nae farther gane, an', indeed, we hae hardly gotten redd up after him yet."

Gil frowned and shook his head at her. But the old witch-wife only chunnered and laughed to herself.

"Hoots," she said to Gil, "it'll be a' the same in a hunner year—or maybe less."

Which was thought among them to be an extravagantly fine joke, and the whole table laughed at it consumedly. For my part I saw not the fun of the jest—nor do I yet—to make such a cackle over the laying of it. But it's easy for the dominie to get a laugh in the school, standing with the taws in his hand.

"What kind o' guids do ye travel in?" asked the old lady when they were at supper, looking over her shoulder at me.

I told her dress pieces—remnants, laces, Welsh flannel, and other things for the good-wives and farm maids of Galloway and Ayrshire."

"How d'ye pay for them at Da'mellington?"

168

"Wi' the siller I got for the last pack," I said, thinking myself wondrous clever. "I hae it wi' me the noo!"

CHAPTER XXVIII

THE BLACK SEA-CHEST

I thought this was my best shot. It was, in fact, my worst, and undid any good that might have accrued to me from the lies that I had told before. It was ever thus. 'Tis little use taking one of the devil's farms. His tacks are so short, and there are no compensations for disturbance.

I had barely spoken when I saw the whole party look at one another, and the little lass steal away with a quivering lip. She slipped quietly upstairs.

"What's that ye're takin' up the stairs?" cried the old woman, sharply.

"Juist a basin o' stew," said the little girl.

"Come here, and let me see it," commanded the old lady.

"Noo, ye'll be tired," said grannie in a little, "and ye had better gang to yer bed, my man, for we maun be up betimes in the mornin'. I like nae lazy banes in my hoose."

I said this accorded well with my own wishes.

At the word she lighted a rush dip candle of the thinnest kind, and showed me into the little back room, the door of which had stood open all the evening. It was furnished with a creepie stool, a bed, and a great black sea-chest.

"And a guid e'en to ye," said the old woman, as she shut the door.

So there I stood, with my brogues in my one hand and my rushlight in the other, and surveyed my narrow chamber. I turned down the bedclothes. They were clean sheets that had never been slept in but once or twice. But I turned down the sheet also, for I am particular in these matters. Something black and glutinous was clogged and hardened on the bed. I turned up the bed. The dark, red stuff had soaked through and dripped on the earthen floor. It was not yet dry, though some sand had been thrown upon it. I did not need to examine further as to the nature of the substance. I turned sick at heart, and gave myself up for lost. But it was necessary that I should make the best of things, even if I were to die. So next I lifted the lid of the great sea-chest.

Merciful Heaven! The back of a dead man, broad and naked, took my eye. There were two open gashes on the right side, livid and ghastly. The rest of the man seemed to be cut up and piled within, as a winter bullock is pressed into a salt barrel ready for the brine.

Now that God who had preserved me from so many perils, and has forgiven me for the lies I told (it may be sending some seraph to take up the attention of the Recording Angel), helped me again in this horrid strait.

At any rate, it is of His supreme and undeserved mercy that I did not swarf away then, or let the lid of the great chest fall with a clang. Indeed, I put it very softly down, took off my coat, and knelt down to pray. I know not if indeed I prayed, but I bent my knees. And as I knelt, I was aware of one that came to the door and spied upon me through the latch-hole, then went and reported what he saw—whereat there was a laugh, as at one who had good cause to say his prayers. As indeed I had.

While I knelt in the still hush after the great guffaw of laughter, I heard the noise of a woman sobbing above somewhere; not the child, but the slower, sharper sob of a woman.

Also somewhere about the house some one whetted at a knife.

As I arose to my feet a folded piece of paper fluttered down as from a crack in the black boards of the ceiling. I took it in my hand as I went shuffling bedward. There was writing upon it.

"For God's sake try the window. You are near your end by cruel men. The Murder Hole gapes wide. A friend writes this."

Then there was written below in smaller characters—

"If by any chance you that read are Patrick Heron, I that write am May Maxwell. And be you who you may, God pity you!"

Again the Lord of Hosts was my help, else had I died even then, so compassed with wonders and so overladen with horrors was I.

The Murder Hole—foul and notorious was its name. There had long been the tradition of such a place in the stories that went about the countryside, and made our flesh creep as we told tales by the fire in the winter forenights. I had never been a believer in such like, accounting it foolish clatter; but now it seemed likely that I should learn something very definite concerning it.

Yet I went to the bed and threw myself down, taking first a look at the window to see what like the fastenings of it might be. They were of thick wood, but looked old and worm-eaten.

As I lay on my bed a whirling universe of thoughts buzzed through my mind. Dark, tremendous clouds tracked each other across my brain. Yet, so strange a thing is man—or at least am I—that I was in danger of falling asleep. Indeed I may have really done so, for I awakened with a start of horror. The cold sweat burst over me as I realised my position. I sprang to the window and tried it. It was fast. I had to kneel on the sea-chest the while, the cold thrills chasing one another up my spine, like darning needles of ice.

I groped round for something to use as a lever. By good fortune my hand touched my own "kent," which Gil had thrown there when he had done exploring the Hog's ribs with its iron prod. I took it, and inserted the point under the frame between the stone wall and the wood. Being glazed only with sheepskin the window made no jangling of glass when it gave outward. I threw myself at the little square of open space. There was a swirl just there, and only a slight cold draught sucked in. Had the opening been on the stormy side, the gust must have roused the men who slept or lay on the floor in the next room.

I was outside in a moment and had replaced the window, that I might have the longer without discovery. I found myself in a narrow passage between the rock of the hillside and the wall of the cottage, which was all but built against the precipice.

Climbing up the rock I crept slowly along the thatch, feeling for an opening into the room whence the letter had fallen. With a throb of fear that was almost delirious, my hand suddenly encountered a hand stretched out in the darkness—a human hand which closed upon mine. It was as startling as though it had come up from the grave; but it was warm and small, and among ten millions I had sworn to it as the hand of May Maxwell, whom my heart called May Mischief.

I pulled the little hand up, but the little hand pulled me down. In a moment my ear was close to her lips. There was only a little skylight unglazed, like the window, but far too small to let any one through.

"Run for your life, Patrick! Oh, they are cruel! They show no mercy!" she said.

"Go I never shall without you," said I. "What! Leave you—you that I came to save?"

"You must," she said. "They will not kill me. And—and—I have a knife!"

"Give me that knife!" said I.

She leapt down like a feather and handed me up a great knife, which was almost like a sword set in a haft.

Readily I cut away the thatch till I felt the skylight about to fall on the floor. "Catch it, May," I said softly; and the next moment the iron frame gave way and fell into her lap, for in the darkness she was holding out her dress, as I had told her.

This also she laid down so that there was no noise.

"But the little maid," she said; "she is in the next room asleep?"

"Her they will not harm. We must get help," I said hastily, to get May away; for, to my shame, I thought only of her.

She tripped down again, swung a bag about her by a strap, and was beside me in a twinkling.

We slid off the roof and found ourselves on the ground in a moment. Then hand in hand we stole out of the lee of Craignairny into the wild war of the elements. The wilder the better for us. I had meant to try the Wolf's Slock, but two things forbade me; first, the murderers knew that was the way I had come; and, second, there was that terrible spout of broken stone which must be crossed.

We stood towards the west along the margin of a loch that was lashing its waves on a rocky shore—a wild, tormented chaos of greyness. This I now know to have been Loch Enoch. Since then I have often and often followed our course that night with men of the hills who knew the ground, so that I am now able to give the names of the localities, which I had not been able to do then when the places were as new to me as the city of Solyman.

CHAPTER XXIX

THE MURDER HOLE

It seemed as though we had only gone a hundred yards when behind us we heard a fearsome crying, "The pedlar has escaped—the pedlar has escaped! Loose the bloodhounds!"

At this perilous outcry May and I instantly set off running at the top of our speed, and by the guiding of Providence we managed to run a long way, keeping our feet somehow among those slippery screes that lie between Craignairny and Craig Neldricken.

It was indeed an uncanny night. The wind shrieked overhead, passing above us in a constant screaming yell, that sometimes sharpened into a whistle and anon dulled into a roar. There was no moon; but the storm-clouds had thinned, and anon the mist lifted. The wind scattered the thick, white clouds and threw a strange semi-darkness over the wild moorland.

Behind us we now heard that most terrible of sounds—the baying of bloodhounds on the trail of blood. May Maxwell ran steadily, with her hand in mine.

"I have another knife; carry you that too!" she said.

"But you may need it," I urged.

"Indeed I may," she said; "but I want to carry my skirt."

I thought I understood women. So do you. We are both in the wrong, my good sir,—we know nothing about the matter.

Behind us on the uneven wind, high above its top note, rose the crying of the hounds.

"How many?" I said, with scanty breath.

"Two," she said briefly.

We came to the bed of a little burn that trickled down the steep sides of the Clints of Neldricken. I went first, feeling with my "kent," striking from side to side like a blind man because of the darkness.

Sometimes as we scrambled down I would catch her by the waist and run with her many yards before I set her down, then on

174

again as though I had carried a feather. So we ran our wild race, and I think gained on our pursuers.

Lanterns began to dance on the slopes above us—that frowning many buttressed table-land, the outlaw's fortress, which we were leaving. Only the booming of the dogs came nearer. We ran on downwards and still down. We seemed to leave the ground beneath us. We passed a little tarn among the rocks which has for name Loch Arron, and then on again among the heather.

Suddenly in trying to lift May Maxwell I stumbled all my length on a heap of stones, dashing myself on the sharp corners till I felt the rough granite dint into my flesh.

I fell with my head on a stone, and knew no more.

When I came to myself May Maxwell had me in her arms, and was trying to stagger away from the place where I had fallen; but it was too much; we dropped together on the heather.

And again I weakly fainted—I that had resolved to do so much. Now I seemed to lie for a long time void of speech and hearing, the blood draining from my head and my brain reeling.

But I had a dream which was more vivid than the yelling of the bloodhounds.

This is what I dreamed, as it were in a flash or great clearness. I thought that May Maxwell took me in her arms, saying, "I will kiss him once before I die. Only once—for I love him and he is mine. He came all alone to find me, and we shall die together."

Then in my dream May Maxwell gave me not one, but many kisses, and so laid me down. But I knew it was a dream. It could be no other.

Then I awoke, and in the brighter light—for the sky was now swept clear of clouds—I saw May Maxwell with a knife in either hand, and so changed was she that I hardly knew her. She crouched as it were like a lithe, wild cat on a spring, and there was glinting fire in her eyes. Down the wind came the baying very near, and the soft gallop of the feet on the heather. Then like a bolt came a great dog out of the darkness, with white fangs dripping froth. Voiceless it sprang at May, but with the knife in her hand this girl, that had held up her skirt as she ran, thrust the steel with more force than many a man into the open mouth of the beast, which fell roaring and snapping upon the iron. Yet she recovered the weapon and struck again and again. Then another brute sprang past her at me as I lay helpless, for it was my trail on which the dogs had been laid. But my bravest girl drove sideways with her knife as the dog came on; yet so heavy and fierce was the beast that it overbore the knife, and would have fallen full upon me had she not thrown herself across my breast. The beast seized her left arm and bit savagely before, with her right hand free, she got home the knife that had been fatal to the first. The brute rolled over, and with a long whine like a puppy whipped in a fault, it died.

Then came behind the dancing rows of lanterns, and I knew that we were doomed indeed. But there was the spirit of an army of men in this girl, for she knelt over me with my bleeding head on her knee, set her back to the rock, and waited.

It had not been good for the first man who should come this way.

Now we were on a platform on the north side of Loch Neldricken, but close down by the waterside. There was a strange thing beneath us. It was a part of this western end of the loch, level as a green where they play bowls, and in daylight of the same smooth colour; but in the midst a black round eye of water, oily and murky, as though it were without a bottom, and the water a little arched in the middle—a most unwholesome place to look upon.

As she knelt over me May Maxwell pointed it out to me, with the knife which was in her hand.

"That is their Murder Hole," she said, "but if we are to lie there we shall not lie there without company."

The lights of the pursuers were dancing now among the heather, and their cries came from here and there, scattered and broken.

In a little, waiting thus together, we could see Gil clear against the sky. He also could see us, for he cried out to the outlaws behind him.

But in that moment of great terror, when my love knelt beside me—who, alas! in that time of need was no better than a log—suddenly something vast and terrible sprang past me—a shaggy beast infinitely greater than the dead bloodhounds, followed by another beast, less in size but even swifter in action. They were the same we had seen together that first night in the kirkyard of Kirk Oswald. These flashed out of sight and disappeared in the direction of our pursuers.

It was the Ghost Hunters that hunted only at the Dark of the Moon.

Gil turned in his tracks and began to flee.

"The Loathly Beasts!" we heard them cry, "the Witch Dogs are out!"

Then there was a shriek of pure animal terror, the lights darkened, and the cries reeled hither and thither—but not now of hunters encouraging each other, rather of men fleeing singly in the deadliest terror and crying out as they ran.

"Oh, the Beasts—they are not of this earth," cried May, holding my hand tightly. "Oh, Patrick, do not faint away again and leave me all my lone."

At this appeal I sat up and looked about. The two dead beasts were lying there. May took a napkin out of her bag and very tenderly wiped my face. Then she put it back and dropped, unconscious herself, into my arms.

So we were lying side by side when suddenly Silver Sand came and found us. So near were we, that the dead bloodhounds had blown their bloody froth upon us in their gasping. Silver Sand brought water from Loch Neldricken to throw on May's face.

"Not from the Murder Hole," I cried in terror, "from the burn."

So he went again and brought it and she awoke.

"What was the terrible beast?" she said, clutching me.

"It was no greater beast than I," said Silver Sand, "my twisted arms are turned the wrong way about for some good purpose."

"But we must budge," said he. "Can ye move?" he asked anxiously.

"I think so," answered I cautiously.

He tried my limbs and got me on my feet.

"Where does it hurt?" he asked.

"In my head," I said.

"That is good," said he, "that's thick aneuch. Try the walkin'."

I soon found that, though misty and dizzy, I could yet walk a little. So we set off—May Maxwell and Silver Sand supporting me.

The night wind blew on my wounded head, cooling it, and May Maxwell's arm was about me. I could have walked to Jericho.

"There's horses at the Gairland Burn," said Silver Sand, encouragingly; "it was touch and go that time, but we'll waur them yet."

CHAPTER XXX

A WOOING NOT LONG A-DOING

It was partly no doubt my wound, but partly also an exaltation of all my faculties, which made me spring forward as though I could not only have walked, but almost flown. The stroke I had gotten on my head, the bitter conflict I had seen, yet been utterly unable to take part in—the sweet dream I had dreamed, all acted on my senses like wine on an empty stomach.

There was no one like May Maxwell, and I had seen her fight for me. This is what I kept thinking. And was there any blame?

We were making down the glen of the Midburn as swiftly as we might. We could hear it hurrying, quite as eager to escape out of the Accursed Country as we ourselves. Silver Sand kept his ears set backwards; and Quharrie, instead of marching before us as was his wont, patrolled behind us, going from side to side, and occasionally taking a scour up over the rugged boulders on the side of Meaul which rose immanent above us.

"I think they have gotten a bellyful," said Silver Sand.

"The Faas?" I returned interrogatively.

"Na—no the Faas," he said, with a sudden and strange temper, "what for need ye be aye speakin' o' the Faas. Yon landloupers were no Faas. They were of the Macatericks—a bad black blood."

"What matter?" said I, mightily contented. Faas or the devil they might be for me, if only they would let us alone.

We passed a great sheep ree on our left. Silver Sand pointed it out.

"Had the worst come to the worst," he said, "we micht hae focht that place again' a dozen Macatericks."

We saw it only dimly through the starlight, so we could not remark the great stones of which it was built, set firm and solid upon a breastwork of the ancientest rocks of the world. But my heart was no more for fighting. There was a smell of blood in my nostrils, and the broad of that poor fellow's back stuck yonder in the sea-chest, lay heavy on my mind. I could not rid myself of it.

Then away we went again, Silver Sand, though both twisted and slender, almost carrying me in his arms, and May Maxwell, saying the while no word, but helping even more than he. We were soon at the spur of Loch Valley, and heard the crunching of the granite sand along its margin underfoot. It was precious to the feet after the miles of heather. The Loch chafed behind us, crisping white on the shore. It seemed to run an incredible way eastward, clapping against the ledges of its rocky basin, while the little waves seemed to applaud our haste. And, indeed, we strove to deserve those soft-palmed plaudits.

A watcher from somewhere cried out a word at us, and in the same tone and tongue he was answered by Silver Sand—the sudden voices sounding startling on the chill night air. But whether he was one of the outlaw breed, or an ally of Silver Sand I did not then know. There was something glimmering before us. This torrent roaring white was but the Gairland Burn seen through the darkness, and I began to speculate on the horses and how far it would be.

"Courage," said Silver Sand, "they are under that star!"

Which was a comfort—but so was Rome.

"If they be not within a mile I am sped," I said, "I can go on farther."

"They are within half a mile," he said gently, as though he had been speaking to a complaining child.

So we went on. May Maxwell was so quickly and readily kind, that the tears rained down on my cheeks to think of her and of her goodness. Even in the starlight she seemed to feel by some hidden or second sight of her own, whenever the red dew on my brow which distilled from my wound, was in danger of running down into my eyes, and she wiped it with linen, soft as a napkin, which she carried about with her. The touch of her hand upon me was gentle as gossamer and cool as the night.

"Horses at the Gairland!" said Silver Sand again, "courage—Laird."

A poor laird, poor as his lairdship. But the pressure of May Mischief's hand was more helpful than the words of Silver Sand.

We heard a whaup crying fitfully in the night down in the narrow darkness by the burn side. Silver Sand paused, put his hand to his mouth like a trumpet, and beat softly upon it with the other. Instantly the tremulous whirr of the snipe when it drops sidelong began in the air above us, so marvellously counterfeited, that even we that saw could hardly believe that it was possible. Yet it was a thing I could do well myself, as you shall hear. For sometime before this we had been descending rapidly, and the exertion of going downward seemed to send the blood to my head. I reeled and quivered in act to fall.

May Maxwell slipped from my arm and went in front of me. "Put your hands on my shoulders!" she said, "and lean on me as you go."

"But I shall hurt you," I said.

"Ye will hurt me far mair if ye dinna," she replied quickly.

Still I hesitated, but Silver Sand, who walked beside me with his arm about me, said, "Do as the lassie tells ye. She has good sense—better than you."

Now I thought that was rather hard on me, who had borne the bitter with the sweet that night, before ever Quharrie and his master came. And the saying grieved me a little, being at the time weak and childish.

Yet it is strange that from the front, whence she could not see me, May Maxwell said, "But Patrick had good sense too, or I would not have been here by now."

She spoke the English, being somewhat moved.

"Good!" said Silver Sand, for all answer.

As we went it was strangely delightsome to lean my hands on May Maxwell's little shoulders, first one and then the other, but the ground was too uneven to permit me to place both there at once. But a strange warm magic—white magic—passed up my arm and settled happily about my heart.

Suddenly we came to ground which was somewhat more level. The terrible pressure upon my wounded head, which came of going downhill, ceased; and some great shapes which moved rose out of the dim starlight.

Silver Sand ran forward and said some words. A man stole off, up the waterside, jumping across it in running skips like a dipper bird. We were on the verge of the little island called Gale Island, and the man ran westward along Loch Trool.

Three shelties stood patiently tethered together. Silver Sand helped me on one.

"Can you sit?" he said.

I could sit, indeed, but felt not so sure of riding.

Then in a minute we were steadily moving along the edge of the Loch of Trool. The path was no more than a peat sledge track, and rough beyond the understanding of southern folk. Silver Sand went first, I came next, and May Maxwell came last and seemed to be lagging.

I turned as well as I could.

"Ride across, May," I said; "this is a terrible road, and no saddle."

But she did not answer a word. Now she had always so ridden in the old days when I went for the milk to Craigdarroch, and she tormented me. But now, though her tongue of old had been so ready, she had not a word to throw at me. But since it was yet the dim starlight, though brightening into the dawn, I think she did as I bade her, at least till we were past the difficult narrows of Glen Trool.

The whaup we had heard before us as we came down the Glen of the Gairland still went on, and its pipe out of the blackness of the fringing birchwood was mightily cheering.

The day was breaking as we reached a great height above the lake and paused for a moment to breathe our sturdy shelties.

"May!" I said softly.

Her pony was behind me, but she did not move forward.

"May!" I said again.

Still she came not, yet she must have heard.

"O my head!" I said, and she was at my side in a moment.

"Does it hurt?" she said; and by the tremble of her voice I am sure she was nigh to weeping for sweet pity. Yet my head was no worse than it had been.

She came up close so that she could touch my brow by leaning over. Her touch healed my head, and after that she rode all the way alongside.

"After all," she said, "it does not matter. It is only Patrick."

Now I shall tell you an extraordinary thing. All this happened on the great height above Loch Trool when the morning star was turning the colour of meadow-sweet in a violet sky. May Maxwell and I never said a word of love—such as asking one another whether we loved each other, as lovers do in books.

But as she leaned to wipe my brow, she was of necessity very near. So I set my arm about her to steady her, and being so near, and she looking up, I kissed her. It can be done if the ponies are good and move daintily. I, that tell you, know.

"I dreamed that in a dream," I said ere I let her go; "it has come true."

Even yet I looked for her to be angry, or at least to make believe. But for so lively and merry-hearted a maid she took it exceedingly sedately, which I liked best of all. Indeed, she kissed me back again fair and frank, without shame, a good true-hearted kiss, which I am proud of—Silver Sand having his back to us, being busy with his pony's girths. Now I am not of them who are for ever telling their kisses, but that one I am proud of, and I care not who knows. But I tell of no more. My tale is of grimmer business.

Now I vow and declare this was all our love-making. Which is strange, considering the coil that is made about the affair in verse-books and ballads. When we made love after that we did it of set purpose, without any pretence that either of us did not like it, which is not at all what I had expected from May Mischief. But one never knows!

The morning broke as we rode through the shallow water of the Trool at Fordmouth, and so came out on the open. Then Silver Sand flung up his cap with the shaggy ears into the air and we all cried, "Hurrah!" For we were clear at last, and May Maxwell was sitting again soberly and properly on her sheltie like a great lady on a side-saddle.

CHAPTER XXXI

MAY MISCHIEF PROVES HER METTLE

We all dismounted by the water-edge, and May came and washed my face like a child's, and bound up my head with strips of linen of the finest. It was warm and soft. Where she carried it I know not. I had one deep cut, ragged and sore, on the right side of my head, and a smaller cut by the temple, which was the one that had distilled the blood and weakened me. These May bathed, and Silver Sand helped her to bind them up. We drank what remained of Mistress Eppie's cheer. Then again mounted and rode.

It was a wide, good road now, especially after we turned south at the House of the Hill and rode towards Cree Brig. There were pleasant farmhouses about us, where the cocks were crowing near and far, and the blue reek went up very friendly into the sunshine. Men came out and looked all around them at the sky, and seemed well pleased. And so were we. I looked often at May Maxwell, and strangely enough at these very moments she always looked at me, though I must have been a bonny sight with my bandaged head and the bonnet cocked on the top of the white rags.

Yet I never saw her look at me in that fashion before. We rode alongside of one another, Silver Sand cantering easy in front, with Quharrie trotting before him again.

I was at May's left hand, and as our horses clattered along ever changing their stride, and making rhythm on the hard road, I took her hand, saying, "This is the hand that saved me."

"Nay, rather say this the hand that drew me out of the House of Murders," she returned.

But she shuddered and lifted up her hand to her face. I saw that upon it which made my blood run cold. Three great fang-marks on her middle arm, from which the sleeve had fallen back as she lifted up her hand.

I was off my beast in a moment, crying out to Silver Sand, who turned at the word.

"What a fool I was not to look," I said; "the dogs have bitten you, May."

Silver Sand looked grave.

"This must be burned," said he, briefly.

"Let me ride on to Cree Bridge," she said; but he would not hear of it.

There was a farmhouse near by, and the name of it is Borgan. Kind folk live there, and it is not far from a bridge where the waters come down tumbling white.

Thither we went, and telling so much of our story as we chose, they took us into the kitchen, and sent out a boy to attend to our horses.

May asked for a knitting-needle, which being brought to her, she heated white hot among the peats, and, turning, looked at me. But it was far beyond me to burn it for her. Which made me ashamed, because I knew that she had done the like for me without the tremor of a muscle—this being the way of women when they need to help those they love. But I was ever a coward in such matters. So May took the needle herself, turned back her sleeve, and with the white point hissing a little, she made a faint blue smoke that sent me down in a swarf on a settle-bed, being yet weak in my head. But she faithfully burned the fang-marks; and then, sitting down beside me, asked quietly for a drink of water, and gave it to me.

The kind people of the Borgan wished us much to stay, but May was keen to get eastward to see her brothers and her father—for I had not had the heart, or indeed the time, to tell her that the old man was dead. This may be thought both wicked and selfish of me, insomuch that I allowed her to ride merrily with me, at times touching my hand, and at other times singing. Yet my heart was heavy as lead for that which I had to tell her. But I could make no other of it, think as I would.

I solaced myself by saying that it had not been wise to tell her when yet we were in no place of safety; but as soon as we sat together in the changehouse at Cree Bridge I told her plainly and tenderly, judging that it was better to have it over. Yet even then she said but little—only that she had judged all the while that something terrible must have happened, since there was no pursuit of her after her capture and carrying off.

Then after a while her tears flowed suddenly, as though she had not at first realised the matter.

"Oh, why did they do it?" she cried. "He was such an old man."

Then she put her hand in mine, and looking up at me in a way that was fair heart-breaking, said, "Patrick, you must not think of me any more. We are not quiet to live with, we Maxwells; and this, I see, will be but the beginning of trouble and bloodshed. My brothers will never rest till my father's murderers are destroyed."

"My lass," I said, "I did not think of marrying your brothers."

"Aye—but," she said sadly, "we are all the same."

"God forbid!" said I—in to myself.

But on the whole she bore the tidings very well, though she looked no more at me, neither gave me her hand any more. Yet when we went out of the changehouse, and from among the strange people that looked curiously at us, she walked very close to me, as though she would nestle her shoulder against mine; which comforted me much, and I think her also.

She did not weep before folk, but when we were once more on the road, the water ran silently down her cheeks; and I think that she forgot altogether about the burns on her arm, or it may be even wished that there were more of them. But all she said was just this, and that over and over—"He was such an old man."

But our horses' feet fell more sadly, and though Silver Sand rode farther ahead there was no more love-making—which I was sorry for, and wished that I had kissed her oftener—so unthankful and selfish is a young man in love.

It came to me, while May thus rode sadly, to speak to Silver Sand concerning the report that we should give in to the Sheriff at Kircudbright.

To my surprise he was much opposed to this course.

"Report me nae reports," he said. "Whatna guid wull the like o' that do ye?"

"But I want it known that there is black murder doing among the hills, and no man the wiser," said I.

"D'ye think the Sherra disna ken that by this time?" said Silver Sand.

"It's easy for you, my man," I said to him. "Ye didna see the puir lad's bloody back in the great sea-chest, nor hear the knives whetting on the sharping stones to cut your ain throat."

"No this nicht, maybe," said Silver Sand; "but see here."

He opened his coat a little, and showed me the blue-white scar of a great wound. "That was a Macaterick knife," he said; "but I reported nae reports. Only," he said, grimly, "I paid my debt."

"And what, then, shall we do?" I said, for I was in a genuine difficulty. I was a laird, though it was of the smallest and poorest kind, and I was not fond of private war, though I had fallen into a good deal of it during the last day or two.

"This is certain," he said; "I ken the Maxwell lads, and I ken the hill sneckdraws—the Marshalls and the Macatericks. Neither will rest till there's mair o' this."

"And the Faas?" I asked, for Hector Faa had made the deepest dint in my own reckoning, and it was with him that I chiefly desired to square accounts.

Silver Sand turned in one of his sudden accesses of temper.

"I tell ye," he said, firmly, "that the Faas hae neither airt nor pairt in the murderings."

I longed to ask him in which camp his heart lay, but for the sake of what he had done for us that night, I had the limited grace to refrain.

"But what, then, was the lass that Hector Faa ran away wi' doing in a house of the Macatericks?"

"That I cannot tell," he said; "of this I am certain—Hector Faa may have had his reasons. But he is no murderer."

"What, then, was that honest man doing pickled in that deil's kist? Friends o' murderers are not so much better that ever I heard."

Silver Sand made answer very quietly.

"It's not well done between friends to speak in that fashion. Surely Silver Sand is well enough kenned by you now, that you might trust him."

Now, I had not thought of Silver Sand at all, but only of Hector Faa, against whom it was small wonder that I was full of anger. I told him this, and his anger, the cause of which I could not then imagine, cooled in a moment.

"Ye're in love, laddie, and that excuses a'."

And from that moment he resumed his ordinary placid demeanour. We passed Kirkcudbright by the sea (which seemed most like a low-lying English town), keeping ourselves all the while upon the crown of the causeway, and were soon within sight of Rathan Isle. I could see the old house shining white across the blue girdle of the sea, and my heart rose within me. Here we met Kennedy Maxwell, and sent him on to announce our coming.

As she went along May Maxwell kept her eyes on the ground, being, I think, afraid of seeing the roofless walls of Craigdarroch with the gables pointing so hopelessly upward, all blackened on the inside.

Half an hour after, as we went by the way, a man came across the fields toward us. He was a well-set-up man in a kind of faded livery, but with moleskin trousers underneath, such as labourers wear. He went up to May Maxwell, who had not looked at him, and with an elaborate bow said to her—

"My Lady Grizel Maxwell's compliments, and she wad be pleased to see you at Earlstoun. She thinks that her house is the best abiding-place for a young leddy of the Maxwells, though but a second cousin."

May looked astonished. It was not so often that a message had come to her from the old lady of Earlstoun. Silver Sand turned sharp round.

"I'll ride with you to Earlstoun yett," he said to Mary. Then turning to the messenger, "An' wha's dog whalpit you?" he queried.

Now this was a distinctly uncivil question, and Silver Sand was always well bred. He told me afterwards that he could not abide anything upsetting from flunkies, and that Quharrie and he always took such matters into their own hands—sometimes, also, in Quharrie's own teeth.

Moleskins, however, was placable.

"Juist the bitch that was your ain dam's sister," said he, pleasantly.

"Served me richt." said Silver Sand; "that's nae flunkie's answer. "What brocht ye into that coat?"

"Juist the same as brings ye ridin' on anither man's beast," said the sturdy serving-man, blinking no whit—"want o' siller to buy yin o' my ain."

Silver Sand looked him straight in the face, and the serving-man looked straight back again, standing with his hands on his hips.

"An' hoo do ye ken that this horse that I ride is no my ain?"

"Juist for the reason that that horse ye ride is Johnny Faa's and cam' frae aff the Border side. I ken the breed by the bonny baisoned face o' him."

Silver Sand took the word patiently, and said only, "Does your mistress wish to keep young Mistress Maxwell by her?"

"I e'en believe such to be her wish and intention."

"You were in the wars, man," said Silver Sand, quickly.

"Aye," said the man, "I rade wi' the wild Bonshaw. Wha rade ye wi?"

"Ye are a man of sense," said Silver Sand; "and men of sense ken when to haud their tongues."

"When it's worth their while," said the serving-man, who had ridden with Bonshaw to the Whig shooting.

"It'll be weel worth your while," said Silver Sand.

"I dinna mean siller," said the other, quickly.

"I never met a soldier that didna. Dinna be blate," retorted Silver Sand.

"Weel, since ye are sae pressin'," said the other.

Something passed from hand to hand. I suspected that it was a guinea or two out of the same bag which had supplied me with mine.

CHAPTER XXXII

I SALUTE THE LADY GRIZEL

So we rode on to the great house of Earlstoun. Its occupant was the Lady Grizel Maxwell, the daughter of old Earl Maxwell, and a woman well kenned and respected through all the Stewartry and farther. She had her especial oddnesses, but she was known to be so exceedingly hospitable that oftentimes her own table was denuded in order that dainties might be sent to those of her poorer neighbours.

She met us at the garden gate. She was a large woman of masculine features, with a prominent nose and a clear and fearless grey eye that looked unwinking at each of us.

It was at Silver Sand she looked first.

"Preserve us, man!" she said; "surely hemp's no sae dear that ye can afford to risk the tow. What do ye in this country?"

Silver Sand was manifestly put out.

"I think your leddyship is mistaken," he said.

"Mistake here!—mistake there!—Grizel Maxwell kens a——"

"Wheesht, wheesht, my Leddy! There's names that's no for cryin' at ilka lodge-yett."

"'Deed, aye," said her ladyship, taking off the broad, blue, man's bonnet that she wore, and showing a beautiful head of lint-white hair rippling away from her brow, "it's one of my name that should ken that."

"Weel THAN!" said Silver Sand for all answer.

She greeted May next. Opening her arms to lift her down, which she did as a grenadier might dismount a drummer-boy, she said—

"My dautie, you an' me has baith lost faithers; it's like the kind o' folk. The Maxwell men are never like to dee in their beds. Na, they ride gaily, and their women folk hear the clatterin' o' their spurs doon the dark valley as they gang awa' to come nae mair back. Ye are wae for yer faither. Come to me an' we'll bide a wee, an' get it bye. It canna be helped, my lassie. Ye see that coat, May, lass. There was a heid ta'en aff close to the collar o' that—ye see the velvet's a wee rusty. That was my faither's heid. That's the way o' the Maxwells ever since they cam' into this Galloway, where, indeed, they had no manner o' business.

Then she turned to me, looking at me fiercely to see how I stood her eye.

"An' wha may ye be, young man, that rides sae free by my cousin's side?"

Ere I had time to speak May Maxwell began to tell how that, when all others had hung back, I had out-ventured and saved her from the most terrible perils, saying nothing as she told it, about her own doings.

"Patrick Heron o' Rathan! An auld name, though nooadays wi' but little to the tail o't. It's nocht the waur o' that. 'Deed, the Maxwells took a' but the bit barren isle, an' I wot they had ta'en that had that been worth their while. Aye, man, I kenned not your faither, but your grandfaither was a mettlesome blade, an' mony a time met me at the end o' the plantin'—just for luck and youth, ye understand; nocht else. He had the bonniest ankle and calf. Aye, laddie, ye favour him aboot the leg, though little aboot the features. Come doon and gie us a salutation."

So I came and very respectfully gave the salute.

"'Deed, sirs, ye favour him but little aboot the moo; but I ettle that'll no be the way ye kiss a bonny lass. Na, an auld cleckin' wife canna look for ocht else at this time o' day. Aweel, aweel!"

We stood before her meek as a flock of chickens, and she held up her apron by the corners as if she had corn within to feed us with.

"But it's a bonny like thing that ye hae to stand here on the steps o' my hoose. I'm an Earl's dochter, ye ken. Didna ye ken? Gin ye dinna, there's Gib Gowdie, that caa's himsel' a butler, he'll sune tell ye—silly auld man, Gib! Will ye come ben, man?" she said to Silver Sand, who stood with his hat in his hand as the gentrice do to a lady. "It's mony a day since I saw ye ride aff wi'—ye-ken-wha——"

But Silver Sand said, "I thank your ladyship exceedingly, but I have much business to transact."

Only us two she took within the portal, and closed it with her own hands, shooting the bars as in a prison. We found ourselves in an immense bare hall with only old buff coats and black armour hanging about, and the faint light filtering down the great staircase.

The Lady Grizel went to the top of the kitchen stair, which opened downwards like a great deep well.

"Jen!" she cried.

"Aye mem; dinna be in a fyke, mem! Canna ye bide a wee? I'll be there the noo."

Her ladyship stamped her foot.

"Come awa' this instant, ye impident hempie!"

"Then your leddyship will hae to come and pook the chucky, an' ye ken ye never were guid at the singin' o't," said a voice from below.

"Jen!" cried Lady Grizel from the stair-head; "this is past bearing. You an' me maun twine."

"An; what for that?" inquired a black-a-vised, good-natured woman of mature good looks, with very red cheeks and dark eyebrows, who looked up at us as we stood at the top and she at the bottom of the kitchen stairs. She had a sheet about her and a great pullet in her hand. "Hoot, yer leddyship, war ye thinkin' o' leavin' Earlstoun?"

"No, Jen, but gin ye canna come at my biddin', I'll hae to pairt wi' you."

"Na, na, yer leddyship, ye ken brawly ye couldna do that. Ye couldna put up that bonny heid o' hair yersel'. Forbye, gin ye dinna ken a guid servant when ye hae yin, I ken a guid mistress."

"Jen, gang to yer wark in the kitchen in a meenit," cried her ladyship, turning on her heel. "Dinna answer me back! I maun e'en mak' shift to show you yer ain room mysel', May; an' you, Laird Rathan, can gang to the reception-room, where ye'll hae company till I come doon."

I went towards the room indicated. The door which admitted me was exceedingly high and opened, like a gate, outwards. There was a great noise within of barking, screaming, and coughing. Here in a large room were a collie dog, a long-haired cat of some foreign breed, a parrot on a stick, and a monkey, or, as the Galloway folks say, a "puggie"—an ugly beast all set up in a red coat, capering about everywhere and keeping the whole room in a turmoil. As soon as I came in there was silence, and the monkey ran to the top of the red velvet curtains, and there showed his head most comically in order to observe if anyone were following me into the room. The action was that of the bad boy of a school looking for the dominie with his taws or birch rod. At this moment I could not forbear laughing.

"Have some manners, ye gowk!" shouted a great voice which startled me, and instinctively I begged pardon. But it was only the parrot, a strange, uncanny bird which I had often heard about but never before seen. So in this room I remained with these curious companions till her ladyship came down to me.

"This lass o' mine tells me that ye saved her frae the gled's clews at the risk o' yer ain life. Ye'll be thinkin' muckle o' that. Hoot, it's naethin' ava. Yer grandfaither had dune as muckle for a kiss and gang-yer-ways frae a bonny lass; but I guess, indeed I ken, that ye hae bespoke the farm and want to life-rent it. Aweel, ye are a decent lad I doot not, though ye haena muckle siller. We'll see, we'll see Paitrick. A Maxwell's no to be picked up ilka day as a hen picks corn. Ye may get her, an' ye may no. What's that ye say, that ye hae gotten her already? Na, my bonny man; gin there had no been slips atween the cup an' the lip, it's no here I wad hae been the day, writin' my name as Papa Priest gied it to me—we'll no say hoo mony year syne!"

CHAPTER XXXIII

JEN GEDDES' SAMPLER BAG

Jen Geddes appeared at the door. She had dressed herself in a black gown of silk, very thick, and her grey hair was over her ears in most elaborate wimples.

"Did I ever see sic a silly auld woman," said Lady Grizel, "at your time o' life, Jen, to dress up for a young man; I'm black affrontit."

Jen said, without turning a hair, "Be my age what it may, it's weel kenned that your ladyship was woman muckle when I was christened."

"Hoot na, Jen, I was but a lassie. I dinna mind on't ava'!" said her ladyship, firmly.

"Na, na, Leddy Girzie, ye ken brawly that it's in your hand o' write that the name o' Janet Geddes stands in the big ha' Bible." This with an air of triumph.

But I went forward, seeing that Jen was a privileged person, and waited for Lady Grizel to introduce me.

"Ye'll ken Laird Heron o' the Rathan, Jen—a mettle spark. He taks after his gran'faither aboot the leg; think ye na, Jen?"

"That your leddyship should ken. I hae heard my faither say he cam' a heap aboot ye. As for me, I'm a deal ower young to mind."

"Hoot na, Jen, ye ken fine that it was you that used to let him in when he cam' tirlin' at the pin, an' that hoised him oot o' the wicket that nicht when his lordship, my faither, cam' on us ower quick."

Jen kindled at the recollection, and was caught.

"Aye, my leddy, an' wasna it bonny to see him ding the sparks frae the iron jackets o' the watchers. Aye, but he was a free lad, and kenned a bonny lass."

"You an' him were ower pack for me, Jen," said her ladyship, craftily. "I like no a man that comes after baith mistress and maid."

"Hoot," said Jen, "there's nae hairm dune, for a gallant lad to tak a bit cheeper frae the maid on his way ben to the mistress; an' what for no? D'ye think the maid is no as guid a judge o' sic like as the leddy; forby whiles a deal bonnier? She canna help bein' whiles mair temptation."

And Jen tossed her stately ringlets before her well-preserved apple cheeks.

"'Deed, Jen, noo that ye hae gi'en in that you an' me is aboot an age, I'll never deny that in the days o' yer youth ye war a weel-faured lass."

Jen held her head high.

"Aiblins I'm nae that ill-lookin' yet," she said.

"An opinion in which I heartily agree," said I, taking her hand in mine, while I held my hat in the other. "Let me claim the privilege of my grandfather, who, I perceive, had excellent taste!"

Whereupon I bowed to mistress and then to maid, who dropped me a curtsy apiece—that of Lady Grizel graceful and sweeping, that of Jen Geddes ample and hearty, as of a tub that rises and falls in a mill-pond.

"Weel bobbit! ye're a plant o' grace," said the Lady Grizel, very much pleased, "an' a lad o' mettle takes the heart o' auld wives mair nor looks."

"But he's weel faured for a' that," said Jen; "I think he's e'en as bonny as ever his gran'faither was."

"An' that was aye your way, Jen; an' a comfortable yin it is. The apple ye *had* was aye the best apple, the bonniest, the reedest-cheekit. That's what it is to be happy."

She sighed.

"As for me," she went on, "the lad I liked best was aye the lad that I couldna get, an' that's maybe the reason that I lie my lane the nicht, wi' only anither auld limmer like mysel' atween me an' the stock."

"Ye micht hae had the Laird o' Rathan," said Jen to her mistress, "and then yer Billie Wattie had never rogueit him oot o' Orraland and Rascarrel an' the bonny Nitwud. But ye war an earl's dochter, an' couldna think to sit in the auld toor o' Rathan and even yoursel' to a commoner."

"'Deed, Jen," said Lady Grizel, tossing her head in a way which reminded me exceedingly of May Maxwell when she is roguish, "it wasna me that was unwillin'. I wad hae gien a' my shapin' claes to sit there' but it wasna to be."

She paused for a moment of thought; then she spoke, waving her hand sideways as though to drive all these things away.

"But they are a' but auld wives' clavers, an' it's Paitrick Heron that's come to my door wi' a bonny lass in his hand, ridin' croose and canty—him wi' a three-cornered dunt on his broo, an' her wi' a scarf on her airm that they hae gotten, ilka yin fechtin' to get the ither. Jen! we'll e'en hae a waddin'. I'se get doon Mass John, an' Jen, ye can air the sheets."

"Great havers," said Jen, "ye were aye for suppin' yer porritch afore they were weel boiled a' the days o' ye. They're Whigs and no o' the religion, and mair nor that the young lass's faither is no lang under the sod."

"Aweel, aweel, Jen," said her ladyship, "it's maybe as weel, but I hae garred this young man's heart gang clinkum-clank this nicht, I wat. Let me hearken!"

And the abominable old woman put her hand on my heart, which was in good sooth thumping with great spontaniety and surprising quickness at the thought.

"A good honest heart," she said, "that hasna been wared on ither lasses. Ye shall no hae lang to wait, my laddie, and I'se butter your bread for ye that day, my man."

And well said. None such a bad old lady was the Lady Grizel.

"D'ye mind," said Jen, "hoo ye used to come gatherin' the bramble-berries, an' then the mistress wad cry ye into the hoose for a bit piece?"

I minded fine, and said so with such an expression of happiness, that Jen was moved to other recollections, while her mistress went out from us.

"She's a wonderfu' woman, the mistress; no the like o' her in the three counties. She micht hae had the wale o' the men—like mysel' indeed; but whenever yin o' them tried ower sair to please her, she turned camsteery wi' him, an' gang in harnass she wadna; and even your gran'faither only pleased her by pretendin' no to care a preen for her."

"She has been very kind to me already," I said.

"Aye, an' she'll be kinder, for she likes you, I can see. My name's no Jen Geddes o' the Parton gin she's no kind to you, far by your thinkin'. But be aff-stan'in' an' contradictious, hot as the mustard, an' flee oot wi' your hat in your hand an' your heid in the air at a word. That's the way to please the mistress; aye, an' the feck o' women. They like nane o' your men that peep and mutter—bena my sister Eppie," she added.

"Your sister Eppie?" I said, a strange thought coming into my head.

"Aye, an' that minds me, my laddie, whaur got ye that bag wi' the bluidy knives intil't lying on the table. I wuss ye haena been at some terrible ploy, you an' the Maxwell lass."

I told her as well as I could our great and wonderful story between her exclamations. Before I had done with the broad back of the carle in the sea-chest, she had to sit down; the two gashes in it finished her, as they had nearly done for me; but she wanted to hear more.

"But the bag; whaur gat ye the bag?" she cried.

Of that I knew nothing. It was one that May Maxwell had brought from the House of Death by Loch Enoch side.

"That's my sister's bag, I can sweer til't," she said. "She's marriet on saft Sammle Tamson o' the Mossdale. It was me that made it an' gied it to her afore she left Parton Hoose. See here!" she cried suddenly.

She ripped away a part of the lining. "JANET GEDDES; HER SAMPLER WORK," was cross-stitched on the inside of the lining.

Then I remembered the story of Marion, and the little lass that we had left with Mistress Eggface and the evil men in the terrible house on the hill of Craignairny.

"The wee bit lass," I said again and again; "an' we left her in that hoose amang the fiends."

My heart smote me sore, as indeed it had no need to do, for of a surety we all had died by torture had we tried to take her with us then. I told myself this, but it did not do a bit of good. Of all the useless, contrary things in the world, conscience is the worst. The preachers say that it cannot do wrong or speak wrong. This is far from being so; for many is the time that I have done something I knew to be right—indeed in which I had no choice but to do as I did; therefore conscience ought to have been satisfied. But was it? Far from that; it kept up such a coil and pother that very often, just to ease it, I went and did something infinitely worse to drown its noise, or in some round-the-corner way cause it to be quiet. This I did now. I could in no wise help leaving the little lass; it was certain that we had only got ourselves all murdered if we had tried to bring her with us; but conscience would have none of it, and I had a sore heart for many days about her. Often have I wished that I had no conscience at all, and that not for evil's sake.

The Lady Grizel now came in.

"I mind," said she, "when you cam' to Earlstoun a wee bit laddie, that ye liked a bit piece wi' butter and the sweet conserves upon it. Noo, ye'll hae to tak' the road soon, for the sake o' Jen's character an' mine. It will no do for a handsome young man to be his lane in the hoose wi' three bonny lasses. Ye war in the Wolf's Slock at dead o' nicht wi' the bonniest, says you; my certes, but ye are no blate to say that to my face. Ye'se no come into my hoose gin ye dinna learn to be ceevil. But it was the bit o' sweetcake wi' conserves that ye likit. See noo, boy, there's a bit o' the like set oot for ye ben in the room there. Gang ben and get it."

So saying, she took me by the shoulders and fairly pushed me out. I entered in at the door, and there before me, standing alone by the window, was my May. I shut the door behind me and looked about for Grizel's sweet cake and conserves.

CHAPTER XXXIV

SWEET CAKE AND CONSERVES

"May!" I said softly.

She turned and came near to me and stood very close against me in a way that was sweet to me, but I knew that she did not wish me to touch her then, but only to stand so. Thus we remained a considerable while, till my heart became very full, aching within me to comfort her. Which at last I did with satisfaction to both of us, and the time sped.

I told her how that I must go to the old Tower of Rathan, and see what matters were like there in the hands of Jerry. I told her, too, about little Marion, who she was; and she cheered me by telling me that the wild and murderous folk were not all unkind to the little child, but that she was treated in that rough and poor place like the daughter of the old woman—as indeed I had seen even while I remained in the kitchen. Also she was not old enough to know their enormities. All which, being the words of my love, eased my heart amazingly, because I did not wish to have a second journey thrust upon me just at that time.

So when we looked about for a place to sit down, for it behoved us to talk together as it were for the last time (for at least a night and a day). There was but one great chair in all that room, though there was much tapestry and some high tables and corner aumries. So we sat down on it with great content, and in good sooth I wist not how I should be able to go from her—so soon does one use to the sight and touch of a dear young lass.

But I knew well that she would be true to me, and she promised to think on me every hour; and asked the same from me again, which made me laugh, for I knew that I should think of nought else the hour by the length and every hour. So I asked her when she would come to the Rathan and stay.

"It is a poor place," I said, "but there is no reason why, with service and good farming, it should not be the bieldiest and happiest of homes for us. We Herons have lived sparely for two generations, and we can afford to spend a little out of the Dumfries lawyer's hands when a bonny bride comes home to Rathan."

I urged her sore, and at last she admitted she would come just when I was ready, for she said, "I have no heart to go back to Craigdarroch, for I ken my brithers, and they are not the men to let byganes lie. There'll be mair and waur red wark or a' be dune!"

"Had she indeed the heart to come to the Rathan?" I asked, to try her; for indeed I knew it before, yet it was so passing sweet to hear that I could not forego a word.

"Deed that I have, Patrick, heart an' body an' a'—juist your ain, when it fits you to call for them."

"Then," said I, "I'll e'en tak' them noo."

At which she cried off, but she was none ill-pleased.

"Hae ye a' the conserves lickit aff the sweetcake yet?" cried a voice from the door, which opened just a little ajar.

We were surprised and answered nothing, and the door closed again as softly as it had opened.

May laughed May Mischief's laugh for, I think, the first time since the beginning of the troubles.

"Have you?" said she, looking at me.

Now we sat in one chair, and though I do not consider myself a clever fellow, and I had no experience, that was good enough for me.

There is nothing to report of the next half hour.

"It's my turn, May," said Lady Grizel, who had been coughing at the door for five minutes; "I'm whiles ta'en wi' the hoast, but I like a bit quiet hour at e'en wi a blythe lad as weel as ony."

"His grandfather, was it no?" asked my witch archly.

"'Deed but ye're nocht but a couple o' birkies that needs turnin' up and skelpin'—and for a word I wad send ye baith to the door. Hear ye that?" said the old lady, greatly pleased.

Then she turned to me.

"Noo awa' wi' ye, Patrick, an' tell thae Maxwell lads that they are welcome to the onstead o' Earlstoun farm to stow their goods and bestial in when they get ony. An' say that there's guid sleepin' in the granary an' stable laft. But there's to be nae fechtin' near the hoose," she added, having, no doubt, in the mind the manners and customs of the Maxwell brothers.

An' anither thing—they maun find their ain caves and hidie-holes for the Hollands an' the lace. I'm no gaun to hae the king's men rampagin' through my hoose, herrying and berryin', at my time o' life. A keg ower the back o' the dyke is yae thing an' cellars full o' brandy is anither."

So I bade them good-bye, kissing them both, and Jen Geddes too at the door, who boxed me on the ear for an "impudent loon, that canna leave a decent woman's kep straucht on her heid."

And this was all the magic I ever used to win three women's hearts.

The Maxwells had heard the whole story of their sister's safety already from Silver Sand, and that much to my credit. So they came about me like bees from where they were working, putting new roofs on their barns and byres. They would have me stay and take the good cheer of the occasion with them, but I was eager to be at the Rathan; so I took their boat and rowed over across the rippling tide that came flowing in as I knew it of old, swirling in the smooth places with an oily underbubble and jabbling along the side of the boat, with the pleasant sound which is always heartsome to me to hear.

I beached the Maxwells' boat at the Shell Cove, at the back of the house, and went up the path, looking as a man looks that has come back from foreign parts and tries to make out the changes about his home. Rathan House looked better than ever I saw it. There was a platform out of one of the windows, which I could by no means tell the use of, and a dark vessel sitting upon it. It was a very silent place, but I heard the hens cackling and pecking at meat newly laid out, so I knew that there was a living soul about it somewhere.

I went quietly about the house till I came to the main door, which was deep set in the wall. It was wide open, and there sat Jerry Macwhirter, peeling potatoes and piping as he worked, "Awa', Whigs awa'," and other unhallowed tunes.

"The Whig is no sae far awa', my lad!—and how do ye like it?" said I.

Wherewith I took him by the back of the neck to shake him, but he twisted himself round, and would have set a dirk in me with exceeding quickness had not he recognised me and dropped it with a hearty cry of joy.

But I still shook him, whereat he kicked my shins.

This brought us back to the point of friendliness, for I had paid him his kane for his insolence at parting. Then I had to tell him all the long story, which made him marvel greatly. There had been, it seemed, a great quietness about Rathan and all the countryside. It was said, however, that the sheriff was organising a party to go against the outlaws, but no one believed it.

On the other hand, the Maxwells were surely setting themselves to prepare for a great raid among the hills. Many had given in their names to Will and Kennedy Maxwell, and it was said that a large body of men exercised every night during the clear of the moon on the farm of Craigdarroch. This much was true at all events, that a party of preventive men from Kirkcudbright had come on a body of fifty horse by the holms of the Darroch, and fled without firing a shot. But these might only be the ordinary Freetraders. The Maxwells had sworn never to run another cargo till the evil beasts were destroyed, root and branch, from off the face of Galloway.

I wondered what the evil beasts had to say to this.

Within doors everything was in such beautiful order that I hardly knew it for the same place. Jerry (to pass the time he said) had so painted and cleaned, that in my heart I thought that the bride might have come home that night—and indeed I wished she had.

When I told him concerning May he looked sulkier than ever I saw him. The further my story went on, the gloomier got he. At last he broke out—

"Then I suppose naething will serve you but you must get this lass ower to the Rathan, set up hoose like a grocer, and tak' the Buik nicht an' mornin'?"

I said that these things were far away.

"But they are comin', I see, an' no sae far away neither—nearer than I like."

"It'll never make any difference to you, Jerry," I said with the innocence of inexperience.

"Whustle on my thoomb!" said he irreverently; "I'm bye wi't; I ken my jug's been ower often at the well. I'll e'en tak' to a tent, like Silver Sand. Him an' me'ill gang the kintry. That's what we'll do. I can at least pent a door. I tell ye what, Jerry'll no mix yer saps an' nurse yer scraichin' brats. I canna bide them."

Whereupon he took me round about, and in a mournful, valedictory manner (which amused me greatly) he showed me all his improvements. He had really wonderfully brightened up the old house. But of course his doings, such as they were, showed me how much must be done before a young bride could come home. I resolved, thereupon, to go to Dumfries the very next day to see the lawyer that had my little property in his hand; but all this time I burned hot and cold in flashes and my head buzzed strangely.

"'Deed ye'll no do that," he said, "I hae a bit sma' job to do mysel', an' gin I kept house for you, ye maun e'en bide for me."

I nodded, asking only when he would be back again.

I told him about the matter of the bag and the little Marion.

"I'll call at the Mossdale on my road to New Galloway, and tell them. It's a thing they should ken, and it'll maybe be better for your health to keep wide o' the Macaterick's country for a wee. I'm but a hirple Dick, an' it maitters little aboot me. There's nocht but the eel's skin on Jerry MacWhirter."

So he sped on his way, with a message that all was right, to Earlstoun, where I asked May to let him have the bag in which the knives had been.

To ease my head I strolled down to where Silver Sand had made his camp by the side of the little Rathan burn. His donkey was there, having been brought to the isle from the other side. Silver Sand looked a little queerly at me as I came up, thinking mayhap that I had asked the Lady Grizel more of his history, which I was far from doing, so long as he did not wish to tell me himself. All about the camp was very fresh and pleasant, and made me very glad, but for the queer humming machinery which was working in my head.

But Silver Sand, as soon as he saw me (for I had wholly forgotten my battered head, being with May and then coming home), ordered me in a loud tone to my bed, calling himself ill-names for not having thought thereon sooner.

So he sent me to bed and himself helped me off with my clothes, and took them away. Then he laid cool, wet cloths on my head, and gave me a draught. Whereat I slept a great sleep of many hours, and when I awakened I could not tell what day or hour of the day it might be. But I was unhappy in my mind, because I had not sent a message to Earlstoun, whereat he went out himself and left me. Outside the salt water sounded cool and pleasant as though it were breaking in spray on my hot head. So I lay, with many earnest thoughts of the goodness of God, as it were between sleeping and waking. Indeed I reproached myself very sore that I had so seldom thought upon the Maker and the Giver of all good. My nature is not to be unthankful, but only of late things had happened so close the one upon the other, that I had forgotten and passed my thanksgivings by. For this now, it may be, I was lying upon my back.

CHAPTER XXXV

SILVER SAND'S WHITE MAGIC

It was the broad light of some unknown day when I came again to myself, for Silver Sand, by his white magic, had put that in the draught which caused me to sleep. But I was marvellously refreshed and my head was cool.

"Give me my sark!" I cried, for I could hear him at the hag-clog where we cut the branches and wood into billets to go into the great fireplace.

"Eppie will bring it from the store-room," said the voice, not of Silver Sand as I had apprehended, but of that sprite Jerry, who sat at the bed-foot and smirked at my surprise.

"Whatna Eppie?" said I.

"Hear till him," said Jerry, scratching his bare foot, "the hound! Hoo mony Eppies do ye ken? Are the Eppies tumblin' ower yin anither i' this hoose o' the Isle o' Rathan?"

But I let the ill-guided loon run on, for there in the doorway stood my kind friend Eppie Tamson of Mossdale, with her comely person and apple cheeks, and she was drying her hands.

"Wi' laddie," she said, "this is blithe seein'—you clothed and in your richt mind. Ye hae had a teuch battle for't on the grey tide where the seeven waters meet, but ye hae won through."

"I want a dish o' porridge," I said, for I was hungry.

She went to the door and cried, "Jen, he's wakkin'; fess the porridge!"

And with that who should put her head in at the door but my own dear May Mischief, who came quietly and sat at the head of my bed and put her head down beside mine on the pillow—which, though a slight thing, went to my heart mightily, so that I thought on it long after she was gone.

Then she told me how that I had been near to ten days unconscious, and had raved on about many things, concerning some of which she said, "I would not have desired any but myself to hear."

But she smiled as she said it.

"And I heard more o' your ill-deeds than I am likely to hear about for the rest o' my life," she said.

Seeing me look a little anxious, she said, "There was nothing to cause me any anxiety, Patrick; for, though I heard everything, you never spoke of any lass but one."

She smiled and waited for me to speak. So, to please her, I asked who that might be.

"It was just daft May Maxwell," she said, looking down at her lap, and then up at me all very simply and sweetly, as indeed was all she did.

"Hoot," said I, "was that a'? I thocht it had been eyther Jen Geddes or Eppie Tamson."

"You're gettin' better," says she, "an' we maun tak' a stap oot o' yer bicker, my lad!"

And in my weak state this seemed to me such a rare witty conceit that I laughed till May, frowning and looking anxious, bade me stop. Then I said that I would get up; but she put her hand on mine and said, "Look, laddie, there'll need to be some days afore that."

And indeed she was right, for my arm was wasted to the flat bone.

"My boy," she said, and I loved to hear her so speak, "thou looks but ill fit to climb the Wolf's Slock this nicht."

Then I asked her of the Lady Grizel and how she did, and she told me that she sent over every day to see how the lad was, and to know when they were coming back, for that the time was long at the Earlstoun without both Jen and May, and with only a common puggy and a common parrot to keep her company. The Lady Grizel was an impolite old woman, I thought.

Also she told me that Mossdale, being on the verge of the outlaw country, was no longer safe; for it was known to the Macatericks that Sammle Tamson had been with me on the links of the Cooran that day, and the gypsies had vowed vengeance against him. So getting the loan of two cars from Clachanpluck, Sammle and Eppie had brought all their belongings to the Earlstoun. Sammle was now with the Maxwells, her brothers, busy making plans for vengeance on the catherans of the hills.

"And Eppie cam' here to nurse you," she said, "but I have done most of it myself, since they let me come," she said, with some little pride that was pretty to see.

All this was news to me, and it took me some time to understand that so much should come to pass in so short a time.

The next day May and Jean went back to Earlstoun, with the promise that Sammle Tamson should bring her (meaning May) over to see me one day in each week till I should be able to go to Earlstoun myself.

Then came Sammle himself to transport the chattels of May and Jen, and with him Kennedy Maxwell, who had a less serious face than the others.

Then I arranged with Sammle Tamson what had been in my mind, that he should come to the Rathan with all his goods, and that the lodge that was by the stable should be his whenever it liked him to go into it; but in the meantime (at least, till the bride that was coming should arrive), Eppie and he were to remain in the house of Rathan itself and look after both me and it. And it pleased me much to have a man of my own.

"To think that you and our May have made it up!" said Kennedy; "that beats a'."

I told him tartly that it beat him at any rate, with his night-hawk traikings and trokings with a dozen hizzies—whereat, rather pleased than rebuked, he did but laugh.

And so it was settled. I was to give Samuel all that he required of bread and meat and ale, four rigs of potatoes, half an acre of barley and an acre of oats, also twelve pounds sterling in the year for the services of himself and of his wife. All which I think very liberal, considering that many a hind is glad to hire himself for two pound and his meat. But I love that in a home which Mary and I looked forward to with so much content, the others who dwell there shall also be content. Besides, with my father's savings I could well afford it.

Kennedy Maxwell told me that the hill folk, meaning the outlaw gypsies, were all agog to revenge the retaking of May and the discovery of their villainy. He told me also that near to a hundred of stout and brave lads had sworn to go in the back end of the year, and root them out of their fastnesses with a great destruction. These men came from all the parishes, from Minnigaff to Rerrick, and from Carsphairn to the edge of Kells. Samuel Tamson had been up raising the men of the head end of the Stewartry, and there were many, even to the Doon Water and the Shalloch-on-Minnoch, sturdy men of Carrick, who would gladly join, having been sore harried by the outlaws in time past.

So the days went by and the weeks brought the harvest, and the reaping of the scanty fields that I had taken so small an interest in. Yet the Maxwells came with others of their company and did it for me; and I wished to divide fair with them, because I needed not so great a store of corn, while they, who were re-stocking their farm, sorely required it. For I had no beasts to speak of save only sheep; and all the corn I had, had been wrought by horse hired from the farmers about, which gave me the less trouble, though also of necessity the less profit. But indeed I cared not much, save that I might grow what was needed for the house of Rathan, having money to get what I wanted in funds and property in the hands of Mr. Erskine, that well-kenned and most honest lawyer in Dumfries.

But all the same I purposed to keep horse in future years, and drain and plough, which should be both for the improvement of Rathan and for its greater usefulness. Also there came into my head a plan whereby the sea being shut out of the narrow gulf where it ran, there might be gained to my estate a great extent of fertile land. All which I have since done, and I mention these things to show that the days of enforced idleness were very fruitful in thoughts for the future.

Also, as I said, I had heart-searchings about my own state of soul, concerning which I perceived that I had thought too little. I intended to go and open my mind to Mr. Macmillan of Balmaghie, who was a leading man among the Societies and a man of great holiness and fearlessness. This also in time I did, becoming a member in good standing, but not till all this brulzie was ended and peace had once more come where now there was only danger and the tuck of drum.

Then, when I could sit up, Silver Sand came and told me tales, teaching me all the lore of the woods, and strange old sayings among the gypsies that made me wonder where he had learned them; but that he seemed to be well learned in everything. He had set up his tent again, and, though I paid him all his tale of guineas, he went back to his trade of selling the scythe sand, all made out of the hardest white grit of the granite where it is ground down and sifted by the rain and the wearing of the rocks on the edges of the lochs in the granite districts.

Three kinds of sand he brought me to see, but not being a scytheman I could not tell the difference. Then, very willingly, Silver Sand instructed me.

"This," he said, running his hand through the fine, white, sandlike meal that he had in one bag, "is the sand which I gather from the edge of the little Loch of Skerrow near to Mossdale that Sammle Tamson kens so weel. This is the commonest kind, yet good for coarse work, such as mowing ordinary grass, or the weeds and girse about a field's edges. This sort also is the cheapest; but this," he said, showing me another very fine sand, "is the sand from Loch Valley, which, when last we passed, I had not time to show you." (It was not indeed likely.) "It is fine, and sticks smoothly on the strake, and is used for corn on the braes, and for short hay that is easy won.

"But this," he said, taking up a smaller bag as if it had been the fine gold, "is the silver sand from Loch Enoch itself. It is the best, the keenest, and lies closest to the blade of the scythe. It is used for the mowing of meadow hay, which is hard to win, because it has to be cut about the Lammas time, when the floods come. Then it is sore work to mow for a long summer's day, and a great swing of the scythe is needed. At that time of year you can hear the 'strake, strake' of the mower in the shade as he puts an edge on his tool, and nothing else is used for this purpose through all Galloway, Carrick, and the Upper Ward of Lanerickshire than the Loch Enoch sand—that is, when they can get it."

He passed it over to me in a canvas bag. It was certainly very beautiful, and I let it trickle through my fingers.

"But how did you get this, Silver Sand?" I said; "have you been back again since——"

"No," he said; "but I have them that can gang for me."

The sand ran through my fingers, clean and dry, till they encountered something like a coin. I brought it out on my palm. It looked very like a token that the ministers give to those who are judged fit to come to the Communion table. But there was no text on it; only some markings which it was beyond me to make anything of. Yet Silver Sand snatched it from me with great instancy, and I fancied that I saw him change colour as he did so.

"God forgive me! How could I have missed it?" he said. Then, having looked at it, he muttered, "So soon!" and was silent.

Now but that Silver Sand had approven himself well, and that I knew him for trusty to the heart's core, I had certainly suspected him of double dealing. Yet he was to me utterly beyond reproach and above suspicion. It was simply not possible that he could be playing "booty," with a foot in either camp. But most certainly he was a man with more secrets of his own, and dangerous ones to boot, than I had cared to carry about without a steel jacket over.

Soon after this he walked away over in the direction of Earlstoun, taking the boat with him to that White Horse Bay which lay nearest to the house in which May dwelt.

When I was well enough to sit again at the high window of my room, for all the windows in Rathan were high, the prospect glass was a great comfort to me. I could see the camp of Silver Sand, with grey Quharrie on guard by the stream, and the flash of the white-peeled *sauch* wand against the black opening of the tent. That was part of Silver Sand's magic. Indeed I often told him that he would be burned for a wizard yet, and that (as they did to Major Weir) they would cast in Quharrie and the peeled wand to keep him company.

"Then there's some o' them will get sair bitten, whatever!" was all his answer.

Yet true it is that when he wanted water to feed the cattle on several parts of Rathan in after-days, it was with this very peeled wand that Silver Sand found the spring, but whether by foreknowledge or some science that was hid from the rest of us, I make not bold to say, for indeed I know not.

Then beyond, over the tide which I watched come and go twice a day, I could see the onstead of Craigdarroch, with the Maxwells busy at their thatching, or working in the fields with their guns standing cocked at the end of the rig, which was a strange thing to see in Scotland at that time of the day.

But what caused me to look oftenest, and that till my eye ached and I had to take it from the eye-piece, was the topmost turret of Earlstoun, and a little bit of the terrace of the Italian garden at the corner beneath, where there was a smooth piece of turf on which May Maxwell often walked and (having so arranged with me) waved a white handkerchief to me for comfort.

CHAPTER XXXVI

THE BARRING OF THE DOOR

So it was no long season before I waxed as strong as ever, and could take my way over to Earlstoun to see my lass. Eppie and Samuel remained in the house, and Samuel occupied much of his time in going over to Craigdarroch to hear the latest plans for the great raid that the Maxwells were to make as soon as the winter frosts came to bind the upland waters; for it was no use to go thither when the bogs and lochs were unfrozen. Boats could not be dragged up to the summits of these wild mountains, and even if the Lowlanders came in force and defeated the outlaws, they would all escape among the haggs, because of their knowledge of the ground.

Now this had been a wild year in Galloway, for His Majesty King George, having so recently come to the throne, many of the evilly disposed seized the occasion to plunder their neighbours. Agnew of Lochnaw took out letters from the Privy Council, and, as the warrant runs, "bought commission of justiciary to pursue and slay the red-handed clans of gypsies and broken men, living in the fastnesses of Carrick and Galloway, who do continually plunder, slay, and put in fear His Majesty's lieges." These clans were the Millers, Baillies, Macatericks, and Marshalls—the Faas not being nominated in the warrandice.

But of this there was no outcome. Agnew stayed in Lochnaw, along with his warrant of justiciary, and the plundering of the Lowland parishes and the terrorism of the upper districts went on as before.

Said William Maxwell of Craigdarroch, when he heard of it, "Lochnaw may scart his fit, his act is but a *flaf* o' wind. Them that's ower far awa' to bear the brunt, are ower far awa' to bring the remead."

By that he meant that Agnew, the King's Sheriff, was too distant to be attacked, and therefore did not feel the need of action. But the Maxwells were not the men to let their burnt rooftree, their lifted cattle, and the splashed red on the white hairs of their father lie unavenged. Yet their scouts, sprinkled here and there on the edges of the wild lands, brought news of the extraordinary activity and boldness of the outlaws—these "wolves and limmers," as in the acts of Council they were denominated.

In these secret councils of the Maxwells my serving-man, Samuel Tamson, was of course deep, having in the business a greater living stake than most. Yet it was through Silver Sand, who took no part in this battle of preparations, that Eppie heard that so far all was well with Marion. The silence of Silver Sand in all this din of war was remarkable. He abode generally very quietly on the lands of Rathan, making only short journeys to sell his sand through the other parishes that lay on the south of the disturbed country. Notwithstanding, it was ever by his means that we heard of the acts of stouthrief and spulzie with which the "wolves of the hills" were charged.

But soon after my recovery a notable day arrived. I mind it like yesterday, nor is it likely that I shall ever forget it.

It was the plashing wet evening of a September day, towards six of the clock, when Silver Sand rode up to the House of Rathan. He came in and shook the raindrops from his coat, standing and warming himself silently with his back to the fire in the hall, for the evening was cold and a fire grateful. The time of the summer fruits was past, and the day of storms was approaching. It had been to me a year of years, in spite of all the pain and the difficulty, for it had brought me a great and continual joy; and, more than all, the hope of May coming to the House of Rathan before the new year, was like sunshine in the gathering night.

Silver Sand stood and looked at me awhile without speaking.

At last he said, "Ye had better hie yersel' awa' ower by to the House of Earlstoun. It's like ye'll be needed there afore the mornin.'

Then I asked him why. But he gave me no answer, saying that he and Eppie were quite sufficient to keep the House of Rathan against all comers.

"But," he added, "there will be no comers here, so tak' your musket and pistolets an' gang your ways. Them that bearded the lion can fecht wi' Grimalkin."

But this last I could not understand. So in some fear I took my arms and the boat, and went over in the direction of Craigdarroch. There were no cattle about it, nor any sign of habitation; but some one whistled to me as I went by in such a way that I knew David Maxwell to be on watch there. So I kept on, hearing nothing but this single whistle coming out of the scattered buildings of the onstead, the new thatch of which shone yellow through the gloaming.

The House of Earlstoun had erstwhile been a baron's castle with a high wall around it and a centre keep; but within the outer wall there were many buildings of stone and lime, roofed with red tiles, which had been built in more settled times, so that now there was only the one great open space in the courtyard, in front of the gate. That gate used in ancient days to be shut nightly, but had not been so for many years; and now it stood open, a mass of useless iron, which the Lady Grizel had often threatened to sell for old metal if the smith would give her sixpence for it to make plough coulters out of.

Lady Grizel had the name of being very rich, yet, though she lived very plainly, and went about the house like one of her own servants, listening to all the clash of the country from Jen and the coachman-butler, she never got the name of a miser. On the contrary, rather the credit of being "juist as free an' hamely as ony plain body." But her father's gold plate (which he had got from Charles the Second for his services to the cause of ridding the country of Whigs) was a favourite theme of conversation over all Galloway, and the House of Earlstoun, having never been broken, was ever counted one of the richest in the countryside.

To me it was the richer because that my lass was there. As I went towards the dark and silent house I looked up at the windows for her but saw no one. There was not a gleam of light about the whole great hulk of the tower. This made me more nervous, lest I had come too late. So I knocked, with some inward quaking, at the door, and one from within asked me who I was, and what I did. When I told there was a noise of voices consulting, and I got my pistols ready in my hands, while my gun swung at my back. For, indeed, I knew not what might have happened.

But I heard the voice of my beloved bidding them open the door, for that it was indeed I, and she could not be mistaken.

So presently, with many creakings and noises of chains and bolts, very rusty, the door swung a little way, and my sweet love's hand came without to draw me quickly in. Then the door went to with a clang, and the bolts were made fast and a great barracado set up again at the back of it.

I was a little bewildered coming out of the windless silence of the night into the bustle of so many men, for I soon saw that the House of Earlstoun was held by no fewer than thirty stout fellows, every one of whom owned William Maxwell for his captain. Yet I could not perceive the cause nor the need of such warlike preparations.

But May took me through many passages till we came to the keep; then up a narrow winding stair, which was so dark that it made it difficult for us to ascend (where only a moment we lagged as lovers use), and so up into a well-lighted room wherein there was a fire, but of which the windows were all barred and bolted and the curtains closely drawn.

Here was the Lady Grizel, sitting with her feet in a great pair of slippers, and toasting them before the fire. Jen Geddes was also here, and May went and sat down by the ingle cheek with a stocking she was knitting.

"Ye are welcome, Patrick. This is an unco-like ploy. Heard ye ever the like o' it?" said Lady Grizel, after I had saluted her.

I answered that I had heard nothing of the purpose of our coming together, save that Silver Sand had sent me, telling me that I should be of use.

"Silver Sand?" said she. "What's Johnny—ah—hum—ah—hum——"

Here she suddenly stopped, and remained a long while in a muse.

"I suppose it's the pairings o' gentrice that's aboot the craitur that gars him to do it, but it's a strange-like thing to stand again yin's ain flesh and blood."

Concerning which Delphic utterance I knew better than to attempt any question.

"Who are here?" I said. "And what can I do, Lady Grizel?"

"There's a' the Maxwell clan here, besides Taits o' the Torr, Maclellans o' Colin, Lennoxes o' Millhoose, Cairnses frae Hardhills, lads frae Balmaghie, Sproats, and Charterses—siccan a crew to eat—but a' men o' mettle, wi' some judgment in guiding a Queen Anne musket half fu' o' slugs."

"And what is all the gathering for?" I asked.

"Jen!" said Lady Grizel.

"Aye, mem," says Jen, who was making a shift for herself and had a pin in her mouth.

"What for are ye speakin' sae mim? Tell Paitrick aboot your lad that cam' to see you this afternoon."

"Bide a wee," says Janet.

Then she carefully stuck pins all over her seam, looking critically at it as she did so, and all of us waited on her time.

"Ye see," she said at last, "I had my wark dune, and had my kitchen sooped up. Then I was e'en makkin' mysel' tidy——"

"Makkin' yoursel' spruce for the lads, Jen," said her ladyship, swaying in her chair and laughing till the floor shook. She ever laughed at but little.

"An' what for no?" said Jen.

"He may come yet, Jen," said her mistress; "ye haena waited lang yet—only forty year to my knowledge!"

"Hoot, I haena lost hope yet, ony mair nor yer leddyship," said Jen, very much unabashed.

"Weel, as I was sayin', I had juist pitten on my kep an' was tyin' the strings whan up cam' a loon to the kitchen door. He had a tarry look aboot him that made me ken him for a sailor.

"'Guid-day to ye, mistress! D'ye want ony sea coal?' says he.

"Noo 'sea coal' has but yae meanin' in Gallowa', an' it's the coal that warms ye in the inside. So I gaed up the stair to see the mistress, for I kenned na but what she micht want a drappie, pitten ower the dyke as the Freetraders gaed by afore the mornie-mornin'.

"Whan I cam' doon again, I took the ither stair that enters by the aumrie.

"My bauchles made nae noise. I juist lookit ben, an' what was my braw lad at but tryin' a' the bars o' the wundows and keekin' in at the spences. He had a fitrule in his hand as weel, but what he was measurin' is mair than I can tell.

"So I gaed back a kennin', an' gied a bit hoast i' my throat and syne cam ben.

"My man was sittin' on a chair by the kitchen table as mim as pussy bawdrons when she has half a pund o' fresh butter in her wame.

"'Ye hae a gran' view,' he says, lookin' oot o' the window, as though he hadna stirred.

"'It's a fine nicht for sowens,' says I. 'Your back gaun doon the loaning wad be a far finer view. Tramp, my lad, I want nae spies and keek-roon-corners in my hoose!"

"Sae he gaed his ways. But afore he gaed he gied me a black look an' a black word.

"'I'll be seein' you again,' says he.

"'Verra like,' says I. 'I gang to a' the hangings. Ye're a braw lad, but ye'll dance the dance withoot steps some mornin' yet—and a bonny tassel at the tail o' a tow ye'll mak'!'

"Then he tell'd me whaur to gang for a witch.

"'Na,' says I, 'there I'll no gang, gin it were only to keep oot o' your gait.'

"Then in cam' Silver Sand wi' a tale o' raid, murder, an' stouthrief, an' in a wee the Maxwells cam' here wi' a' their band, an' I had my leddy's orders to let them in. That's a' I ken, save and except that we are just three puir women that's to be murdered."

There was silence after Jen's tale, and May set me something to eat and drink, the which I swiftly despatched, and went out—for it was not meet that on such a night I should taigle with the women, even though one of them was my own dear May. She came to the door with me, and told me as all women do when their men go out to weir or danger, to be sure to take good care of myself for her sake.

"I wad come wi' you," she said, "an' help, as I did on the Gairy o' Neldricken, but my lady says I'm to bide wi' her in the keep."

So with some little pain but a great eagerness, I bade her for that night farewell.

Then I sought Kennedy Maxwell, who was my chiefest friend among all the brothers of my maid. He was on watch at a window opposite to the great iron gate that stood open. I said I should covet to be near him through what was coming. So he told me to go and speak to his brother Will, who was the captain and originator of the band. Accordingly I did so, and in a little was at my window within a couple of yards of Kennedy, whence I could see down into the courtyard, and also over the main wall of the castle out upon the fields. I could even see the gravelled walk sweeping away through the trees of the avenue.

It was nearly pit-mirk, for the stars were dimmed and forwandered in the thin cloud overhead. As we stood to our posts, steadily and clearly in a gallery behind a clock struck the hours.

Once I thought that I heard horses, as though an iron shod had slipped on a stone; but again it might only have been in the stables of Earlstoun, the noise of a horse rising to its feet.

"What think ye they can want?" said I to Kennedy, "It canna be Hector Faa seekin' May again?"

"Hector Faa—my fit!" he said, in a contemptuous whisper; "this is a bigger job than the liftin' o' your jo," he said. "They're after the auld wife's rents an' mails, and maybe they jaloose that my faither's brass kist is here as weel."

I was at once relieved and disappointed to hear that Hector Faa had nothing to do with the raid.

"Mind you there's them in this business," continued Maxwell, "that hauds their heids high. This is nae Macaterick's ploy—though of coorse there'll be baith Macatericks and Marshalls there. But the wale o' the Solway Freetraders will be ridin' through that door afore the mornin', an' you an' me wull eyther be suppin' oor parritch in Earlstoun kitchen or gettin' oor kale het in anither place, according to circumstances an' upbringin'."

"What set them on her?" said I, for the Lady of Earlstoun had always been well thought of as one of the old stock, and never forward in setting on the dogs of justice.

"Guid kens," said Kennedy, "mostly greed an' ill bluid. Forbye they hae a pick at us, an' they ken she has gi'en shelter to May. So they think, nae doot, that she is airt an' pairt wi' us."

"I kenned brawly how it wad be," continued Kennedy, in a discontented tone. "Oor Wull is aye sae fond o' keepin' within the law, an' he craved permits frae Sir Andrew Agnew to pursue an' mak' an end o' the outlaws o' the hill country. So of course he got it for the askin', an' thank ye kindly—for the Government o' King George has aneuch to do in the north no to be pleased to get ony jobs like this aff its hand. But the warrant was posted in Edinburgh, an' as soon as word o't cam' to Carrick an' Gallowa', I kenned they wad be a' doon on us, bizzin' like a bees' bike."

CHAPTER XXXVII

THE SILVER WHISTLE BLOWS

"Guid guide us! D'ye hear that?" said Kennedy.

A clear jingling came over the moor.

"That's a horse beast shakin' its bridle reins," said I.

Indeed I cannot say that I liked the business at all. It was eery to sit by the unglazed narrow window with one's ears on the strain, and every bird that cried on the moors making the heart jump. A corncrake among the long grass cried "Crake—crake!" But there was something in the tone of it which told me that the bird wore a buff jacket and steel cap, or I was the more mistaken. An owl flew by with a soft waft of the wing, and if I had not seen it, I should not have believed in the hoot it gave from the centre tower where Neil Cochrane stood on guard. He was an Ayrshireman, and I heard him say, "Shoo, you beast!" below his breath.

My nerves were tugging at my arms, and had a cat crossed the courtyard I declare that I should have loosed off my musket at it. It was but little that I could see from my window, save the blackness of the courtyard, and the glimmering grey space of the great open doorway where, if anywhere, danger would come.

Suddenly something black, like a four-footed beast, appeared in that grey space. I had my gun at my shoulder to fire, but a familiar aspect took me, and I dropped it. I recognised the spread of the hind legs. It was Quharrie, and I am sure it was his master that stole like a shadow across the grass plot behind him.

Whither could he be going? Was he warning the enemy or acting as our advanced guard? The questions which had tormented me ever since Silver Sand took our matters in hand came up again with new and overwhelming force.

Was it still possible that Silver Sand was playing booty? Could it be that he was, through all his twistings and secrecies, working for the interests of our cruel and revengeful enemies?

I had indeed good cause to think so, but then again I simply could not believe it. Once and again Silver Sand had held the whole of us in his power. Had he wished to destroy us on this present occasion, all that he needed to do was simply to lie in his camp and the stroke had inevitably fallen. Yet he had saved us. But why did he for ever hang about the skirts of the fray? How was it that whenever it came to a tulzie and the swords were sharpened for war, Silver Sand disappeared and was no more to be found, reappearing only to cover the retreat of the foe? I found no answer, and, indeed, none was possible for me to find at that time. That matter was far beyond me at the moment, depending on something which I never suspected. So I need not have troubled myself that night by the open wicket of the tower of Earlstoun as to the solving of the problem.

Yet I knew that the enemy could not be far off, for Silver Sand was ever a stormy petrel of danger. But the night shut down again, and I grew deadly weary of inaction. I heard Kennedy softly cursing the universe, and particularly his brother Will, because he was numb with cold and had been forbidden to smoke or so much as to spit—a dire prohibition to the untamed Galloway man who spits in his sleep, and still more especially in church, regurgitating all through the sermon like Solway tide in the narrows of Rathan.

Outside the corncrake cried as though it were beneath the wall. There was more of the steel cap in the sound than ever. The fellow was near by, under the wall mayhap. Then farther off a heatherbleat, whose note is the clan call of the wolves of Buchan, whinnied as though to it once had been given a soul, now lost without hope, which nevertheless it continued to seek over the breast of the moorland.

Now I had imitated all the moorland sounds and those of the sea fowl for many a day as I lay on the smooth green turf of Rathan, till there was no bird that I could not summon to me, save the snipe (which is called the heatherbleat) alone. So, as a lad will, I practised the cry night and day, till the bird itself would come nearer and fall beside me like a falling star, or (as I thought) a cherub with a broken wing. So proud was I that I never made soup of him, but sent him off, a very astonished bird, to bleat again after his lost soul upon the waste. At this business I thought that I could beat even Silver Sand.

So utter weary did I grow of this time of tension that I put my head out of the window to look about me, thereby inviting a shot had any enemy been near enough; for, indeed, I never put risk against pleasure all the days of me but I chose without hesitation the pleasure. For some long moments I drank in the night air, and it was sweet to my soul. Again the bird whinnied in the air. I looked narrowly for him, for it was yet early for the snipe to be astir, even in the nesting time of the year.

Before I knew it my pride came upon me. With my tongue vibrating upon my palate, and my hand directing my voice upward, I let the weird sound float out three times on the night air. So exactly did I give it, that even I was touched with the pathos of it, and tears stood in my eyes for the lonely bird seeking its soul. That is the way I thought of it, and that is the reason I was able to do it so truly. First there was the sough in the air as the bird mounted, then the quiver of the stoop, and the sharpening *crescendo* as the bird caught itself up again and began to ascend. Never had I done it better. Indeed I did it overwell, and had Will Maxwell known then what he will know now, if any one takes the trouble to read this tale to him, he had come near to taking my life. But even Kennedy at my elbow was deceived, and cursed heartily at the noisy bird, which pleased me more than keeping all the commandments.

But what happened thereafter still more astonished me. The crake I had heard before immediately cried three times beneath the wall with a human sound. The fellow deserved a bullet in him for doing it so poorly. Yet the quality of steel cap in the corncrake's tones gave a jar to the nerves that went down one's back, and I shuddered in spite of the poorness of the performance. Only the heatherbleat which I had answered went on crying. Again I sent my voice up into the dark lift, and again steel cap cried "Crake!" I called once more with drowsy whimpering wing—the true nesting sound, and then all soft and mellow out on the waste, clear as a flute, a silver whistle blew.

Then knew I that at last the fat was in the fire, and I looked carefully to the lock of my piece.

I heard Will Maxwell speak behind me.

"Fire when the gate darkens!" he said, and passed on, a keen soldier with the eye of the Duke of Ramillies himself.

Then suddenly was the Great House of Earlstoun with all its entrances and approaches belted in a ring of noise. Hoofs clattered up the pebbled avenue, feet stirred about the wall, and from the other side, where the office-houses were, came the sound of a forehammer thundering on a gate.

A deep voice cried, "Open!" But from the dark of the wall upon the hither side no voice came back. The hammer again thundered upon the wood somewhere with hideous clamour. Then with a crash the gate gave, and there came a rush of trampling feet.

Horse iron clanged on the hard pavement beneath the gate. A man on a gigantic horse filled up the doorway.

"Hector Faa, as I'm a living soul," said I within me, and so fired. The echo from the little wicket through which I had set my gun deafened me. I did not hear the noise of any other shots, but I am told that as soon as my piece had given the signal, there came from all about the house a dropping and irregular fire, first from our side at the ports and wickets, and then a return from the enemy without.

I saw that the man in the doorway had fallen, and lay across. Then those without the gate drew the horse away, and in the darkness I could see the man trying to crawl clear as though to lie down in the shelter of the wall.

But now, riding two abreast, a crowd of men drave right into the quadrangle of the court from the entrance. They had been astonished by their reception, never dreaming that the tower was garrisoned. Yet they were not the men to be dauntoned. So they rode in. Why they came on horseback, when it had been better generalship to come on foot, I know not; but so they did. For one thing the outlawry men never cared to trust themselves far off their horses while they raided into the low country, and every Lingtowman upon the shore kept a swift beast as the main tool of his craft.

At all events they trampled in upon their garrons till the courtyard was nearly full, and on the strong main door by which I had entered the sledges began to thunder.

"Fire!" cried Will Maxwell at last, and almost as one the guns went off, and men tumbled right and left among the horse' feet.

"Load with lead drops!" cried the voice of Will Maxwell, high up on the tower.

"Let me do it for you as I did in the cave!" said a voice in my ear, softly. It was May Maxwell, standing with shawl over her head in the stone passage.

Without a word I handed her my piece, and the flask and lead lay on the stone sill. Was she not a soldier's daughter—a Maxwell—and about to become the Lady of Rathan?

What right had I to forbid? Her kind had stood behind father and husband for many a day, with the powder-flask in recent years and before that with the dirk. May was good with either, as I had reason to know.

The next volley came irregularly, according as the Maxwells and their men had facilities for loading. The drops scattered wide among the animals, and the whole courtyard became a leaping and plunging hell of maddened horses. They blocked the gate. They fought with each other, biting and kicking. The breaching blows upon the great door ceased. The strikers with the sledge hammer were swept away, likely under the feet of the horse, for I heard confused cries and groans as the turmoil swept beneath me. It was pitiful, but I thought on the beef in the sea-chest, for that broad, cold, white expanse with the two red gashes in it had ridden my memory ever since. So I hardened my heart again and fired (as it were) into the brown, May handing me my piece the while as deftly and calmly as a man-at-arms.

The tide now set through the gate, and though the men had seemed a long time in getting within, the rush of the maddened horses carried them out swiftly, and the courtyard emptied itself like the White Horse Sands when the ebb surges back through the gut of Solway.

But there were three men and a horse that lay still on the red flags to rise no more. One of the men was groaning, but I thanked God that the horse was dead. Dumb brutes in pain I never could bear.

"Gin that wasna the Miller o' Barnboard that I pat a shot intil, my name's no Kennedy Maxwell," said a voice. "The foul thief—he owes us for fower kye!"

CHAPTER XXXVIII

THE SECOND CROWING OF THE RED COCK

May had silently stolen away from my side during the outlaws' retreat, without doubt to carry the news to the Lady Grizel. Again there was a time of waiting, and it was weary, as in the heart of action such times ever are. But the next that we knew of the attack was from the side which I could not see. First there came a thick smoke drifting and eddying round the tower, and then the uncertain flicker of flames, casting red reflections upon the already crimson-splashed courtyard. The ghastly men lay there with black masks across their brows; but one, in the corner beneath us, had in his agony torn off his, and revealed the features of Gil Macaterick, whom I had seen last by the "Murder Hole" on the side of Craig Neldricken.

We were waiting thus when Will Maxwell cried from the top of the battlements for ten men to come from the north side to the high tower wall. I sprang away to get before Kennedy, for I knew that one of us would surely be sent back. Now it seemed that Kennedy was certain to get before me, being able to reach the stair first, so I said, "Kennedy, hae ye your ramrod?" which made him search, whereupon I sprang before him, setting my hand on his breast and giving him a push; and so left him using, as was his custom, the language for which our soldiers were noted in Flanders. For this may I be forgiven.

From the tower top there was a sight worthy to be seen. Men were hurrying about the outhouses with bundles of faggots, and half a dozen of our pickled marksmen were shooting at them as at running deer—mighty pretty to see, as one and another dropped his man.

So here, on the top of the keep, I stood still in wonder, till Will Maxwell came and gave me a great clap on the back, ordering me to cower behind the wall, and do some good shooting for my board and lodging. He kept marching up and down, and must have made a conspicuous mark to those below, for just as I dropped behind the stepped battlements a bullet came "spat" against the wall by which I had been standing, driving most viciously, and fell flattened and frayed at my feet. It was quite warm. Will Maxwell was rolling up one arm with a napkin, using the other hand and his teeth, but looking all the time mighty coolly at the men running round the office-houses with firebrands. The ball had just nicked him and gone its way.

The burning sticks crackled and a great smoor of reek arose, especially from the back of the stables, where we could hear the poor horses plunging. But the enemy now kept carefully under cover, and though we continued shooting at them I could see no manner of good being done.

"This is the second time I hae heard the Red Cock craw," said Will Maxwell; "the third I'll be chanticleer mysel'."

He stood on the tower top looking abroad as calmly as though he had been setting out a day's work at bigging dykes, and then said—

"This will no do, boys; we'll hae to get oot by at them!" So with that he took twenty of us (of whom, alas! I was not one), and set them ten and ten to go out by opposite doors, with orders to run round the back of the byre and stables to slay all who opposed them, while himself and other three active men scattered and put out the fires already kindled.

So this they did, while two of the Maxwells kept the gates.

I was not on the roster of those who were to sally forth from the walls, but nevertheless I slipped out after them from the lesser door on the south side at which the outlaw men had first come. It was great Nick Haining of Dalsleuth who was leading our sally, and the men scoured away to the corner of the barn, dropping on their knees to take aim when they rounded it—no doubt raking the enemy sheltering there with a severe cross fire, for at that moment Will Maxwell's party began to shoot from the corner by the carriage house. I did not trouble my head with either party, having no arms with me save my pistols, but ran at once to the stables, where I loosened the plunging horses and turned them out, for I could not bear to see the poor beasts burnt and hear their crying. They were driven fairly wild with the noise, the flickering lights of the torches, and the smoke. Being strange to me, they would on no account let me come near them, but almost knocked out my brains against the wall with their flying heels. However, from the ancient corn-crib that stood in the corner and had a good high lid, I swung myself up among the rough joists; and so with my great jockteleg knife I leaned down and cut their halters one by one, scrambling perilously the while among the rafters. Whereat each turned and made for the door, I giving them a sound scud on the hip as they went past for the peck of trouble they had cost me. So in a trice the stable was emptied and I went on to see after the cows.

The smoor of reek was thicker in the byre, but luckily all the cows were out and only one little late-dropped calf was in its stall, bleating most piteously. It also I loosed and turned to the door. But no sooner had I done so than I saw our men, with Will Maxwell at the head of them, drive like stour across the yard and in at the open gate, which clashed in the face of the crowd of men that hung upon their tails. It was so quickly done that I could not see well, and in the uncertain light of coming dawn and the flickering of the dying fires I could not clearly make out their numbers. But it seemed to me that there were only eight of them. Several, therefore, must be dead or taken.

As I thought upon my position it seemed to me exceedingly likely that there might be still more missing at roll-call, and that one of them would be myself.

The men who had rushed after Will Maxwell's small band to the sally port turned as quickly and ran back whence they came; for a gun or two cracked from the walls, and a man stumbled and came down on his hands and knees, crawling away painfully on all fours. For me, I lay a long time stretched out on a beam in the byre, and as the beam was untrimmed and of rough tree, it galled me exceedingly. I thought every moment that I must drop for very pain, half of me on either side of the wretched contrivance. I forgot that byre joists are not meant for places of concealment.

Suddenly there was a noise without. A man came and looked every way about the byre, standing fair in the doorway. I could easily have shot him from where I lay, for I saw the whites of his eyes. He walked stealthily, and the dancing lights without glinted on the blade of the long knife which he carried. He glided within with a bowing slouch that was most unwholesome to see. These things I did not distaste so greatly, but I hated the red gleam of the fired stack which shone in the man's eyes through a narrow wicket of the byre as he looked about. A man has been hanged only for showing a face like that in broad day; but in the dark of a cowshed, and with the whites of his eyes flickering red, and his upper lip pulled high over his gleaming teeth, I thought it had been the devil himself looking for me. I think that if Hector Faa had come into the byre just then I should have fallen upon his neck.

There came again the tread of a light foot at the door, and my gentleman of the red eyes leapt swiftly under me with his knife point down, and sprang into the darkness of the hay-mow at the end of the byre. Then there was stillness. But what a stillness! My heart beat against the beam like a hammer of wood. I listened till I could hear the spiders spinning their webs. I heard the mice creep, and the slaters and little beasties running among the thatch. I almost heard my own flesh crawl on my bones—as indeed I well might, for I think it must nearly have got down by itself, leaving my skeleton hanging there on the joist.

How long this suspense might have continued I cannot tell, for the light noise at the door went on. Something bellowed outside, but weakly; and I could hear my gentleman of the eyes and teeth quake among the hay.

At last the grey oblong of the door was filled up with a living shape.

"Patrick!" said a voice I well knew, in a whisper. Gracious Providence above be merciful! *It was May Maxwell!*

With a quick snarl like a wild beast, the creeping rascal sprang from the hay-mow at the end of the barn. As he sped underneath me I could see his knife gleam when he turned the blade upwards to strike. But he never reached the door, for one of my pistols went off in my hand, more by instinct than of intention. He staggered a moment, and then fell forward, all standing as he was, and so lay, spread abroad on his face in the gutter of the byre. His knife flew ringing to May Maxwell's feet. Down I leapt, and taking her right hand with my left as she stood amazed, and with my undischarged pistol in the other, we ran to the little postern door swift as ghosts and hammered thereon.

The keeper of it was no doubt at his wicket, for it was some moments before we were spied and could make them understand who was without. Inside I heard Jen raging like one possessed for some man to come and help her to turn the key. It had been jammed with a bar to keep any from turning it with nippers from the outside. For the keyholes at the Great House of Earlstoun one might put his fist into, and one key was a back-burden for a sturdy lad.

It was only a moment or two that we stood there in all, but it seemed to us an eternity. For even as we waited, quaking, for the opening of the door, certain men ran in front of the byre to find what the shot was, and as the first man crossed the threshold he cried aloud flinging up his hands. Then one turned and observed us at the

postern, for he levelled his piece at us. I saw the straight gleam of
the gun barrel drop to a black dot, and with all my force I thrust May
behind me. A horrid burning pain in my leg and a jerk to every nerve
and muscle that threw me back, told me that I was hit somewhere. I
never heard any report at all, but I knew that May had caught me and
dragged me within even as the door opened.

Jen was there with a candle, and with all haste they ripped away
my stocking and saw the wound. It was a mere nothing. A shot had
gone clean through the fleshy part of my calf, happily without
injuring either bone or great muscle.

The wound was not serious, as even May saw. So they washed
it and bound it up, and I insisted on going back to my wicket with
my gun again.

But the great raid was over. The Red Cock would crow no
more. The day was dawning, and the outlaws and their friends drew
themselves away like the grey night-wolves that they were. But as
May and I looked down we saw a strange thing. Each dead man
seemed to rise of his own accord and crawl backward towards the
gate. We remained stiff with terror, rooted to the spot with fear, and
in a little nothing remained in the courtyard but the red splashes and
the broad, shallow pools of blood. How they managed it I know not,
but probably, under the cover of a cloud, they sent some of their
smaller and more dextrous thieves to carry off the dead for fear of
discovery. These, getting beneath, may have glided off with the
body, which in the darkness was at once a protective shield and a
terror to the onlooker. However it be, I know that not a shot was
fired. For me, I would as soon have fired at the corpse at a funeral as
at these dead men come to life again, who went crawling off, trailing
their blood behind them on the slippery flags of the courtyard.

The silver whistle blew time and again, farther and farther
away. Then the morning came and the sun rose. There was a great
silence about the uncanny house till we heard the cocks crowing
upon the midden-stead at the byre end. It was passing strange that
they had slept safely through all the clamour of the Red Cock
crowing. To these answered the cocks of Craigdarroch in distant
whoopings, and from the Rathan Isle methought I heard my own
noble rooster crowing tinily and airily, like a cock in fairyland when
the bells are ringing for the little folk to come home.

Then we went out in a body to see what we could find.

In the courtyard there were only the stiffening pools of blood,
scarlet splashes blackening rapidly to crimson and puce—

unwholesome and horrible. The marks of the forehammers were on the spiked and plated doors all about the handles and keyholes. The windows in the inner dwellings were all broken with bullets, the sashes being splintered. On the roof the flagstaff had been hit and hung by a shaving in a very sad and melancholy manner. The dead horse in the corner, with its eyes wide open, lay on its side. It was well caparisoned, and the mounting of the harness was of silver, both plain and good but wholly without crest or motto.

"That's no hill-country horse!" said Will Maxwell.

"I think I hae seen the like aboot Barnboard," said Kennedy, lifting up the head; "an' I'm thinkin' that gin we opened the beast's wame we wad find some o' oor ain meal."

And true it is that the Miller of Barnboard was never more seen on the countryside—neither at kirk or market, holy fair or cock-fighting.

On the threshold of the byre door lay the knife of the man with the teeth, which I secured and still have on the wall above me as I write here at Rathan. My wife took it down from over the mantelpiece and put it in the aumrie of the spence where she never goes; but I found it and brought it back again. That is the difference between her and me. I had almost said between men and women, but that might not be wholly true. For she likes not to think on these old dangerous black days now when all is peace, and Galloway is once more a sober place to live in. But, contrariwise, I love to think on every old memory, except only on the white beef in the great sea-chest. That scunners me.

CHAPTER XXXIX

THE EARL'S GREAT CHAIR

It was six weeks before I was myself again, though I lay up at the Great House of Earlstoun under the eyes of Jen Geddes and the Lady Grizel. It was wild weather and the winter was setting in earlier than usual, as it ever does when we have a summer season by ordinary good—"two summers in a year," as the folk say.

There was indeed nothing to take me over to the Rathan, for the Dumfries masons and joiners were in, putting such improvements upon it as the age of the house and its ancient construction would allow. Eppie was on their backs all day long (so Silver Sand told me), flyting and raging at them for useless, handless loons. I imagined I could hear her, and thought myself well out of the stour and the noise, especially as May Maxwell with her own hands bandaged and bathed my leg each day. She had got back much of her gay spirits, and it was an entirely pleasant thing to have her look in upon me with a smile and a bright word as she went up and down the stairs with a duster or such like in her hand.

Then I would call to her to come to me for a moment. Whereupon it was her custom if it were morning and she had her house business to do, to tiptoe round and kiss the top of my crown where the parting of the hair is. Now as I have little parting but only a wiry wisp of bristles, any one may judge if this mode of kissing is not a mightily unsatisfying thing. But it was no use to complain. There I sat in a great black oak armchair, which was not a whit the more comfortable because of the fact (of which Lady Grizel and Gib Gowdie reminded me twice a day) that three Earls had died in it. It was a monstrously cumbersome article of furniture, and there was no mode of getting round to the back of it which I could compass with my leg on a stool; so that May Mischief was kissing her hand to me at the door before ever I could move, and saying in a tantalising way, as she imitated my tones, "Wasna it nice?"

The wretch!

But it was not always so, for I played fox several times, pretending to be in pain, which with one harder-hearted than May was a game which would soon have spoiled itself. But she never quite knew whether I might not be suffering in earnest, and so (perhaps desiring a little to yield) ventured at long and last within reach. Whereupon she retired for a time and a time and half a time into the depths of the Earl's chair.

"There's a difference in folk," she once said, merrily. "Jen says that three Earls hae sat here; but I'm thinkin' gin twa o' them sat thegither at yince in it, they had hardly agreed so weel as we."

Which made us agree yet more and better.

So I abode in the snug shelter of the great house, and in the forenights Kennedy Maxwell would slip over and tell me tales of how the great raid on the outlaws was progressing. He told of mighty doings. There were preparations being made on the skirts of the Kells. Bands of men from Minnigaff and the edge of the Shire were to be led by one of the MacKies of Glencaird. They were all to move as soon as the hard weather set it, for the only time to hunt the broken men out of their fastnesses was in the days of a black frost and in the bright time of the moon.

Now it was into November before I could get out at all, and I was still a little lame in the middle of the month. Yet by the first week in December I could run with any of them up the Rathan Hill. However, I still stayed on in the great house by the command of Lady Grizel, who now openly assured us of her intention of leaving her whole estate to May Maxwell and her heirs for ever.

"So it will depend on how you behave yoursel', Patrick my man, whether you an' yours gets ony benefit. Men are no to lippin to, an' I'll get Rab MacMonnies the lawyer to fettle it doon sae that gin ye are no a guid wean, May can set ye to the door wi' a bare 'Guid-e'en to ye!' That's the lilt o't, May, my lass."

But May, being of Scots bluid and far from reckless, said to this no word of bad or good.

Whereupon the old lady would say, "Ye're a' alike, you women, afore ye get marriet; your ain lad is aye 'the wee white hen that never lays away'; but after—my certes, ye never quat dabbin' at his kame."

But for all Lady Grizel's kindness I do not think that either May or I thought anything would come out of her good will and even her promises. For me, I have never been desirous of great possessions, and the old house at Rathan has quite contented me, and to this day I hold that there is no place in the world like it. For I have the warm feeling for the soil which nurtured and upheld me in my youth very close round my heart. And May thinks so too.

But during these weeks there was ever a shade on May's brow, and I knew what was causing it. She was acquainted with the preparations for the great raid on the den of the Wolves; and she, that was the daughter of Richard Maxwell, did not dare to say a word to dissuade me from taking part in it. Yet I felt that she was anxious for me. I knew it from the way that she would hang on the words of Kennedy when he came in the evening and we all sat by the fire.

On the other hand Kennedy and the rest of the Maxwells anticipated this raid as the great pleasure and excitement of their lives. They had taken out a Privy Council warranty for the extirpation of the outlaws as one might take out a license to shoot game in these present peaceful times, and they cleaned their guns joyously and jested upon probable sport. Yet with William Maxwell and some of the elder hands there was a deep and even a kind of perverted religious earnestness in the ploy. They had black scores of death and burning against the outlaws. They had a deeper, keener, even a religious hatred also, for the Faas and the Marshalls had been recruited by the remnants of the wild Highland Host that ravaged the Lowlands a generation before, carrying away all that it could carry and burning whatever would not lift. It was always believed that in the gypsies' country there were hoards of the rich plunder of halls and the poor heirlooms of cots, reft away in the terrible years that preceded the unforgotten and unforgiven "Killing Time."

There was once a minister in Balmaghie who used to add a rider to the prayer, "Forgive us our trespasses as we forgive them that trespass against us," by saying as often as he used this petition, "But for Thy glory tak' the Laird o' Lag an' a' the lave o' the Malignants in Thine ain hand, lest they repent and it be forgiven them!"

So the great raid was in train by the 17th of December. From all sides the men of the Lowland parishes were to close in upon the outlaw country. There was mustering and accoutring along the Solway, and there was no doubt that the Marshalls, Millers, Macatericks, and all the hideous crew that gathered about them knew what was in store for them, for the most part of their women were sent into Ayrshire, and out along the Freetrade routes to Edinburgh and Glasgow. Many of these were put in hold by the Sheriffs of Ayr and Lanark as sorners and limmers, and were safe gaoled when the blow fell on the men whose worthy mates they were. Only a few of the most indurated and cruel, like my friend Eggface, remained to bide the brunt of the storm.

CHAPTER XL

THE BREAKING OF THE BARRIER

It was a chill morning in the shortest days when I took my fighting harness on my back, girt my sword by my side, kissed my lass, and swung into stirrup with a sinking heart within me and wet eyes behind me. Right often did I vow that if only I were once safe home again in the old tower of Rathan (from the chimney of whose kitchen I could see the blue reek go up so homely and friendly, yet so far away), I would never wear leather jerkin more, nor yet belt the weary broadsword on again.

Never did soldier more unwillingly ride to battle than I for the first three miles. But when I met with long Samuel Tamson, accoutred with sword and pistol like the best—unmounted, but moving his legs as fast as a horse could trot, I somehow changed my mind. I saw a strange glint in his eye, and I thought of the little Marion whom only I had seen, and only May Maxwell had spoken to, since she was lost on the Silver Flow of Buchan so long ago. I was mustered into Will Maxwell's company, and fell in behind him in the front rank with Kennedy. Three or four young lads, pretty fellows with good horses that were brisk jumpers at fences, went on before as vedettes.

It was a cold, dim, raw day, with a thick yellow haze in the air, and a grim grip of black frost underfoot. The horses' feet fell on the hard road as on a pavement, and sounds carried far. There was a sough of snow in the air. The wind came in little gusts and swirls, flicking the blood into our cheeks as though they had been switched with the ravelled lash of a whip.

I had risen late after a long night's rest, for none knew when we might sleep again, with so much wild work before us; and now, when I was fairly on the road, I found strapped to my saddle-bow, within a soldier's blue military cloak that an Earl had worn, many things good and pleasant, which proved comfortable to a hungry man in a winter campaign.

It was mighty touching to me to think of one of the very last things May said to me through her tears—

"See an' keep your feet dry. There's a pair of socks in your left pistol holster."

And that was as precious to me as many endearments.

We were now riding westward to meet the men of Lower Minnigaff at the bridge of Cree. As we went the air became extraordinarily bitter. The wind indeed dropped as we passed Cassencary, where in the estuary the tide rolled full—a turbid yellowish brown. As we rode clanking into Cree Bridge the small snow began to swirl about us. I believed that we were in for a great fall, and gave my word like a faint heart to turn back, or at least to shelter for the night. But the movements had all been concerted, and to pause meant nothing less than putting off the attack indefinitely. Moreover, Will argued very truly that it was a question whether we should ever be able to get so many men and horses to come together for the same purpose again.

So we went on, and after a little I was not so very sorry, for the thought of having to go through the parting with May (and also the screwing up of my courage) all over again, lay very heavy on my heart, so that I became as eager as any to go through with it at once.

It was arranged that we were to leave our horses at the Lodge of Eschonchan near Loch Trool, where my Lord Galloway had a post, and kept his men at all times of the year—paying, of course, mail to the Marshalls to escape skaith, and in name of protection. Here we would leave a guard and push northward to cast the die once and for all.

We counted upon having the young moon, but it now seemed that a moon we should certainly not have to light us on our way, though she ought to have been in the sky by seven o'clock.

The snow flew thicker but in a curious, uncertain way, as though little breezes were blowing it back from the ground. A flake would fall softly down till it neared the earth, then suddenly reel and swirl, rising again with a tossing motion as when a child blows a feather into the air.

As we went along the pale purple branches of the trees grew fuzzy with rime, which thickened till every tree was a wintry image of itself carved in whitest marble.

In truth I liked not the day, and I liked it ever the worse as we went on, though I had said all that I could say with honour. For the yellow mist packed itself dense and clammy about us as we advanced. It had a wersh, unkindly feeling about it, and as we rose higher up the water of Trool it hung in fleecy waves and drifts against the brows of the hills. But what I liked least was the awesome darkness of the sky. The mist was almost white against it wherever there was a break, yet itself was dark and lowering. A dismal, uncanny light that I cared not to look upon pursued us and just enabled us to see. I cannot say that it cheered us.

The feelings of most of us were expressed by old Rab MacQuhirr who had long been herd on the Merrick and was now our guide.

"Guid save us an' sain us!" said Rab; "I like not this day. This is a de'il's day! Nae day o' God's makkin' was ever like this!"

Which indeed may seem a foolish if not unreverent thing to say, but then had you been there and under the skarrow of that ugsome cloud, maybe a belief in the all-ordering Providence would not have served you quite so well either. It is easy to thole the boots when your neighbour is put to the question.

The Glen of Trool was dark and narrow as we went down into it along the waterside, and the loch itself lay black as night at the bottom of its precipices. It might have been the mouth of the pit of blackness itself. The faintly falling snow had not lain on its surface, which made me wish that I could unbind my father's Dutch ice-runners from the saddle-bow. He had brought them home with him from the Low Countries as curious things for folk to wonder at; and with them I used many a day to disport myself on the White Loch o' the Clonyard, or upon the Orraland mill-dam when I cared not to go so far from home.

I fetched them with me, knowing that when we had to storm the fortress of the isle in Loch Enoch, my life might depend on my speed. Moreover, ice-running was an accomplishment seldom tried in Galloway at that time, and I hoped to come back having gained not a little honour and reputation thereby.

After a long and weary plod up hill and down dale the Lodge of Eschonchan rose before us close by the waterside, a place which the Lords of Galloway had used for a hunting lodge ever since they came to be overlords of that part of the Forest of Buchan—for of old only Cassillis and the Kennedies bore the rule there. It is not a large, but it is a strong-built house—though with hardly any articles of furniture, except bowls and platters of the roughest, because it is not wise to trust aught of value to the gypsies, even under the protection of the payment of mail. So my Lord the Earl keeps not his muniment boxes and treasure chests at the Lodge of Eschonchan by the water of Trool. Here, therefore, we had some refreshment, and rested an hour. Then, leaving a guard with the horses just sufficient to protect them in case of attack, we pressed on with most of the younger men.

Our way lay up the same Gairland Burn by which May, Silver Sand, and I came down in such pain that morning long ago. Yet I think I was heavier of heart to go up it under that gloomy winter sky, for now every step took me farther away from all I loved. I tried to think that it must be for the best, which was no doubt true; but somehow the thought did not affect the state of my courage, which had (as usual) sunk down into the pit of my stomach. It was, in truth, cold comfort.

We marched in close array with skirmishers flung far up the slope to touch any hidden enemy, while the rest came by the narrow path by the waterside, where the burn roared and swirled about the great gray stones.

We were soon deep among the hills, and yet not a shot had been fired at us. Not a dry red bracken had waved. The rime lay close and thick, and the brown heather kept the feet quiet. Only a scabbard rang now and then on a jutting point of granite, or a nail in some brogan screamed stridently against a stone, harsh and slippery with frost. No whaup or peewit cried. Only on a rock high on the Clints of the Nether Hill of Buchan, a black corbie croaked his dismal anticipative song.

It was not cheering, all this, yet I felt some real elevation to think that we were soon to come to grips.

We were just at the corner of the burn where, under a great black face of rock it is hemmed in a deep defile, when our scouts on the hillside set up a great crying, the cause of which we could not at the time understand.

"Come up!" they cried. "The water's broken lowse!"

Our herd guide and I took the hill at once, and so did many who were acquainted with the wild lochs and precipices about us, and with the nature of the wilder men whose lives were forfeit to the law.

Suddenly we heard before and above us a tremendous roaring noise, as though the bowels of creation were gushing out in some great convulsion. The hills gave back the echoes on every side. I found myself climbing the brae with some considerable verve and activity till I was fairly among the higher rocks. So active was I that I ran straightway into the embraces of a hairy savage with matted locks, whose weapon was in his hand—the long dirk of the

Highlander. But he had not expected any one to come at him over a rock in so remarkable a manner. He took my inroad as a dangerous assault, conceiving that I must have men behind me to be so bold, for he instantly threw down his knife and up with his hands in an attitude or supplication.

"Hursel' be a puir Gregor lad, an' no doin' ony harm!" was his statement.

Behind me came our guide, Rab MacQuhirr and Kennedy Maxwell, at sight of whom my captive, taking heart of grace, plunged upwards weaponless among the rocks, and as it was a rough place, with many *yirds,* or hiding-places between the boulders, he was out of sight in a moment. Of which I was glad, for had Will Maxwell come upon him and his dirk, that hour had been the last of "hursel" the puir Gregor lad."

But the MacGregor dirk I set in my belt as a trophy.

The great roaring noise still continued. Indeed the whole of the foregoing since I took the hill passed in a brief tale of seconds. Suddenly we that were up on the side of the Gairy saw a wondrous sight. A great wall of water, glassy black, tinged at the top with brown and crowned with a surging crest of white with many dancing overlapping folds, sped down the glen. Our array was pent in the narrow passage—all those, that is, who had not taken the hill at the first alarm. As the wave came down upon them there was the wildest confusion. Men threw away their guns and took blindly to the hillside, running upward like rabbits that have been feeding in a bottom of old grass. From where we stood the water seemed to travel with great deliberation, but nevertheless not a few of our men were caught in the wash of it and spun downwards like corks in the inrush of the Solway tide.

The black, white-crested wave being passed, the great flood ran red again in a moment, with only a creamy froth over it, and we could hear the boulders grinding and plunging at the bottom of the burn.

Then upon us, scattered as we were in confusion over the brae face, there broke a storm of bullets from behind the rocks higher up the Gairy. It was the first sign of the enemy we had found, and we resented it exceedingly.

A strange sense of the unfairness of the proceeding took hold of me. We had come prepared to give battle and to deliver an assault; but we wanted to do it in our own way and on our own terms. We felt that it was most perfidious (indeed unfair and scoundrelly) thus to scatter us over a great area of ground, and then have at us when we were least prepared.

But Will Maxwell had some of the spirit of a general. Standing on a rock, he sounded his pipe, calling all down from the bare hillside, where each man was a mark for the guns of the outlaws into the closer cover of the burnside, thick sown with boulders. The flood was still running, but was evidently past its strength. The great roaring sped farther and farther down the valley. We gathered off the hill, running like foxes about the stones, and taking advantage of the chance cover as we went. Bullets spatted uncomfortably among the rocks, but the fire of the hill men was not good, and the light was becoming uncertain, so that very few of our men were wounded.

As soon as he had us all collected in the valley, our captain began moving in loose skirmishing formation along the side of the burn towards the loch. The outlaws above us also kept parallel with our march, shots cracked, and on the hillside there was a noise of cheering. But we held on our way, and so far no one was seriously hurt, which showed that the aim of the enemy had been bad. But we knew not if our own were much better.

CHAPTER XLI

A RACE FOR LIFE UPON THE ICE

When we came to the southern side of Loch Valley, whence the Gairland Burn issues, we saw a strange and surprising sight. There was a deep trench, the upper part of which had been cut through recently by the hands of man, for the rubbish lay all about where the spades had been at work. The ends of a weir across the outlet of the loch were yet to be seen jutting into the rushing waters. This had evidently been constructed with considerable care and certainly with immense labour. But now it was cut clean through, and we could see where their sappers had first set their picks; the power of the flood had done the rest. So great had been the force of the water that the passage was clean cut as with a knife down to the bed rock. The deep knoll of sand and jingling stones, which lies like a barrier across the mouth of the loch, had been severed as one cuts sweet-milk cheese, and the black waters were yet pouring out from under the arch of ice that spanned the loch as out of a cave in some frozen Tartarus.

But as we looked over the black and glistering expanse of hollow ice which swept away to our left, bright cracks began to play like forked lightning across its whole surface. The water had been sucked from beneath it, and it held up only by its own weight. The hills echoed the deep-voiced roaring as the cracks and rendings ran across and across. Gradually the play of this flashing and thundering turmoil centred at a point beneath our eyes, and fair in the middle of the loch. An intensely black spot began to yawn there, from which the white, roaring cracks rayed out like the spokes of a wheel from the hub. On the edge of the loch we stood as it were on the rim of a whirlpool, for the ice sloped down from our feet every way into the black centre. Had any one set foot upon the verge of it they had been carried down to the yawning hole, for the entire ice of the loch was giving way as the roof of a great cavern slopes and sways before it falls in.

Then with a crash that shook the ground the ice cave fell in upon the water in a thousand pieces, sending the white foam mixed with dark lumps of ice high into the air, while underneath the broken fragments tumbled and crunched against one another like bergs in a heavy sea (such as I have heard the whalers tell of). Then little by little, groaning and wheezing, the turmoil settled down; and Loch Valley, with its shivered covering of broken ice, went to sleep ten feet beneath its level of the morning.

Hardly elsewhere in Scotland had such a thing been possible; but the outlaws took advantage of the higher barrier of sand and shingle which had so long dammed back the waters of the deep rock-bound lake. It was a true stroke of generalship, and showed us that we had others than ignorant red-handed Marshalls and bloody Macatericks to deal with. It was so well thought on that it did not seem like the rough-and-ready knife-and-bullet method of the common catheran.

And, indeed, nothing more calculated to shake one's nerve could well be conceived. We were glad to draw together our scattered force, but there is no doubt that by this time most wished themselves well out of it. For me, at least, that six-foot breast of black water and the shining whirlpool of rending ice had taken away any desire for revenge.

Nevertheless, as the darkness settled deeper, we drew down to the old sheep *rees* by the Midburn, which are solidly built of great granite stones like a fortress, based upon the unshaken ribs of the hills. There was room for us all here. By nature the place was strongly protected—on the other side by the roaring and dangerous Midburn, and on the other it is fenced in by a morass. Here we hoped to abide in some sort of peace, if little enough comfort, through the long winter night. We had all our plaids wrapped about us; and my friend Kennedy had carried strapped about him, half for the warmth and half for the good things of my Lady Grizel which it contained, the Earl's great military mantle. Both cloak and comforts we had agreed to share together.

But this consummation was not at all what I had expected. My chances of glory were few, and the raid seemed likely to end in disaster. To run uphill and take prisoner a shaggy catheran (who immediately escaped again), to be penned like one of a score of hogs in a granite sheep-ree, were not at all to my mind. But how could I better it?

The outlaws on the hill had given us no farther trouble, and indeed their demonstration against us had been confined to the moment when the rush of the escaping waters of Loch Valley made us give back and scatter.

"The Carrick men should be coming on by now," said Will Maxwell. "Oh, if only we had some one to go up and see what they are doing!"

The old shepherd of the Merrick knew the country best, but he was stiff and old; and, besides, cared little about the matter. About as little cared I, save to burn the Shieling of Craignairny and get that accursed sea-chest out of my dreams. But I think the devil must have tempted me suddenly and successfully, for I called out among them all that I would put on my ice-runners and go. At which they cried admiration and astonishment. Yet I was grieved the next moment and silently called myself a fool for my pains, and that many times over; but my accursed pride would not let me take back the spoken word.

May Maxwell says now that that was the wickedest thing I ever did, because I forgot my plighted word and promise to her—I might have let one of the others go. All which I own is true, but then no one of the others would have offered, and so we had all come home with our fingers in our mouths.

But all the lads of the raid cried out upon me, and said that I was the bravest of the brave, and other things which please a young man. So I took my ice-runners in my hand—which, as I have said, my father had brought from Holland. Kennedy Maxwell and four others, all proper young men with well-grown beards on their faces, whom for this cause I often envied, came to see my safely off, for I proposed first to circle Lord Neldricken on the ice, that I might be sure there were no enemies lurking about it. This I did, not because I thought that the outlaw men would encamp there, but that these young men, especially Colin Screel and Kennedy Maxwell, who had formerly despised me, might see me start off alone into the night. Such a thick-skull was I, and so void of common understanding! For I ever loved to be admired and to be exclaimed upon for doing that from which others held back. And this same quaint kind of cowardice, for I had little real courage, has often carried me through with credit. I am of the faction of the old soldier who said, when complimented on his bravery in battle, "We are all black afraid, only—we do not all show it!"

So I had enough sense to keep my fears to myself at that time. Now it does not matter, for I am a man of middle years, and such is the power of reputation that I cannot do away with this repute myself, so that even this plain confession of weakness will not be believed; which is perhaps, after all, the reason why I make it here. So apt is man at deceiving others—and himself.

But sally forth I did, binding my ice-runners of curved iron to my feet at the little inlet where the Midburn issues—too strong and fierce ever to freeze, save only at the edges where the frost and spray hung in fringes, reaching down cold fingers to clasp the rapid waters.

Away to the left stretched Loch Neldricken, the midmost of the three lochs of that wild high region—Valley, Neldricken and topmost Enoch. I set foot gingerly on the smooth black ice, with hardly even a sprinkling of snow upon it, for the winds had swept away the little feathery fall, and the surface was smooth as glass beneath my feet. Each of the young men shook me silently by the hand. I suppose they thought me at once brave and mad, for I had lost no cattle and had a sweetheart at home to make a bride of. Yet there was I, setting off into the black night in the face of dangers unknown—dangers to which the close-packed well-fenced camp in the sheep-*ree* was as one's own fireside.

I struck out from the edge with great strokes, moving my hands with each sway of my body as my father had taught me. In a moment the four lads sank behind me and I was alone on the black ice; yet I had that feeling of high defiance which all swift motion gives. The ice whirled behind. Following the southern edge, I was between the narrows in a minute. Here a jutting promontory of land—a mere tongue of sand and boulder—cut the loch almost in two. There was a fire kindled on the south shore nearest our camp, and on the opposite side as I sped by I seemed to see two men standing with muskets in their hands; but so dark was it that of this I could not be sure. If they saw me (which with the fire on the shore opposite to them and the passage through which I went not more than twenty yards wide, they could hardly fail to do) they must have thought me the evil one himself, flitting by as it were on the wings of the wind.

I sped away with the irons on my feet, cutting crisply through the thin-sprinkled snow, the immanent mass of the Black Gairy casting a gloomy shadow overhead. An odd flake or two of snow came into my face as I bent low to look sideways up the hill. I went slowly, moving only my body and hardly making a sound, as the night parted before and closed behind me.

It took but little time to make the circuit of the loch and come back to the narrows; but as I passed I put on speed, for I knew that it was dead earnest this time. The watchers would now be on the alert and might very properly bethink themselves that the devil did not use iron runners, but leathery wings like the bat. So I bent low and scudded through the strait with the dying fire on one side and the land closing in to trip me upon the other. I was just in the middle and running my best, when a couple of shots went off, and the bullets tore past behind me screaming like plovers whistling down the wind.

I was so excited with my escape and proud of my daring that I shouted as I flew; but I had better have held my tongue, for a moment after I saw that the force of my impulse was taking me out of the region of sprinkled ice among a low forest of dense green reeds. As swift as thought I turned, but my impetus was too great. I was carried among them, and there, not twenty yards before me, like a hideous black demon's eye looking up at me, lay the unplumbed depths of the Murder Hole, in which for the second time I came nigh to being my own victim. I remembered the tales told of it. It never froze; it was never whitened with snow. With open mouth it lay ever waiting like an insatiable beast for its tribute of human life; it never gave us a body committed to its depths, or broke a murderer's trust.

The thin ice swayed beneath me, but did not crack—which was the worse sign, for it was brittle and weakened by the reeds. The lip of the horrid place seemed to shoot out at me, and the reeds opened to show me the way. I had let myself down on all fours as I came among the rushes; now I laid hold of them as I swept along, and so came to a standstill but a little way from that black verge. Here I hardly dared to move, till, by slow degrees, pulling myself forward and pushing backward, I got once more upon safe ice; then I made directly for the shore, for the Murder Hole was more dreadful to me than a tribe of Faas armed to the teeth.

In a few moments I had unshipped my runners, gained the heather, and was making the best of my way over the Ewe Rig towards the great barrier of Craig Neldricken, behind which Loch Enoch lay. As I went I heard the moor-birds cry—the wild whirl of the whaup and the croak of the raven. Now I knew well that most of these must be the signals of my foes answering one another, because the gypsies can imitate any bird that flies; besides which, the whaup is but seldom seen on these moors in winter and the snipe never. A thought struck me. I set my hands to my mouth in the way that I have already described, and made the whinny of the heatherbleat palpitate across the moor.

Instantly, as on the night of the blowing of the silver whistle, I was answered from either hand; my summons had aroused a whole colony. Only towards Loch Arron, lying straight in front of me, there was not a single sound. So I called again more persistently and, as it were, querulously; and immediately set off running headlong upward in the direction of Loch Arron, which I judged to be my best chance of safety.

More than once I had to crouch among the rocks to let a man run past me, so efficacious and imperative had my second call been. It was a blessing that almost everywhere over all that country there is a capable hiding-place within each half-dozen yards; else had I been ten times a dead man.

I skirted Loch Arron without putting on my ice-runners, because it is little more than a mountain tarn, and I knew that if there were any guards in the direction I was travelling, they would be up at the Nicks of Neldricken, or at the Slock of the Dungeon—the passes which are the usual roads to the tableland of Enoch. Without a moment's hesitation, therefore, I set my feet upon the rugged Clints, hoary with rime and slippery with frost.

Born by the shore of the Solway, with heuchs at my door, and gulls' eggs for my playthings, I was at home wherever there was a chance of holding by my arms. Dark or light did not make any great difference to me, and but that my fingers thrilled with cold as they caught the rocks, I cannot say that I was agitated by the perils of climbing the Clints of Neldricken.

CHAPTER XLII

THE FASTNESSES OF UTMOST ENOCH

Yet there was that in me as I went, which told me I should never again see the day fair and the sun shining on my own house at home. I had not so much hope of success as a kind of anger against the pride that had carried me up here among the hills where I had no business. I might well have bided in my walled dwelling of Rathan, and, with the credit I had, have taken my wife into my bosom. But I must needs, for the pride of being spoken about, be climbing here on the rigging of creation like a tom-cat on the tiles. And for what? Just that the young men might wonder and wait, and the message flee athwart the country that none was so brave as Patrick Heron! Which, indeed, was no truth; for even now the heart within me loathed my own deed, and I had a most cowardly spirit—the spirit of a mouse, and even of a poor mean mouse.

Yet must I go on, because the hunters were behind me as well as before. I gripped the icy clints of the granite rock tighter, and set my face to the thick-sown bank of stars above me, for the night had blown clear. Or perhaps, since the cliff was so high, I may have risen above the frosty mist. At any rate it was a place of deadly cold, and my fingers became numb. Then they seemed to swell and thrill with heat so that I thought they were dropping off.

Presently I was on the topmost ledge of all, and crawling a few paces I looked down upon the desolate waste of Loch Enoch under the pale light of the stars. It is not possible that I should be able to tell what I saw, yet I shall try.

I saw a weird wide world, new and strange, not yet out of chaos—nor yet approven of God; but such a scene as there may be on the farther side of the moon, which no man hath seen nor can see. I thought with some woe and pity on the poor souls condemned, though it were by their own crimes, to sojourn there. I thought also that, had I been a dweller so far from ordinances and the cheerful faces or men, it might be that I had been no better than the outlaw men. And I blamed myself that I had been so slack and careless in my attendance on religion, promising (for the comfort of my soul as I lay thus breathing and looking) that when I should be back in

Rathan, May and I should ride each day to church upon a good horse, she behind me upon a pillion—and the thought put marrow into me. But whether grace or propinquity was in my mind, who shall say? At any rate I bethought me that God could not destroy a youth of such excellent intentions.

But this is what I saw, as clearly as the light permitted—a huge, conical hill in front, the Hill of the Star, glimmering snow-sprinkled, as it rose above the desolations of Loch Enoch and the depths of Buchan's Dungeon. To the right the great steeps of the Merrick, bounding upward to heaven like the lowest steps of Jacob's ladder. Beneath, Loch Enoch, very black, set in a grey whiteness of sparse snow and sheeted granite. Then I saw in the midst of all the Island of Outlaws, and on it, methought, a glimmering light.

So I set me to crawl downward. I went now as though I had left fear behind me sticking to the frosty Clints of Neldricken. The space between me and the loch was hardly a bowshot, and I found myself putting on my runners on the edge of the ice behind a great logan-stone, or ever my heart had time to beat faster. Then I was not at all afraid, thinking that on the ice so black and polished I could distance all pursuers, for none had that art in Galloway save myself.

The ice sloped away from the edge, and there was a little quiver within me as I slid downwards, lest I should be slipping into such another chasm as I had seen open for me at the Murder Hole of Loch Neldricken.

But only the great flat met me, and I struck out softly. It was beautiful ice, smoother than I had ever seen, having frozen early, and by the first intention, as it were, being close up under the sky—with a skin on it like fine bottle glass. But withal so clear and still was now the air that, do as I would, I could not hinder the ringing of my ice-runners, and the whole loch twanged like a fiddle-string when one hooks it with the forefinger and then lets go. Yet as I swept along, swinging my arms nearly to the ice, and taking the sweeping strides of the Low Countrymen, I had a sense of pride that nothing in Galloway could come near me for speed.

So sure was I, that with a sweep like an albatross (as I told myself) I circled about to the island whereon was the dying fire. As near as I could observe it the light was in a kind of turf-covered shelter—not a claybuilt house with windows like that in which I had spent a night of terror on the slopes of Craignairny. There were men crouching around the fire, all looking out to the loch, from which no doubt there came the strange ringing of my ice-runners, the like of which was never heard there before. Suddenly these men seemed to take alarm, and like a brood of partridges dispersing when one sets random foot among them, they sped every way into the cover. I laughed within myself. But I laughed not long, for as I went I had that sense of being hunted, which comes so quickly and is so unnerving. I heard not, saw not my pursuer. I knew not whether the thing were man or beast, ghost or devil. But I was being followed, and that swiftly, silently. There was that behind me—I knew not what—something that my nature feared, perhaps just because it knew not what. In wild terror I clenched my hands and flew. My runners cut the smooth ice in long, crisp whistlings. The black shores sped backward. On my track I heard ever the patter of feet galloping as a horse gallops, yet noiselessly, as though shod in velvet. As I turned at the eastern end of the loch something grey and fierce and horribly bristling sprang past open-mouthed, straining to take me; but overshooting the mark with the impulse of extreme speed, the beast shot past with all four feet hissing taut on the glistening ice, yet looking back with fangs gleaming white.

So to and fro there was the rushing on the glassy ice of Enoch—the beast that hunted me gaining ever on the straight, and I at the turnings. After a time or two I regained my composure in some degree. It was a boy's game this, and I had played it before on the ice, though not with such a fearsome playmate; nor yet with savage men scrambling and watching among the stones at the edge, dirks in their hands and murder in their hearts.

But I clearly saw that I had only the advantage so long as I could keep up my speed. Did I slacken or trip but once, the fangs were at my throat.

Likewise, though the nights were long, the morning must come at last, and then I would be but a poor hare waiting for the shot of the huntsmen, driven by the hounds to die. Yet this I did not mind so much, had there only been some one there to tell May Maxwell and the people of my country how I took my fate.

But very suddenly the end came, even as I darted between two isles that stand out of the middle of the loch—my runner scraped the edge of a long ridge of granite, and I pitched over on my face. In a moment I felt the horrible breath of the beast on my face, as it came rushing after and drove headlong upon me.

I had my knife out in a moment, and struck wildly again and again at nothing till my arm was seized as in a vice.

Then I heard the sound of men's voices, but faint and far away, as though I were hearing in a dream. The light of a lantern shone upon me, and a band of men came clattering over the ice to me. But there was something that stood between me and the stars, something black and large and panting, which faced towards the men who came, standing across me like a lion that guards its prey. Yet had the beast done me no harm, so far as I could feel, saving (it might be) that my arm was a little stiff.

As the men came nearer the beast emitted many short, hoarse growls from deep within. Its body seemed to quiver with rage, but whether with rage at being interfered with in the disposition of its prey, I could not tell.

"Quharrie, good Quharrie, come here!" said a voice from the group which halted three yards away.

"*Quharrie at Loch Enoch!*" I thought, and it all came clear to me. If Quharrie were at Enoch, Silver Sand was also there, and I was betrayed! That was my thought. Yet I was not the more afraid. On the contrary, the conviction put into my heart a certain dumb and proud anger, and I began at once to compose, even as I lay on the ice, the speech that I would make when I met my false friend face to face. For this was my nature. It was a good speech and cutting, and it made me feel that it was a fine thing to die. I was ready to be a martyr, but I was resolved that every one should know how I had been brought to the death—and more especially Silver Sand, who had been my friend. I was determined not to be dumb. I should speak my mind once.

The men about me kept calling to Quharrie—now threateningly, now as one that fleeches, coaxing with promises. But the great wolf-dog only growled the fiercer, standing across my body with a wide-arched stride.

One of the men wished, I think, to do the dog a mischief, but the others withheld him, putting their hands upon him to deprive him of his pistol. Then two came from opposite sides to snatch at me as I lay, a little stunned with my fall; but this so excited the fierce beast that he wheeled this way and that, roaring and snapping, and made such dangerous swift charges that they were compelled to desist.

Then two men came by themselves over the ice towards us from the island. As they entered within the shining circle of the lantern light I saw it was Silver Sand and another. The men made way for them. Silver Sand strode through them, and I thought he had never seemed so large and strong. I saw him coming long before he knew me, and I hugged myself at the thought of what I should say to him.

"Give me the lantern," he said.

As he came, Quharrie left me and fell in behind his master. His work was done. I looked around and regained my knife. But not to strike. Silver Sand came up and shone the light of the lantern on my face, where I was now sitting up.

I took the dagger by the point, and offered it to him, saying, "Silver Sand, true friend, here is a knife; strike quickly at my heart, and make a swift end. Thou knowest where to strike, for thou hast lain against it many a time."

This I thought mighty fine at the time, and original; but now I know that I had heard my father read somewhat like it out of an old book of stage plays.

Silver Sand looked at me, coolly and cruelly as I then thought, nobly and gently as I know now.

"Patrick!" was all he said.

"Aye," said I, "the same—Patrick Heron of Rathan—where the tent of Silver Sand has stood any time these seventeen years—and stands now ready for him—after—" (I said, nodding my head)— "after——"

"Can you walk?" he said, briefly.

I took off my ice-runners and stood ready.

So without word spoken we went back to the famous island on which I set foot for the first time. There on the grey-green grass were many turf huts and shelters. Into these we did not go, but only into the wider sod-built shelter, open to the sky, where the fire I had seen was yet smouldering.

As we went Silver Sand said to me neither good or bad. I thought I knew that his conscience was busy within him, and I rejoiced like a chidden child who says he will die, and *then* his mother will be sorry.

The dusky followers crouched around, talking together in whispers, casting meantime deadly enough looks at me. I sat on a stone and warmed my fingers at the embers. I was so full of getting, as I thought, the upper hand of Silver Sand who had been my friend, that (though I knew that I was as good as dead) I acted a part at that fire among the outlaws as willingly as in a stage play.

Then one sprang up and made a speech, pointed often at me, and as I imagined denouncing me. I knew not what he was saying, much of the talk being gypsy gibberish. But I knew that the gist was that it was I who had been in the Hut of Craignairny—I who had been their undoing.

Another and another spoke their minds, and Silver Sand was yet silent. The dark man who had come with him over the ice whispered to him.

Then the outlaw that had spoken first, the lout of the kitchen, took his knife and came over to me as if to make an end. Suddenly the fashion of the countenance of Silver Sand was changed. He sprang to his feet, and stood before them straight and proud as I had never seen him stand.

"To me, Faas!" he cried. "Back, or I will blast you with the black curse of Little Egypt, Roderick Macaterick!"

The man slunk back; but, as it seemed, dourly and unconvinced before the threatening finger.

Of the men that stood by, some ten gathered themselves about Silver Sand. The others clubbed the closer together, crouching with their heads forward in a bunch.

"Who are you," said their spokesmen, "to come among us after these years, when you have taken no part in the danger, and to think to lord it over us now?"

"Silence, hound!" said Silver Sand, with consuming vehemence. "Well you know who I am. I am John Faa, of the blood royal of Egypt. Well you remember why I left you: because I am not of them that do murder. Well you know that I have kept free not from the danger, but from the plunder. Now that the plunder is done with, and the danger come, I am here. Is it not so?"

There was no answer, but his own followers gathered closer about him.

"I am here," he cried again, "and here is this lad—Patrick Heron of the Rathan. It is true what he says, that I have eaten his bread for seventeen years, and my tent stands now with the peeled rod before it by the side of the water on Rathan Isle."

"And you would break the clan to save this lad that comes to spy on us and destroy us!" cried another voice from the thick of the adverse crowd, with great bitterness, and, I am bound to admit, with some measure of reason.

But Silver Sand had this of the royal blood in him, that he took the true attitude of the man of action. He commanded; he never explained.

"Down, dog!" he cried; "who dares to thwart John Faa—by the king's belting, Lord and Earl of Little Egypt? Not you that are no Egyptians, but scattermouches and unwashed ruffians from the four seas? I will hunt you with the Loathly Beasts. I will press on you with the Faa's curse. I will dwine your flesh on your bones, for I am your king, John Faa, and the power is mine, alone and without bound among this people of Egypt."

The man who had hitherto faced him would have uttered something, but the power was not given to him. His words withered on his lips.

"Roderick Macaterick," said Silver Sand, solemnly, "on the grave of him that ye slew by the Loch of Neldricken when he was forwandered in the moss, stand the white wraith that curses and the Grey Dog that waits. I deliver your soul to them!"

The man fell moaning on the ground.

Then Silver Sand took to speaking in the language which I could not understand, but chiefly, as it seemed, to his own people. Me he took by the arm and drew me away. So in a body those that clave to him moved off from the island and out upon the ice. Some of the others started up to follow.

Silver Sand turned and faced them.

"Him that sets his feet on the ice to follow us shall be blasted quick and sure. He shall never see good days more. You had best scatter and save yourselves, for a heavier hand than the Lowlanders' shall fall before to-morrow upon you for your murders and iniquities."

The men stood still, hesitating and afraid, and we went our way.

It was towards the Hill of the Star that we went, Silver Sand leading. When we came to the verge of the loch Silver Sand turned to his followers.

"Faas," said he, "and you, Hector, bide not here. There shall no assault be delivered by your enemies, but one more sure and terrible by the Almighty. The judgment for murder and crime comes swiftly. Go not back to take part in it, for I foresee that no one shall escape. Haste ye up Doon Water. Stay not for pursuer nor turn aside for foe, but scatter over the country as soon as ye have passed the marches!"

The men stood silent and irresolute.

"I know that ye obey me only because I am your master, John Faa, and your chief. Ye obey without question, like Egyptians of the pure blood. Ye have done well. Go now and be honest, or as honest as ye can, for never more shall you or I dwell in the dens of the Dungeon of Buchan. Fare ye well!"

"And who is to be chief?" said Hector Faa.

"I that speak am chief. As long as I live I cannot be other than chief, but I give to you my hand and my authority, Hector;" and he added, "It is a poor throne, that of Little Egypt, and no wise man would covet it, but such as it is you stand next to it."

So on the side of the Star Hill they parted from us, diving into the black night, and we were left standing alone—Silver Sand, who was John Faa, King of the Gypsies, Patrick Heron of the Rathan, and Quharrie, that had hunted me like vermin an hour agone, and afterwards fought for me like a blood brother.

CHAPTER XLIII

THE AUGHTY ON THE STAR HILL

We clasped hands in the darkness.

"Now we shall go to the Aughty!" he said.

I knew not where that might be, but I was content to go there, being dazed and quite deprived of speech. Quharrie as ever went before.

"And the Maxwells?" I said. "I must get back to them."

"They waited not for you," he said; "they are all back at the house of Eschonchan by this."

"But they were to attack to-night," I said; "they waited only for my return."

"Well, Patrick, I tell you they are waiting at the house at Eschonchan, but with tankards of ale before them. Be at ease about them. They will be glad to see you when you come, but they thought it better to bide warm at the Lodge of Eschonchan than cauldrife in the snow in the ree of the Midburn. In which they showed their judgement."

So saying he put aside a matted covering of heather, which drooped down the face of a rock, and a light for a moment flashed through the opening, and fell on the bleached grey-yellow bent.

"An' it's as weel!" said he, dropping into the Lowland Scotch, "for there's sic a storm brewing as has never been seen in your days nor mine."

The air was chill and damp, but gusts of warmish wind blew at times, and in the south there was a luminous brightness. Just before I entered the cave I looked over the hip of the Merrick, and there, through a cleft of a cloud, I saw the stars and the flickering brightness of the northern lights. They shone with a strange green the like of which I had never seen.

"This," said Silver Sand, "is the Aughty of the Star. Ye have heard o' it, but few have seen it since the Killing Time. It is the best hiding-place in all broad Scotland."

THE AUGHTY ON THE STAR HILL

I looked about at the famous cave which had sheltered nearly all the wanderers, from Cargill to Renwick—which had been safe haven in many a storm, for which both Clavers and Lag sought in vain. My father had told me also how he and Patrick Walker the pedlar (he that scribes the stories of the sufferers and has them printed), went to seek for the Aughty; but, though Patrick Walker had lain in it for four nights in the days of the Highland Host, he could never find it again.

"And how came you here, and what came you to do, Silver Sand?" I asked, as we stood in the flickering light of the wood fire.

"Will ye hae it bit by bit or a' at a meal?" said Silver Sand.

"I'll wait," said I.

"An' that's best," he answered, curtly.

The Aughty was a commodious shelter, most part of which had been fashioned by the hand of man. It had a little platform before it, twelve feet wide, in the summer green with grass; but (save for this) from the very door the precipice, scarred and sheer, fell away both above and below. It was, in fact, set on the face of the hill that looked towards the Dungeon, and one turned into it by a sudden and unexpected twist among the rocks. Within it had been roughly floored with small logs, and arched above with the same, so that, though only about five feet in height in the highest part, it yet resembled the inside of a very small claybigging, or ordinary cottar's house, more than I had thought possible in a mere hill shelter. There was a fire at one end, the smoke of which found its way up through the matted heather in such a manner that but little of it appeared at the outside, seeking out unnoticed along the face of the cliff. It was the custom of the wanderers, however, to half-burn their wood at night, and then when cooking was needed during the day to make a clear fire of the charcoal—a very excellent plan, and one I should never have thought on myself.

I had not been long in the Aughty before Silver Sand gave me something to eat and drink, which, indeed, stood ready in a goblet, only needing to be set on the *grieshoch*[1]—a kind of stew, very like that which Eggface had made on Craignairny, but richer.

"Hoo hae ye keepit the secret o' this place sae lang?" I asked of Silver Sand.

---

[1] Red embers.

"Verra simple," he said. "I never told a woman. But it'll no keep lang noo, for ye'll tell yer May, as sure as shootin'."

I had a retort at my tongue tip, but it was struck away by a thought, which made me feel myself a heartless brute.

"What's come o' the bit lass?" I asked, for speaking of my own lass had minded me of her. "What's come o' Marion Tamson?"

"Save us!" said Silver Sand. "I'm but a gomeral to forget the bit thing."

Outside the storm burst at this moment with exceeding fury. We had to draw nearer to hear ourselves speaking above the roar of the elements.

"It's a peety that we didna think on't suner. We'll hae an ill job noo, I doubt," said Silver Sand.

I asked where she was.

"She's in the clay hoose o' Craignairny," said Silver Sand.

That I liked least of all—to turn from the Aughty warm and safe, to face that terrible storm at the house of Black Murder, which I had such good cause to mind.

"An' the suner the better," said Silver Sand, "for lang afore the mornin' we shall be corked up as tight as if we were in a sealed bottle."

Through the matted covering which formed a door I thrust my naked hand, and so close and fierce was the storm driving, that it seemed to me as if I had thrust my arm into a solid wreath of snow.

"Is there no other way of it?" I said, for indeed I had had enough.

"No," said Silver Sand; "the morning will be ower late. She's no wi' guid or provident folk, an' the Lord's arm reaches far."

Which seemed to me at the time an inadequate way of putting the character of the inhabitants of the House of Craignairny.

In a moment we were out facing it. In a step we had lost one another. We were blinded, deafened, blown away. I stood and shouted my loudest. When I got my eyes open I saw a fearsome sight. The darkness was white—above, around, beneath—all was a livid, solid, white darkness. So fierce were the flakes, driven by the wind, that neither the black of the earth nor the dun of the sky shone through. I shouted my best, standing with outstretched arms. My cry was shut in my mouth. It never reached my own ears. So standing, I was neither able to go back or forward. A hand came across me out of the white smother. Stooping low, Silver Sand and I went down the hill, Quharrie no doubt in front, though it was all impossible to see him. I heard afterwards that as soon as Silver Sand had stepped out he had fallen headlong into a great drift of snow which had risen like magic before the door in a few minutes.

We went blindly forward through the storm—yet with judgment, for after descending into the valley we saw, as through a partial break, the eastern end of Loch Enoch with the snowdrift hurtling across it. The black ice, swept clean by the fierce wind, showed dark in bars and streaks. We came to sleeked hollows which we crawled over on our faces, for we knew not how far down they went. We stumbled blindly into great wreaths, and rolled through them. In a little we were breasting the ridge of Craignairny.

"We're on it now," yelled Silver Sand, putting hand to my ear.

I had set myself against a great heap of snow, and was cowering for the leap upon it when Silver Sand stopped me. We stood against the cot of Craignairny—the House of Death itself. Eggface and all her crew lay within—under my hand, as it were.

Leaving me where I was, Silver Sand went round the house to reconnoitre. I stood, rather sheltered in the snow, on the side at which the shieling was built against the rock. There was a swirl in the wind, the place was bieldy, and I had time to think. In a little while Silver Sand came back. He signed to me to give him a lift upon the roof. Up he went till he reached the window from which I had leapt that terrible night in the summer of the year. Above it was the skylight through which May had followed. We had come now for the little one who had been left behind—the thought of whom had lain heavy on my heart many a time.

The skylight was barred with snow, but Silver Sand cautiously cleaned it away, pulled it open, and again came sliding down.

"If there's onybody sleepin' there, they'll think it's blawn open an' rise to shut it," I could hear him say in my ear.

The window was not shut. We could hear the wind whistling on the iron edge of it, as though it were playing a tune.

Again Silver Sand mounted. This time he put a knife between his teeth, and, raising himself on his hands, dropped lightly within. Then a few terrible minutes ensued in which I waited. The wind was so loud that had Silver Sand been murdered within I could not have heard a sound. I only leant against the end of the clay hut and thought what a fool I was and of how many various sorts.

In a little Silver Sand put his head out again and beckoned me up. I mounted upon the roof, my knee sinking among the waterlogged, evil-smelling thatch. When I reached the skylight Silver Sand suddenly thrust out something to me wrapped in a plaid. It was heavy, warm, and soft. The child, Marion Tamson herself, lay in my arm, but wasted and thin. She was no great weight for all her seven years. We were out and down in a trice. The skylight was again shut behind us, and the snowstorm blinding and shrieking about us. Quharrie I saw now. He had been sitting on the rigging of the house, looking into the skylight all the time that Silver Sand was within, a statue graven in the granite of the hills, his wild wolfish front shaggy with driven and frozen snow.

Down among the drifts we stumbled—up again over the hill, not a word spoken all the time, leading time about, the hindmost man carrying the little lamb that was too frightened to cry in the wild roar of the storm and the darkness of the plaid neuk. But loving arms held her, and I think she knew it.

Quharrie led us straight to the mouth of the Aughty. Without ceremony he shoved his sharp nose under the covering of matted heather and sprang in. Before we could cast a plaid, loose a button, or even take our little stolen lamb out of her bieldy nook, Quharrie had curled himself about upon the hearth and gone to sleep, as though it were a fine night and he had just come in from a friendly turn on the hill after the rabbits.

Then, all wrapped in her shawls, clean as everything about Eggface was clean (to give the devil his dues), we got little Marion out. I took her on my knee and talked to her, for I had ever a way with children, as even May allows. At first the child watched with eyes full of terror; yet it was not long before I won her heart, and she was cheerily talking of brighter days. But in the midst of it all, even whilst she was laughing merrily, her head would fall on my shoulder and she take to crying as though her little heart would break.

Now this I could not understand, for I thought the worst was past, yet I had sense enough not to ask any questions, but only to rock her on my knee and hush her to sleep. Silver Sand made up a bed of warm blankets for her before the fire, and she rested there very simply and sweetly, though her hands twitched and pulled at the coverings, and once or twice she waked out of her sleep with a sharp cry.

Then I cursed them that had caused the innocent bairn to do the like and said to myself, "Wait till we hae ye a year at the Rathan, Marion, we'll gar ye forget a' this o't."

This also came to pass, by the blessing of God.

On the morrow the great storm was in no way abated, but nevertheless we abode here in the Aughty with much content. We had plenty of good baconham and meal, tons of water outside for the melting, loads of peat fuel from Kirreoch moss. We were in no wise unhappy—though I had the grace to be continually thinking about them that must be anxious concerning me. But yet I was over young to think much even of that. Hardly any man is thoughtful for others till he is well past thirty. May Maxwell says "Not then!"

That night, while the maid slept, Silver Sand began to tell me all his story which I marvelled much to hear.

CHAPTER XLIV

THE SIXTEEN DRIFTY DAYS

Without, the hurricane drove ever from the south. It was the first of the famous Sixteen Drifty Days which are yet remembered over all the face of the hill country, when of sheep and cattle the dead far outnumbered the living. The snow drove hissing round the corner of the Aughty and faced against the entrance in a forty foot wreath. Looking down in the breaks of the storm we could see only the wild whirl of drifting whiteness in the gulf of the Dungeon of Buchan.

But it was warm and pleasant within. The fire drew peacefully with a gentle draught up the side of the rock, and the heather couches on the floor were dry and pleasant. Even the House of Rathan had hardly been more homelike than the cave called the Aughty, on the north-eastern face of the precipice of the Star.

It was here that Silver Sand, that was John Faa, belted Earl and Gypsy, told his story.

"There was never," he said, "I think, any man so strangely driven as I of the gypsy blood, who am yet an earl of this realm of Scotland; I who am of the reiver kin have ridden with the king's men and worn the dragoon's coat; I that have looked on at many a killing of the poor Whig folk, have lain at Peden's hip in the caves by the Crichope Water—a true-blue Whig mysel'!

"I that was Richard Cameron's man and proscrivit by the Government of the Stuarts, have likewise lain under ban by the Government of the Whigs for the riding and reiving of my clan. King's man or Hill Whig, Society man or Lag's rider—the Faa has ever been at the tow's end; and never, save as puir Silver Sand that maks his living by the keel and the scythe sand, has he ever rested sound in his bed.

"I was but a young lad when the riding time began, an' there was screevin' and chasin' over a' the Westland after the Whigs. All this to a gypsy of the blood royal was but the squattering and quackin' of ducks upon a mill-dam—a matter for themselves. But I was in Dumfries on a day, and standin' on the brig-end o' Devorgill, wha should come by up the Vennel but the red-wud Laird o' Lag.

"'There's a proper lad that should be nae Whig,' he cried, as soon as ever he saw me standing there; 'I ken by the cock o' his beaver bonnet wi' the gawsy feather intil't.'

"The troop that was riding with him, three files of King's troopers, and some young blades o' the country lairds that cam' themselves wi' twa-three led horses to ride wi' Lag—maistly lads that hated the Kirk for meddlin' wi' their gentrice richt o' free fornication, cried oot for me to mount an' ride wi' them.

"'Wull ye tak' service wi' the King, His Excellent Majesty, an' wull ye curse the Whigs?' they said.

"That last I was fain to do; indeed I loved them little, for they had held my father's sept down wi' an iron hand all through the thirty years of their greatness. But to ride wi' the trooping men and bite bread wi' them, was just as little to the stomach of a Faa.

"But needs must when the devil drives.

"'Fess him on till the bonny braes o' the Brigend!' cried the laird; 'he can mount an' hunt, or he can bide an' blood when we get him there.'

"So they carried me across till we came to a wide grassy place where the broom was growing and the wind blowing. It was fresh and free, and the innocent birds were singing.

"Lag halted his troop.

"'Noo, bonny lad,' says he, 'we hae little time to pit aff wi' the likes o' you, but ye can hae the free choice. Here's a silver merk, for the King's arles, and here's Sergeant Armstrong's file wi' twal unce o' the best lead bullets. Three meenites to tell us whatna yin ye'll hae.'

"The birdies whistled on the yellow whins, and the wind waved the branches they sat on. The summer airs blew soft. The green leaves laughed drily. They were beech-leaves, and their talk is aye a wee malicious.

"In three minutes I was mounted on a grey horse o' the wild laird's, and that nicht they drank me fu' in the auld Lag's Too'er, where to this day that same laird, that has his hand black with blood, sleeps in his silken bed under the safe conduct o' the Government—while I that have been under a dozen Governments nor done ill to yin o' them, am a broken man and the King's enemy to this day. But then I am but John Faa and an Egyptian.

"But sae we rade an' better rade at the tail o' the wicked laird, an' as for his ill-doin' and ill-speakin' there was nayther beginnin' or end to it.

"He wad ride up to a farmhouse an' chap on the door wi' the basket hilt o' his broadsword.

"'Is the guidman in?' says he.

"'Deed, he is that!' says the mistress; 'he's gettin' his parritch.'

"'Haste him fast, then,' says Lag, 'for the Archangel Gawbriel' (nae less) 'is waitin' to tak' his fower-'oors[1] wi' him, an' it's a kittle thing to keep the likes o' him waitin'!'

"Then in ten minutes that wife's a weedow, an' gatherin' up her man's harns in a napkin!

"Ridin' under the cloud o' nicht to droon the psalm wi' the rattle o' the musket shot; oot on the wide uplands, where there are but the bumbees an' the heatherbleats, stelling up a raw o' five or six decent muirland men on their knees, as yince I saw at Kirkconnel, some wi' the white napkins roond their broos, an' some lookin' intil the gun muzzle, it was waesome wark—waesome wark! An' the curse o God Almichty has lain on a' that had a hand in it—savin' that de'il's knight, Sir Robert himsel', wha's iniquities the Almichty is most surely reckoning at compound interest, for he sits snug an' hearty to this day in his hoose at Lag's Too'er, while in muckle Hell the de'il banks his fires and heats his irons for him.

"But there was yae mornin' that I gat my fill—heathen gypsy though I was. We had lain a' nicht at Morton Castle, an' it was daybreak or we set hip to saddle leather. There was a bairn that we cam' on by the gully o' the Crichope—a laddie o' ten. He was sittin' by his lane in a bit bouroch when we cam' up till him, whistlin' like a lintie. He had a can o' the guid sweet milk an' a basketfu' o' bannocks. He was close by the mouth o' the Linn. It behoved, then, that he was takkin' them to some cave whaur the outlawed minister was hiding.

"It was just like the laird to get the lad to inform. It was sic a bit o' de'il's wark that pleasured him weel an' also David Graham that they had made Sherra o' Gallowa' in the place o' the Agnews o' Lochnaw. They war a bonny pair. They feared the bit boy, half daffin, half in earnest, till the wean was blae wi' fricht.

---

[1] A meal taken at four o'clock in the afternoon.

"Lag gruppit him by the collar and shook him by the coat-neck ower the Linn, like a bit whaulpie that ye micht lift by the cuff o' the neck.

"'Tell,' he says, 'whaur lies auld Tam Glen, or ower ye gang.'

"The bit laddie lookit doon, an'—O Paitrick! me that is an auld man can see the terror glint in the e'e o' him as he saw the great trees nae bigger than berry busses at the bottom. Syne he lookit up at us that sat oor horses ahint the laird and the sherra.

"'Hae nane o' ye ony wee laddies at hame that ye should let a bairn dee?'

"He had a voice like a wean I yince kenned, and at the word o' him, I that was but a youngster, an' no lang frae the mither's milk mysel', burst out in a kin o' gowl o' anger.

"Lag turned quick, the de'il's dead-white thumb marks on ilka side o' his nose.

"'What cursed Whig's that?' says he, in his death voice.

"Then I canna tell whether the bairn's bit coatie rave oot o' his hand, or whether Lag let him drap; but when we lookit again there was Lag's hand empty, an' up the Linn cam' a soun' like a bairn greetin' in the dark his lane.

"Lag stood maybes three heart-loups in a swither. I think he hadna juist bargained for that, but he turns an' cries wi' a wave o' his ruffled lace band—

"'The corbies will hae sweet pickin' aff that whalp's bones!'

"But I had had aneuch an' mair—a bellyfu' to settle me for yince an' a'.

"I was aff my horse an' doon amang the busses on the Linn side wi' a great clatter o' stanes.

"'Wha's that?' cries Lag, ower his shoother, for he was turned to ride awa'.

"'Gypsy Jock,' says yin, 'deserted——'

"'Give him a volley, lads. I never thocht the loon true man!' cried Lag.

"But the riders had little stomach for the shootin'. The wee bit laddie lay on their hearts, and in especial his words, for most o' them had bairns o' their ain, though some no juist owned wi'. So but few shot after me, an' them mostly Hielan' men that kenned no English except *'Present! Fire!'* whilk they had heard often aneuch in a' conscience since they rade wi' Lag.

"I was doon at the laddie afore the troop had ridden away. But he was bye wi't. A bonny bit laddie as ever ye saw. I carried him till his mither, strippin' aff the regimentals as I gaed, but keepin' the sword, the musket, an' the brass mounted pistols. His mither met us at the gable end. The bairn had the empty can claspit in his wee bit hand. O sirce me! sirce me! Paitrick! gin I could forget it——"

And Silver Sand set down his head on the rude shelf in the Aughty and sobbed till I feared he might do himself a hurt.

"An' his mither took him oot o' my airms, that am but a rude man; an' she said never word, neither did the tear rin doon her cheek, but bade me come ben as ceevil as gin I had been a minister. She set before me to eat, but ye may ken what heart I had for victual. I juist roared an' grat, but she pat her hand on my shoother, an' hushed me as gin I had been the mourner. Syne she laid him on the bed.

"'My wee Willie,' says she, as she smoothed his bonny broo an' kaimed his hair that was lang and yellow an' fell on the sheet in wavy ringlets.

"'Even so,' she said, 'Lord, I had thocht ye micht hae spared this bit boy to me for company, seein' he was the last. But it's no be. Yin at Drumclog, yin at Kirkconnel, an' yin by the bonny links o' the Cluden. I thocht the Lord wad hae spared the widow's yae bit hindmost lamb. The wull o' the Lord be dune.'

"She turned sharp to me.

"'Hoo died he?' she asked, as calm as 'What's-o'-the clock?'

"I tried to tell her, between the sabs—her waitin' till I cam' to mysel' an' giein' me a bit clap on my shoother—me that am but a sinfu' man, as if I had been her ain bairn himsel'.

"'Noo na—noo na,' says she, aye fleechin' like.

"O wae's me! wae's me!" Silver Sand cried, sinking his head on the table board. "The Lord forgie the sins o' my youth."

I was weeping too by this time, and I think the King himself had wept as well to hear the tale.

Silver Sand went on.

"She stood ower him a gye while, sortin' him an' touchin' him an' straikin' him.

"'He was a carefu' boy,' she said, 'an' that guid to his mither, my bit boy Willie! Ye helpit her ilka day, an' ye sleepit in her bosom ever since her ain guid man won awa'. Aye, Willie, my wean, ye sall sleep this yae nicht in her mither's airms, for they shall never meet aboot onything that is the desire o' her heart in this world mair. Even this yae nicht ye shall lie in the airms o' her that bore ye, an' that close again her side, where she carried ye the black year she lost her man.'

"She turned to me with a kind o' anger.

"'An' what for no?' she said, as if I had forbidden her. 'An' what for no, I wad like to ken? Pit your hand on him, man; he's warm an' bonny—no a mark on him that the yellow lint locks canna cover, an' that I can wash. What for shouldna he sleep by his ain mither? He will sleep soond. I'll no wakkin' him gin he be tired. This mornin' I raise on my bare feet that he should get a langer lie and a soond sleep—aye, an' a soond sleep he's got, my laddie, O my laddie!

"'An' ye were a kind boy to your mither, Willie—a kind, kind boy—an' I hae nae mair; it's a sin to mourn for them that the Lord has ta'en. But O he was a carefu' boy Willie, an' the maist thochtfu' for his mither. See man, see—he has brocht his mither's bit can safe hame in his hand——'

"O, waes me! waes me!" wailed Silver Sand, rocking himself to and fro, so that little Marion woke, and seeing us weeping, wept too, like a young child that knows not why.

Then there was a long pause, and the fire flickered and the wild storm raved outside the Aughty. And the storm within our bosoms sobbed itself out, and we watched little Marion silently till she slept again, our right hands being clasped each in the other.

CHAPTER XLV

ALIEN AND OUTLAW

"So that day," continued Silver Sand, "made me a believing man—that is, so far as a gypsy and a Faa may be a believing man.

"But it was a long time before I was trusted by the moormen, because I was known for a gypsy and a red-hand follower of the chief persecutor. I was even as Paul at Damascus to them; yet in time they believed, and treated me not as a spy but as a brand plucked from the burning. Yet it was my lot to be cast among the extremer sect, who were the followers of Richard Cameron.

"As you may have heard, these received but scant justice at the Revolution, so that when all was over, and I went to what home I had, I found that they of my own clan had been attainted, and were under worse condemnation than ever, for their lawless deeds whilst I had been away from them.

"It was not likely that I could take part with them now, for the order of the King's council caused them to become worse outlaws and reivers than ever—though, I think, no murderers.

"Yet I could not live with them; nor, being a Faa, and the chief, could I betray them. Nor yet, for my father's sake and my name's sake, would I claim any indulgence that might not be extended to them. So I took to the hills and to the trade of selling the bonny scythe sand and the red keel for the sheep. And though I have not where to lay my head, I am a better and happier man, than the man who witnessed that sight by the Linn of Crichope ever deserved to be. But I have dwelt with my Maker and humbled myself before Him in secret wood and lonely fell. The men of the hills ceased their hiding in the mosses and moors near forty years agone—all but one, and he a persecutor, a heathen man, and one whose hand had been dyed in the blood of God's saints. For forty years I have dwelt where God's folk dwelt, and striven with the devil and the flesh in many a strange place—often not sure whether indeed I had gotten me the victory.

"And I fear me that in these later troubles I have taken too much to do with carnal things, for which I must be constant in prayer that the Lord will forgive me—an unworthy man and an aged. But I have not steeped my hands in taking of blood; and, so far as I may, I have both been faithful to my friends and to my name. But the task has not been light, and sometimes I have suffered from the unbelief of both."

I stretched out my hand, and humbly asked him to forgive me my unjust words and unworthy suspicions.

"And I cannot call you aught but Silver Sand, and you will still come and camp by the Water of Rathan?" I said.

Silver Sand assented with a sweet smile, and took my hands and kissed them; for a gypsy has strange ways.

But there were many things that I desired to have explained.

"Why did you, being the man you are," I said, "threaten warlock threats to the men down there the other night?"

Silver Sand smiled.

"In Rome I must do as the Romans," he said; which, however, I did not think a very sound exposition or deduction.

"But could you indeed perform these things?" I asked, still doubtfully.

"They believed I could, which is the same thing. You see," he went on, "I have been forced to practise simple stratagems to keep myself safe between a wild clan and an unjust law, and there are many things that are easy to do and hard to make others understand. My arms which were twisted in the torture of the Star Chamber before James, Duke of York, have served me in that I can run like a beast, and when we hunt as the Loathly Dogs, Quharrie and I fear the foolish folk out of their wits."

"Indeed, I think you are no that canny mysel'," I said, with a kind of awe on my face.

"Weel," said Silver Sand, "I doubt not that gin some o' the landward presbyteries got me, I micht burn even at this day, as did Major Weir. Yet is all my magic of the simplest and most childish—even as simple as keel and scythe sand."

I asked, had he ever applied for grace for Government.

He told me no; for that there were none in any Government who would believe that a Faa could be other than a sorner and a limmer. That grapes do not grow on thorns nor figs on thistles is good Government doctrine.

"An' to tell the truth," said John Faa, "I am none that anxious, for I am a man that has been so long at the horn, that I could not lie happy were I hand in glove wi' King's men and baron baillies. I love best the fowl o' the air that cackle and cry on the moorland, the spotted eggs o' the pee-wees an' the great marled eggs o' the whaup, the fish frae the burn an' the haddock frae the salt sea flats. All these and the taking o' them are marrow to the bones o' Silver Sand."

I asked him again (but not continuously, for we had plenty of time for our converse, during the sixteen days and nights of the great storm) among other things, what he thought of the Freetraders. He gave me a queer look.

"I think verra much what your faither thocht," said he, "in his latter days. I dinna meddle wi' the stuff mysel', but I lay no informations on them that hold otherwise. I hae nocht, for instance, to say aboot your freends the Maxwells—only (a word in your lug) gin I war you I wad pit my fit doon again them using the cellars o' Rathan for their caves o' storage."

He nodded significantly.

"Ye dinna mean that they hae dune that!" I said, with indignation.

"An' what else?" said Silver Sand. "They are as fu' as they can stick o' French brandy, and Vallenceens; an' gin ony o' Agnew's men were gaun snowkin' roond, it micht cause misunderstandings atween them that's in poo'er an' you that's sic a grand King's man."

"And are you quite content as you are, Silver Sand?" I said to him again, to pass the time. Little Marion, to whom the quiet of the cave was heaven, sat at our feet and played with the quaint toys which Silver Sand had made her.

"Content!" said Silver Sand; "what for shouldna I be content? I ken nane that has mair cause to be. I look on the buik o' God a' the day under His wide, high lift for a rooftree, an' often a' nicht gin the storms keep aff. I hae God's Word in my oxter forbye—see here!"

He pulled out two dumpy little red-covered Bibles, with the Old Testament divided at Isaiah, and the Psalms of David in metre, very clean, but thumbed yellowish like a banknote at the end.

"What mair could a man want?" he said.

"But sellin' the sand an' the keel can only tak' a sma' part o' your time—what do ye do wi' the rest when ye are awa' frae the Rathan?"

Silver Sand smiled and made a curious little noise in his throat, as May does when she calls the hens for their "daich."

"I play at bogle wi' the lasses," he said, "aboot the cornstacks."

I looked at him, and was silent with surprise. He had just been telling me that his aim was to be a godly man according to his possible.

"Did ye never hear o' the Brownie?" he said, seeing my surprise.

"Aye," said I; "but I believe nothing in freets. There's nae siccan thing." For being young I knew no better.

"The first starlicht nicht after we are back at the Rathan I'll show ye," said he.

"Tell me noo," I said, "Guid kens there's plenty o' time in this auld Aughty."

"Tell on," said Marion, who was awaking quickly from her daze, and beginning to take an interest in many things.

If I could have forgotten the great rambling house where the women-folk waited—May and Eppie and the Lady Grizel—these days in the Aughty, with the wild men and the wild storm alike shut out, with the peril past (or so I thought) had been as happy and memorable as any in my life. I have often noticed that an unexpected experience of bodily comfort, as coming to a house wet and weary and finding a welcome, a warm fire and dry socks, clings to the heart longer than anything else, and is oftener recalled than many greater kindnesses.

So the Aughty comes to me whenever the winds howl and the shutters clatter. I think we were all happy in the Aughty, and certainly little Marion gained in beauty and fearlessness every day. At first it was sad to see her shrinking when any one moved suddenly near her. But this also gradually ceased.

To this day I can hear the soft *swish* of the snow against the flap of heather curtain, the roaring of the wind above, the crackle of the heather roots and broom branches on the fire. I can see the red loom of the peats at the back—indeed all things precisely as they were on these days of storm when the winds drifted the snow for sixteen days, till in many of the hollows the wreaths lay a hundred feet deep, and over half of Scotland one sheep out of every two died—as well as many men that were shepherds and wanderers. Once we heard a great roar as though the mountains were falling, and we all instinctively cowered and prayed that the Destroying Angel might pass over our heads.

"That's a most michty hurl of stanes somewhere," said Silver Sand.

"I wish the Star Hill bena comin' doon on our heids," said I. But it was not the Hill of the Dungeon.

We waited for a long time, but we could hear no more of it, and from the doorway we could only see the great tide of snow-flakes running steadily up the Dungeon o' Buchan far below, and occasional swirls entering into the sheltered bend in which the mouth of the Aughty lay. The snow was not falling now, but blowing uninterruptedly north with the mighty wind, as level as ruled lines on a copybook.

So we let fall the flap, after having taken Marion to the door that she might wonder at the white driving world of snow.

"I think I could float in it like a feather," she said—a feeling which I had myself.

It is but little to read the gypsy's strange relations, or for the matter of that to write them, in the bien comfort of one's own dwelling; but it was quite other to hear them told in the slow, level voice of Silver Sand himself, who was Johnny Faa, the bloody persecutor and Cameronian gypsy—for such things were never heard of before in broad Scotland. All this, too, while the greatest storm of the century raved without, and the winds of the Sixteen Drifty Days sped past outside like fiends that rode to the yelling of the damned.

It was comfortable too at meal-times to hear the bacon skirling in the pan, and smell the canty smell of the oatmeal fried among it. Sometimes Quharrie would rise from one side of the fireplace and walk solemnly round to the other, whither Marion would presently follow him, and lie down beside him with her head on his mighty flank. Then he would lift his head and look at her like a great benignant wolf (the first of that race); and because he loved her down in his rough-husked heart somewhere, he licked her on the point of her nose, which seemed to turn up a little on purpose.

Then at night it was pleasant to draw about the fire while Silver Sand read out of his book—often from John's Gospel, oftenest from the Apocalypse, which somehow appealed strongly to him. Then all kneeling upon the hearth, he poured out his soul in prayer—such a prayer as he had heard from Renwick and Shields in the last days of the sufferings when John Faa was yet on his prohibition. He would often fleech on me to take part in the exercises, but though my heart was very much attuned to do it, I never could come at the performance of it till I was in a house of my own.

CHAPTER XLVI

THE BROWNIE

"Ye want to hear mair aboot the Brownie?" said Silver Sand. "Aweel, ye are gye far ben wi' me, an' I'm gettin' ower auld to play sic tricks an' pliskies. Ye think, nae doot, that my life hasna been a verra usefu' life. I am o' a different opeenion."

I had no such thought, and said so.

"Aweel, ye mind the year afore last. Wha was't, do ye think, that cut an' stookit the feck o' the Maxwell's corn in the short days so far in the year, when the lads had to gang awa' to the Isle o' Man for the first cargo for my Lord Stair?"

"I heard some word o' its bein' the fairies," said I.

"And there ye show your penetration, Paitrick, but maybes ye didna discern, you that was so far seein', that it was Silver Sand wi' his bit scythe an' his lang shauchelt airms. An' wha was't that gathered a' yer sheep intil the buchts the nicht afore the great storm o' February-was-a-year?"

"I aye jaloosed it was the Maxwells, but they never wad own wi't, but I thocht little o' that, for Kennedy thinks no more o' tellin' a whud than o' slappin' a cleg that nips him on the hench bane."

"That he disna!" said Silver Sand, with conviction.

"But," he continued, "he tell'd the truth that time by accident whatever, for it was juist me an' Quharrie that buchtit the Rathan yowes, an' the neist nicht dippit them, rubbin' tar an' butter amang the oo' to mak' it grow flossy an' lang."

And Silver Sand went on to tell us of nights out on the fells and in the green parks about the farm-towns. How he delved the old wives' kail-yards, as he said, for the pleasure of going round the next morning to hear their wonderings.

"'Ye'll no be wantin' ony sand for yer heuk, Betty?" he would say to some old dame at her cottage door.

"Na, no the day, Silver Sand," says Betty.

"Ony news, Betty?" he would say.

"News!" quo' she—"News! What think ye o' the gentle people bein' in my garden yestreen, nae farder gane, an' left it a' delved, an' no as muckle as the dent o' their feet!"

"And that," said Silver Sand, "was likely, seeing the trouble I was at to tak' the footmarks oot wi' an iron-teethed rake."

"It's maist wonderful indeed, Betty; but what wad Maister Forbes, honest man, say to yer hae'in' sic dealin's wi' the fairies? Think ye that' canny, Betty, my woman?"

"Canny here, canny there, as lang as I get my garden delved an' my tawties howkit for nocht, I'se seek nae Maister Forbes! Maister Forbes, indeed! it wad be a lang time or ever he howkit a dreel o' my tawties. He's fitter at eatin' them, great fushionless hoshen that he is!'"

Thus Silver Sand carried us over the storm with wealth of tales. I listened eagerly, my toes cocked to the comfortable fire on the hearthstone (for there was a good hearthstone in the Aughty), and one ear bent to the outer moil of the storm as I nestled down with my right and left side time about to the fire.

"Then," continued the story-teller, "there were nichts on the corn rigs when the shearin' was at its height, and the farms lay sleepin' under the cool, clean air—nichts when it was juist heaven to work amang the sheaves, and hear the *crap, crap!* of the short-bladed reaping-hook driving through the corn. Every sheaf was like a friend. Every stook added another to the weel-buskit army that made glad the heart and exercised the brain of the bit farmer body, when he cam' oot in the mornin' an' gaed dodderin' aboot the oothooses, an' syne cam' dawnerin' doon the field to plan the wark for the day.

"'Hi, Rab!' he would cry to the cotman, as he saw my handiwork, 'come ye here.'

"Then Rab would come oot, dichting his neb frae the byre, belike whaur he had been preein' the sweet milk-can, or else the moo, o' the byre lass, wha kens—gye sheepish and shamefaced whatever.

"'Rab! d'ye see that?' his maister wad say (me up in the muckle tree a' the time).

"Rab looks. Rab better looks. The fashion or his countenance changes.

"'The Lord preserve's,' he cries, as he catches sicht o' a dizzen mair rigs cut, past eh mark whaur he had finished at the gloamin' o' the nicht afore—'the midnicht fairies hae been here. I'se gang hame. I'se no work wi' Broonie.'

"'Ye muckle nowt,' says his master, 'be thankfu' that Broonie thinks so weel o' the place as to work on it. A licht heart an' an untired leg has the lads aboot the bit whaur Broonie works. Heartsome be his meal o' meat, puir falla'!'

"So the neist day at e'en there's a basin o' parritch an' a great bowl o' milk set oot at the barn-end. Then I tak' my great sheepskin coat aboot me, that keeps me warm on the cauldest nicht in a hedge-root, if need be, an' up the loanin I gang my ways. There'll be some muckle gomerel o' a half-grown loon that wants to get credit wi' the lasses. He's watchin' for Broonie. I can hear his knees playin' *knoit* thegether at the back o' the hedge.

"'BOO-HOO!" says I, billying like a bullock.

"Up gets Hobbledehoy, an' rins wi' skelloch on rairin' skelloch to the farmhoose, where the lasses are biggit in threes about the back o' the door, fair wat wi' fear.

"'Never was there sic a thing!' Gomerel threeps. He has seen Broonie. He can describe him. He is as big as the barn, an' beltit wi' a curly hide. He has horns as lang as my leg. Then on the morn whatna bizz there is in a' the kintraside. Frae far an' near they come to hear Rob Gomerel tell aboot the Broonie that billied at him in the hedge. Rab tells the tale, and tells it ower again. An' every time he tells it there's twa yairds on till the length o' the beast, an' at least yin to the horns. It's a fearsome beast afore a's dune."

Silver Sand laughed his silent chuckling laugh, and went on.

"Then there are the trysts o' the lasses an' the lads. There was an ill speldron o' a loon that had mistrysted wi' twa lasses already, an' he cam' to the kirk-stile to speak to wee Margaret Lauder that is an innocent as a lamb. I saw the colour come an' gang, an' the bit heart loup. And my bauld birkie saw it too, for he eined wi' the denty wee lass to meet him at the Myrestane black-yetts at the back o' the wood. But he never gat there to this day. Brownie met him as he cam' steppin' sae gawsy across the dry stanes at Sandy's Ford. There Brownie stood an' shook his horns at the great scoundrel frae side to side like a govin' beast, wi' a kind o' elricht *yammer* that near feared mysel' as I made it.

"Flat doon fell the speldron, for ill-doers are a' ill-dreaders. Syne Broonie comin' a wee nearer, he gat him on his feet an' ran hame to his stable-laft wi' the cauld ice water drappin' aff him.

"Then wha but Silver Sand an' no Broonie ava' saw hame the bit lass to her mither, an' took the chance o' reddin' up the loon's character on the road. I'se warrant he gets a flea in his lug the neist time he gangs to yon toon!" said Silver Sand, triumphantly.

"Dod, man, Silver Sand, but that was guid!" cried I, hitting my thigh in my delight. For he made us see the whole business by his manner of telling it.

"But there's better than that," says he, blinkin' kindly at me across the red glow of the Aughty fire.

"Mony is the time," he went on, "in the auld days when Craigdarroch ingle-cheek lowed bonny, an' the lads o' the countryside forgathered in the gloamin', I hae played bogle there an' seen strange things. There was a lass (I'se no tell ye her name, so dinna ask) that I hae seen wi' thae e'en o' mine, comin' slippin' sae denty to the door, an' gaun doon by the soughin' grey willows that turned their white undersides to look at her in the gloom of the gloamin' as she gaed by the three thorns, hastening as though she were gangin' to a love tryst."

I began to understand, yet I so loved my lass that I had no fear of what I might hear from this recording angel of the night and the fields.

"An' wha, think ye, cam' to see her—this bonny lass that left the braw wooers ahint, speakin' about the nowt to her daddy?"

I shook my head.

"She stood by the side o' the Solway, wi' the tide washin' up to her feet, and she lookit ower at the auld Hoose o' Rathan, where there was a licht at the high window, and whiles a bit fire doon on the shore. That was the camp o' Silver Sand. Maybe it was at the camp she lookit, an' maybe it was for the sake o' Silver Sand that she gaed doon there by hersel'—an' maybe no!

"At ony rate it wasna juist the safest to be gaun there, wi' Freetraders an' Yawkins an' sic like cattle aboot; So Quharrie an' me we made it our business like to see that she wasna disturbit.

"But whatna cuif was the lad she likit to bide in the Rathan when the bonniest lass in the countryside cam' doon to keep tryst wi' nocht but the bit fardin' candle in the Hoose o' Rathan?"

"But I never jaloosed—hoo was I to ken?" I say, for I am indeed ashamed.

"Hoot awa', man! Ye surely wore your e'en in the tail o' your coat! Ye micht hae kenned by the way she flyted on ye!"

"O man, Silver Sand, ye should hae telled me," says I.

"Na, na, Laird Rathan, Silver Sand is nae tale-pyet. A bonny-like thing gin a young lass trusted me an' the stars wi' the innocence o' her heart's chamber, an' I should rin clashin' to a great hulk that hadna the gumption to find the road in for himsel'."

Silver Sand shook his head at the thought, but I took no offence for all the ill names he gave me. Contrariwise, I was exceeding glad; because I wanted to believe that her heart was mine before the night of the Dungeon and the fight by the Murder Hole.

"There's yae thing mair," said he, "that for your peace I may tell ye, though ye but little deserve it. It was the day ye waur sae ill wi' the brain heat when it turned to a raging fever, frae the cloor ye got up by the Neldricken. The doctor that had been ridden for to Dumfries, had gien ye up an' gaen awa' to order your coffin, belike. It was waefu' to hear ye. They say that they could hear the cryin' o' ye at the Orraland through the open windows that terrible nicht.

"Weel, man, I was there by the water edge, and what think ye I saw? I saw a bit lassie that had been wearin' hersel' oot to help ye, come awa' oot into the nicht air, an' afore I had time to rin, doon she clapped on her knees close by me, an' by chance (because I couldna help it) I heard the prayer for you she thocht only the Almichty listened to. She prayed lang and sair for ye, Paitrick, my lad. Ye ill deserve the like o' her. She asked that the Lord micht tak' her an' leave ye a wee bit langer, 'for he's but young,' she said, 'an' hasna had time to bethink himsel'.'"

"The God of Jacob bless her!" I said, solemnly, for I could hardly speak. And small wonder.

Silver Sand said "Amen!"

But a thought struck me.

"An' what," I said, "micht ye be doin' doon by the shore at that time o' nicht? Were you no at the prayin' too?"

"O," said Silver Sand, lightly, "I was juist throwin' chuckie-stanes in the water!"

CHAPTER XLVII

THE LAST OF THE OUTLAWS

On the morning of the seventeenth day, when we were becoming anxious for those whose anxiety for us we dared not think upon we looked out, and lo! the great blast—the greatest of a century—had blown itself out. We gazed abroad on the face of the world, and the sight made us both fear and quake, and that exceedingly.

It was a clear, bright morning when we put aside the mat and looked out. The brightness was like the kingdom of heaven. There was a chill thin air blowing, and the snow was already hard bound with frost. We looked down into the Dungeon of Buchan. Its mighty cauldron that had the three lochs at the bottom, was nearly full of snow. The lochs existed not. The Wolf's Slock was not. The night before we had only seen a whirling chaos of hurrying flakes of infinite deepness. The morning showed us the great valley almost levelled up with snow, from Breesha and the Snibe to the Range of Kells.

We stepped from the door upon the first wreath. It rose in the grand sweep which curved round the angle of the hill. We set foot on it, and it was strong enough to bear us. So closely had the particles been driven by the force of the wind, that as soon as the pressure was taken off, the frost bound the whole mass together firm as ice and smooth as ivory.

Then as we stood on the top there was a wonderful sight to be seen. A wide world of wreathed snow. There was no Loch Enoch to be discerned. The dazzling curve of the blown snow ran clear up the side of the great Merrick Hill. There was no Loch-in-loch. There was no Outlaws' Island. The same frost-bound whiteness had covered all. The old world was drowned in snow and there was no Bow of Promise to be seen. Perhaps because we had offered no sacrifice.

"God help them that are under that!" said Silver Sand.

But indeed we saw at a glance that all who had been without rooftree during the great storm were long past our help.

Only on the Dungeon Hill opposite, under the hanging brow of

Craignairny there was a great pit mark like a stone quarry, in colour red and grey—the granite showing its unhealed edges, set about with the white snow. This landslip we had not seen before.

Bidding Marion abide in the Aughty till we returned, we set out to explore. We bound kerchiefs about our brogues to keep the loose particles from balling; but, both of us being light on our feet, we sank only a very inconsiderable way. And Quharrie did not sink at all, but lightly passed over, and so went before. He was a thoughtful but not a morose dog. Only this morning the snow seemed to get into his sedate brain, and he whirled about after the stump of a tail so short, that as he turned, he only saw it rounding the uttermost curve of a very far away turn. A stern chase in his case was not only a long but a perfectly hopeless one. Yet he spun round nevertheless. He overturned himself in the snow. He slid on his back down the great snow wreaths—in fact did everything except bark. Then suddenly he would take himself up, as one may see a dignified baillie or magistrate surprised in a game of romps, look about to see whether any one has observed him, and then walk off with an air as though he were mightily surprised at the lightness of the walk and conversation of the man next to him. So Quharrie on the great snow wreaths that filled up the valley of the Star Hill.

Before going out we looked to our arms, although Silver Sand sighed and said, "I misdoot me that all the arms we shall need the day are picks and shovels."

The wreaths of the snow were bewildering and of exquisite beauty, rosy where the sun touched them—a pale faint blue in the shadow, and with such a delicious play of wavering light where the sun and shade met that it was like the sun shining through deep leaves and throbbing in the clearness of a shaded mountain pool.

As we went we sounded each step with our great poles tipped with iron. Silver Sand went foremost, because I knew but little about snow; for by the sea edge of Solway it lies but seldom and that never deep. Sometimes we set foot on a snow bridge between two stones—so fell in and had to pull one another out. Sometimes we would start a rush of snow sliding downhill, which always made Silver Sand very grave, knowing the danger of it.

First we went towards the Isle of Enoch, from which we had set out the night we came to the Aughty. So level was the buried loch that it was only by very carefully observing the landmarks that we could tell when the frozen water lay beneath us. But the side of the Merrick above us was clear in patches, where it rises too steeply to hold the snow.

Soon we came to where we thought the Isle of Loch-in-loch to lie, but nothing told us that any abodes of human beings could be beneath. Looking westward to the side of the Merrick from the highest part of the snow, we saw what seemed to be an excavation of an oval form.

"There!" said Silver Sand, pointing with his ironshod 'kent.'

So he went upward and I followed him, till we came to the edge. I shall never forget what I saw, though I must hasten to tell it briefly. It was a great pit in the snow, nearly circular, built up high on all sides, but specially towards the south. The lower tiers of it were constructed of the dead bodies of a great multitude of sheep piled one on top of the other, forming frozen fleecy ramparts. But the snow had swept over and blown in, so that there was a way down to the bottom by walking along the edge of a wreath. Looking in, we saw protruding from the snow—here the arm of a man and there the horn of a bullock.

I understood at once. We were standing above the white grave of the outlaws of the Dungeon. They had died in their hillside shelter. With our "kents" we could do little to unbury them, and give them permanent sepulture. It was better that they should lie till the snow melted off the hill. But we uncovered many of the faces, for so much of the work was not difficult. As each white frozen face came in view Silver Sand said briefly, "Miller!" or "Macaterick!" or "Marshall" as soon as he looked upon them.

But there were no Faas among them.

"The Faas have done my bidding," he said, "and they have at least a chance for their lives."

Quharrie marked the spots where the dead were to be found by digging with his forepaws, throwing the snow through the wide space between his hind legs, and blowing through his nose as a terrier does at a rabbit hole.

But we found seventeen and no more, all under the great south wall of sheep, which the starving wretches had built to keep them from the icy *bensil* of the snow wind. I wondered why they had not abode in their little cots and clay biggings; but Silver Sand said that to gather into great camps with their cattle, and collect materials for a vast fire in the midst was ever their custom in time of storm. But the Sixteen Drifty Days had been too much for them.

It was a mighty storm, and the like has never been seen in

Galloway to this day. Afterwards when men came to bury the dead, they found good proof that they had warred it out till the tenth day, when their food and their fire alike gave out. Then here and there they had laid them down to sleep, and so awoke no more. Thus we found them, and thus, poor wretches, we left them.

They looked strangely happy, for the whiteness of the snow set their faces as in a frame. I saw the rascal that would have killed me in the cot of Craignairny. He looked quite a respectable man. Which made me think that some ill devil had, mayhap, long hirsled and harried an innocent body against its will. So may it be. The good God knows. The Day of Judgement is not my business.

Then we went towards the House of Craignairny itself. But when we got there we found not the house, and we found not the landmarks. The great gash on the Dungeon brow, which we had seen from the Aughty, had been made by an inconceivable quantity of rock, which had fallen, crushing its way down the hillside and followed by a multitude of smaller stones mixed with snow. The lirk of the hill in which the ill-omened House of Death once stood, was covered fathoms deep in rock, as though the very mountain had hanged itself, Judas-like, so that all its bowels gushed out. Thus was the surprising judgment of God made plain and manifest. It was the roar of that great downthrow which we had heard when we were in the Aughty, and thought that the Star Hill was about to fall upon our heads.

No man ever saw hilt or hair of Eggface or her sons, nor of any that had been seen in that ill house, save only the man that would have knifed me, whom I saw in the great Pit of Sheep under the lee of the Merrick. The place is now all overgrown with heather and the brown bent grass; but it is still plain to be seen, and the shepherds call it the Landfall of Craignairny. They say that no sheep will feed there to this day. but I know not the truth of that.

We had, however, seen enough. So we went back to the Aughty till night, for the sun was rendering the snow too soft even on that keen December day to make travelling easy.

CHAPTER XLVIII

THE EARL'S GREAT CHAIR ONCE MORE

After taking council together we decided that we should wait till the night fell and the young moon rose. Then when the frost had bound the snow we should march. We found Marion very content, playing with a doll which she had made out of a piece of wood and some rags which lay in a corner. It was quaint to watch her hushing it to sleep.

Silver Sand spent the most part of that day in putting the Aughty to rights, stacking what of the fuel was not yet consumed, and making the abode as habitable and tidy as when we entered it. "Otherwise," he said "I should have no heart in coming back to it."

It was nearly six in the evening before we started upon our way. Silver Sand said that we would go by the Wolf's Slock and the Links of the Cooran, but I liked not the name of either.

"The Wolf's Slock is a made coach road the nicht," he said. But till we came to the edge of it, I knew not what he meant; then I saw and understood.

The gale from the south had swept the snow into the wide Wolf's Throat of Buchan, and from top to bottom all those many hundreds of feet a smooth and equal slope extended, most beautiful to see in the faint moonlight which glinted and sifted into it from the east. We had little Marion with us, carrying her most of the way, but letting her run at other times when it was level and there was good going for the feet.

Yet I sighed and was afraid, for I knew not how we were to win down that great precipice, taking the bairn with us. But my companion soon showed me how little I knew about the matter. He let me see a trick the outlaws used in the times of snow among the hills.

Silver Sand took a rope from his shoulder and bound it round my middle—afterwards about his own. Then he took out his great red kerchief and spread it on the snow. Whereupon he sat down on it with the corner fastened to his hempen waistband. He bade me to do the like, with my legs forked on either side of him. Between us he set little Marion, telling her to fasten her hands in his belt and hold tight. Then, with my arms one on either side of her and clasping Silver Sand, we softly slid over the edge. It was a wild ride in the moonlight—slow at first, then quickening with a rush. The snow streamed on either side of us, driving past with a *whish* like the spray from a boat's nose when she has much sea-way. There was a strange feeling somewhere low down within me as if I had left all my vital parts sticking to the snow where we set out, and I feared that I might be inconvenienced for the lack of them when we stopped. But withal there was a wild exhilaration; so that when we were but half-way down little Marion laughed out a rippling, girlish laugh which did us good to hear. We slid almost instantly down the steep place and glided out upon the long, sweeping, downward curve, beneath which the Cooran lane lay buried. At last, far out on the plain, we stopped, and Silver Sand stood up and shook himself.

"What think ye o' that, you that's a shoreman and kens everything?" he said, with a calmness that struck me with fresh admiration, as he dusted the snow from about little Marion and then from his own legs.

That was the end of all worth writing about—at least, all that I have room to write of in this place; for the carrier has forgotten to fetch me my new supply of paper to the Orraland, and I have been writing for the last twenty pages on empty sugarbags; but my wife is losing patience, for she keeps her garden seeds in them.

But indeed there is little more to say.

We got horses at the Clattering Shaws, and when we reached the Great House of Earlstoun it was gloaming of the next day. I hope never to be so tired again till I lie down and die. It was, by the marvellous providence of God, Eppie Tamson and not my May Maxwell that opened the door to us. Her sister Jen was over at the Rathan, where her tongue could keep the joiners and masons in better order. There is always a wild set of such men about Dumfries. Once they put out a legend on a shop door in the Brigend: "Coorse meal for Dumfries masons." Whereat the masons crossed Devorgill's bridge and broke many windows.

I had little Marion in my arms at the time when Eppie opened the door, and I had thought it a mighty fine thing just to hand her into Eppie's arms; but Silver Sand thrust me back with his strong elbow, setting it so suddenly in my mind that I had enough to do only to gasp and recover myself.

"Eppie," he said, "be verra quiet. Can ye break the news to

May—Paitrick's bit lassie here?"

"Aye," said Eppie; "are ye risen frae the deed?"

"Safe an' soond," said Silver Sand; "no a ghaist amang us."

"Come ben!" says she.

"Is Sammle in, Eppie?" says he, in a whisper.

"He's in the kitchen wi' Kennedy an' a' the Maxwell loons."

"Is he weel? Can ye tak' some news to him? D'ye think he can bear it?" said Silver Sand, cunningly.

"What is't?" cried Eppie, gripping him by the lapels of his coat and shaking him so that Silver Sand vows that she hurt him. But not grievously, I think.

"This!" said I, stepping past him and putting Marion into Eppie's arms, sound asleep, just as we had taken her from before Silver Sand on the horse.

"Hush, woman; dinna wakken' her!" said I, holding up my finger.

Eppie gave me a look of mingled adoration and scorn. I had brought back her life to her—but that I should think that she would waken her treasure!

Silver Sand afterwards said that it was one of the happiest inspirations of my life.

I wanted much to ask concerning May and where she was; but, of course, there was so much fuss made about the bairn that I had to go and look for her myself.

I went up to the great room in the tower which the Lady Grizel made so comfortable in the winter months. I knocked very gently. The strong voice of My Lady bade me enter. I came into the bright glow of the great wood fire.

The old lady threw up her hands. "The Lord preserve us, Paitrick!" she said.

She rose from the chair and came towards me. She took my hand, and I declare but she kissed both it and me, though she was an Earl's daughter. Then she minded something, seeing me look around.

"Aye, laddie," she said, "what am I thinkin' on—ye hae nae use for auld wives like me."

She stepped to the foot of the stair that went up the tower.

"May!" she cried, quickly.

There was a stirring above, and then a light foot on the stair which made my pulses dance. Lady Grizel slipped out, shutting the outer door with a clang so that I might know that she had gone. She was ever a considerate woman—few like her.

The stair door opened, and the flicker of the fire shone on a fair lassie, pale as the lily flower is pale, who stood framed against the darkness of the turret.

I held out my arms towards her. "May!" I cried, even as the Lady Grizel had done, but in another fashion.

She put her hand to her breast and came toward me slowly, as though dazed and uncertain for two or three steps. Then suddenly crying out, and the light fairly leaping in her eyes, she broke and ran to me. So I gathered my love within my arms.

And now a "Fair-guid-e'en" to you all that have come so far with us. There is no more that I have to say, and no more that you need hear. Mistress May Mischief and I love you for your kind curtesy, and we pray you that, like the dear Lady Grizel, you will take the door with you as far as it will go, and leave us thus in the firelight, with only the Earl's great chair for company.

THE END

By the mercy of God this account of our many trials and their happy end is finished at our house of the Rathan, on the first day of Aprile, 17——, being the second anniversary of the birth of my son John Faa Heron, my daughter Grizel Maxwell being now in her seventh year, and my dear wife entering her thirty-third—but, as I think, bonnier than ever.

GLOSSARY

A

A' .... all
Abide .... tolerate
Aboot ....about
Aff .... off
Afore .... before
Ahint .... behind
Aiblins .... perhaps
Ain ....own
Airt and pairt .... closely connected
                          with
A-kennin .... a little, somewhat
Alane .... alone
An' .... and
Aneath .... beneath
Anent .... opposite
Aneuch .... enough
Arles .... earnest money to
                          bind a bargain
Argie-bargie .... dispute
Auld ....old
Aumry .... cupboard
Ava .... at all
Awa .... away
Aweel .... well
Awesome .... fearful
Aye .... always
Ayont ....beyond

B

Baggonets .... bayonets
Baisoned .... having a long white
                          mark on the face, said
                          of an animal
Baith .... both
Bauchle .... a slipper
Bawbee .... halfpenny
Bawdrons .... a cat
Bees-byke .... bees nest
Beetle .... mallet of wood used for
                          various domestic
                          purposes
Begrutten .... exhausted with crying
Behove .... obliged
Ben .... inner apartment
Bena .... besides
Belike .... probably
Belly-flaught .... falling flat forward
Bent .... a coarse grass
Bensel .... bleak, cold (as of wind)
Berried .... hurt
Besom .... contemptuous term for
                          a woman.

Besom .... a broom
Bestial .... cattle
Bide .... remain, stay
Bien .... flourishing, wealthy
Bieldest .... most sheltered
Bicker .... wooden bowl
Big .... build
Bigging .... a building
Billie .... brother, companion
Birkies .... lively fellows
Birl .... quick motion in walking
Birling .... drinking spirits, &c
Birk .... birch
Birling .... making a sound like
                          falling water.
Billied .... bellowed
Black-affrontit ..... greatly affronted
Black-a-vised ...... dark complexioned
Blaff .... downcome
Blae .... blue
Blastie .... an ill-disposed person
Blate .... shy
Blateness .... shyness
Bleeze .... blaze
Bobbit .... curtsied
Bogle .... to play a romp or game
                          in a stockyard
Bood .... must
Bool .... handle of pot or bucket
Bouroch .... a small knoll, a small
                          house children build in
                          play, often among
                          bushes
Bracken .... fern, generally *Pteris
                          Aquilina*
Braid .... broad
Braw .... fine
Brawly .... finely
Breeks .... trowsers, breeches
Brew .... juice, infusion
Briers .... briars
Brogan .... a light kind of shoe
Broken-men .... outlaws
Brogues .... shoes of half-dressed
                          leather.
Broo ....forehead
Brulzie .... broil, disturbance
Brownie .... a domestic goblin
Bucht .... sheepfold
Buckie .... any spiral shell
Bum-bees .... humble bees
Bum-clock .... cockchaffer
Buik, The ....The Bible, used of
                          family worship

GLOSSARY

Burnie .... a small stream
Buss .... bush
By .... past
By-ordinar .... uncommon
Byre .... cow-house

C

Caa' .... call
Cadge .... to act as a pedlar
Caird .... sturdy rascal
Calf-conceit .... the conceit of youth
Callant .... lad
Caller .... fresh
Callevine .... lead pencil
Calm-sough .... quiet
Camsteery .... unmanageable
Canna .... cannot
Canny .... careful
Canty .... lively, cheerful
Carl .... gruff old person
Carritch .... catechism
Catheran .... freebooter
Cauldrife .... chilly
Certes .... faith, *my certes, by my faith.*
Chancy .... not safe, dangerous
Chapping .... knocking
Cheat-the-wuddy . defrauding the gallows, a term of reproach
Cheep .... creak
Cheep .... kiss
Cheeper .... a slight kiss
Chirt .... squeeze
Chucky .... a fowl
Chucky-stanes ..... pebbles
Chunnered .... laughed internally
Clachan .... small village
Claes & Claiths ... clothes
Clap .... lie down
Clash .... tittle-tattle
Clatter .... talk
Clattering .... noisy talk
Clavers .... idle talk
Cleckin' .... talk
Cleg .... horse-fly
Clickie .... crooked head on staff
Clinkum-clank ...... beating strongly
Cloot .... hoof
Clottered .... mixed up
Coaties .... petticoats
Coggle .... to move unsteadily
Collieshangie .... quarrel, row

Coo .... cow
Cooshairn .... cow dung
Corbie .... raven
Corklit .... a kind of lichen
Corpse-clout .... winding-sheet
Cosy .... comfortable
Creepie .... small stool
Cries .... proclamation of marriage
Croose and canty lively and cheerful
Crown o' the causeway .... middle of the street.
Cuddy .... donkey
Cuif .... simpleton
Cutty-sark .... a short shift

D

Daffin' .... thoughtless gaiety, joking
Daft .... mad
Daich .... dough
Darned .... concealed
Daudin .... dangling
Dawtie .... darling
Dee .... die
Deein' .... dying
Deavin .... deafening
Denty .... dainty
Deray .... disorder
Dichting .... wiping, dusting
Ding .... strike, a blow
Dinna .... do not
Disjeestion .... digestion
Dodderin' .... walking unsteadily
Dominie .... schoolmaster
Dook .... to bathe
Doon .... down
Door-cheek .... side of door
Douce .... sedate, not frivolous
Doup .... the bottom
Dour .... morose, stubborn
Dourest .... severest, hardiest
Dowsed .... beat, conquered
Drappie .... a small quantity
Drookit .... drenched
Droon .... drown
Drovin' .... driving cattle
Dune .... done
Dunt .... a blow
Dwam .... fainting fit
Dwine .... decay
Dyke .... wall

282

GLOSSARY

E

Een .... eyes
Eery .... dreary, ghost-like
Eidently .... attentively
Eined .... a meeting of lad and
                        lass by appointment or
                        otherwise
Elricht .... weird, unearthly
Elshin .... an awl
Enbra' .... Edinburgh
Erne .... eagle
Ether .... adder
Ettled .... intended
Even .... compare, equal

F

Faain' .... falling
Faceable .... likely
Fairings .... presents given at fairs
Far-ben .... as far away as possible
Faulds .... folds
Fause .... false
Favour .... to be like in features
Feared .... afraid, frightened
Fearsome .... fearful
Feck .... part of anything
Feckless .... feeble
Fecht .... fight
Fechter .... fighter
Fess .... fetch
Fettle .... to put in order
File .... to dirty
Fit .... foot
Flaf .... puff
Fleechin' .... coaxing cajoling
Fley, ... startle, frighten
Flinders .... splinters
Flunky .... footman, manservant
Flyting .... scolding
Foo .... drunk, full
Forbye .... besides
Forenicht .... early in the evening
Forgathered .... met
Forritsome .... forward
Foul-thief .... the Devil
Fower-'oors .... meal taken at four
                        o'clock
Freets .... superstitions
Freen' .... relation, friend
Freit .... observance
Fushionless .... pithless, weak
Fyke .... fidget

G

Gaed .... went
Gait & Gate .... road, way
Gar .... make, compel
Garron .... a small horse
Gang .... go
Gaun .... going
Gaun-bodies .... travelling folk
Gaunting .... yawning
Gawsy .... jolly, plump
Gear .... goods of any kind
Gellock .... an earwig, sand
                        jumper.
Gentle people ...... fairies
Gentrice .... gentry, gentility
Gibin' .... taunting
Gie .... give
Gied .... gave
Gin .... if
Girse .... grass
Glaur .... mud
Gled .... hawk
Gleg .... handy, smart, quick
Glet & Glit .... oily, sticky matter
Glint .... glance
Glinting .... glancing, shining
Glisk .... glance
Gloamin' .... twilight
Gollying .... bawling
Gomeril .... fool, idiot
Go-off .... beginning
Gorroch .... mix, spoil, trample
Gowk .... fool
Gowpenfu' .... two hands full
Grat .... cried
Greet .... cry
Greeting .... crying
Grieshoch .... hot embers
Grooing .... desire
Gruesome .... horrible
Grupped .... caught hold of
Guid-e'en .... good evening
Gumption .... understanding
Gye .... tolerably, shortly

H

Hae .... have
Hadna .... had not
Haena .... have not
Hag-clog .... block for cutting wood
                        on
Hagg .... slough, pit in moss

GLOSSARY

Halewar................ whole
Hallan.................. partition between the door and fireplace.
Hame.................... home
Harns................... brains
Harry.................... rob
Haudin'................ holding
Hauf .... chief place of resort
Haun' .... hand
Havers................. nonsense
Heatherbleat .... snipe
Heather-cat .... wild cat
Heid.................... head
Hellicat .... wild, wicked
Hempie .... roguish girl
Hench................... to throw stones by jerking the hand along the haunch
Herryin'
and berryin' .... robbing and breaking
Heuch.................. a ragged steep cliff
Heuk.................... reaping hook
Hilt and hair .... the whole of anything
Hind ....farm servant
Hinderend............ afterwards
Hirple.................. walking lame
Hirsled .... moved about restlessly
Hoast................... cough
Hoised.................. assisted, pushed up
Hoo .... how
Hoolet .... owl
Hoose................... house
Hoshen................. stockings without feet, used as a term of reproach.
Howe.................... hollow
Howkit ....dug
Hullion................. sloven
Hurdies .... posteriors

I

Ilka .... every
Ill......................... bad
Ill Bit................... hell
Ill-thief................ the devil
Income................ bodily infirmity
Ingle.................... fire in a room
Ingle-cheek.......... fireside
Ingle-nook .... fireside-corner.
Intil..................... into
Ither.................... other

J

Jabble.................. a noisy motion of water
Jaloosin'.............. suspecting
Jockteleg.............. a large clasp knife
Jookin', Juikin' ... shifting, turning actively
Jock-my-jo........... a romping game of young men and women

K

Kail-yard.............. cabbage garden
Kaim .... a hill fort, crest of a hill resembling a cock's comb
Kale...................... broth
Kamed.................. combed
Kane..................... tribute paid in kind
Keek...................... look
Keel...................... red chalk, ruddle
Ken....................... know
Kenna................... know not
Kenning, a .... a little
Kenspeckle.......... conspicuous
Kent...................... a rough stick
Kep....................... cap
Kilted ....tucked up
Kin' .... kind
Kintry................... country
Kist....................... chest
Kitchen .... something to give food a relish
Kittle.................... nice, difficult
Knapping............. knocking
Knoit.................... a smart stroke
Knowe.................. hillock
Kuitled ....tickled
Kye....................... cows

L

Laired................... stuck in a bog
Lairin'.................. being bogged
Landloupin'......... rambling (used as term of reproach)
Lang-nebbit......... long-nosed
Lapper.................. to beat gently (as water)
Lave .... the rest
Leal .... loyal
Lees...................... lies
Licht..................... light
Lichtlied............... slighted

GLOSSARY

Lick,..................... beat, a blow
Lift .... sky
Liftin'..................... stealing
Lilt......................... a song
Limmer .... a slighting term (used of a woman).
Lingtow............... a rope used by smugglers
Link....................... a division, a piece
Linking .... walking quickly
Lintie.................... a linnet
Lippened............. trusted
Lirk .... a hollow in a hill
Loaden .... load
Lochan .... a small lake
Loanin' .... a lane
Loathly-dogs .... ghostly hounds
Loon...................... rogue
Loup...................... jump, leap
Lowe .... flame
Lowed.................. blazed
Lown..................... calm, sheltered
Lowse.................. loose
Lug....................... the ear
Lunted.................. smoked
Luntin' ....blazing and smoking

M

Mails .... rents, tribute
Maist.................... most
Mair, Mae,.......... more
Marriet................. married
Maun.................... must
Maybe .... perhaps
Mess John............a name for a priest
Midden................. dung heap
Mind..................... remember
Minnie.................. mother
Misca' .... abuse
Mischance............ accident
Misdooted............ doubted
Misleared............. ill-bred, evil-intentioned
Mislippen............. to overlook, mismanage
Mistrysted............ deceived
Mither .... mother
Moiderd .... dazed, stupid
Mony.................... many
Moo...................... mouth
Mools................... earth
Moss-hag............ deep gully, or pit in a moss
Muckle................. large, much
Muirburn.............. burning heather

Mutch................... woman's cap

N

Nae....................... no
Nane..................... none
Napkin .... handkerchief
Neb....................... nose
Neffy.................... nephew
Neist..................... next
Neuk..................... corner of anything
Nicht .... night
Nicky Ben .... old familiar term for the Devil
No.......................... not
Noo .... now
Nowt .... cattle

O

On-ding............... noise, turmoil, heavy fall of rain or snow
On-stead.............. farm buildings
Ony .... any
Ony-gate .... any way
Oo.......................... wool
Oor .... our
Oot ....out
O't......................... of it
Or .... before
Orra .... odd, not matched
Ower .... over, too
Ower-by.............. over the way
Oxter .... arm-pit, arm

P

Pack...................... intimate
Paddock .... frog
Paidled ....to walk with short irregular steps, to dabble
Pairtrick .... partridge
Partan.................. crab
Pawky .... sly, wily
Pech...................... pant
Peching .... panting
Peep...................... a feeble sound
Pelloch ....porpoise
Pent .... paint
Pentit................... painted
Pick .... offence
Pickle ....a small quantity
Pit, Pitten .... put
Pit-mirk................ pitch dark

GLOSSARY

Plenishing............ household furnishings, &c.
Pliskies................. mischievous tricks
Ploy...................... employment
Puggie.................. monkey
Pooch....................pocket
Pook...................... pluck
Preein'................. tasting
Preen...................... pin
Professor.............. religious
Put-on................... dressed

Q

Quag...................... bog
Quakin-quas .... shaking dangerous bogs
Quat...................... quit
Quean................... wench
Quey..................... heifer

R

Rade...................... rode
Rale...................... real
Rampagin' .... prancing about in a boisterous way
Ramshackle .... ruinous, tumble-down
Randy................... scolding, disorderly
Rape...................... rope
Rave...................... tore
Reamin' .... foaming
Red cock,............. craw, to gar the, fire-raising
Red-up .... cleaned, tidied
Reddin'-up........... cleaning up
Ree .... a stone enclosure for sheep
Reek...................... smoke
Reesled .... wrestled
Remead............... remedy
Reived................. taken by force, stolen
Reivers................. robbers
Richt...................... right
Rig........................ a wild adventure
Rig and fur .... ridge and furrow in ploughing or weaving
Rigs...................... ridges
Rive...................... a worthless lot
Rogueit .... driven by force
Roon.................... round
Routed................. bellowed
Routh .... plenty

S

Sabbit................... sobbed

Sae....................... so
Sain .... to bless against evil influences
Sair....................... sore
Sant .... saint
Sark .... shirt
Saugh ....willow
Scarfit................ scratched
Scart................... scratch
Schule .... school
Scoup...................to run off with
Scraichin'............ screaming hoarsely
Scrauchlin' .... scrambling
Screed .... a piece torn off, a rag
Screeving............. shooting swiftly
Scrive................... piece of writing
Scroggie............... stunted
Scrunt.................. meagre
Scunner............... disgust
Shapin-claes .... best outfit
Sheltie.................. small pony
Sherra.................. sheriff
Sheuch .... a trench, ditch
Shippen................ cow-house, byre
Shoother.............. shoulder
Shootin'-airns...... firearms
Sib........................ related to
Sic .... such
Siccan.................. such
Siller.................... money
Singin' .... singeing
Sirce-me.............. an exclamation = dear me
Skaith................... harm
Skarrow................ shadow, reflection
Skelloch................scream, squall
Skelpin'................ beating
Skillet.................. a drinking cup
Skirling-pan..........frying-pan
Sleekit .... smooth, shining
Slecked .... miry
Slithering............. sliding
Sloyt.................... a lazy dirty fellow
Sma'..................... small
Smoor.................. smother
Snod.................... neat, in good order
Snore-up .... ascend
Snowkin' .... smelling about
Sonsy .... fat, comfortable
Soop.................... sweep
Sorning .... spunging
Sough.................. a sound
Soughin' .... sighing of wind

GLOSSARY

Souter.................. cobbler, shoemaker
Sowens................. flummery (a common Scottish dish)
Spang ....to spring up
Spate .... a flood
Speaned............... weaned
Sped ....exhausted
Speer.................... ask
Speerin'................. asking
Speldron.............. awkward fellow
Spence.................. parlour
Spulzie ....spoil
Spurtle.................. stick for stirring porridge &c.
Stance.................. station
Stap .... stave. A *stap oot o' yer bicker*, a reduced quantity
Stark..................... strong
Steading ....farm buildings
Sted .... place
Steeve.................. strong, stiff
Stock .... fore part of a bed
Stookit.................. put up in shocks (stooks)
Stoor..................... dust
Stot........................ a bullock
Straikin' ....laying out a corpse
Stouthrief..............robbery
Straucht............... straight
Streekin' .... going in the direction of
Sumph.................. a soft stupid fellow
Swap .... exchange
Swarf.................... faint
Swither................ hesitate

T

Taws.................... leather strap for punishing schoolboys
Tarry-breeks........ term for sailors
Tale-pyet............. tell-tale
Tangs .... tongs
Taigle.................. detain
Tawties .... potatoes
Teuch .... tough
Thack .... thatch
Thole.................... endure
Thoom................. thumb
Thraw.................. twist
Thoucht............... thought
Threepit............... to aver pertinaciously
Thruch-stone .... flat gravestone

Till........................ to
Tirlin' at the pin.. twirling at the door-latch
Tocher.................. dower
Tod....................... fox
Toom................... empty
Toom................... place for shooting rubbish
Toon..................... town
Toor, ... tower
Toorock, ... little tower
Tow, ... rope
Town .... farm-house and buildings
Tow-rope .... halter
Towrow............... noise, confusion
Traiking .... following closely
Troking .... dealing
Tryst..................... appointment
Tuck .... beat
Twa .... two
Twal.................... twelve
Twine................... to part
Tyke .... a dog

U

Ugsome................ ugly
Uncanny.............. dangerous, ill-boding
Unco.................... strange, unusual
Unsonsy ....bad-looking, unlucky
Uptak .... understand,-ing
Unkempt .... in disarray

V

Victual .... grain

W

Waa .... wall
Wad..................... would
Waddin' .... wedding
Wae...................... sorry
Waefu' .... sorrowful
Waft .... a hasty glance
Wakkin' .... awake
Wale..................... choice, the remainder
Wall-e'e............. spring in a bog
Wame.................. the belly
Wan..................... obtained, got
War .... was
Warrandice.......... warrant
Wasna .... was not
Wasterfu' .... wasteful
Waur .... vanquish, destroy

287

GLOSSARY

Wean.................... child
Weared................. bestowed
Wee wee German
lairdie.................. His Most Sacred
                                Majesty King George
Weel-faured......... good-looking
Weir .... war
Wersh................... insipid, raw
Wha...................... who
Whalp.................. whelp
Whalpit .... brought forth
Whammilt............ overturned
Whaulpie .... puppy
Whaup.................. curlew
Whaur .... where
Wheen.................. few
Whiles.................. sometimes
Whish................... a buzzing sound
Whinger............... a short sword
Whud .... a lie
Wile..................... to entice, to force
Win .... get
Wirricows............ bugbears, devils
Wraith.................. apparition
Wuddy .... gallows
Wull ....will
Wullcat .... wild cat
Wuss .... wish

Y

Yae....................... one
Yammering........... making a loud outcry
Ye......................... you
Yestreen............... last night
Yett .... gate
Yeukin .... itching
Yin ....one
Yince.................... once
Yirds .... caves, hiding-places
                          (said of "*fox-earths*").
Yon .... that, yonder
Yowching .... barking
Yowes.................. ewes

NOTE

Some of the words above given are used metaphorically or obliquely, and are peculiar to Galloway and other adjoining parts in the south of Scotland, e.g., *Streckin'*, "going in the direction of", the proper meaning of the word is stretching, and is generally applied to laying out a corpse; *Birl*, "quick motion in walking", the proper meaning is to drink plentifully, generally in company; *Grooing*, "desire", properly "to shudder, to shiver", &c. The meaning of the words given in the Glossary are in accordance with the meaning of the text, and perhaps may not be so found in Jamieson's dictionary or other glossaries. The spelling of the Scotch words used by the author are sometimes different from the usual form e.g., *Hauf*, is usually spelt by Scott, Burns, and others, *Houff, Howff,* &c.

July 1894